Accidents
Happen

ALSO BY LOUISE MILLAR

The Playdate

Praise for *The Playdate*

"British author Millar's engrossing debut offers an unsettling, realistic view of friendships, gossip, and loneliness. . . . What starts as a quiet story about neighbors soon builds into a gripping psychological thriller."   —*Publishers Weekly* (starred review)

"Millar's well-drawn characters and impeccably structured plot instantly grab the reader and may leave parents wondering who to trust with their children. A supremely accomplished debut thriller by a writer to watch."   —*Booklist* (starred review)

"A disturbing psychological thriller that probes the insular lives of social misfits in a London suburb."   —*The New York Times Book Review*

"A must read that will tap into every mother's primal fears."
—Sophie Hannah

"Millar's gripping thriller has anxious moms in its crosshairs."
—*People*

"Louise Millar's novel sucks the reader in like quicksand to the surprising ending. I did not want to miss a page!"
— Lee Woodruff, *New York Times* bestselling
author of *Those We Love Most*

"Like the best thrillers, it is quietly creepy and expertly crafted. Add it to your book club reading list now."   —*Stylist* magazine

"Taut, page-turning, and surprising."   —Cleveland *Plain Dealer*

"Sinister, yet beautifully written and very real, *The Playdate* is a modern Gothic novel with echoes of du Maurier. You will slip into the lives of its London cast but your allegiances will shift throughout. Louise Millar plots her story so skillfully, you will distrust the characters to the point where you cannot even trust yourself. But you will read to the end, madly. And when you put this book down, you'll wish there were more."
— Ann Bauer, author of *The Forever Marriage*

Accidents Happen

✳ *A Novel* ✳

LOUISE MILLAR

EMILY BESTLER BOOKS

ATRIA

New York London Toronto Sydney New Delhi

ATRIA PAPERBACK
A Division of Simon & Schuster, Inc.
1230 Avenue of the Americas
New York, NY 10020

First Emily Bestler Books/Atria Paperback edition June 2013

EMILY BESTLER BOOKS / ATRIA PAPERBACK and colophons are trademarks of Simon & Schuster, Inc.

For information about special discounts for bulk purchases, please contact Simon & Schuster Special Sales at 1-866-506-1949 or business@simonandschuster.com.

The Simon & Schuster Speakers Bureau can bring authors to your live event. For more information or to book an event, contact the Simon & Schuster Speakers Bureau at 1-866-248-3049 or visit our website at www.simonspeakers.com.

Designed by Jill Putorti

Manufactured in the United States of America

10 9 8 7 6 5 4 3 2 1

Library of Congress Cataloging-in-Publication Data
Millar, Louise.
Accidents happen / by Louise Millar. — First Atria Paperback edition.
    pages   cm
1. Single mothers—Fiction. 2. Widows—Fiction. 3. Psychological fiction.
4. Suspense fiction. I. Title.
   PR6113.I548A65 2013
   823'.92—dc23

                                                        2012047980

ISBN 978-1-4516-5670-1
ISBN 978-1-4516-5672-5 (ebook)

For Andy, with love

In 1962 music teacher Frano Selak from Croatia was a passenger aboard a train that derailed and crashed into a river.

In 1963 he was blown out of the door of the first plane he'd ever flown in, and landed on a haystack.

In 1966 a bus he was traveling on crashed into a river.

In 1970 Frano Selak's car caught fire as he was driving on a highway. He escaped just before it exploded.

In 1973 his car caught fire again in a freak accident, burning away most of his hair.

In 1995 Frano Selak was hit by a bus.

In 1996 he met a truck head-on on a mountain road, and escaped just as his car crashed down a three-hundred-foot precipice.

Frano Selak then went on to win $1,000,000 in the lottery.

Accidents
Happen

1

Something had happened. Something unexpected. He could tell by the maverick puff of gray smoke that hung above the M40 motorway; by the kaleidoscope jam of cars glinting under an otherwise blue sky; by the way the drivers craned their necks out of windows to see what was up ahead.

Jack kicked his soccer boots together in the backseat, feeling carsick.

"Where are we?"

"Nearly there. Oh, will you get out the bloody way! What is wrong with these . . . ?"

He glanced up to see his mother glaring in the rearview mirror. Behind them in the slow lane, a truck jutted up to the back of their car, its engine growling.

"Him?"

Kate nodded crossly. "He's right up my back," she complained, clicking on her indicator and looking for an empty space in the adjacent lane.

Jack rubbed his face, which was still sticky and red from running around the soccer field. The May afternoon hot air that blew in the window was mucky with exhaust as three thick rows of traffic tried in vain to force their way toward Oxford.

"I can't even see his lights now. . . ."

A sharp spasm gripped Jack's stomach. It made the nausea worse. He returned to his computer game. "Mum. Chill out. They probably have sensors or something to tell them when they're going to hit something."

"Do they?" She waved to a tiny hatchback in the middle lane that was flashing her to move in. "What, even the older ones?"

"Hmm?" he replied, pressing a button.

"Jack? Even old trucks, like that?"

He shrugged. "I don't know. I mean, they don't *want* to hit you, Mum. They don't *want* to go to jail."

Without looking up, he knew she was shaking her head.

"Yeah, well, it's the one who's *not* thinking that you've got to worry about, Jack. Last year, this British couple got killed by a French truck doing the same thing—he was texting someone in a traffic jam and ran right over them. He didn't even know he'd done it, they were so squashed."

"You told me," Jack said. He flicked the little man back and forward, trying to get to the next level, trying to take his mind off his stomach.

"Oh, God—I'm going to be late," his mother murmured, glancing at the car clock.

"What for?"

She hesitated. "Just an appointment at six."

"What, the doctor's?"

"No. Work related."

He glanced at her. Her voice did that thing again, like when she told him the reason she took the train to London last week. It went flat and calm, as if she were forcing it to stay still. There were no ups and downs. And her eyes slid a tiny bit off to the right, as if she were looking at him, but not.

A flicker of white caught Jack's attention in the side mirror. He saw the offending truck indicate to move in behind their car again.

He watched his mother, waiting for her to see it.

"Mum . . ."

"What?"

He saw her glance behind them angrily.

"Oh, Jesus—not again . . . What the . . . ?"

Jack banged his boots together, watching dried mud sprinkle onto the newspaper she'd put down in the back.

"Mum?"

"*What?*"

When his voice came out, it was so quiet he could barely hear it himself over all the straining car engines.

"I could have come back in the minibus. You could have picked me up at school like everyone else."

He saw her shoulders tense up.

"I wanted to see you play—it was the tournament final!" she said, the shrillness entering her voice again. "What, am I an embarrassing mum?"

"I didn't say that," he protested.

"Maybe next time I'll come wearing my underwear on my head."

She made a silly face at him in the mirror. He smiled, even though he knew that the silly face wasn't hers. It was stolen property. He'd seen her studying Gabe's mum when she did it. Gabe's mum did it a lot, and it made them laugh. When Jack's mum tried, it was as if the corners of her lips were pulled up by clothespins. Then two minutes later, her face went back to the usual frown that suggested she was concentrating hard on something private.

"It was nice to see Gabe today," she said. "Why don't you ask him round soon?"

Jack carried on playing his game. After what she'd done to their house this week, he'd never be able to ask anyone around again.

"Maybe," he muttered.

"Oh . . . there's the problem . . . Can you see?"

He leaned over and looked out the passenger side of the car and saw a flashing blue light around the bend to the left.

"Police," he murmured, straining his head forward. "And . . . a fire engine."

"Really?"

She looked so worried. He sighed quietly and put down his game.

"Oh, Mum . . . I've got something really good to tell you."

"Uh-uh?"

"Next term, Mr. Dixon wants me to play reserve for this team he runs after school."

"Does he?" She glanced at him. "That's brilliant, Jack. . . ."

"But I'll have to train on Wednesdays after school, as well, so perhaps I can go to . . ."

She wasn't listening. In the mirror, he saw her eyes dart wildly back and forward between the blue light, and the truck now crossing lanes to sit behind them again.

"Mum?"

"What?" She sounded bewildered.

"Why don't you move into the fast lane? Trucks aren't allowed in there."

And she'd be farther away from the burnt-out car that was currently coming into view around the bend on the hard shoulder.

His mother stared at him for a second as if in a daze. Finally, she focused again. Then the clothespin smile returned.

"Good idea, Captain," she said brightly. "But we're fine here. Don't worry about it, Jack."

He saw her force a smile, causing her eyes to crinkle at the sides, just like Gabe's mum's did. Except Gabe's mum's eyes were warm and blue, offset by laughter lines and friendly freckles, whereas Jack's mum's eyes were still, like amber-colored glass. They sat in skin as white and smooth as Nana's china, except for two dark shadows beneath them.

He knew his mum's extra-crinkly smile was supposed to reassure him that there was nothing to worry about. He was only ten-and-three-quarters old, after all. She was the grown-up. She was in charge, and everything was fine.

Jack rubbed his stomach and watched the truck with a careful eye in the side mirror.

Oh, God. She was so late. She couldn't miss this appointment. Now the motorway traffic had concertinaed into the city and jammed that up, too.

Kate turned off the packed ring road, and sped through the backstreets of East Oxford, taking routes the tourists wouldn't know. Bouncing over speed bumps, she dodged around shoals of cyclists and badly parked rental vans evacuating ramshackle student houses for the summer. Where there was only room for one vehicle down streets so narrow cars parked on the pavement, she forced her way through, waving with a smile at oncoming queues of drivers, ignoring their mouthed insults.

"They're here!" Jack shouted as she made the last turn into the welcoming width of Hubert Street.

Damn. He was right.

Richard's black four-by-four was parked in its usual gentlemanly way outside her house, leaving the graveled driveway free for her. A box of pink tissues on the dashboard announced Helen's presence. Of course they were here. They would have been here at the dot of five. Desperate to get their hands on him.

"So they are," she said, turning into the drive and braking abruptly in front of the side gate. She pulled on the hand brake harder than she meant to. "Right—run. I'm late."

They spilled out of the car, hands full of plastic bags of Jack's school clothes, the empty wrappers of postsoccer snacks, and his homework folder for the weekend.

"Hi!" Jack called out, waving. Helen was mouthing "hello" from between Kate's sitting-room curtains, her smile strangely girlish for a woman in her sixties.

Kate pursed her lips. Why hadn't they waited in their car? That house key was for when they were looking after Jack, not for letting themselves in when she was late. Mentally, she tried to visualize what the house had looked like when she left this morning. What state was the toilet in? Had she tidied away her bras off the radiators?

Then, with the recoil of a trigger, she remembered what was upstairs.

Oh, no.

Her cheeks burned. She looked down at the ground, slammed the car door, and locked it. She was supposed to tell them before they saw it. She needed to explain.

She marched after Jack and up to the front porch.

"Hello! Have you grown again, young man?" Helen called, flinging open the door.

"Not since last week, I don't think, Helen," Kate exclaimed from behind them. Why did she say these things? They all knew he was small. Pretending he wasn't was doing Jack no favors.

"Gosh, you're going to be tall like your dad." Helen laughed, ignoring her. She placed her arm around Jack, and led him through the hall to the kitchen.

"Everything OK, Kate?" she called back. "Traffic?"

"Yup. Sorry." Kate gritted her teeth as she closed the door behind her.

"Let me take those."

She turned to see Richard striding toward her, his hands outstretched, oblivious to her chagrin that he had just let himself into his daughter-in-law's house. His imposing frame filled the hallway. "How did you get on? Traffic?"

"Yes, sorry," she said, giving him Jack's homework. She could smell Richard's usual fragrance of pipe smoke.

Kate looked up into Richard's serious and questioning brown eyes, waiting for them to check that Jack was out of earshot. But they didn't. Instead he turned on his heels and followed after Helen and Jack into the kitchen, grinning through his gray-flecked beard at the sight of his grandson.

"So did you beat their socks off, sir?" he boomed at Jack, who was stuffing a muffin in his mouth.

Kate glanced up the stairs.

It was still there.

Richard hadn't seen it.

She checked her watch. Five twenty. The woman wanted to see her at six sharp in North Oxford. The traffic was so bad, she was going to have to cycle. Kate quickly worked out a few figures.

Thirty-four . . . Eighty-one—or was it eighty-two? Damn it, she needed that new computer. The chances were high, anyway.

She shook her head. It would have to be OK.

She followed Richard through to the kitchen, opened a cupboard, and bent down to find her helmet.

"Helen, do you mind if I rush off?"

"Of course, dear," Helen chirped, filling up a jug at the sink. "Sound interesting?"

"Um—just a woman who might have some renovation work," Kate said, avoiding Helen's eye.

"Where?"

"In Summertown."

"Oh, well, good luck, dear."

"Thanks."

Kate turned to see Jack, his mouth still too full of muffin to answer his grandfather's question about the match score this afternoon. He was grinning and sticking up two fingers like Winston Churchill.

"Peace, man?" asked Richard. "It's the nineteen-sixties, is it? No! Two-all, then? No? What? A bunny rabbit jumped onto the field?" Richard chortled, his arms wrapped around his rugby player's chest, as his grandson shook his head at his jokes. "What? Two-nil then?"

Jack nodded, laughing, dropping crumbs out of his mouth.

"Aw—well done!" Helen clapped, cheeks as pink as cupcakes.

"Good lad!" Richard exclaimed. "Was he good, Mum?"

Kate grabbed her helmet from the back of the cupboard and went to stand up. "He was. He made a good save, didn't you?"

As she spun around, the sight of Helen and Jack together took her by surprise.

A pit of disappointment settled in her stomach.

Jack was a clone of her. You couldn't deny it.

Kate buckled up her helmet, watching them. However desperately she willed his hair to darken and thicken like Hugo's, or for his green eyes to turn brown, it was Helen and Saskia who Jack took after. As he sat beside his grandmother, the similarities were painfully obvious. The same pale hair that was slightly too fine for the long skater-boy cut he desperately wanted; delicate features that would remain immune to the nasal bumps and widening jaws that would wipe out his friends' childhood beauty; the flawless skin that tanned so easily and would remain unmarked by Kate's dark moles or Richard and Hugo's unruly eyebrows.

He was nearly eleven and nothing was going to change now. Jack would be a physically uncomplicated adult, like his grandmother and aunt, with none of the familiar landmarks of his father.

Kate stood up straight and made herself stop thinking. She walked to the fridge and opened it.

"Oh, by the way, Helen, I've made this for tonight," she said, pulling out a casserole dish and lifting the lid. "It's just vegetables and lentils. And some potatoes . . ."

Kate stopped.

She stared at the stew. It was an inch or two shallower in the dish than she'd left it this morning.

"Jack, did you eat some of this this morning?" Kate asked, looking around alarmed. He shook his head.

The kitchen window locks and the back door were all intact. She turned to check the window at the side return—and came face-to-face with Helen, who had come up behind her.

Watching her.

Helen took the casserole gently from her, replacing it in the fridge.

"Now, don't worry about us, Kate. We stopped at Marks on the way over. I got some salmon and new potatoes, and a bit of salad."

Kate saw the salmon sitting in her fridge on the shelf above the casserole, and felt the waves of Helen's firm resolve radiate toward her. "Oh. But I made it for tonight. Really. There's probably enough for the three of you if you have it with some bread. I'm just confused at how so much of it has disappeared. It's as if—"

"Oh, it'll have just sunk down in the dish when it was cooling," Helen interrupted firmly, shooting a reassuring smile to Jack. "No, Kate. You keep it for tomorrow."

Kate stared into the fridge. Was Helen right? She tried to see a faint line of dried casserole that would prove its original height.

There was nothing there.

"OK," she heard herself say lamely. She shut the fridge. They could eat their bloody salmon. Jack didn't even like it. He only ate it to be polite.

"Now, you're probably starving, darling, aren't you?" Helen said to Jack, taking Kate's apron off a peg to put on. There was a fragment of canned tomato on it, left over from making the stew this morning, Kate noted, that was about to press against Helen's white summer cardigan.

She started to speak, and then didn't.

"OK, then . . ." Kate hesitated, checking the clock. "By the way . . ." They both looked at her. Jack looked down at the table.

"I've . . . have you been up . . . ?" She pointed at the ceiling. They shook their heads. "No, dear," Helen replied. "Why?"

Jack slowly chewed his muffin.

"Well, I haven't got time to explain, but anyway, don't worry about it. It's just . . ."

They waited expectantly. She realized Jack's jaws had stopped moving.

"I needed to do it. And it's done now. So—see you later."

And with that, she marched out the door of her house—her house—cross that she had to explain it all.

2

It was a warm May evening and Oxford was bathed in a pale-lemon tint. Kate pushed her bike across Donnington Bridge, then coasted down the steep path on the other side to cycle the path along the river.

It was busy this evening. She set off, cycling around a woman with two big, wet dogs, and a student on a bike who had clearly not yet learned to drive and wasn't sticking to the left side. Kate pumped her legs hard, averting her eyes from the water on her right, trying to clear her mind of what she was about to do. She pushed against the resistance of each pedal stroke, changing gear when the journey along the flat path became too easy, till she could hear her own breath whistling gently on the early summer breeze.

A swarm settled around her head like tiny flies.

One out of five. Twenty percent, she thought, trying to ignore it.

She hit a steady pace around Christchurch Meadow. Across

the river, the grand old college looked especially beautiful to-night, with its stone façade, soft and pretty in the low light.

The grass in front of it glowed that rich, saturated Oxford green suggesting high teas and country estates. It was scattered with groups of the cheery, hardworking students who imbued the air in Oxford with their optimism and best efforts; who sprinkled its streets and parks and alleyways with goodwill, like bubbles of sweetness in a fizzy drink. Who made Oxford feel safe.

No, on nights like these, she hardly missed London at all.

After Folly Bridge Kate cleared the crowds, and sped up again. She sailed past the waterside apartments at Botley, and the circus-colored canal boats moored around Osney Lock. Behind Jericho, she ducked under a graffitied bridge, and carried along the canal path till she could cross into North Oxford.

Dismounting to cross the bridge, she checked her watch. Twenty-five minutes flat. She could still make it for six. She had done it.

As she set off, pushing her bike along the pavement to Sum-mertown, the enormity of what lay ahead overwhelmed her.

She stopped, the anxiety hitting her like a wave.

She was here, finally. She was actually going to do it this time.

Before she could change her mind yet again, Kate made her-self walk on, pushing the bike along the quiet side streets, then bursting into the rush-hour traffic of Woodstock Road and Ban-bury Road, where she crossed to arrive in a leafy Summertown avenue.

Peace descended as she entered the exclusive Oxford enclave. The houses were spectacular. Imposing Victorian detacheds, with grand pianos in grand bay windows and walled gardens.

Inspector Morse streets, as Helen would call them. As far from the clattering noise and cheerful chaos of East Oxford as you could be. The kind of leafy avenues Helen and Richard assumed Kate would use her inheritance to buy a home in when she and Jack moved from London.

With a gulp, she wondered whether her parents-in-law had been upstairs yet back at Hubert Street, and seen what she had done. She would have to deal with that.

To keep her mind from the task at hand, Kate glanced at each house as she passed, looking for a feature Hugo would appreciate. The houses were Victorian Gothic revival. Not his period, but she bet he would have known the correct name for every architectural detail on their elegant frontages.

Before she knew it, the sign was in front of her. Hemingway Avenue.

Kate stopped. Her watch said 5:55. She had made it.

She was nearly there.

The urge to run overwhelmed her. She steadied herself against a wall.

She was outside number one. If she carried on to 15 Hemingway Avenue, there would be no going back.

"You are going to do this," she whispered, pushing herself off the wall.

And on she went, taking smaller and smaller steps as she walked toward the house.

It was even more impressive than its neighbors. One gable jutted in front of the other. Ivy grew around medieval-style stone window frames. The glass revealed nothing inside but the red silk fringe of a lamp, then darkness beyond.

Kate pushed her bike into the driveway and locked it. She removed her helmet and ran her fingers through her hair. It fell forward, thick with the Celtic blackness Mum told her she had inherited from an Irish aunt, blocking out the early evening sun for a second. She threw her head back and straightened her hair back down to her shoulders, then, with a deep breath, forced herself up the stone steps to a white, carved portico. The front door was magnificent. Hugo would have loved it. An eight-foot-high, Gothic revival arch, wooden, with roughly hewn baronial black metal hinges and a thick knocker.

Kate paused.

Before she could run away, she banged on the door.

The sound resonated around the front garden like a shotgun. The huge door swung open and standing there was a blond woman in her sixties. She was as tall as Richard, and broad, with a matronly bosom. Her hair was drawn up into an elaborate bun, which looked as if it had first been created in the '60s. She wore a green print dress, with a strong turquoise necklace.

"Kate?"

Her voice was pleasant and soft, like ripe fruit.

Kate nodded, feeling like a child.

"I'm Sylvia. Come in."

"Thanks."

Kate walked into an elegant hall. The floor was covered with gold-and-blue geometric Victorian tiles. "Do you want to leave your helmet there?" Sylvia said, pointing to a mahogany table adorned by a giant vase of lilies.

Kate nodded again.

"I'm so glad you finally made it," Sylvia said.

Kate looked at the floor.

"I know. Sorry. Things just kept coming up."

"You managed to get someone to look after your son then?" Sylvia said, opening a door and guiding Kate through.

"Yes, I did, thanks. His grandparents. My in-laws."

The sitting room was even more impressive than the hall. It was furnished with antique tables, bookshelves, and over-stuffed chairs and sofas. It smelled of polish. The wallpaper looked original Victorian, too, or at least one of those expensive reproductions Hugo used to buy through specialists. Sage green with an intricate spray of curling dark stems and ruby-red roses.

Sylvia gestured toward an armchair.

"Please, have a seat, Kate."

But Kate couldn't.

She stood in front of the chair. She was here now. It was time to start.

Looking Sylvia in the eye, she made herself speak the words. The voice that came out didn't sound like hers. The words were half-formed and uncertain, as if she had left off the hard edges, and spoken only the soft bits in the middle.

"I told them I was seeing someone who was doing renovation work on their house."

Sylvia nodded as she moved to the sofa.

"I see. Well, that's something we can talk about, Kate."

There he was again. That weirdo.

Saskia stood second in line at the Tesco on Cowley Road, watching the student in front of her put through two micro-waveable hamburgers-in-buns, three cans of Vienna sausages, and a large pack of Curly Wurlys.

Yum, she thought, touching a French-polished fingertip on the chilled bottle of sparkling rosé she had placed on the belt. Some lucky girl was going to be wined and dined tonight.

She checked him out carefully so that he didn't notice what

she was doing. It was the first time she had seen him up close. It was his height that had originally caught her eye a few weeks ago. Not that he was particularly taller than any other man she knew. Dad, for instance. His legs just seemed overly long, perhaps due to the shapeless black trousers he wore. His shirt was black, too, and too short, revealing a white slice of soft, out-of-shape belly each time he moved. Inside Tesco, the student looked even odder. His outdated spiky, dark-blond hair and bad glasses marked him out from the cool indie kids from the Poly—or Oxford Brookes University as Saskia was now supposed to call it on her CV. Or Oxford Puniversity as Hugo used to call it to wind her up.

Five minutes later she left Tesco with her wine, and found herself behind the student again as they both wound through the backstreets of East Oxford. He was doing that strange walk again. Bouncing along on his oddly long legs, his upper torso bobbing with the motion. It gave the impression of awkwardness and arrogance. His strides were so much longer than Saskia's that by the time she reached the corner of Walter Street, he had disappeared from sight.

Saskia stopped to look in a real-estate agent's window, pausing on her reflection for a second. With the early evening sun behind her head, it looked like she was wearing a halo, the white-blond tips of her hair melding into its rays. She flattened down the front of her pale-blue summer dress, wondering if Jonathan was missing her at all.

With a sigh, she checked the property values. Hubert Street was holding its own. That was good. Something, at least, for Jack's sake.

Oh, no. She looked herself in the eye, in the window.

Jack.

He would be waiting for her, desperate to know her decision.

On impulse, she dived into the newsstand next door and searched the boys' magazines to find one she hadn't bought him yet. That would distract him till she decided what to do. Because if she did it, Kate would kill her. If she didn't—well, things were bad enough as it was for her nephew.

At the last minute she grabbed some cough drops for her presentation at work on Monday morning, and headed back outside, popping a cough drop in her mouth. There was a flash of movement to her right.

Saskia jumped.

What the hell was that?

A large, black shape was moving between two cars.

Walking fast, she waited till she was at a safe distance to turn around.

She could see a black-clad backside between the cars. A slice of white, flabby skin hung gently over the waistband.

The weirdo. He was crouched down, looking at a row of houses across the road.

Why was he behaving so surreptitiously?

Saskia surveyed the house opposite. It looked like a normal residential house. No piles of bikes or posters in the window to suggest that students lived there. A well-painted red door. Cream curtains half-closed. Faint classical music drifting out of an open window, inside of which a woman with a brunette bob, who looked to be in her thirties, could be seen.

Saskia heard a faint click, and then another.

A camera?

Was he watching someone? A woman?

Oh, that was gross.

Then, Saskia felt a tickle of cold air at the back of her throat—and coughed.

The student moved.

"No, I'll get some pizza," she exclaimed, walking off and talking into her hand as if it were a phone, realizing too late that a woman with a stroller was coming straight at her, and staring curiously.

Saskia continued quickly toward Hubert Street. She better tell Kate. As if they needed any more problems.

Saskia turned onto Hubert, trying to shake off the sense of unease caused by what she'd just seen. Kate's semidetached Edwardian house looked pretty in the evening sunshine, the freshly whitewashed windowsills sparkling, the burnt-orange passionflower that Helen had planted trailing around the front door. Saskia glanced at the house next to it, to which Kate's was attached. It looked like the unidentical twin. Whereas Kate's frontage was tidy, her bins behind a wooden fence Richard had erected and stained a pale lilac Helen had chosen, the one next door was undoubtedly a student house. It was worn and tired; its windowsills also painted white, but the paint sloshed cheaply over the joins and onto the windowpanes. Bikes lay in heaps on the overgrown lawn, chained together. A garbage can was half-open, trash bags bursting out, the faint smell of rubbish detectable even from where she stood.

That was the best thing about living in a village. There were no students. Not for the first time, Saskia wished Mum and Dad had insisted Kate not rush into buying when she moved from London. If they hadn't been so wary of her pain-in-the-ass moods, they might have at least suggested she check into who lived next door.

Steeling herself, as she always did on arrival at Hubert Street, Saskia walked up to the door and pressed the bell.

"Hello," came a deep voice from behind her. The "oh" was pronounced as "aw," with a long, Scandinavian vowel.

She turned and saw the weirdo walking through the gate next door. He looked at her impassively from behind his glasses.

"Hi," she said as coldly as she could.

She felt his eyes still on her.

Creep.

He'd probably followed her up the road, taking photos of her backside.

To her relief, Jack flung open the door, grinning.

"Hey, Jackasnory!" she exclaimed in relief, walking inside and shutting the door. She held her hands slightly forward, in case he wanted to hug. She was never sure these days. Boys of nearly eleven were fickle.

Luckily, her nephew was in the mood. He came straight to her, wrapping himself tightly around her waist. She put her arms around him and moved his body gently from left to right. He stayed there happily. Or was it desperately?

"God, you give the best cuddles. Did you win?"

"Two-nil," Richard shouted from the sitting room. "And he's in the reserves for a junior league team next term."

"Oh, are you now? Smartie bum." Saskia grinned at Jack's beaming, upturned face.

The smile quickly disappeared and was replaced with a meaningful stare.

"What?"

"Please?" he mouthed, holding his hands in the praying position.

"Oh." She glanced through to the kitchen where Helen was lifting a pot. That was odd. Her mother hadn't even looked up, never mind a cheery hello.

"No. Not now. Later. You'll get me into trouble, Snores. I'm still thinking about it," she whispered, pushing him toward the sitting room. "Take this." She gave him the magazine. "Go and keep Granddad company."

Jack obeyed, as he always did, with a thrust of his lower lip to make her laugh.

Saskia looked at her mother again in the kitchen, seemingly unaware that she had arrived. What was different about her? Her shoulders? They looked rigid. And even from here, her face appeared rosier than normal.

Saskia went to hang her bag on the balustrade.

There was a silver flash above her head.

She tried to process what she had just seen.

As she stood staring, her father walked out of the sitting room and placed his hands on her shoulders.

She turned and saw his usually jovial face as serious as it had ever been.

"*What. The. Hell?*" she mouthed, incredulous, pointing upstairs.

"Later," he murmured, nodding toward the sitting room, where Jack was.

As he headed off down the hallway, her big, powerful dad, with his shoulders hunched, Saskia now realized her mother was crying. It was all she could do not to shout, "Kate?" and run off around Oxford looking for her stupid bloody idiot of a sister-in-law.

3

It was a while before Kate began to talk to Sylvia. They sat in silence, as she knew they might. It was an old-fashioned silence, Kate thought. Inside these thick walls, there were none of the normal city sounds. No kids shouting after school. No sirens. The silence felt thick and upper-class and dusty.

She scanned the room. In the center was an oversized stone fireplace, its heart blackened and empty. A Chinese urn sat on an oak table. This was the type of house a housekeeper ran, Kate thought. She couldn't see elegant Sylvia kneeling down and scrubbing away coal dust.

Sylvia sat opposite her on a sofa. The fabric was strewn with a faint orange-and-green botanical print. Just the right tone of faded, Hugo would have said.

She looked up at an oil painting of a woman in a wine-colored velvet dress, with blond hair like Veronica Lake, sitting with her hands in her lap.

"That's amazing," Kate said, gesturing.

Sylvia smiled. "Thank you."

Kate shifted in her seat. She crossed her legs, then her arms, then tried to uncross them again. That was amateur stuff. Everyone knew that. The defensive move.

Sylvia kept looking at her. She had a face both long and broad, with generous cheekbones. Her lips were painted a confident red. Kate suspected she was a woman who had grown comfortable in her large frame in later years.

She tried to find something to say. "It reminds me of those old horror films where you move around the room, and the eyes in a painting follow you."

Sylvia nodded.

Kate sighed. This was hopeless.

The ticking of a grandfather clock gave the room life, by way of a heavy heartbeat.

"It is going to sound silly," Kate finally said.

"Why don't you try?"

"OK. Well, it appears . . ."

She was aware of Sylvia's steady breath as she spoke.

". . . that I am cursed."

Immediately, nervously, she laughed at her own admission.

"Oh, God. I'm sorry. That just sounded funny. You know, with the painting, and everything."

Sylvia smiled.

"Like I'm in a Vincent Price movie, or something. . . . You know, 'I'm *cursed*, I tell you!'" She rolled the syllables like a comedy horror actor, curling her fingers like talons beside her face.

Sylvia held her gaze.

"Sorry. I'm a bit anxious," Kate said. She stopped fighting her arms and let them wrap around her chest.

Sylvia dropped her head to one side, like a bird.

"Can you tell me what you mean by 'cursed,' Kate?"

How could she explain this? It sounded so crazy. "OK. Well, I mean, that I'm someone to whom bad things are meant to happen."

"What kind of bad things, Kate?"

Out of the blue, a tear pricked at her eye. Damn. Where had that come from?

Kate swallowed hard. "Uh, it happens all the time. For instance, ten days ago I was burgled. Someone broke in the back of the house when I was out at a work meeting, and stole my laptop and my son's Wii."

Sylvia nodded sympathetically. "I'm sorry to hear that. But it's not unusual to be burgled, of course."

Kate pushed her hands into her knees. "Right, but it's the second time in five months. Every time I come home, I'm paranoid it's happened again. I keep thinking objects have moved. I can't find anything. I'm convinced that doors I thought I left open have been shut."

"Burglary can be traumatic." Sylvia nodded. "It's an invasion of your space, your home."

Kate tried not to sound irritated when she said, "Yes, but it's not just that. It's not just the burglary. You asked for an example. I was just giving you one. No one else on my street has been burgled this year. Out of fifty houses." Sylvia's face remained impassive. "Oh. I don't know how to explain it. . . . OK. You know how most people will never be in a train crash, but a tiny number will be in two? Well, I'm always the person who's in two train crashes."

Sylvia nodded. "Could you give me another example?"

Kate sighed. This was harder than she'd imagined.

"Well, five years ago my h—"

She stopped. Tears threatened to betray her, to expose the soft wounds beneath toughened bones.

She tried again. Sylvia waited.

"I find it difficult to say the word."

"Take your time."

She swallowed hard and forced the syllables out. "My husband." The word came out strangled, like her throat was sore.

"Your husband?"

Kate let herself exist in the moment, a second during which Sylvia thought Hugo was alive.

The tears burst forth and ran freely down her cheeks.

"Please." Sylvia leaned forward offering tissues.

Kate took one. She sniffed and wiped her cheek.

"My husband . . . was killed."

The memory of violence, a flash, silver and sharp. She automatically touched her stomach.

"Oh, Kate. How terrible for you. I'm so sorry," Sylvia said.

Kate held up one hand, and took a deep breath to compose herself.

"And my parents," she whispered, the tears welling. "Sorry."

"It's fine to cry, Kate."

Kate shook her head vigorously. Suddenly, she was angry.

She *did not cry anymore*.

She *would not*.

"One thousand." She forced herself to count internally. "Two thousand . . . Three thousand . . . Four . . ."

The heave of her chest settled gradually.

Sylvia watched her carefully. "I can see how difficult this is for you. Would you like to tell me what happened?"

"No," Kate said, gratefully feeling her composure begin to return. "It was years ago. Anyway, that's not why I'm here. Not right now."

She sat up, determined. She looked Sylvia straight in the eye.
It was time.

"I do sums."

"Sums?"

"Yes. Obsessively. All the time, in my head."

"Could you tell me what kind of sums?"

Kate shrugged.

"I calculate stuff. Constantly. To stop more bad things from
happening to us."

"You and your son?"

"Yes. Jack."

"Could you give me an example?"

"Well, I could. But before I do, I need to know something."

"Please."

Kate sat forward. "If I tell you, do you have the power to take
away my son?"

Sylvia paused.

"Yes, if I feel a child is in immediate danger, I have an obli-
gation to take some action. But the fact that you are here, seeking help in relation to your son, makes me think you are a good
mother."

Kate nodded, surprised. "I try to be," she said.

"Well, why don't we concentrate on you? Can you tell me
more about these sums?"

"OK, there was a lot of traffic tonight so I decided to cycle.
But before I cycled, I did a sum. Because it's May, my chance of
having a bike accident is higher than in winter, and eighty percent of accidents take place during daylight hours. But because
more than half of cycling fatalities happen at road junctions,
I knew if I went off-road, I could lower that chance dramatically. So I did. And I also worked out that because I am thirty-

five, I have more chance of having a cycling accident than another woman in Oxfordshire in her twenties, but because I was wearing my helmet, I have—according to one report I read, anyway—about an eighty-five percent chance of reducing my risk of head injury. Then, when I was cycling I balanced my chances of having an accident with the fact that by doing half an hour of sustained cardio cycling, I could lower my risk of getting cancer. Of course, that meant I increased my chances of being sexually attacked by being alone on a quiet canal path, but as I have roughly a one-in-a-thousand chance in Oxfordshire, I think it's worth taking.

"And then when I was cycling here, I kept doing calculations. When I passed through Osney Weir, I didn't think how pretty it was, I looked for the tree I'd cling on to if I accidentally fell in, and planned how I'd swim with the current, not against it, because if you plan your escape you improve your chances of survival by a third. And when I passed the waterside flats at Botley, I didn't think how lovely it must be to live there, I thought about the flood risk. Same when I passed the cottages backing onto the river path at Jericho, I thought about how your chances of being burgled are higher if you have open access to your garden. . . ."

Her breath ran out. She'd been talking so quickly, she'd barely gotten any air.

"They just come at me like swarms. I can't explain it any other way. They come out of nowhere."

"Where do you get these figures from?"

"I collect books on survival, insurance Web sites, newspapers. Every day the newspapers have new figures about how to lower or increase the chances of things happening to you."

"And you compile them, what, into lists?"

"Yes. But when my laptop got stolen, I lost all my statistics, so I've been trying to remember till the new one is delivered next week. I use my iPhone when I can. But I'm worried that I might be getting some figures wrong. Like today, I picked my son up from soccer because my car has the best safety record, and his PE teacher is in his twenties, which increases his chances of an accident. But my phone battery needed charging, and I couldn't remember the risk of a minibus crash in comparison to a car, so I picked Jack up anyway, in front of his friends, and he just looked so . . ."

She felt exhausted.

"Oh, God. I know what it sounds like."

"What does it sounds like?"

"Crazy," she said. "It sounds crazy."

"Crazy that you want to protect your son?"

Kate looked up, surprised. She wiped her eyes again.

"My in-laws think I'm crazy. They don't understand that's all I'm trying to do. After his dad . . ." Her voice faded away. "I see their faces when I talk about these things, especially in front of Jack. But I want him to know about the statistics. I want him to be careful because I'm so scared of anything happening to him, too. And yet at the same time, I know it worries him, and I shouldn't burden him with that." She wiped her nose. The words she'd hidden for so long were coming thick and fast now. "The thing is, I find it hard to judge anymore if I'm being rational or not. Like a few days ago, I spent over a thousand pounds in a private clinic in London having a whole-body scan. I'm not sick or anything. I do one every year to check I am not getting ill, that I don't have even the start of a tumor. Because catching it early would increase my chances of survival. I have to be there for Jack, now that Hugo is gone." She pushed the wet tissues below her eyes as if physically holding back any more tears. "I mean, is that normal? I don't know anymore." She placed the tissues on her lap and sniffed. "When Hugo was here he'd rein me in. When my parents died, and Jack was a baby, I was all over the place, but he never let it get out of hand. He'd let me melt down when I needed to—but then he'd also expect me to be normal sometimes, too. That made me expect it, too."

Sylvia nodded. "He gave you perspective."

"Mmm. I had bad days and good days, eventually more good days. But now, it's not even about bad days. It's gone so far past that it's like I'm in free fall. I worry I'll never get back."

Kate put her head in her hands. From between her knees, she heard the forbidden words emerge from her mouth.

"I miss Hugo so much."

Sylvia let the words hang, echoing around the room.

They sat together silently for a while.

"I'm sorry," Kate said finally. "I'm all over the place today."

Sylvia regarded her warmly. If she thought Kate was mad, she was hiding it well. "First sessions can be very emotional, Kate. You've waited a long time to talk about some very private and distressing feelings."

Kate nodded. "Thanks. You must think I'm a complete lunatic."

Sylvia sat very still, giving nothing away with her body language, Kate noted. She wondered if she'd ever had a client with such a crazy-sounding problem. "I certainly don't think you're a lunatic. I think you have been very brave coming here. From the little you've told me, I think you are a young woman who has experienced extreme trauma and has understandably been left with overwhelming feelings of anxiety. But you're here now, and that's the first step."

Kate licked her dry lips. "Really?"

Sylvia nodded. She smiled suddenly, looking as if she herself had relaxed into the session a little. As if she knew where she was with Kate, and where she was going to go with her. "Absolutely. Now, before we go on, can I fetch you a glass of water?"

Kate nodded gratefully.

Sylvia stood up. She walked out of the sitting room, leaving the door ajar.

Kate sat back into the comfortable chair. She looked around the room again. This wouldn't be a bad place to sit for an hour or two a week. This woman might really help her find her way back to Jack.

Kate heard murmured voices. And laughter drifting from a room in the back of the house.

She could hear a man, laughing.

She could hear Sylvia's voice and a male voice, and tried to make out what they were saying, but then, abruptly, it went quiet.

She sat up straight.

Sylvia had spoken to this man at the back of the house, and then he had laughed.

About her?

A second later, she heard Sylvia's heavy footsteps. She appeared with a glass of water and shut the door.

"Sorry about that, Kate. I thought we had the house to ourselves tonight."

Kate stared at her. "So someone else is here?"

Sylvia sat down. "Actually, that's something I should clarify. As you know, Kate, I hold my appointments in the evenings, but because I work from home, I must explain that there may be people around at that time. But I can assure you that nobody can hear our discussions. Everything we say in here is confidential."

Kate paused to choose her words carefully.

"You were laughing with someone."

Sylvia folded her hands on her lap. "Oh. Kate. You heard my husband laughing. I'm afraid he was just walking through the garage door as I went into the kitchen, and was talking to his colleague on his mobile. My appointments normally don't start till seven o'clock, so he didn't realize that I had a client here so early. I must also reassure you that the door to the back of the house is shut at all times when I'm working."

My husband.

Kate flinched. When this woman said the word "husband," it didn't stick in her mouth. It didn't hurt. It spoke of a life where husbands came home early, not of a life where they never came home.

Kate stood up.

Sylvia looked confused. "Kate, we still have forty minutes left."

"You know," Kate said, "when Hugo died, they told me not to start bereavement counseling too early. They said I needed to process things first. And by that point, it hurt so badly, I didn't want to talk about it. I didn't want to cry anymore. And I still don't. Maybe this was a mistake." She pulled out some money. "I came here for my son. I tell you these awful things, that I've told no one in five years, and you go into the kitchen . . ." She gave Sylvia an astonished look ". . . and I hear laughing. And right now, I don't care who was laughing—I just heard laughing."

Sylvia stood up. "Kate, I am so sorry. This is so unfortunate. Please sit down and we can talk a little more."

"No," Kate said, putting the money on the oak table and walking to the door. Sylvia's expression was full of concern. Kate looked around.

"You know, I imagine some of your clients might feel intimidated by this house. But the irony is that, if I wanted, I could buy it. That's what happens when all the people around you are killed. You'd be amazed at how much money people give you. Like this horrible consolation prize. But you know what? I'd give it all up to escape from this." She pointed at her head. "To feel like I used to, even for one day. To be a normal person again, and a decent mother."

A lump came into her throat. Why did she tell this woman so much? What had she been thinking even coming here?

"Kate," Sylvia exclaimed, standing up. "Please. I can understand why you're upset. Could we discuss it a little more?"

Kate held up her hand. "If you tell anyone what I told you, or talk to anyone about my son, I'll deny I was ever here."

With that, she marched into the hall, picked up her helmet without caring whether it scratched the table or not, and slammed the door behind her.

Saskia came downstairs, shaking her head in disbelief. She entered the kitchen where Richard was reading a newspaper. Helen stabbed potatoes with a knife.

"Have you talked to Jack about it?" she asked quietly.

Richard carried on reading, raising his eyebrows.

"Dad tried but he just looked embarrassed, poor pet," Helen replied. She stuck the knife in again. "Oh, help, I've overdone these. Sorry, you lot."

Her pale-green eyes were watery.

Saskia rested her hands on her father's chair. "But it's ridiculous," she whispered. "We've got to do something."

"Not now," Richard murmured, nodding toward the sitting room.

"He can't live like this."

"I said not now, darling."

Saskia turned. Jack was sticking his head around the door frame, watching. The theme song from *The Simpsons* blared in the background.

"Five minutes, Snores," Saskia called cheerily. "Go and wash your hands."

He nodded and disappeared upstairs.

"What do you want me to do?" she asked.

"Set the table, will you, darling?" her mother said. "I'll have to mash these to dry them out." As she carried the pot to the sink, Saskia could see she was struggling not to drop it.

She was sick of it. Seeing Dad, the powerful businessman who took nonsense from no one, walking around Kate on eggshells. Him and Mum summoning bright smiles and constantly calling her "dear" and "darling," in an attempt to diffuse the tense atmosphere their daughter-in-law created. Well, if they weren't going to force some sense into Kate, she would.

Saskia looked at a closed door beside the sitting room. She checked the clock. Kate would be back after seven.

That would do it. Send a message.

Quietly, Saskia took down a tray from above the fridge, and placed glasses, a jug of water, and cutlery on it. Then she walked past the kitchen table where her father sat, and carried it to the hallway.

She turned the handle of the closed door. As she expected, it was now locked.

"Sass, darling, don't . . . ." she heard her mother whisper loudly from the kitchen. "You know what she's like."

"I'm doing it, Mum," she said, reaching above the door frame for the new key. She saw her father shake his head.

She turned it in the door, and pushed it open.

It was the smell that hit her first. Fresh paint and a new carpet, incarcerated for four years in this locked room. Forced to ripen into a chemical reek, now complemented by the sweet tang of fresh putty.

Shutting the door gently so Jack wouldn't hear, she walked to the window and pushed the curtains farther apart to brighten the room. It had little effect. The room was naturally somber. Like that gloomy parlor in the eighteenth-century cottage she and Jonathan had rented in North Wales one Easter that felt as if bodies had once been laid out in it before funerals. Or perhaps it had just been a foreboding about the fate of their marriage.

She placed the tray gently on the long walnut Georgian table, one of the few beautiful pieces Kate had kept of Hugo's. How many times had she been in here? Once? Twice? In four years? The room was painted the same white Kate had chosen for the rest of the house. Not the careful shade of off-white Hugo would have spent a month tracking down. This was Kate's white. An I-don't-care, this-will-do shade of white. The fresh putty used to fix the window broken by the burglar was lighter than the rest. She ran a finger over it. It was dry.

Curious, Saskia looked around. There was nothing in here apart from a four-drawer oak sideboard with turned legs that she remembered from the Highgate house, too. It was a piece Hugo had salvaged from one of his restoration projects.

She knelt down on the unused carpet, and opened a door in the sideboard.

A silver Georgian-era epergne stared back at her, its delicate arms and tiny bowls once ready to shine as the centerpiece of a lavish dinner party, now tarnished and unloved.

Her hand shot out to touch its cold surface. She hadn't seen this for years.

A rush of memories of dinner at Hugo and Kate's came at Saskia, unexpected and pungent.

Opening the door farther, she found the sets of gold-plated bone china that Hugo collected; his exquisite silver soup terrine, found in a cellar in a derelict property in Bath and polished to within an inch of its life, now blackened and dull once again.

She saw it all for a moment. Friends seated along the Georgian table, silver cutlery, laughing, eyes shining under Hugo's prized candelabra. Hugo pouring the wine so generously that she'd find herself emptying half-drunk goblets into the sink at the end of the night, with Kate growling something about "there goes our bloody pension down the drain." Hugo the fabulous host. The spirit of Hugo.

Now all locked in a cupboard in a forgotten room.

She took out a modern, taupe table runner that she recognized from their casual suppers around the kitchen table in the basement. A musty smell arose from it. She ran her fingers along it then stopped.

There was a dark gray stain on it, the size of a two-penny piece. Red wine, perhaps.

Why hadn't it been washed off?

A glint of glass below the china caught her eye. What was that? Kneeling down, Saskia pushed her hand into the back, trying not to knock over a set of cut-glass crystal. It was a bottle. Grimacing, she delicately placed her fingers around its neck and pulled it out.

As soon as she saw it, she knew what it was.

Saskia froze.

It was a dusty bottle of red wine, half-drunk, with a stopper in its top. Not a particularly good wine, either. In fact, one she recognized as the high-end limit of the corner shop where Hugo and Kate lived in Highgate. She had bought it in there enough times on the way to visit if she was late.

Kate had kept it. Hugo's last bottle of wine, from that night. The one he must have been drinking when those people came to his front door.

Saskia opened the wine and sniffed its faint, rotten tang.

She surveyed its label, sad that her brother, the generous connoisseur, had been subjected to this bottle of crap as his last.

Just as it was unjust that Hugo's son, who had inherited his father's fun-loving spirit, was having it squeezed out of him, drop by drop, by Kate.

"Hugo," she whispered into the bottle. "Don't be cross at me. I promise you, you wouldn't know her now."

There was a noise to her right. Someone was opening the door.

Saskia shoved the bottle back inside, and looked up.

Jack appeared. His eyes were wide. He looked around the room and back at her.

"We're not supposed to eat in here."

"Snores," she said, standing up. "Leave it to the grown-ups to worry about things like that. Anyway, you know that thing we were talking about?"

His expression changed.

"Yeah?"

"You know what? I've decided to let you do it. But if you tell anyone, I will seriously kill your head."

4

Oxford High Street was packed with people out enjoying the early summer evening. Kate pushed her bike home over Magdalen Bridge, behind a young couple who had just bolted out of the hatch door in the giant wooden gate of one of the university colleges like rabbits from a secret burrow. Kate tried not to look at them but couldn't help herself.

Clearly they had just tumbled out of bed. They stalked along on long, skinny-jean-clad legs, their arms moving from waist to shoulder then back again, fluidly, as if they were so high on each other they couldn't stop touching every part. The girl's hair was long and expertly teased into a perfect *Vogue*, bed-head ponytail. The boy wore pointed Chelsea boots and had a black quiff. They spoke in loud, confident voices. Oxford University, King's Road, Val D'Isere, Barbados, Kate thought. She knew that type of student.

They weren't her favorites.

She preferred the odds and sods. The girls in shapeless floral shirts and denim shorts, legs self-consciously covered with dark tights, pointlessly long hair pulled back off spotty faces; the delicate-framed boys in glasses dressed in white chinos and striped shirts, who looked as if their brains had developed so fast, their bodies had never had time to catch up. The students with the awkward gaits and brilliant intellects who would spend a lifetime searching for like-minded souls.

That type was easier to bear right now.

Kate crossed the bridge and entered East Oxford. She pushed her bike up the relative peace of Iffley Road toward home, trying to shake off the humiliation of her aborted session with Sylvia.

She had been ready to talk, finally. After months of nearly calling Sylvia and preparing what to say, she had gone there and let it all out at last. Now she had to shove it back inside, to be hidden away again. Her fear had been confirmed. Her problem was ludicrous. Laughable. No one could help her. And even if she had misunderstood and overreacted at Sylvia's, which she was starting queasily to suspect she might have done, she'd never be able to go back anyway, after that outburst.

With no hope for her, what about Jack?

Kate looked up the road ahead. And as if it wasn't bad enough, Helen and Richard would be there when she got home, Helen plumping her cushions without being asked. Richard bellowing in his exhausting manner, asking how her fake appointment with a client who needed renovation work went as if it was the most important job anyone had ever pitched for, and asking difficult questions about what she had done upstairs.

Kate walked wearily into Hubert Street a few minutes later, and put down her bag.

Something was different. She listened. Voices drifted forth from the back of the house. The kitchen light was off.

"Hello?" she said, taking off her helmet and peering into the sitting room.

"Hi, Mum!" Jack shouted.

She stared at the dining-room door.

Putting down her helmet, she turned the handle.

It was unlocked.

She pushed the door open with a growing sense of dread.

They wouldn't have dared.

She walked into the room to find Richard, Helen, Saskia, and Jack sitting at the table.

Her dining-room table.

The dining-room table where Kate and Hugo and her own parents should have sat a hundred times, enjoying Christmas dinner, and family weekend get-togethers, and birthdays and anniversaries.

And now, Richard, Helen, and Saskia had forced their way in and taken their places.

The tabletop was laid with plates and cutlery from the kitchen, along with Hugo's bone china serving dishes from the sideboard. Everything was illuminated by his candelabra, the flames flickering above the old table runner from Highgate.

She saw the stain immediately.

There was a row of cards down the middle of the table.

Helen twitched nervously, a smile stuck on her face. She avoided Kate's eye.

Saskia, however, glared at her defiantly.

"We thought we'd sit in here tonight," she said. "Have a family meal."

"Jack, could you go up for your bath, please," Kate said as calmly as she could.

"Mum—look at this trick Granddad showed me!" he exclaimed, jumping up, his green eyes flashing in the candlelight. He took her arm and tried to lead her to the cards. "You've got to choose cards, and put them into two piles, and at the end I can turn one pile into red and the other one into black. Really."

Kate took his hand and held it firmly in hers.

"I said now, please, Jack. Bath."

He looked at Saskia and his grandparents, put the cards on the table and walked out, closing the door gently behind him.

Kate stared at the dreaded triumvirate.

"Let me get you a drink, darling," Richard said, picking up the bottle of rosé.

"No. I don't want a drink, Richard. Thank you."

Helen nibbled at a piece of bread.

"How did it go? Any good, do you think?" Richard continued, replacing the bottle. He pulled out a chair. "Have a seat."

Kate shook her head as she sat down. "I don't think so. When I explained the work placement situation she wasn't so keen."

How could they do this?

"Not keen on having the local ruffians buffing up her floorboards, eh?" Richard was babbling now, filling the unpleasant silence with meaningless chatter.

Kate felt her voice grow weaker as she said, "They're kids from deprived backgrounds, Richard." This wasn't the time for a sparring match about how she chose to use Hugo's money.

She couldn't believe they'd ransacked her home and displayed her and Hugo's belongings, private posessions, without permission. She felt Saskia's eyes boring into her.

"Anyone else want a refill?" Richard asked.

What was wrong with Saskia? Was she drunk? Her cheeks were pink like her mother's, and her eyes flashed dangerously in the candlelight. Kate looked at her steadily, trying to control herself in front of Richard and Helen. In the old days, when she and Sass had been best friends, they'd peppered their own conversations casually with swearwords, but never in front of Richard and Helen.

"How very lovely the dining-room table looks, doesn't it?" said Richard beaming. He waved his hand across the table exuberantly. "Hugo would always . . ." His voice just cut away. His smile extinguished.

"Was this your idea, Sass?" Kate said quietly.

"I think we're the ones who should be asking questions, Kate."

Kate looked at her, incredulous. She hadn't even been invited this evening. She just turned up, as usual. And now she was questioning her in front of Richard and Helen, and in her own home.

"Sass!" she said, shocked.

Richard raised his hand to stop his daughter from saying more. "OK, that's enough, Sass." He turned to his daughter-in-law. "It's just that it is a little unexpected, darling. What you've done."

"Unexpected? It's complete bloody madness, Dad! At what point are you and Mum going to stop pussyfooting around her, and tell her this has to stop?" Saskia was exasperated.

Richard's expression turned cold, but Saskia's voice only grew louder. "Are you afraid she's going to stop you and Mum from seeing Jack? Is that why you put up with it?"

Kate could only sit in shock. After the trauma of Sylvia's, a fight between Hugo's family was the last thing she needed.

"Look, I did it in case they come back," Kate finally said, trying to keep her voice calm.

"But you've just spent thousands on a new alarm when the one you had worked perfectly well!"

Kate wondered what in the hell her sister-in-law was doing.

"Sass, I'm sorry, but this is none of your business. The old alarm wasn't perfect. It went off a few times when there was a storm or it was really windy—so if anyone broke in, the neighbors probably wouldn't even notice, because they'd already heard it go off in the middle of the night. So why take the chance?"

"Oh, for God's sake. This is *bloody ridiculous!*" Saskia said. "And then there was all that money on putting in the internal locks downstairs. And now this bloody thing," she exclaimed, pointing upward. "I mean, Jesus, Kate. How much did it cost? What the hell would Hugo say?"

Kate gulped hard. "Sass . . . don't even . . ."

"And then tonight, Snores tells us you're not letting him go to the local secondary with his friends because you're scared he's going to be stabbed or something—you're thinking of sending him to some fee-paying private school on the other side of Oxford where he'll know nobody. I mean, for God's sake, Kate, what is *wrong* with you?"

"He's called *Jack*," Kate said, her voice rising to meet her sister-in-law's.

Saskia stood up, eyes blazing.

Richard and Helen stayed silent. Why were they not stopping this?

Kate stood up, too.

"Actually, Sass," she said, her voice icy, "if you must know, though I don't think it's any of your bloody business, someone from that school was threatened with a knife. A sixth-former. At a party last weekend in Cowley."

Richard finally spoke up.

"Listen, Sass. This isn't helping. Sit down, darling."

He waited till she begrudgingly obeyed, then turned to Kate, who sat down, too.

"Look, Kate, the thing is, these things happen," he said, taking Kate's hand into his, which was large and warm and comforting, like her own father's used to be. Hugo's hands had never reached that stage. They had been too strong and busy and vital at his stage of life.

"I know you're just trying to protect him, darling, we all understand that. And you know, I'd be absolutely delighted if you wanted to send the boy private . . ." In fact, Richard had never stopped going on about it since she and Hugo had announced they were sending Jack to the local state primary school in London. ". . . But I think what Sass is trying to say is"—he glared at his daughter—"and perhaps not in the best way, is that perhaps things have gone a little too far. You have to prepare the boy for life, not hide him from it."

Kate shook her head. It was all too much. The session with Sylvia, and now this.

"I'm sorry," she said, holding up her hands. "Richard, Sass, Helen—I appreciate everything you have done for me, I really do. And I know not everything is right in my life right now. But Jack is my child and, really, I'm sorry, but this is no one else's business."

The room fell silent. She focused on the runner. On the stain on the runner.

Tears began to prick the back of her eyes again. She was exhausted by the effort it took to hold them back.

Saskia shook her head. Her cheeks were flushed and her eyes flashed with anger.

"OK, darling, listen, everyone's getting upset." Richard looked at Helen. "Why doesn't Mum make us some coffee— we'll discuss this another time, when everyone is calmer?"

Helen cleared her throat. "Actually, Kate, I think it is our business."

They all looked at her in surprise. In fourteen years, Kate had never heard Helen speak with such authority.

"It's gone too far, Kate. You've gone too far. We've stood by for years now watching this . . . letting you mourn in your own way, but this?" she said, pointing upstairs to "it." "It's, it's . . . lunacy. And for your information, Sass," Helen continued, "I have already spoken to social services anonymously about what is happening in this house, and what my rights are as a grandparent, and no, I am not worried about Kate not letting me see Jack."

Kate stared at her.

"Helen, how could you?" she asked desperately.

"I won't let you do this to my grandson anymore, Kate. After the terrible thing that has happened to him, this little boy deserves love and reassurance and happiness. But instead, you've turned him into a nervous wreck. Do you know he tried three times tonight to stop us from eating in here? He was so anxious about what you would say. I mean, for goodness' sake, it's a dining room."

Kate was bewildered. What on earth was Helen doing? She waited for her mother-in-law to return to her benign, fragrant self. To apologize. To keep the peace.

But Helen continued, her voice cold.

"I think he should come and live with me and Richard for a while."

Kate was horrified. "No!" she cried.

"Richard can run him into town to school, and pick him up."

"Richard?" Kate said frantically, pleading.

Richard sighed. "Darling, you haven't been yourself for a while. The thing is, Helen and I feel a strong responsibility to you, but we also need to think about what Hugo would want us to do, for Jack."

"You think Hugo would want you to take him from me?" Kate spluttered. "Jesus. How long have you been planning this?"

Richard shook his head. "We're just offering to take him for a while to give you a chance to start thinking about how to improve things. . . ."

"And if I say no?"

Helen met her eye. "My next call to social services will not be anonymous."

A stunned silence descended on the table.

"Helen." Kate gasped. "How could you say that?"

Helen sat upright. "I've never interfered, Kate. Not once, with all the alarms and hospital visits and the irrational rules, and this obsession with . . ." She stopped. "Because Richard said we needed to give you time after what happened. But you don't even seem aware of your behavior. You lie to Jack constantly. You told him last week that you were in London seeing a friend, but we know you were at the hospital because you left the letter in the drawer where the clothespins are. And this business tonight, frightening him by saying someone had been here, stealing your casserole?"

No. No. This couldn't be happening.

"Some of it had gone out of the dish. . . ." she whispered.

"It had *not* gone!" Helen exclaimed, dropping her delicate, pale hand on the table. "You imagine these things, Kate! Constantly! And now he's copying you, for goodness' sake!" Helen stopped to draw a breath. "I mean, this business about hearing noises in his wardrobe. Richard had to check inside three times the other night when you were in London. Jack was terribly anxious."

Kate looked at her mother-in-law with confusion. What was she talking about?

Helen shook her head. "He's nearly eleven, Kate! When are you going to let him go to the shop, or walk to school on his own? What do his friends say? Nearly eleven, thinking there are bad men hiding in his wardrobe." She saw the lack of understanding on Kate's face. "Oh, you don't even know, do you?" She looked at her husband. "The boy hasn't even told her, Richard."

Kate felt the shame of Helen's exposure that they knew more about Jack than she did. Helen continued. "Can you even see what's going on here anymore, Kate? You're his mother. Some opportunist, probably a drug addict, smashed a window, came in and snatched your laptop. It happens. You need to reassure Jack that's all it was. Not talk constantly about crime and accident and burglary statistics! The poor little chap's lying there in the dark, terrified that sinister figures are hiding in his wardrobe because of this constant anxiety of yours, and he can't even tell you, because he knows it will make you worse!" Her face broke into a horrified laugh. "I mean, this is intolerable! You should be fixing this for the boy. Not making it worse, Kate! Not after what he's been through."

Desperately, Kate tried to think. "You're right. I know I'm anxious. But I am trying to fix it. I just didn't want to tell you," she said.

"What, darling?" Richard asked.

The lie was bitter in her mouth. "I've started therapy."

"When?" Saskia asked, dubiously.

"Tonight. That's where I was. In Summertown."

Richard and Helen glanced at each other.

"That's convenient," Saskia murmured.

"She's at Fifteen Hemingway Avenue. Look her up if you like. My GP recommended her. And she said she can help me," Kate continued.

"When?"

"Next week onward. I'm going once a week, on Tuesdays, indefinitely. At seven thirty. She says that it's all a reaction to the trauma of losing my parents, then Hugo. It's just anxiety. She says it's normal, and that she can help me. And I can talk to her about Jack, too. Find ways to help him, too."

"Well—that's fantastic," Richard said, using the overly jovial voice he used to cheer everyone up. "Well done, darling."

Saskia looked Kate straight in the eye. "OK then. I'll babysit for you. When you go." There was a challenge in her voice.

She nodded.

"So, every Tuesday, at seven thirty, I'll be here," Saskia added.

"Helen?" Richard said.

Helen began to rub at the stain on the runner with her finger. Kate watched her mother-in-law, her expression sad and serious, and she knew in that moment that Helen, like Kate, knew that the faded red mark was not wine.

"If this is true, Kate, then I am glad. But I have to tell you, there will be no going back for me now. Perhaps I should have spoken up sooner. But the situation is that I have lost one son, and I won't allow my grandson to be lost, too. He is not your parent. You are his.

"If you are unable to start behaving as a present, engaged parent, and control your constant anxiety around Jack, I will interfere as I see fit. So, let's call it a start. Let's see how it goes."

Kate nodded.

"And now I would like you to go and get me the key."

"The key?" Kate stuttered.

"To that thing."

Humiliation washed over Kate yet again. As she looked into Helen's eyes, she knew that Helen, her sweet, chirpy mother-in-law, was now a serious foe.

Kate went upstairs to the ceiling-high steel cage that ran fifteen feet along the length of the upstairs landing, took the key from the door that locked her and Jack safely behind it at night, and brought it slowly back downstairs.

5

It was Monday morning, a school day. Normally, Jack would be tucked up under the duvet, buried in the deep hormonal slumber of a preteenager.

But things weren't normal. For an hour now, he had lain awake, ignoring the growing pressure in his bladder.

He rolled over to face the wall and picked at the Blu-Tack behind his Arsenal poster. Rows of red-shirted players stood shoulder to shoulder, the goalkeepers in yellow perched above them. Thoughtfully, he stretched his feet toward the bottom of the bed, and his arms in the other direction. Nana had said he was "about the same" height as Dad when he was ten-and-three-quarters, but that wasn't strictly true. On the back of the airing cupboard door at her house, he'd discovered the names "Hugo" and "Saskia" written against little black marks measured in inches that climbed up the door like a ladder. He had run his finger along a faded date in 1984. Dad had already been three inches taller.

He turned to the old fitted wardrobe beside the fireplace. The doors were firmly closed, as he had left them last night. His bright-red electric guitar was where he'd left it propped up. "What would his friends say about him being scared of burglars in his wardrobe?" he'd heard Nana say last night through the stripped floorboards. Like he was ever going to tell Gabe and Damon that?

He reached up and took down the little snow globe from his shelf and shook it. Glitter floated down over a little plastic mountain.

He waited, then shook it again. Finally, he heard the noise he had been dreading since seven o'clock this morning.

His mother's bedroom door opened. A pad of bare feet toward the stairs.

He rolled onto his back, stuffing his fingers in his ears.

"Jack," she called gently. "Are you up? We've slept in."

"Hmm," he replied, removing his fingers a fraction.

"You'll have to get dressed quickly. What do you want for breakfast?"

He looked at the ceiling.

"Nothing. I'm not hungry."

"You need something. Do you want a bagel?"

There was a click. He stuck his fingers back in his ears so hard, his nails scraped the skin inside. But it was too late. He had heard it.

"OK," he shouted, willing her to go away.

She was opening the gate. Trying to do it so he wouldn't hear. Trying to pretend she hadn't locked it again with that padlock he'd seen in her shopping bag on Saturday. Even though he'd heard Nana tell her not to on Friday night.

Jack looked up at the plastic stars Aunt Sass had stuck on his ceiling when they moved here from London when he was six. His blood thumped inside his ears. *Boom, boom, boom*, it pulsed. He imagined he was swimming under the ocean among those shoals of baby rays he'd seen at the Aquarium in London with Nana and Granddad.

He stared hard at the poster and imagined saving a penalty shoot-out for Arsenal in the FA cup. Six-foot-two, Dad had been. Still smallish for a professional goalie, but possible. He needed to eat more to try to catch up to Dad.

The faint aroma of toasted bagel floated in.

With a grunt, Jack pulled himself out of bed, and swept his hair out of his face. He took off his pajamas, found his school uniform in a drawer, and put it on. He removed the guitar from in front of it, and opened the wardrobe hesitantly.

Rows of clothes appeared, above two fitted shelves Granddad had made at the bottom, to put his shoes on. Checking quickly that Mum wasn't behind him, he swept a hand behind the clothes, touching the wall to check no one was there. He went to pick up his sneakers for PE from the bottom shelf, then stopped.

They had moved again.

He was sure of it.

He had chucked them in the other day, and now they sat neatly.

Jack grabbed them by the laces, and stood up. Had Mum tidied them up when she was putting away his clean laundry?

He hunched his shoulders and went to open his bedroom door, knowing he couldn't ask her. She'd just start going on again about someone eating the casserole and look more worried.

The bars of the cage glinted in the morning sun. They were as flat and wide as his school ruler, embedded into a long bracket on the ceiling above. The door had been pushed back quietly into its hook in the wall, leaving the entrance open to the top of the stairs.

Jack ran to the bathroom, peed and washed, then walked through the open gate quickly, trying not to look at it.

"What do you want on it?" his mother shouted as he came downstairs.

"Peanut butter, please," he said, walking toward the kitchen. He would make himself eat it. Perhaps when he measured himself again secretly on Nana's door this Saturday, there would be a difference. Sometimes he measured himself two or three times on the same day, hoping for growth.

Kate turned, unsmiling, spreading his bagel. He sat at the table, and watched her. Her shoulder blades were showing even more clearly than before through the worn cream silk of the nightie Dad had given her, like two L-shapes, back to back. He looked down at her legs. White string with knots in the middle.

Jack sipped the tea she'd made for him, and tried to think about something else.

"When's the new laptop getting delivered, Mum?"

She groaned as she placed his bagel on the table. "This week, I hope. They tried to say they'd delivered it on Tuesday but obviously they didn't because I was in London—when I went up to see Patricia, our old neighbor?" she added swiftly, glancing to see Jack's reaction to the lie. "So they're sending another one on Friday. I should have just gone to the bloody shop. I've got to get some figures off to David in London by next weekend for a house auction."

She wrinkled her brow, and returned to the sink. Jack took a reluctant bite of his bagel, thinking. If he got Gabe to invite him around after school, they could use his mum's computer and see if Aunt Sass had done what she promised.

He looked up and saw Kate watching him from the sink.

"Jack, you're not getting one. Please don't ask again. There are reasons that ten is too early."

He shrugged. "I know. There are weird people looking at the Internet. They told us at school."

She nodded, surprised.

"Good." She came over, and sat down with a cup and no food. He could smell the hot raspberry from her tea. He saw her take an uncertain breath.

"I like your hair like that," she said. "Bet the girls do, too."

"No," he said awkwardly. "They like Gabe. He's taller than me."

Her brow immediately wrinkled with worry.

"It doesn't matter. Don't worry about it, Mum," he told her. Why was she frowning? Being small was his problem, not hers.

Out of nowhere, Jack suddenly felt very, very cross.

She had locked that stupid, embarrassing gate again last night, even though Nana had told her not to. She had completely lied to Nana. Done the opposite of what she'd promised. And now he knew that she'd lied, and Nana didn't, and if Nana asked him when he went to stay this weekend, and he told her the truth, Mum would be cross.

He glanced at his mum, but she was lost again, somewhere off in her secret place.

Why did she always have to make everybody so upset?

Why could he never tell her he was scared of the strange noises he heard in the wardrobe at night? Or of his stomach-aches, which he suspected might be caused by the same disease that boy had on Children in Need? Or of the year-eight boys who were scaring him and Gabe?

Why could he not tell Mum any of this without her stealing

his worries and turning them into her own, making it worse, not better?

Jack sat back.

A second wave of anger engulfed him.

A thought took Jack by surprise.

Right now, this minute, he hated her.

He wasn't just cross. He actually hated her.

Jack leaned forward at the table, savoring this new, strange feeling, while glancing at his mum. She stared out of the kitchen window into the garden, sipping her tea with a little hissing noise.

Thoughts began to pile into his head, one after the other. Yes—he hated her. Hated her stupid nightie that she wore all the time even though it had little holes in it like wounds. Hated the way she never listened to him and always made his worries her worries. Hated the way she kept talking about people breaking into their house and other bad things that made him lie awake at night, seeing shadows and hearing creaks. Hated the way she lied to Nana, and was allowed to make their house gray and quiet all the time, just because she was the adult.

Jack put down his bagel.

The hate suddenly made him feel brave.

"Mum?"

She glanced up.

"I want to go to secondary school with Gabe and everyone else."

Kate stirred her tea even though she hadn't put any sugar in it. The circles under her eyes were even darker than usual, he noticed.

"I don't want to go to that private school."

He waited for her reaction.

Kate sighed. "Well, you don't have to."

"Really?" He bit his bagel again, his appetite returning a little.

"No." She took a sip of tea. "Jack, listen, I made a decision this weekend. You know we moved to Oxford so Nana and Granddad could help me after Daddy?"

He nodded.

"Well, I think we're better now."

He stopped chewing. "What do you mean?"

"I mean, I think it might be a good time for us to go back to London."

Jack tried to swallow the lumpy, soggy dough but it seemed to swell up and lodge in his throat. He tried again, but it stuck there, refusing to move forward or backward. In a panic, he took a mouthful of tea and gulped as hard as he could. The hot liquid forced the soggy mass down his throat, but it hurt.

Perhaps it was because he was gasping to clear his mouth, that when he spoke it came out in a panicked rush.

"No!" he yelled.

The sides of his mother's face drew back like curtains.

"Jack!"

His voice had been so loud it shocked him, too. But there was something about the shout that felt good. Before he could help it, he knew he wanted to do it again.

He jumped up. "No!" he cried.

She looked bewildered. "Why are you shouting?"

He didn't know. He just knew it felt good. He tried the new voice again.

"Because I'm sick of you always making me do what you want to do!"

Her eyes watched him, round and wide; cold, amber glass. Jack realized that he wanted to smash that glass, and make her eyes move. Make them move like Nana's. Make them do something.

"Jack!" Her voice sounded scared. "What's got into you? Why are you speaking like this? Has Nana said something?"

Tears were seeping into her eyes.

Furious, the little boy slammed both his hands down.

"No!" he yelled. "Don't cry. You always do that! I'm not looking at you anymore!"

His mother looked shocked. "Jack. I'm not crying! I try very hard not to cry."

He jumped up, with no idea where he was going. He just knew he wasn't doing this anymore. Clenching his fists, he stalked out of the kitchen and into the hallway. He sat on the stairway, pulled on his shoes without undoing them, and grabbed his book bag.

"Where are you going?" Kate said, following him.

"School!"

"But it's only eight o'clock. Gabe won't be ready to walk with you yet."

He could hear the panic in her voice. "I don't care. I'm going on my own. Everyone else does. Everyone else's mum doesn't think they're going to get killed by a car or a murderer!"

He saw the dismay on her face. He didn't care. His voice increased in volume with every sentence. Every time he did it, it felt like he was blowing things up.

Pow! Pow!

It was exhilarating.

He didn't care if his mother was upset. She never helped him. The truth was sometimes he felt a bit scared about the idea of walking to school on his own, but she should be making him feel better about it, not more worried. Helping him.

Jack saw his sneakers by the stairs and grabbed them.

"Jack. Please. You haven't even done your teeth," she said.

She was trying to stay calm, saying grown-up things in a voice that was all wobbly and confused and hurt.

As he took his blazer off the banister, he looked up and saw the stupid cage.

He was sick of it. Everyone feeling sorry for him. For his dad. For having a weird mum, and now a stupid house.

He turned and scowled at Kate.

"You go to London!" he yelled, unbolting the door. "I'm not staying in this stupid house anymore. I want to live with Nana. She said I could. I heard her. Nana's kind." And, then, before he could stop himself, "*And* she lets me go to the shop on my own."

Kate gasped. "She *what?*"

"She lets me go!" he yelled defiantly. "*Every* Saturday at twelve o'clock when the village baker opens, to get bread for lunch!"

"Bloody Nana," she spat. "How *dare* she? I *knew* this had something to do with her. What else has she done? What has she said?"

He shook his head furiously. "It's *not* Nana. It's *you*. You're . . . you're . . . just the worst mother *ever!* I just . . . *hate you!*"

Turning to find the key for the lock, he saw that his mother's face looked like it had dried onto her bones.

At that moment, the little boy realized with a strange curiosity that she was not in control after all. The power had always been his to take. He could blow her up whenever he wanted.

He turned and shoved the key in the lock, and tried to turn it.

Behind him came a low moan. He stopped.

He had seen her worried, furiously blinking back tears, but he had never heard that noise before.

A picture came into his mind of that terrible earthquake he had watched with Granddad on the news, where everything was blown up and broken, and the people on the news said that nothing would ever be the same again.

A painful cramp tightened in his stomach.

What had he done? He'd told her about Nana letting him go to the shop in the village. And now they'd fight about that, too.

To his shame, Jack felt tears coming into his own eyes. Desperately, he tried to grab the doorknob and get out before she said anything else.

"Jack!" His mother gasped. "No!"

He turned the Chubb key and a piercing sound exploded into the air.

Jack jumped.

It was the burglar alarm.

She hadn't turned it off this morning.

The earsplitting din filled his ears, and he lifted his hands automatically to cover them. At the same time he felt her hand grab the shoulder of his school shirt, pulling him back from the door, but he jerked away from her. This movement threw him off balance, and he veered sideways. He felt her try to grab him tighter to stop him from falling, but she couldn't.

Jack saw the hall radiator coming toward him out the corner of his eye. His forehead hit the side of it. It was sharp, and it hurt.

"Oh, my God—Jack!"

He landed on his knees, and stayed there for a second, stunned. He touched his forehead and felt something wet. It was blood.

The house alarm was squealing at full pitch now, stabbing at his ears.

It all felt too much. All this blood and power and noise and destruction.

Kate jumped up, ran to the alarm box under the stairs, and punched in a number.

Silence abruptly descended on the hall again.

Jack leaned back, shocked.

Kate grabbed his face, looking at the cut.

"Jack. I'm so sorry," she whispered. "I was trying to stop you from setting off the alarm."

She wiped blood from his cut with her fingers. It smeared across her skin. Nana would do it with a tissue, Jack thought, moving his head away. Nana always had a clean tissue. Nana would put a gentle arm around him that smelled of flowers, and talk calmly, not swipe at the blood with bare fingers as if it were attacking her, and look at him in terror.

"I didn't mean to pull you so hard," Mum was gabbling. "Is your head sore? Do you feel dizzy?"

He shook it.

She stopped speaking and let her hand drop. He saw her rub his blood between her fingers. She had retreated again. Lost in her head.

"Stay there. I'll get a Band-Aid."

She went in the kitchen, with her hands over her mouth. Jack sat in the hallway, fighting the tears that threatened to come properly now.

All of a sudden, he felt annoyed with himself. He was sitting on the floor, trying not to cry like a baby, with a little scratch on his head. He looked up and saw himself in the hall mirror. What if Dad was watching him? Granddad had told him he was supposed to be the man of the house now that Dad was gone.

And just like that, Jack's hate for Kate disappeared as quickly as it had come. As she hurried around looking in cupboards, her lips were forming words as if she were having a conversation with someone invisible.

It took him a moment to work it out.

"You have to stop this," she was saying to herself. "You have to stop this."

Jack felt bad.

What had he done?

"Let me . . . do it . . ." She came and knelt down and dabbed at his cut with an antiseptic cream that stung a little and then placed a Band-Aid over the cut. He could smell raspberry tea on her breath.

"Are you sure you feel OK?" She made him follow her finger to be sure. "Oh, Jack."

She sat back and surveyed his face. He saw her gaze working hard, like she was thinking.

She took a sharp breath. "Jack. Listen." She looked him in the eye. "If anyone asks you how you got the scratch, I need you to not tell them that you hit your head on the radiator."

He watched her.

"The thing is, they might not understand that it was an accident. Nana, for instance. Or your teacher. So, if it's OK, you could just say you fell off your skateboard. Is that OK?"

There was such a pleading tone in her voice, that Jack shrugged.

She leapt toward him and threw her arms around him. He was too surprised to resist. "Jack. I'm so sorry. I don't know what is happening to me, but I will make this right," she murmured. "I just . . ." She sniffed. "I just want you and me to be safe." It was such an unfamiliar sensation being in her arms again that Jack let his face press against his mother's shoulder, and watched, curious, as a trickle of watery pink blood from his forehead seeped into the fabric of her shoulder strap. He found himself hoping the stain would finally force her to throw it away. He stayed there, even though he knew the embrace was to make her feel better, and not him. Knowing that she was trying.

The thing was, if he kept being angry like this, and destroyed her, he would also destroy any chance that his old warm, funny mum who he was starting to forget would return from behind those amber glass eyes. He had to do it for Dad, in case Dad was watching, counting on him to look after Mum. He had to be here waiting for her in case.

So he stayed there, still, inside Kate's embrace, trying to stay hopeful that the real her was in there somewhere.

It was after nine by the time Kate had cleaned Jack up. She dropped him at primary school, nervously watching his year-six teacher's expression through the window as he entered the classroom. Kate left before Ms. Corrigan could call her back. She knew, under scrutiny, her eyes would expose the lie about the skateboard.

She drove home, ran upstairs to her office and sat at her desk and fixed her gaze on the rich green leaves of the magnolia tree outside that had months before shed its pink flowers onto the lawn.

She sat there for an hour, doodling tight-knit webs and tee-tering towers onto white paper. Then for another hour.

Jack's face haunted her. The blood dripping from his fore-head, his angry voice, his look of disgust when she asked him not to tell Nana what had happened.

Social services. That was what Helen had said on Friday.

A memory of her mother-in-law drifted back to her. It was the first time Kate had visited Richard and Helen's house with Hugo for Sunday lunch. Helen had come behind him, drying her hands on a tea towel. Kate smiled nervously as she reached the bottom of the stairs, ready to hold out a hand.

"Ah, my precious boy," Helen had said, ignoring her, instead reaching up to Hugo's face with hands that had been moisturized into soft creaminess. She touched his cheeks tenderly, while Kate stood to the side, feeling stupid. Hugo had shot her a wink over his mother's head. "How are you, my darling?" Helen asked.

Hugo took her hands in his own, physically turning her to the left. "Good! Mum! This is Kate."

Kate knew from the emphasis he placed on her name that he was introducing her to Helen as someone significant. Someone he and his mother had already discussed. But as Helen turned her pale-green eyes on Kate, Kate suspected, already, that she'd failed. Right there, in her jeans and scuffed boots, with her Shropshire accent and her state-school education, she knew that everything Helen, in her grand riverside house, had been hoping for, had not appeared this morning.

"Hi," Kate said, holding out her hand. "Nice to meet you."

"Hello, Kate," Helen said, taking it. She gave a modest smile. The smile stretched as she turned back to Hugo, only to find him watching Kate, mesmerized.

Later, Kate would wonder if that was when Helen decided that whatever concerns she had about Kate's suitability for her "precious boy" were to be packed away immediately. If the glow in her son's eyes as he looked at Kate told her this was serious. That there was no going back for him.

Certainly, Helen had never treated her like that again, to the point where Kate had convinced herself that she'd imagined that first encounter. Blamed it on her hangover.

Till now.

She looked out the window as the sun disappeared around the back of the garden. What if that malevolent undercurrent she'd glimpsed in Helen on their first meeting did exist. Had always existed, but been hidden for Hugo's sake, then Jack's.

On impulse, Kate sat back and opened a drawer in her desk to take out a photo. It was turned on its front, not faceup as she had left it on top of her work diary.

Nervously, Kate glanced around her office. Had she been burgled again?

Helen's irritated words flew back to her about the casserole. "It had *not gone*."

She stopped.

"Must have been Jack," she reassured herself.

She removed the photo, propped it on the desk, and met Hugo's eyes. It was a good photo. Saskia had taken it secretly through the kitchen window of their Highgate house. Unaware, Kate was lying back on Hugo's chest, his hand casually lying across the breast of her shirt. She was wearing a head scarf from painting Jack's room. Her face was tilted up, laughing. He was trying not to smile at her bad joke. Behind them was the magnolia tree, just a baby then, in a pot, its first pink blossoms yet to burst through.

"Don't laugh at me," Hugo had been saying, putting on his hurt voice.

His fingers played on her rib below her bra, slowly, with no intent, while he used his other hand to write on a pad.

"But how can I help it? You're so funny. See? I can't stop laughing at you. . . ." Kate opened her mouth as if to laugh—then froze. "Oh, wait—yes I can."

"Fuck off."

He pinched her skin under her top, and carried on writing.

She lay back looking at the baby magnolia tree they had just bought, sitting in a pot.

"What are you writing?" she asked.

"Instructions for your assassination."

"No, really."

"Instructions for your assassination."

"Oh, that's a nice way to talk to your poor orphaned wife."

She felt a catch in Hugo's breath as he went to laugh, shocked at the barbed nature of her joke, and tried to stop himself.

To Kate's joy, she felt a tiny reverberation in his chest.

"Some notes for the refurb on Algon Terrace," Hugo grunted, trying to hide it.

She sat up sideways to see one of his neat sketches of a room dominated by a Georgian fireplace.

She lay back again, wondering where to plant the magnolia. If they put it just to the right, it would grow under Jack's bedroom. By the time he was eight or nine, the bloom would reach his window.

"It's not that I think you shouldn't do it . . ." Hugo started.

"But . . ."

"Well, I just don't want you to do it."

"Hugo," she groaned, hitting his chest. "Honestly. Don't start. It's what I want for my thirtieth. You can't say no."

"What about Jack?" he said, grabbing her hand and playing with it.

"What do you think's going to happen?" she exclaimed, running his fingers through her own. "I thought you wanted me to get back to normal again. Have some fun."

"You are back to normal." He dropped his voice to a stage whisper. "Normal for a weirdo, anyway."

She dug her elbow into his rib.

He shifted his weight to release it. "Really. I just don't think it's a good idea."

Kate tried to sit up. "You're not serious?" she asked.

He shrugged, and sipped his beer. "I've just got a bad feeling about it."

She threw her hands up. "Says the man who's bought a car that looks like a penis."

He pinched her harder, and carried on sketching.

"What do you think about all this, Sass?" she said as her sister-in-law wandered outside, waving a camera.

Saskia settled herself on Kate's thighs gently, and leaned back. "Don't know, don't care. Look . . ."

Hugo and Kate peered forward to see the image of themselves, with Kate laughing at her own joke, and Hugo trying to hide his grin.

"You were laughing!" Kate sang childlishly.

"Right. That's it. Both of you, off," Hugo grunted, pushing off the combined weight of his wife and sister. "I'm not sitting here being harassed. What time is your film?"

"Half-eight?" Kate and Saskia said in unison, checking with each other.

"Right. I'm going for a quick drive in my penis car then."

That had been the summer, five years into their marriage, when she had finally emerged from the darkness of her parents' deaths. The year she knew who she was again without the solid mooring of their existence. She was turning thirty, and found renewed strength in the idea of a new decade. Even broaching the idea of a new baby, now that Jack was starting primary school. Hugo had stopped tiptoeing around her, trying to make something better that could not be made better. With unspoken relief on both sides, they had found their way back to the easy rudeness of old. She had even made a joke—not about her parents' death, but about the way she had been after her parents' death. It was over, the joke said. A sign to Hugo that she felt ready now, finally, to move on.

Kate sighed and looked at the photo closely. The contours of her body and his ran into each other, without borders. What had it felt like to be that physically intimate with another person?

She looked at the baby magnolia tree. They had never planted it, of course. Four hours later, Hugo died.

"I don't know what to do," she said to the photo. But the low resolution of the camera blurred the sharpness of Hugo's pupils, robbing her of the chance to interpret some peace and understanding in his gaze.

What would he say, anyway? Tell his mother to keep her nose out of Kate and Jack's business? Or would he stand beside Helen as her ally? Would his face say that he now realized his mother had been right in that brief moment in her hallway all those years ago, when she first met Kate? Had she been correct to be disappointed? Kate had proved to be a failure after all. She fell apart in a crisis and was a terrible mother to Hugo's son.

At one time, Kate would have known, of course. Years' worth of Hugo's reactions and opinions, she had discovered after his death, had been safely wired into her head, ready to draw upon in his absence. It had been a comfort. But that was from another time; already he was five years younger in this photo than she was now. Those reactions and opinions belonged to then, not now. Hugo never saw an iPad or a Twitter page. He belonged to a different time. He was disappearing from her view, like the man overboard in the wake of a ship.

Kate dropped the photo on the desk, and looked at the clock. Nearly eleven.

Jesus.

She glanced at her work schedule on the wall. David needed her funding proposal for a new renovation project in Islington by the end of the week. She had to get out of here or she would never start work.

She jumped up, grabbed some papers, and walked downstairs, pausing to lock the gate with the new padlock. Checking that all the windows, and then the inner doors, were locked manually downstairs, she grabbed her bag, turned on the alarm, and left, double locking the front door.

She looked at the strong sun that had now moved to the front of the house. Should she drive or cycle? Statistics about road accidents began to swarm around her head. Mixed up in them were half-remembered percentages to do with air quality and skin cancer.

Ninety percent of skin cancers are caused by direct sunlight!

She caught herself, and pinched her palm hard with her other hand.

"Shut up!" she growled, bringing Jack's shocked, bloodied face from this morning into her mind.

Forcing herself to ignore the numbers, she marched down the road, toward the center of East Oxford.

Helen's words returned to her. "The next time I ring social services it will not be anonymous."

Nobody could help her. She had to do this by herself, and it had to start now.

*   *   *

Magnus heard the front door bang next door. He looked down into Hubert Street from his upstairs window. The skinny woman from next door was going out again.

He picked up his camera and took a quick shot from behind.

Skinny, but not bad looking. Dark hair like the girls back home, thick and lustrous. She even had the upturned nose.

It was her face that was a put-off. She always looked miserable. In need of a good cheering up.

He closed the laptop Kate had been expecting last Tuesday, and turned it off. It hadn't been difficult to procure it. In fact, he was quite pleased with himself at how he'd managed it. Hacking into her e-mails had allowed him to discover that she had a hospital appointment in London the day her new computer was due to be delivered. So, all he'd had to do was lurk at her front door waiting for the delivery van, wearing a baseball hat without his glasses and holding front-door keys in his hand. Then he'd signed for it cheerily using an indecipherable signature before pretending to enter Kate's house. It had been funny afterward to read her angry e-mail exchanges with the computer store, when she came home to find no missed-delivery note. It was even funnier when the store accepted that their driver had clearly mixed up her delivery with someone else's and accepted fault. A replacement computer, Magnus noted cheerfully on Kate's e-mails, was winging its way to her house this week.

He'd let her keep that one.

It was a good computer, this one. Better than the one he'd taken five months ago from her house. She'd upgraded—probably to make room for all those weird pages of numbers she kept on it. He might even keep this one instead of trying to sell it.

Speaking of which . . . better check she was really going out, and not just popping in to see a neighbor. He watched out of the window till the woman reached the end of Hubert Street, counted to fifty, then bounced down the worn stair carpet, pulling on his black T-shirt from yesterday, enjoying being reacquainted with his own pungent smell. The kitchen was empty. It smelled slightly of damp, not that that bothered him.

"Hello?" His shout echoed around the cheap units and into the hall, where piles of post for former student tenants lay in messy heaps.

No one replied.

Lucky, the other students were out. Not that they spoke to him anyway. The short one with the sharp face had complained just last night about him singing drinking songs when he arrived home at two in the morning. No one knew how to have a good time in this bloody town.

Magnus went out the front door and walked up to Kate's house to check that it was empty. He rang the doorbell, twice, ready with a fake question about the rubbish collection day. No answer.

Good. Quickly, he returned home, and climbed up to his bedroom.

He shut the door and locked it, just to be sure, then went to the heavy wardrobe that stood against the wall he shared with Kate's house, and moved it, grunting, a shoulder against the edge.

It traveled with a deep scraping noise across the laminate floor, leaving a fresh new gray skid mark on top of a previous faded one.

In front of Magnus was a hole in the wall, just above the skirting board, two feet by three feet. It had taken him three days to create, chipping away with a rock hammer when both households were out. A scouting trip to steal the first laptop five months ago had told him the best place to do it.

In front of Magnus, on the other side of the hole, was a piece of plywood that he had painted white to blend in with the wall next door, and inserted across the hole with two clips. Carefully he unclipped it and pushed it into the empty space beyond, then turned it diagonally and pulled it back through the hole. Then, as he always did, he tested the wooden lintel he'd placed for stability along the underside of the top of the hole, which in turn rested on two vertical lintels either side of it. To his satisfaction, nothing budged. In front of him now lay a gap into the bottom of a fitted wardrobe, which was presently covered in shoes and boots. There was a shelf just above his head.

Magnus pulled the shoes out of his way, lay on the floor, put his long arms into the hole, and pushed the wardrobe doors ahead of him open. As usual, there was a thud as he put his head through the hole, and pulled his body after him, into the wardrobe then out through the open doors on the other side.

It was a tight squeeze, but he did it.

Magnus pulled his big body onto all fours, then stood upright, brushing off a scattering of dust from his shoulder.

He stood the electric guitar upright again from where it had fallen, and surveyed Jack's bedroom.

6

Kate was trying. She really was, as she stomped to the center of East Oxford. But the numbers wouldn't leave her alone. They buzzed inside her ears, their collective high pitch almost as unbearable as the house alarm this morning as they screamed, "Danger!" at every curb. At every road crossing.

Listen to the figures, a voice said in Kate's head. It'll make you feel better. Let them in, and everything will be OK. You'll be back in control. Safe. Calm.

Clenching her fists, Kate double-checked at each junction, till she reached the bustle of Cowley Road.

At least there were people here, and sights to distract her.

She looked up at the shimmering minarets of the mosque, and the inert mothers in front of it in the play park, grabbing a few seconds' rest on benches as their toddlers ran around. She stared hard at the O2 Academy announcing a gig by a band she vaguely recognized from long ago. She dodged the crowds with their carrier bags from Tesco, and stared in the windows of a packed row of restaurants offering everything from South American to North African to Thai.

Concentrate, she thought. Concentrate on the menus. Beef *picanha*, *pimentos piquillo con alchachofas*, steamed mussels with chili and Thai herbs. Don't think about numbers.

Be normal. Be normal like those two girls walking along in vest tops, hands flying as they exchange stories of the night before. Like the man in the jester's hat cycling down the pavement, whistling, hands not touching the handlebars. Like the elderly lady remonstrating with her Jack Russell for peeing on a trash can.

Kate blinked hard. The sun was raw and sharp in her face, burning her pale skin, blinding her.

A terrible desert thirst grabbed her throat.

Kate coughed. She felt her chest flutter.

And then, without warning, she simply came to a stop.

Right on the pavement, with no warning.

Her feet were stuck. Rooted. Refusing to move.

She put out a hand, frightened. It touched a door frame. She leaned into the wood.

Her eyes settled on a small patch of dirt by the doorway.

The patch looked like road dust mixed with mud from shoes and old chewing gum. It was ground-in, year-old grime, jammed into a corner, where door frame met window frame. Too hidden to be cleaned by the owner or swept away by the street cleaner.

Nasty and stuck and horrible.

The perfect place for her.

As she stared at the patch of dirt, a nagging thought entered Kate's mind. What if she could never get a grip on the anxiety? What if she could never shake off this sense of impending danger for her and Jack? Of being cursed? What if Richard and Helen really take Jack from her?

Kate grimaced in despair. They would give him everything, there was no doubt of that. Love, reassurance, and fun. But Jack would never be able to stand up to Richard like Hugo did. He would never escape. He would become like Saskia, pulled in by the gravitational force of Richard Parker's world.

The thought of losing Jack filled Kate with such grief, she clutched her stomach and bent over farther.

What if she couldn't stop it, though? Was it just inevitable she would lose him now? Hugo, her parents, Jack . . .

Kate stood there, head hanging, exhausted from trying to ward off a monster she could never see.

"Are you all right there?"

Kate jerked her head up.

A girl was looking at her, concerned.

Kate realized the girl's head was peering out from behind the door frame on which Kate was leaning. She saw a sign. It was a café she didn't know.

"Can I get you some water?"

Kate shook her head. "No, I'm fine, thanks." Beyond the glass was a simple, white-walled room, with wooden tables.

"Do you do coffee?"

"It's a juice bar, I'm afraid."

The girl's skin was makeup free and flawless, apart from a few freckles. She had long legs under a black miniskirt, and a white blouse. Her long auburn hair was twisted into a thick ponytail that hung down one side of her chest. Her smile was so friendly that Kate wanted to follow the girl inside. She wanted to leave behind the patch of dirt and the thoughts of losing Jack.

The café smelled fresh and sharp inside, like citrus fruit.

Only one table was occupied, by a man with a pierced nose holding hands with a girl with pink hair. Pop music played over the speakers. A blackboard menu announced a variety of juices with names like Superfruiter and Detox-alula.

"We've just opened so there's a special of fifty percent off a juice of the day," the girl said brightly.

The urge to sit down was overwhelming.

"Thank you." Kate nodded.

"It's strawberries, peach . . ."

"That sounds fine," Kate said, holding up a hand.

As the girl piled fruit into a giant juicer, Kate sat at the long counter along the front window and tried to gather her thoughts. The numbers came at her again.

Forty percent of catering staff don't wash their hands after going to the toilet.

Exhausted, she grabbed the printouts of her funding proposal for David from her bag, hoping it would help.

Working often calmed the numbers. God knows why, but it did. She stared hard at the property details of the house David wanted to buy at auction, and the estimates from each member of the renovation team, noting which ones she still had to chase down.

The house was a dilapidated Georgian terrace in Islington that was being sold by a housing association to fund a brand-new block of fourteen apartments elsewhere. She looked at the exterior, knowing Hugo would have loved it. Three original fireplaces remained, as did the original wooden floors beneath stained brown carpets and cheap laminate. There was a major dampness problem coming from the basement, a fairly serious crack in the back bedroom, and a suspicion of woodworm in the floors, but nothing David and the team hadn't seen before.

Suddenly she realized what the house reminded her of.

*   *   *

"You've what?" Kate had exclaimed, spinning around to look at Hugo. Hugo was leaning on his car's hood in front of the four-story Georgian house in a tiny square in Highgate. Opposite, there was a pretty little garden with a bench in it. He'd told her they were going for a walk on Hampstead Heath to talk about their plans for the summer, then unexpectedly pulled off the road.

"I've bought it," he said, laughing, and flashed the mischievous smile he used when he knew he was pushing her to the limit of her patience. "Well, I've put an offer in, anyway."

"But how . . . ?"

He grabbed her arm and pulled her in against him, both of them facing the house. It was in serious need of renovation. Gray paint was peeling off the façade. The front door had been replaced with a cheap, wooden one with DIY-store-stained glass. Terrible double glazing had been put in, presumably without planning permission. She could tell from here that the roof was in serious need of attention.

"Dad came through with the start-up loan."

Kate's mouth dropped. "No way. He gave in?"

Hugo nodded at the house, pleased. "Yup."

"Seriously? He's accepted you're not going to join the business?" She stroked his arm. "Oh, God, Hugo. Well done!"

Hugo squeezed her tightly. "Anyway, it's enough to get it with an interest-only mortgage. Then, if me and David do a good job on it, we'll use it as a show-house for new clients. You and I could live in it after the wedding. The idea is to remortgage it and use the equity to get the business up and running. You can start work with us when you get back from abroad."

Kate spun around. "You're not coming?"

"No. I want you to go and have some fun without me. This is my fun. Trust me, if this takes off, me and David will need you flat-out when you get back to help us set up the next project."

Hugo was beaming. He looked exactly like he had, Kate noted with a flush of love, when he'd announced to all their parents last month at Richard's favorite London restaurant that he and Kate were getting engaged. He sighed. "So, do you like it? Can we do it?"

She wrapped her arms around his arms, which were across her chest, forming a tight double embrace. "It's amazing. I love it. You're an arse for not telling me, but you're very clever, too."

He'd squeezed her tight. "God. It's happening, Kate. Finally . . ." He kissed her ear, and she dipped her head to the side to let him nuzzle her neck. "I tell you what, I feel lucky. Too bloody lucky, sometimes."

Kate shut the property details, and took a sip of her juice. Hugo and David had increased the value of the house so rapidly that the business had been racing ahead of them and within two years, Richard's loan was repaid. Their passion for, and expert knowledge of, the Georgian period and their decision to use only the most-skilled craftspeople to restore the original details had quickly gained them a reputation with discerning—and wealthy—buyers.

"I feel lucky."

Hugo's words echoed in her head. Lucky, yes. Richard had helped at first. But it was Hugo and David's passion and hard work that made their business work. Kate looked at the Islington house again. And as a silent partner, she would benefit financially from this project, too, as she had from all the others, because of Hugo's hard work. But Hugo would never be there to enjoy it with her and Jack. The unfairness of it all was almost unbearable. Deciding what to do next, she looked around her.

That was odd.

Where had that come from?

A paperback lay three seats away from her on the counter, beside the café door. It had been left upside down, and open about halfway through, like someone had been reading it then walked away, abandoning it.

Kate looked around again. It was still just her and the New Age couple, and the cheerful waitress who was humming along to Dusty Springfield.

A word jumped out at her from the book's cover.

Odds.

Odds?

Intrigued, Kate cocked her head so she could read the rest of the title. *Odds . . . Change . . . Beat the Odds and Change Your Life.*

Was this a joke? Or had she actually started to hallucinate?

She leaned over and lifted up the paperback where it was open.

"How to Choose Which Airline to Fly With" the chapter heading said.

Oh, my God.

Kate moved closer, and flipped quickly through the book, checking to make sure no one was watching. As she read more, she could feel the number swarm building in her mind with all this new ammunition. It was incredible. There were so many statistics! Some she recognized, some she'd never heard of before. And that wasn't all. She looked at the other chapters, hungrily. "How to Improve Your Chances of Avoiding a Road Accident." "How to Improve Your Chances of Avoiding Dying Prematurely."

It was all here. Everything she needed. She and Jack.

"Enjoying that?"

Kate saw the reflection of a man in the window. She turned around. He was walking toward her from the back of the café. The toilet door by the counter swung shut behind him.

"Oh. Sorry, I was just . . ." She trailed off.

The man smiled. He was tall, with light-brown hair cut short into a crew cut. He was wearing a T-shirt with jeans. There was a faint stubble around his jaw and his eyes were such an intense blue she had to stop herself from staring.

"No. Go ahead," he said, gesturing toward the book. His accent was Scottish.

She hesitated.

"It's fine. Here," he said, passing it to her.

"Oh. Thanks," Kate said shyly. "I'll just copy down the title, if that's OK?"

"Absolutely."

She grabbed her pen and began to write. In her peripheral vision, she saw the man finish his juice and take a cell phone from a leather bag he had slung over his body. He stared at the screen, reading something.

He tapped a number in his phone.

"Hi, Liam," she heard him say. "It's Jago."

While the Scottish man talked on the phone, Kate opened the back flap. Staring back at her was a photograph of the man in the juice bar. Professor Jago Martin of the University of Edinburgh, the caption read.

Kate looked up, astonished.

The Scottish man was ending his call. He looked back, slightly surprised.

"Done?" He pointed to the book.

"Yes. Thanks," Kate repeated, wishing she could think of something else to say. The man took the book from her, smiled, and turned to walk out.

As she watched him go, an irrational, overwhelming need to stop him overcame her. Why, she wasn't really sure. She just knew she had to.

"So, um, you wrote the book?" she called out in what she realized too late was a slightly hysterical tone.

The man turned back, amused. "Uh. Yes. I did."

Kate shrank back. "Sorry. I saw your photo. . . ." She waved vaguely at the book. "Do you mind if I ask you something? Since you're an expert in this kind of thing."

"Sure."

"I just wondered, that section on how to improve your chances of not being in an air crash."

"Uh-huh."

"How do you work that out?"

"The chances?" The Scottish man wrinkled his brow. He appraised her with his blue eyes, as if he hadn't really seen properly the first time, then leaned back against a stool. She cringed. He must think she was mad.

"Well," he started. "We checked airline safety records. Maintenance levels. Pilot training. Weather conditions. That kind of thing. Actuaries do it all the time in the City to calculate insurance premiums for airlines."

She found herself fixated by his eyes. They had unusually dark rings around the irises. Wrinkles appeared when he smiled, making her think he'd lived a little, possibly in the sun, despite the studenty jeans and T-shirt.

"But doesn't that make you scared of flying? If you've seen all those records?"

Immediately she regretted her question. The crew cut and easy way he held his body gave him the look of a lean boxer, a man who wouldn't be scared by much.

"Sorry. I didn't mean to . . ."

"I'm just wondering. Is this a professional interest?"

Kate shook her head. "No. It's just I never know who to fly with. The one who's crashed recently, because the chances are they won't again? Or the one who's never crashed, but what if a crash is due?"

The man looked thoughtful. "You know what? I'm maybe not the best person to ask."

She spotted a thin leather band just below the neck of his T-shirt, the type traders sold to tourists on beaches in India and Thailand. It sat on a tanned neck, adding to the impression he was someone who traveled. She looked up and saw him watching her, and flicked her eyes away, embarrassed. "But you wrote the book. . . ." Her voice sounded more abrupt that she meant it to.

He hesitated. "Ah, but you see, with my work, I travel all over the world for conferences. Sometimes on airlines that don't have the best safety records."

Kate stared. "Even though you know they have a high chance of crashing?"

"Well, higher, yes. Not high."

She blinked. "How do you do that?"

Just as she said it, the Dusty Springfield song that was play-ing finished. Kate's question blasted into the silence it left in its wake. Her tone was so pleading that the man, the New Age couple, and the waitress all glanced at her warily.

"Sorry," she said, lowering her voice, "I just meant . . ."

The man held up his hand to stop her from explaining.

There was a glimmer of concern in his face. "I just don't think about it."

This man's words reached out and wrapped themselves around Kate.

She couldn't explain it.

They pulled her in like safe, warm arms.

For a reason she couldn't explain, she thought those words might hold the key to her survival.

"So, does that help? Have you got what you need?" he said.

"Uh. Yes. Thanks." Damn. Where was he going? She tried to think of an excuse to stall him.

"Actually, can I just . . ." she started desperately, not even knowing what she was going to say.

His phone rang, interrupting her. He smiled apologetically and started a conversation with someone called Mike about a seminar he was teaching at the university that afternoon. Kate waved him on, even though she didn't want to. He waved back. "Nice to meet you," he mouthed, walking out the door. Kate craned her neck to see him unlocking a bike with one hand, as he spoke on his phone.

"Cor . . ." The waitress giggled, coming up and lifting the man's glass.

"Sorry?" said Kate, jerking back. The waitress watched Jago, twisting her long auburn ponytail in her fingers. She must have been fifteen years younger than him.

"You didn't hear him say what college he lectured at, did you?" Kate asked as casually as she could.

The waitress gave her a look.

"It's a work thing."

The girl grinned. "No, but let me know if you find out! Mmm, that accent . . ." She fanned herself dramatically.

Kate looked back out the window and saw the man speeding off down Cowley Road precariously, still with the phone at his ear. For a second, she imagined jumping on a bike and following him into the traffic.

The thought took her completely by surprise.

Kate never cycled in traffic.

7

The presentation went well. Better than she'd expected.

Saskia watched as the suave man from the London marketing agency wrapped up his pitch impressively. His smile was fixed firmly on Dad—Saskia's suggestion—as he reiterated the importance of the Richard Parker Agency prioritizing marketing to head off the effects of the current economic downturn. Richard's business would do well to concentrate on winning new clients with a viral campaign incorporating social media.

At the end, Richard clapped loudly, the rest of his staff joining in on cue. "Well done, sir! Impressive stuff," he said. He turned to Saskia. "Good job, darling."

Saskia smiled demurely as Richard's staff gave her a round of applause, as if they had any choice. She was Richard Parker's daughter, after all.

"Well done, Sass," Richard said again as he picked up his car keys from his desk. "Right. I'm off to work at home. Playing golf with Jeremy after lunch, if you're looking for me. Can you talk to the chap about fees and contract conditions?"

"No problem," she said, patting his arm. She went into her own office, shut the door, and sat down.

She had done a good job. She knew she had. Another success. As Dad often told his friends and clients, usually loudly and embarrassingly in front of her: "Don't know what we'd do without our Sass. Bloody place would fall apart without her!"

She sighed and opened up her laptop. It wasn't exactly true. And anyway, with the salary her father paid her, there would be nowhere to go to. She must be the best-paid office manager in Britain.

Saskia looked at the screen and saw the note she'd left herself: "Snores."

Right.

Checking that Dad was gone, she summoned Facebook and started the process of creating an account for Jack. Ignoring the age-limit warning, she created an account linked to her own e-mail address under her nephew's name, adding three years to his age and a photo of him wearing dark glasses where he could easily have been thirteen.

When the nagging doubts surfaced, she pushed them away. If her sister-in-law was really going to dump poor Jack in a new school, it was the least Saskia could do to help him keep in touch with his old friends. She and Hugo had moved schools enough times as Richard built his bloody business empire for her to know how it felt.

Her finger hovered over the "submit" button for a second. Saskia exhaled and clicked. Jack's Facebook page went live.

She opened up an e-mail message to the marketing agency

to request agreements in writing, her mind still on Jack. He was sensible. He wouldn't do anything silly, would he?

Saskia started typing, blinking hard.

Oh, well. Too late now, anyway.

The minute the Scottish man left the café, Kate felt the urge to run straight to Blackwell's to buy his book.

No.

The book was a test of her resolve, and she was going to pass. Buying it would completely contradict what she'd set out to do this morning. If she didn't get a grip on her anxiety, she was going to lose Jack. What was more useful was to focus on what the Scottish man had said.

"I just don't think about it."

How the hell did you do that? She put David's proposal in her bag. Well, work was the best way to start.

Waving to the waitress, she left the café and headed down Cowley Road into central Oxford, crossing Magdalen Bridge above students and tourists punting in the river below. The elegant greenhouses of the Botanic Gardens appeared on her left. She swiftly turned into the entrance.

In the cool walled garden, a welcome feeling of calm descended upon her again. As Helen had once said, it was like a private park in here. No dogs or soccer balls flying around. Just a lush lawn among the thick boughs of centuries-old exotic trees. Unless there was some rare disease communicated by a mulberry white or honey locust tree that she didn't know about, the odds of something bad happening here were very low. The swarm of statistics rarely followed her in here.

Kate settled on the grass, and pulled out the proposal. She sat

under the black pine that had been J.R.R. Tolkien's favorite, and
made herself concentrate on the various cost breakdowns and
lists of planning submissions they'd require due to the Islington
house being in a conservation area. It was difficult to do without her laptop and the Internet, but she managed, enjoying the
change of pace of working outside with a pen.

After she'd done that, she pulled out a list of teenage ap-
plicants for work placements through the foundation she and
David had set up in Hugo's name. The first girl caught her eye
immediately. She was sixteen, and close to the end of a difficult
childhood in and out of foster care. She had been nominated by
an eagle-eyed art teacher who'd spotted the girl sitting quietly
on the South Bank on a school trip to the Tate Modern gal-
lery, doing beautifully detailed drawings of St. Paul's Cathedral
across the Millennium Bridge, while her school friends ate their
packed lunches and messed about by the River Thames. Kate
smiled. Hugo would have loved this girl. Her application was
diffident, despite the teacher's obvious help, but her passion
for art and architectural history shone through clearly, and the
drawings she'd included were exquisite.

Kate flagged her application for David to consider. Perhaps a
summer work placement at the Islington property would be a
good start for the girl.

She smiled mischievously, thinking of Richard and how
much he hated her helping what he termed "bloody no-hopers"
with Hugo's money. And how much Hugo would have loved
her for it. Their own little rebellion against Richard's conserva-
tive, money-obsessed ways.

Suddenly, the Scottish man's book infiltrated her mind again.
It slipped in as if it had been by the door all afternoon, waiting
for the opportunity.

She checked her watch.

Jack had cricket practice until five. He said something as she left him this morning, white-faced and quiet, about going to Gabe's for tea. She hadn't even bothered to argue. How could she?

She put down the proposal and lay back on the lawn. A plane breezed across the summer sky.

She thought about how David had offered her and Jack his house in Mallorca this summer. It had been the third year he'd offered, and the third year she'd turned him down. But with that book, she could find out the safety records of the airlines who flew there, and make a calculated decision about the risks. Three weeks away in Mallorca, without Richard and Helen's constant interference, might just be what she and Jack needed to find their way back to each other.

Kate's mind went back to the other chapter headings she had spotted.

Hang on.

She tore at the grass.

If she had the book, with all its research on statistics, all the facts she'd need would at least be in one place. If she proved too weak to keep her addiction at bay completely, the book would at least stop her endlessly scouring newspaper Web sites and insurance sites for figures. It would help her break the habit. Like a smoker using nicotine patches.

She sat up abruptly.

Perhaps it wasn't realistic to try to stop this by herself all of a sudden.

She could just cut down.

Yes. The book would help her cut down, and at the same time concentrate more on fixing things with Jack.

Before she could stop herself, she jumped up, excited, packed up her proposal, and hurried out of the gardens. She marched right up Longwall Street toward Blackwell's on Broad Street.

She could have that book in her hands in ten minutes.

Kate's strides quickened. She broke into a half run, so fixated was she on whether the book would be in stock or she'd have to order it and suffer an agonizing wait. Everything in front of her became a blur of faces, of pastel tops and bare calves and rucksacks and sunglasses, and then one close-cropped head came into focus.

Kate stopped.

It was the Scottish man from the coffee shop.

Jago Martin.

He was crouched down outside the gates of Trinity College a few feet ahead of her, talking to a young male student.

Kate pretended to look at a display of science books in Blackwell's window, keeping him in her peripheral vision all the while.

The Scottish man and the student were looking at the tire of his bike, which was flat. He stood up and looked at his watch, with a slight shake of his head, and said something. The student took back the pump and shrugged. They waved at each other as the student climbed onto his own bike and set off down Broad Street.

All of a sudden, Jago stood up and looked around him.

Kate stood still. She felt his eyes pass over her, and then look back in recognition. She shrank with embarrassment.

"Hello again," she said nervously, walking toward him and waving awkwardly.

"Oh, hello. What are the chances of this, eh?" He grinned.

Kate smiled. "Have you got a flat?"

He surveyed the tire. "I have. I'm just wondering if it's the little bastard whose paper I just failed."

"Seriously?" Kate said, aghast.

"Nah. Hope not, anyway. Think I went over some glass on Cowley Road."

"Oh."

"I don't suppose you know any bike shops round here?"

Kate looked around her. "I don't. I know there's one back on Iffley Road, the one parallel to Cowley Road. That's the one me and my son go to, anyway."

Kate kicked herself. My son—why did she say that?

If the man noticed, he didn't show it. He turned around 180 degrees and looked toward the High Street.

"Actually, it's quicker this way. Through the backstreets," she replied, pointing in the opposite direction.

"Seriously?" he exclaimed, banging his forehead with the flat of his hand. "I've been going that way all term."

"Well, I'm going to Iffley Road in a minute—if you like, I can show you the shortcut."

Oh, God. He'd think she was flirting with him.

Or worse, that she'd followed him from the café.

What was wrong with her?

"I mean, you don't have to, I just—" she stuttered.

"No. That would be great," he said. Self-consciously, she pushed her hair behind her ears.

"So, where are you off to?" he asked.

Kate pointed at Blackwell's.

"I was just going to . . ." She blushed, trying to think of a lie and failing. "Actually, I was just about to go and buy your book."

"Were you?" The Scottish man looked incredulous. He rubbed

a hand over his close-cropped head, revealing a tanned bicep. "God, well, that's nice of you but it's not published in the UK till the summer, just in the States. But hang on . . ." He pulled the copy from the café out of his bag. "Here you go. Have this one."

"Really?"

"Absolutely. I get some free ones from my American publisher that I lend to my students. This one was for the student in question who may or may not have slashed my tires. But as his family apparently owns half of Wiltshire, you're very welcome. Let him get his own."

He frowned. "Hang on. Your family don't own the other half, do they?"

Kate laughed and shook her head.

"Good." He raised his eyebrows. "I tell you what, I'm going to get myself into trouble round here. My prol roots coming out. Anyway, here you go. Call it a thanks for stopping me from going a mile in the wrong direction for the rest of the summer."

Kate took the book gratefully. Just feeling it in her hands sent a thrill through her. It was all she could do not to rip it open and consume the figures in great gulps.

"Thanks," she said. "So the bike shop's this way."

He took his bike by the handles and pushed it alongside her.

"I'm Kate, by the way," she said, holding out her hand.

"Pleased to meet you, Kate," he said, taking it. She liked his voice. It was relaxed and friendly, each word confidently enunciated, as if he were in no rush to finish it off before heading to the next one.

She looked at him shyly. "So, what *are* the chances of this? How would an expert in probability explain this, then? Meeting a stranger twice in one day."

They crossed back into Holywell Street, past a row of seventeenth-century terraced cottages with heavy, studded oak doors and fairy-tale windows.

"Ah—well, let's see," Jago said. "Where do you live?"

She pointed ahead of her. "Where we're going. East Oxford."

"OK, and I'm staying here, at Balliol, back there." He pointed to the college next to Trinity. "So we work and live and shop within, what, a mile or two of each other? I've been here for eight weeks. We probably pass within three hundred feet of each other every few days. It's just today, we recognize each other's faces." He paused as if he'd had a thought.

"Now—that's actually a good project for one of my lazy undergraduates. Pick a stranger in the center of town, and see how many times you see them again in a fixed period of time. I should make them do it just to get them out of their bloody beds in the morning."

Kate smiled. "Do you mind if I ask why you are in Oxford? If you teach at Edinburgh?" They turned into the long curve of Longwall Street, back toward Magdalen Bridge.

"Good question. Actually, I'm on a one-term guest lectureship. Because of the book."

"Really?"

"Uh-huh, well you know, there's a trend at the moment for popular books about science and maths, written by academics. Brian Cox on the universe, that kind of thing."

She nodded. "My son, Jack, loves them."

"How old is he?"

"Nearly eleven."

He nodded. "Good for him. Well, there you go. This idea of chance and probability is big news right now, especially in the States—I was teaching and doing research there for a few years, by the way." She nodded. "Anyway, it gives your university a bit of kudos when you write a bestseller. Suddenly everyone wants a bit of you. So here I am, enjoying my fifteen minutes of fame."

Kate nodded. It was so long since she'd walked along chatting with someone like this. A stranger. A man. Desperately, she stumbled around for something else to say. "And do you like it? Or do you miss Edinburgh?"

"I do. I particularly miss the rain."

"Really?"

"No."

She glanced sideways at him, confused. He smiled.

"Sorry."

"No—don't apologize. I'm being an arse. Seriously? I like the students here. They keep you on your toes. What about you—what do you do? Hang on. Let me guess. . . ."

He screwed up his eyes as if thinking. "OK . . . are you the person who injects new ink into recycled ink cartridges?"

Kate laughed out loud. She couldn't believe the sound. It was so unfamiliar.

"No?" he continued, as she tried to gather herself. "Detective superintendent?" Kate giggled again, unable to stop herself. "OK. Greek Orthodox wedding planner?"

"No!"

He winked. "You see, eventually if I go on, I'll get it. That's probability for you."

"Ah, I see. Well, actually, I do some project managing for a historical renovation company," she said, checking for cyclists in the bike lane before they crossed at the end of Magdalen Bridge. "And I run a foundation attached to it to help kids from deprived backgrounds get into architectural studies and renovation work."

"Do you now?" Jago said, looking impressed. "Good for you. I should tell my sister about that. She teaches in a big inner-city school. You should see her. She's ace. Five foot, and feisty as shit. She's always saying it's hard for some of the kids to get a break."

Kate nodded. She liked the way he spoke about his sister. It reminded her of Hugo.

They stopped at the end of the bridge, and she looked ahead. Damn.

They would be across the roundabout in a minute, then into Iffley Road. Kate looked up ahead and saw the bike shop. Soon he would be gone.

"Jago. Do you mind? Can I ask you something? About the book again?" she asked.

"Uh-huh."

"You know what you said earlier, about flying with less reputable airlines. That you put it out of your mind. Can I ask how do you do that?"

He stopped outside an Indian restaurant just before the bicycle shop, and scratched the stubble on his chin. She looked up at him. He was different physically than Hugo. A few inches shorter at around six foot, and lean and muscular, where Hugo had been broad like Richard, with some softness around his stomach thanks to all that good red wine. As Kate looked at Jago, she noticed their reflection in the window of the restaurant. They looked like a couple. The image of her with a man again was so strange, she couldn't stop glancing at it.

His face grew more serious.

"Well, what I meant is that you can't control these things. You can make an educated guess that might lower or increase your chances of something happening but in the end, you can't control everything. Nothing in life is certain apart from the fact that we're all going to die. You can spend all day trying to work out which is the safest airline, then choke on a peanut in the departure lounge. And personally, I think life's too short. Don't know about you but I'd rather be lying on a beach somewhere."

He regarded her with his intense blue eyes. There was a spark of interest in them she hadn't seen earlier.

"Right, I'd better get this tire fixed," he said. "It was nice to meet you, Kate, and I hope you enjoy the book. But don't take it too seriously. Remember, it is meant to be a bit of fun."

"I won't," she lied, knowing that the minute she left him she would go straight to the juice bar and begin reading.

"Anyway, as we've now established, I expect I'll bump into you again." He touched her on the arm pleasantly.

Kate wasn't ready to let him go. Not yet.

"Jago?" she called, not even knowing what was coming next.

He turned.

She thought frantically. "Listen, if you're new to Oxford . . . you know, I'd be happy to show you round. Me and Jack only moved here a few years ago ourselves, so I know what it's like."

She saw him hesitate, and glance at the wedding ring she could never take off, probably trying to work out what was going on here.

She cringed. What was she thinking? He was probably planning to drop off his bike and head off to ask out the gorgeous young auburn-haired waitress in the juice bar. Not some worn-out, thirty-five-year-old mum with—she noticed, to her discomfiture—a rip in the knee of her jeans.

"Uh. Well," he said carefully. "To be honest, the students at Balliol were ordered to take me on enough tours of Oxford when I arrived to last me a lifetime. It's all very nice but, I don't know, maybe a drink one evening? That would be good. You could tell me a bit more about your work with the kids."

Kate almost stepped back in surprise. "Sure, sounds great."

"OK. What about tomorrow tonight?

Tomorrow was Tuesday. Saskia was booked to babysit so that Kate could go to her nonexistent therapy session with Sylvia. She appraised Jago. He had already given her more to think about in five minutes than that woman probably would in three months.

"Would it be OK to make it quite early—about seven thirty? I've only got a babysitter till about nine."

"Yup. Absolutely." She was happy to note that he still didn't flinch at the mention of the fact she had a child. "I'll leave it to you where we meet."

Kate blanched. She couldn't possibly decide that quickly. She'd need time to work out the safest place to meet and the safest way to get there.

Jago took in her expression. "Tell you what, here's my number," he said, taking out a pen and scribbling on a piece of paper. "Just text me where you want to meet."

"Perfect," she said, relieved.

"OK—see you," Jago said, pushing his bike inside.

"Good luck." Kate smiled.

"Actually, Kate," he said, turning back. "If we're meeting tomorrow, can I keep that copy of the book? I was going to go straight to the library after this. I'll dig out another one from my room tomorrow for you."

She held the book tightly in her hand.

"Sure," she said, fighting to control her impulse to cling to it, and handing it over.

"I won't forget, promise." He smiled.

She waved and walked up Iffley Road fighting the urge to beg him for it back.

Maybe this was for the best. It would be a test of strength.

All of a sudden, a thought hit her.

Her mind hadn't summoned up a single statistic about arriving home safely since she met Jago Martin on Broad Street.

Not one.

And, for the first time in a long time, she'd actually enjoyed a conversation with someone, too.

She looked up Iffley Road.

What if she could get home without thinking about any numbers?

Steeling herself, Kate picked up speed, summoning up Jack's anxious face to spur her on, trying to forget about Jago Martin's book.

8

The clock on Gabe's computer in his bedroom said 5:45 P.M. Jack looked at his new Facebook account on the screen, eyes glowing. With Gabe's help, he already had eleven friends: ten from school, and Aunt Sass, who had insisted that if she was going to go behind his mum's back, she was at least going to see what he was up to. Gabe's mum had made him do the same, so at least Jack wasn't the only one with a smiling grown-up on his list. As long as Sid at school didn't start writing rude things on his page. Aunt Sass was cool but even she'd be shocked at some of the stuff Sid showed them on his phone at playtime.

"Mum says you can stay for tea, J!" Gabe shouted from downstairs.

"But you've got to phone your mum and tell her, Jack," came Gabe's mum's voice from the kitchen. Her voice always sounded relaxed, like it was lazing on a beach. "You know what she's like, yeah?"

"OK," Jack called. He frowned. He knew Gabe and his mum

would be making faces at each other about his mum. He picked up his phone, thinking. He wasn't ready to speak to her yet. He felt too guilty. She'd only be at home, worrying again, more probably because of what he'd said this morning. No—he knew what he would do.

"Hi mum," he texted. He sat for a moment, listening to Gabe fighting with his brother downstairs, and Gabe's mum shouting "You two!" and "Enough!" Jack swept a curve of fine blond hair away from his face. It would be nice to have a brother so it wasn't always just him and Mum. He supposed he would never get one now.

Kate's phone buzzed as she walked in the house.

hi mum. gabes mum says i can stay for tea. can i?

hi jack, of course, have fun

She made herself text back, fighting the urge to tell him to ensure Gabe walked him home afterward. She sighed, imagining Jack in the loud, happy chaos of Gabe's house, wishing he never had to come home. She was just about to plug her phone into the charger in the kitchen, when a new text arrived.

are you ok mum?

The unfamiliar concern of his words took Kate by surprise.

yes of course!

But just as she was about to send it, she stopped.

She sat down at the kitchen table and stared at the screen, looking at his question.

are you ok mum?

After their awful fight this morning, and the lie she made him tell his teacher, the least she could do was answer truthfully.

She thought for a moment, then tapped in a different reply.

honestly jack? no. not really. but it has NOTHING to do with you. it's me, and i promise i am trying to fix it. really, really sorry about your head.

She pressed the "send" button and grimaced. Was it too much? She sat nervously biting her fingernails. His message pinged back.

im sorry 2

He was trying to talk to her! After all this time, he was trying to talk to her.

Sitting upright, Kate tried to think fast.

no jack. you've done nothing wrong. it's me, and i know some things have gone wrong and I promise that I'm doing everything i can now to make it better . . .

Nothing happened.

More minutes passed.

Damn, she'd scared him. She couldn't expect him to go from never talking about the terrible thing that had torn their lives apart, to an open, frank discussion, just because she had decided it would be good for them. She decided to take a risk.

maybe you can help me?

This time, the reply was almost immediate.

i dont know what 2 do.

"Oh, Jack," she said sadly.

u cd tell me what I'm doing wrong.

She waited.

but then you get upset.

She sniffed.

sorry. jack—I didn't realize.

She thought for a minute then typed again.

you know, it's so good to talk about this with you. could we talk about it more when you get home?

She waited and waited.
His message pinged back.

Gabes coming, bye.

Kate put her phone down. She was reeling but this was good. This was a start.

She thought about Jago Martin. She didn't know why, but somehow ever since she'd met that man this morning, she felt different. Better. A tiny bit hopeful.

"Just don't think about it," he'd said.

And she hadn't. Not about a single statistic. She'd managed it all the way home.

Out of nowhere, an impulse overtook her. She ran upstairs, unlocked the padlock to the gate, grabbed it, and marched into the study. Without stopping to think, she unlocked and flung open the window.

It was time. Things had to change. Today.

With a grunt, Kate threw the padlock as far as she could into the garden.

"Fuck off!" she called out.

There was a sound to her left. Somebody was clearing his throat. It was a man sitting in the garden next door, holding a beer bottle, looking up at her. He had very long legs splayed out in front of him, and was dressed in black, with deathly pale skin and bad glasses. One of the students, presumably.

"Oh. Sorry," she said. "Not you."

"OK, then! Everybody's happy!" he said, raising his bottle. His accent was musical, each word sounding as if it were formed carefully to incorporate unfamiliar vowels. He was swaying a little as if he were drunk. He kept looking at her, as if he were trying to get into focus. His eyes, she noticed, were an odd shade, silvery pale blue. The color of a husky's.

"Well. Bye," she said, withdrawing and shutting the window.

She locked it again and went to run a bath.

She stayed in the bath for a while, using her hands to create waves of warm water to wash over her body, thinking about Jago Martin.

Jesus Christ. She was going for a drink with a man.

A man with interesting blue eyes who had awakened something in her that she couldn't even begin to describe.

As she lay back in the bath, she noticed the vanilla hand lotion that sat on the bathroom windowsill.

She blinked.

It was a quarter empty.

She had only bought it on Saturday yet it was almost a quarter empty. Surely she hadn't used that much? Kate looked around the bathroom. Was it an old one she'd forgotten about? The familiar sense of unease settled on her.

Helen's words came back to her about the casserole. "It had not gone."

"For God's sake! Stop this," Kate said to herself. What was

wrong with her? She had obviously just used more than she'd realized.

A door slammed downstairs, making her jump.

"Mum?"

Jack was back.

"I'm in the bath. Are you OK?" she called out nervously, sitting up. She fought the urge to ask if Gabe had walked him home.

"Yeah," he shouted up. "Can I watch *The Simpsons?*"

"Got any homework?"

"No."

"OK. See you in a while."

There was a pause.

"Gabe walked back with me, by the way," he shouted up.

She berated herself in the mirror. "Oh, OK."

Ten minutes later, she went downstairs to find Jack lying on the sofa, the Band-Aid still on his head.

She wondered if maybe they'd continue the conversation they'd started earlier but he just glanced up at her, then looked back at the TV.

"Hi."

"Hi."

"How's your head?"

"OK, thanks." He shrugged.

"Anyone ask?"

"Mrs. Corrigan. I said it was my skateboard."

"Oh. Sorry," Kate said, guiltily.

"S'OK."

The barrier was back up. She sat uncertainly on the arm of the sofa, pretending to watch the television. Helen's words came back to her. "You are his parent, not the other way round."

Whatever she suspected now about the danger of Helen's

feelings toward her, on that point she had been right. Which is why Kate had lain in bed this morning, forcing herself to do what she never did: delve painfully into the bank of memories of their life before Hugo died. Trying to find something she could use. One flashback from the kitchen in their old house in Highgate had given her an idea.

Would he go for it, or was he too old now?

"Jack," she said.

"Hmm?" he replied, grinning as Bart showed his butt to Principal Skinner.

"I was thinking of making some brownies or something for Nana and Granddad, for you to take with you this weekend. You don't fancy helping, do you?"

He turned, unsure, and she saw him trying to judge whether she meant it or not.

"Now?"

"Hmm."

"Have we got stuff to make them?"

Kate shrugged uncertainly. It was so long since those Highgate days when Jack stood on a stool to reach the counter, the pair of them chatting, as they baked for Hugo's lunch box. "Isn't it just butter and flour and sugar?" she said. "And . . . hang on, we don't have any chocolate."

Jack scratched his nose. "We could go and get some at the shop."

She realized he was trying to hide a smile.

And then, to her delight, there he was, finally. In Jack's expression, just for a second—Hugo's hidden grin. Just like in the photograph on the terrace in Highgate as he tried not to laugh at her joke.

9

It was six thirty the following evening by the time Saskia finished work in central Oxford and made her way slowly to Hubert Street.

She walked along thinking crossly about work.

The contracts had come through from the marketing agency this morning, and she'd spent the day sorting out a Twitter account. By six, she'd managed to attract thirty-seven followers, five of them potential clients.

"Look at that!" Dad had exclaimed in the office, summoning a few others to look at Saskia's screen, to her embarrassment. "Don't know how you get the hang of these technical things so quickly, Sass."

Saskia stomped onward. It was a Twitter account, not rocket science. Dad could have done it himself, in no time. He wasn't an idiot. She reached Hubert Street and looked up apprehensively.

At least Kate would be going out to her therapy session, but first they had to face each other.

They hadn't spoken since Gate-gate, as Saskia was now calling Friday's showdown. She hadn't spoken to Mum about it, either. Just spent the weekend having a drink with her book group in the village, and going through her divorce papers from Jonathan, desperately trying not to ring and beg him to reconsider.

Nervously, she rang the bell.

Kate opened the door. "Hi."

"Hi," Saskia said, meeting her eye awkwardly. She did a double take.

Kate appeared transformed. She was wearing dark skinny jeans that actually fit her instead of the old size sixes that hung from her loosely, and a tailored white summer shirt Saskia hadn't seen before. She was wearing makeup, too. Just a touch, but it was there. Soft blush on her cheeks, a touch of eyeliner and mascara. Perhaps that was what had put a new light in her eyes. The little flecks of gold that had been tarnished for so long were sparkling again.

"Come in," Kate said. Sass followed, taken aback. Kate's dark hair had been blow-dried and sat silkily just above her shoulders. From the back, the jeans reminded her what enviable legs Kate had. The shirt was doing wonders, too, to cover up her corset-thin waist and the bony protuberances of her shoulders and arms. Saskia blinked. She hadn't seen Kate dressed up like this in years.

That old sense of insecurity reawakened inside her.

It had been difficult when Hugo arrived back from university, enthralled with this self-assured girl from Shropshire that he brought with him. Those first times the five of them went out together, Dad sweeping them into a restaurant or on a birthday visit to the theater, she had realized that it was Kate who people—both men and women—looked at before her.

But after Hugo died, that light within her was extinguished.

On the street, men had started to glance at Saskia first. Sometimes they didn't look at Kate at all. It was as if Kate's beauty had died with Hugo. Water drained from the flower.

Saskia followed Kate into the kitchen, uncertainly, and sat at the table.

"So . . . ?" she said tentatively, watching Kate pull a bottle of white wine from the fridge.

"Yes?"

"Well . . ."

"I don't want to talk about it, Sass."

Saskia sat back. "Look," she started awkwardly, "I was really cross with you about that fucking gate. I mean, for God's sake, Kate. But I had no idea Mum was going to turn into Ninja Helen. . . ." She lifted her arm in a karate chop.

"I don't want to talk about it," Kate repeated.

Saskia blinked hard and poured them each a glass of wine. Kate worked around her, clearing up the mess from tea and putting out a plate of pasta with pesto for Saskia.

"So how angry are you with me? On a scale from one to ten."

"To be honest, I don't know what I feel," Kate said, sitting down and sipping her wine. "I just know I can't talk about it with you right now."

"OK, but you're going to see this woman. Tonight?"

"I'm getting help, yes."

Kate took another sip and put down her glass. They surveyed each other.

Perhaps it was seeing her dressed like this, but Saskia found herself wishing for the old Kate in a way she hadn't in a long time.

She ran a finger down her wineglass, imagining telling Kate

that she'd sat outside Jonathan's office at lunchtime in a café just to catch a glimpse of him. Imagining telling Kate the truth about the mess of her marriage, and about how fed up she was working for Dad but could see no way out. For an agonizing second, she pictured curling up with Kate on the sofa and talking till their honking laughter woke Hugo and he came downstairs, crumpled and cross, and told them to be quiet.

But the chill emanating from Kate told her not to even think about it.

"Is it all right to stay over tonight?" Saskia said in the end, motioning to her wine. "I left the car at the village station."

Kate nodded. "Of course."

"Can I borrow some knickers tomorrow?"

Kate stood up and shut the dishwasher. "Help yourself—you know where they are.

"Actually, if you're staying, do you mind if I stay out for a while afterward? One of the school mums is having a birthday drink at a bar on Cowley Road later."

"Not at all." Kate, going out? Well, at least that was something positive she could tell Mum. Kate seeing friends and going to therapy. It might defrost the situation before Helen had any more earth-shattering notions about taking Jack away.

Kate hung a cloth over the tap.

"Thanks. I better go. I have to be there at half-seven. Oh, and I'm not expecting anybody tonight, so can you not . . ."

Kate stopped midsentence, the word teetering on the end of her tongue.

". . . answer the front door when it's dark," Saskia finished for her. "Don't worry. I know the house rules."

Kate turned away. "It's not a house rule," she retorted over her shoulder.

Saskia shrugged. There was no point inflaming the situation.

"And can you make sure Jack's in bed by nine?"

"Yup. Will do."

The mention of Jack made Saskia feel guilty. She had checked his Facebook page before she'd left the office and seen how quickly he'd been swamped with friends. She'd also seen a quiz on his page posted by someone named Sid called "Is Jack a dick—yes or no?" with his friends, including Gabe, all apparently "jokingly" agreeing that Jack was.

"Thanks—see you later," said Kate, grabbing her jacket and finishing her wine in one gulp. She shouted, "Bye, Jack!" into the sitting room, before stopping by the front door to grab her bike helmet.

Saskia picked up her own glass and turned to find Kate checking her reflection in the hall mirror. It was so long since Saskia had seen her pay the slightest attention to her appearance that she couldn't stop staring.

Tonight men would be noticing Kate again, she realized. With a pang, Saskia thought of Hugo. One day his self-assured girl from Shropshire would not be his anymore. She would belong to another man.

This made her sad but she had to be positive. Think of Jack and keep trying to support Kate—not upset her. And the good thing was, it looked like the therapy was already helping.

It had not been an easy choice, but in the end Kate had picked the Hanley Arms just a quarter of a mile from Hubert Street. It was close enough to home that she could cycle back along the quiet pavements later tonight, and avoid thinking about traffic accident statistics, but far enough that Sass wouldn't catch her lying.

She arrived to find Jago locking his newly repaired bike to a lamppost outside. "Good timing," he called.

He looked up at the pub. "Your local?"

"Kind of," she lied, locking her own bike to a railing. She had been in here once with Saskia. You had to know people in a pub for it to be your local. "New tire, then?" she ventured pointlessly.

"Yup. Thanks for the recommendation." Jago smiled, opening the door for her. She passed through with a nervous "Thanks."

He was wearing jeans and a slim navy shirt that made his eyes look even bluer, and properly exposed the thin leather band around his neck. Suddenly, Kate felt completely tongue-tied. What had she been thinking? She couldn't think of one word to say to this man.

It didn't help when she heard jeers coming from inside the pub.

"What do you want to drink?" Jago asked.

"Um, white wine, thanks," she said, glancing at the source of the jeers. A group of five men in soccer shirts, their bodies and faces moving jerkily en masse, swore and bantered with one another, all the while throwing back pints and laughing loudly.

She was so preoccupied with the men that she didn't realize what she had done at first. It was only when Jago turned and asked "Ah—Chardonnay or Sauvignon Blanc?" that she realized she was about to order her second glass of white wine tonight. Which would push her daily limit over three units and increase her chances of cancer.

"Sorry. Actually, could I change that, could I have a soda and . . ."

Just don't think about it. That's what he had said. Don't even think about it.

"A what?" he asked.

"No, actually, either's fine," Kate said. "I'll get a table."

She moved as far away as she could from the men, who were watching soccer on a raised television near the bar. She wound her way through ten empty tables till she could go no farther, and stopped at the toilets.

She saw Jago looking for her, then finding her miles away. He shot her a playful, curious look.

"Is this a special table?" he asked after he'd wandered over.

"No . . . Sorry. I just thought it was quieter."

He sat down and looked around. "No. It's fine. Nice and close to the toilet. And"—he pointed at the wall—"the fire extinguisher."

She smiled, despite herself. "Have you been teaching this afternoon?"

He nodded and regaled her with a story about a supersmart but cocky student of his who he had noticed kept bouncing his knee up and down, because, it turned out, he was wearing earphones under his beanie during the lecture.

"And to cap it off, when I question him about it, he says he's listening to a recording of my lecture from last week, cheeky little bastard. Anyway, tell me about the project you're working on."

Kate tried to gather her thoughts. But they kept slipping to the other side of the bar. "Get in there!" one of the soccer fans growled, standing up and throwing an arm at the television screen, as his friends yelled behind him, then clapped.

"It's a house in Islington that my colleague David's going to turn back from three flats into a house. . . ." she started, forcing herself to recall details about plans they had to restore the stonework at the front, trying to ignore the way each shout made her chest tighten.

"So what kind of work placements do you give these kids?" Jago asked politely.

One of the soccer fans staggered toward them, eyes bleary and unfocused. As he went through the door into the toilet beside them, he burped loudly.

Kate tried to ignore it. She tried to explain to Jago about how the kids had a chance to work with each member of the renovation team, from the architect to the craftspeople like the stonemasons, to the high-spec interior decoration at the end, to see which area of the renovation they enjoyed. And how if they really took to it, the foundation would sponsor them through A levels, and then maybe a degree in a relevant subject, like architectural design or art history—Kate's own subject—or, if they were really committed, even architecture.

In turn Jago asked intelligent questions, which she tried to answer. But it was no good. Every instinct was telling her to get out of this pub. To run as far from these men as she could.

She listened to Jago, desperate to beat back the panic rising up inside her. The conversation turned back to his experience of publishing a book, and then to his lectures at Oxford.

"Term finishes next week. Then there's a summer school I'll teach for a while before I head back out to the States for August."

"You fuck-ing wank-er!"

Kate jumped. The largest of the men had leapt out of his seat and was shaking his fist at the telly, while the others jeered in a chorus.

"What are you doing in the States?"

"I've got a bit of personal stuff to tie up in North Carolina where I was teaching, then I'm heading over to Utah with friends to do some mountain biking."

"Oh," she said, looking at the men again. "So, where did you say you lived in Oxford?"

"I've got a room at Balliol."

"At Balliol? Really? Is it nice?"

He drained the bottom of his pint. "It is nice. All stone steps and bay windows where I can stand and smoke a pipe. If I actually smoked a pipe."

Kate nodded, distracted. "So is your room nice?" she repeated inadvertently, glancing back over at the soccer fans.

Jago didn't reply, and she saw he was watching her.

"Kate, why did you really choose this table?"

"Because it's quiet."

"You mean, not near those guys?"

She shrugged. "They're quite noisy—don't you think?"

Jago leaned forward onto his elbows. "I hope you don't mind me saying but you look really nervous."

Kate was horrified, and on the verge of tears. She swallowed hard to make them go away.

"Do you know them?"

She shook her head, defeated. "No."

"You look terrified of them."

She shrugged. "They just seem a little aggressive."

"Do they?" He looked over. "So, you're worried about what they might do, rather than what they have done."

"Yes." It was time to go. She was a disgrace, a mess. She couldn't even have a quiet drink in a pub without this bloody nonsense ruining everything.

Jago stood up. He was holding out his hand. She took it. It was dry and warm.

She stood up, too, trying to hold herself together. He understood, she realized with gratitude. He was taking her out of here and to another pub.

Jago led her through the bar toward the front door. To her bewilderment, he veered toward the men.

Kate's heart skipped a painful beat, and she began to fall back. But Jago kept leading her firmly.

With her hand in his grasp, Jago approached the largest of the group. The man was huge, with cheeks as wide as a pig's. His eyes were lost between folds of skin, his head shaved around the back, with a spiked black do on top. Forearms the size of Kate's thighs burst out of the sleeves of his soccer shirt.

"Don't," she whispered.

Jago walked up to the man and slapped him on the back.

"How's it going, lads?" Jago said, pointing at the screen. "What's the score?"

Kate's legs began to shake.

The man put down his pint and surveyed Jago belligerently with his tiny eyes. Jago met his stare face on. The man's mates watched, beers suspended in midair.

He opened his mouth.

"Two-nil, mate—fucking beauty, that last one." He lifted up his arm as the crowd on the screen cheered the opposition's run toward the goal. "Mark him, you fucking wanker!"

Jago smiled as he took Kate's hand again and led her past toward the door. "Thanks, lads."

"See you, mate," the man called, raising his pint. He regarded Kate, who was now pale with fright. "Night, love."

Her heart was hammering so hard in her chest that it was difficult to breathe properly. Her legs felt as if the muscles and bones had been removed and she might collapse.

She put out a hand to steady herself against the wall.

Jago turned.

"Kate! What the fuck? You're shaking," he exclaimed.

She caught a couple of deep breaths. "Why did you do that?"

He took her shoulders. "They're just lads out for a drink,

celebrating the end of the soccer season. They're harmless. I just wanted you to see that."

To her horror, she couldn't hold the tears back.

He looked down at her, concerned. "Oh, shit. Are you sick?"

"No." She wiped away the tears, feeling pathetic.

"What did you think they were going to do?"

She shook her head, hating herself. He held her shoulders gently. Self-consciously, she pulled back. It was strange to be so physically close to a man after all these years. She shook her head. "I don't know. I know they seem OK to you, but to me . . ."

He watched her carefully.

"I can't explain it, OK?" Her voice sounded strident and ugly. "I'm a freak." She pulled away from him. "That's all I can tell you, Jago. I'm sorry I suggested a drink. It was a really bad idea."

She started to put her helmet on but in her rush, dropped it on the pavement with a crack.

"Bloody hell!" she cried. She had to get out of there.

"Kate," Jago repeated calmly. He leaned over before she could, and picked up her helmet, but didn't give it back to her. "Why would you say that about yourself?"

She shook her head. This was dreadful. "I'm sorry. I just don't want to talk about it. I've got to go."

But he wouldn't move out of her way. "Not till you tell me."

A pit of disappointment began to settle inside her. He was going to cycle off in a second, and that would be it. In all the years she'd lived in Oxford, he was the first person she'd had any type of real connection with. And it had given her hope. For whatever reason, he was the first person she'd felt able to talk to since losing Hugo.

And now, thanks to her fucking anxiety, she was scaring him off.

Kate shook her head angrily at the thought that she had ruined whatever chance she'd had of getting to know this man. "Look. I'm sorry. I just can't be around other people right now. It's complicated. It's me, not you. I better go."

She reached for her helmet but Jago put it behind his back. "I want to help you. Let's talk about it."

She shook her head. "You don't want to know."

"Why don't you let me decide that?"

She looked at him defiantly. He held her gaze. She sighed and shook her head. What the hell? She'd never see him again anyway, so what did it even matter?

"OK. Well, to start . . . It's hard for me to be around people like that. . . . Because my husband . . ."

Jago glanced quickly at her wedding ring. "Oh, right. I'd assumed that you . . ."

"No. My husband—he died."

Jago was clearly surprised. "Oh, I'm so sorry."

"You couldn't have known. I just . . . I shouldn't have come. I'm sorry. I just—when we spoke. It seemed to help."

"With what?" Jago cocked his head to the side. It was such an understanding gesture, one she had seen Sylvia make during their session. She felt a lump in her throat. "It'll sound crazy."

He touched her arm. "Come on. Trust me. I'm a doctor. Of mathematics, but it's worth a try."

The falling darkness threw their faces into shadow. She looked at Jago waiting patiently for her to speak.

"OK. It helped because I spend a lot of time doing this. A huge amount of time, actually. Worrying about what might happen. I constantly obsess about the chance of bad things happening to my son and me."

He screwed up his eyes. "I see . . ."

But she could tell he didn't.

"You know, 'you have a fifteen percent chance of having a bike accident if you cycle on a weekday compared to ten percent at the weekend.' So I'm hesitant to ride during the week. That kind of thing."

"So that's why you wanted the book."

She nodded. "And if you want to know the truth, it's ruining my life."

Kate couldn't believe he wasn't laughing at her, or suddenly remembering he had to be somewhere else.

Jago turned and sat on a low wall. "Bloody hell. Kate, I was just talking to my publisher in the States about this last week. There's a psychologist working on a book about exactly that."

Why hadn't Sylvia known that?

"It's an emerging phenomenon, apparently—people trying to gain a sense of control over their lives by using statistics to do with safety or health. Living with a constant fear of imagined danger. He said it's a kind of obsessive-compulsive disorder." He stuck out his lip like a naughty boy. "Kate, I'm so sorry. I feel awful. Is that why you were asking me about how to put these things out of your head?"

"Anyway," she said calmly, knowing it was time to end this encounter before she humiliated herself any more. "I think I better just go . . ." She waited for him to hand over the helmet.

"Go?" Jago said. "No way. I feel a bit responsible now. Right. Just give me a second to think." He paused. "Right. I know."

"You know what?"

"Get on your bike," he said, giving her the helmet.

He jumped on his own bike—without a helmet, she noticed

queasily—and set off to the end of the street, where the road turned into an alley that she knew led to the river.

"Come on," he shouted, without turning back.

Jago disappeared in the darkness. Damn. If she didn't follow him, she might lose him altogether and then he'd think she was not just a freak but rude, as well, for just leaving. Shakily, Kate unlocked her bike, put on her helmet, and headed toward the alley.

10

The evening light was fading quickly. Kate turned right, then left. Jago was waiting for her fifty yards up ahead on the riverbank.

As soon as she got close enough to ask him what was going on, he just turned and started cycling again, with a gesture to follow.

Kate kept going apprehensively, pushing hard on the pedals to negotiate the bumpy towpath. As they moved away from Oxford, the path grew quieter. She cycled past the silhouette of a dog walker; two students jogging, with swinging ponytails sticking out from baseball caps; a lone rower heading for home, his oars creating rippling silver pyramids in the water.

She thought Jago might never stop. This was ridiculous. She looked back. They must be a mile from the pub now. In a minute they'd be in the countryside.

They'd gone too far to go back now alone, so she turned on her lights and pushed on.

Eventually they stopped passing other people. They did pass

three solitary canal boats moored for the evening, smoke drifting from their chimneys, and a heron on the bank.

She cycled on, taking in the unfamiliar sights. She never came
out here on her bike. She had to admit that the ride through
the still evening felt oddly calming. It was beautiful out here.
Looking behind her, she saw the disappearing sun had cracked
orange along the horizon, turning the ferns and ducks black
against it. A meditative pace took over in the motions in her
legs. An unusual lightness filled her body.

She was leaving Oxford behind, for what reason, she wasn't sure
yet. She became aware of everything falling away, even for a short
time. She left the trouble with Richard and Helen, Jack and Saskia in
the opposite direction of the river's current. For a few exhilarating
seconds, Kate felt freed up. She could've cycled like this all night.

In the end, it was another five minutes before Jago started to
slow down. She saw him up ahead, in the dying light, coming
to a stop beside a gate.

"Here!" he shouted, and disappeared. She dismounted and
pushed her bike through a gate off the towpath, onto what
appeared to be a single-lane country road overhung with
branches. There were a few gated houses set discreetly back
from the road, a forest behind them.

Within moments, Jago was back on his bike, cycling ahead.

Kate jumped on hers again. Right. Now she could catch him
and tell him to stop. This was starting to make her very nervous.

She pedaled fast, only to see Jago turn right again, this time
down an even narrower lane with a rough, unserviced surface.
He pulled over after fifty yards.

Kate came up behind him in the dark.

"What are you doing? I had no idea you were going . . ." She
drew breath. "Where are we?"

Jago put his finger to his lips.

"What?" she said quietly, looking around.

He threw his bike down in a ditch and motioned for her to do the same. There was only one streetlight back at the top of the lane, so she could hardly see his face, just the curve of his cheek from behind.

"This way." He motioned her to follow.

"No way!" she exclaimed as he began to climb a gate that was over ten feet high.

But Jago kept going. She peered up and saw he was already halfway up. Through the iron railings lay a sprawling country hall, Gothic peaks silhouetted in the sky.

"Jago. What are you *doing?*"

He reached the top of the gate, put his leg over, and started climbing down. "Come on," he dared her as he reached her at eye level on the other side.

"Absolutely not," she said furiously.

"OK. Suit yourself." He turned and began to melt into the darkness beyond.

Where was he going?

Kate peered behind her at the lane, and then into the forest. She wasn't bloody staying here by herself or cycling back down that empty, dark river path alone. Crossly, she reached up to the bars, and began to climb, her legs shaking. Jago emerged from the shadows and gently helped her down.

"Quick," he whispered, grabbing her hand again. "Before anyone sees us."

She looked around. Who was he talking about? Her heart thumping, she allowed her hand to settle into his, self-conscious at the touch of his skin. Jago led her around the boundary hedge, staying in the shadows, away from a gentle light being cast from the ground-floor windows of the grand hall.

Kate inhaled. The air was fresh and warm, filled with the scent of blossom and cut grass.

"I think it's round the back," Jago said. She didn't ask what.

He led her along the hedge till they cleared the illuminated patch of lawn, then bent down and scurried like a soldier on maneuvers toward some stone steps. She copied him, entering a network of vegetable and flower beds.

"There it is," he said quietly.

In front of them was a square pond surrounded by an old stone wall. Lilies floated in black, silky water.

"Glowworms!" Kate pointed in delight at the tiny fluttering green lights glowing in the gaps of the wall.

Jago smiled. He pulled out a sweater from his bag, and laid it on the grass. They sat next to each other. He sighed contentedly and lay back on the grass.

"What is this place?" she whispered. "It's beautiful."

"It's cool, isn't it? Someone at Balliol told me about it."

"But what is it?"

He winked. "Now that, I'm not going to tell you."

"Why?"

"Because I've taken you somewhere you know nothing about, so you can't make any calculation. And I've distracted you from the anxiety hopefully. It's a guerilla experiment—the kind of thing my department head keeps threatening to sack me for." Jago sat up on his elbows. "OK, so you're sitting in a strange garden with a guy you know nothing about, miles from anywhere. No one knows you're here. Are you scared?"

Kate watched the light of the moon in his pupils and waited for the fear to come. She shook her head slowly. "No."

"And why do you think that is?"

She paused. "Because I haven't had time to think about it."

"And there you go," he said, and lay back down.

Neither of them spoke for a while.

Kate let her eyes adjust to the darkness. She scanned the garden, looking at the branches of a weeping willow and a statue behind it.

"Well, it is beautiful. Whatever it is."

" 'Nothing can cure the soul but the senses, just as nothing can cure the senses but the soul,' " Jago said.

Kate waited for him to tell her where the quote was from.

Instead he asked, "Kate, can I ask what happened? To your husband."

The glowworms flitted like fairies. She found a small twig and dug it into the grooves of her sneakers, which were caked with mud. She tried to find the voice to tell him but knew she couldn't. She shook her head.

"Sorry," Jago said. "I didn't mean to be nosy."

"It's fine. I just don't really talk about it."

"Why?" He wasn't giving up.

"Well, I used to. But I just found it didn't help. People would say the wrong thing. Not on purpose, they just did. They'd say: 'How do you feel?' really kindly. And after a while I realized that, yes, they did care about me, but underneath they were actually more terrified by what had happened to me. What they actually wanted to know was not 'How do you feel?' but 'How bad do you feel? How bad is it? Will I be able to endure it if it happens to me?' "

She paused. Jago didn't push her for details. His silence was like Sylvia's, relaxed and unhurried. It made her want to talk more.

"Then," she continued, "after an hour of me talking, I'd see them thinking, 'God, get me out of here. This is depressing.' Not that I could blame them. I'd see them five minutes later chatting on the pavement to a friend about getting their highlights done. Back in the real world." She glanced back at Jago. "Where I felt I couldn't go anymore. And it was difficult. So I stopped."

Jago stayed silent. They were two feet apart, side by side on the damp grass, listening to the trickle of water from the pond, and a splash of fish jumping.

He plucked a piece of grass and put it in his mouth. "OK, but can I ask if that's when it began? This obsession with numbers? Because of your husband dying?"

Inside, Kate felt all the words she'd prepared so carefully for Sylvia bubbling back up, trying to escape from her mouth again, desperate to be heard now that someone was finally willing to listen. Jago was lying down, chewing grass like a chilled-out student at a festival. If he had worries of his own, they didn't show. What would that be like? What would it be like to spend time with someone like him, with his easy, boyish laugh and comforting demeanor?

"I feel like I'm in a therapy session," she said, laughing nervously.

Jago chuckled. "Really? My ex-girlfriend would think that was hilarious. According to her, I am 'the worst fucking listener in the world.'"

Kate glanced at him curiously. Ex-girlfriend. "Ha. Well, trust me, you're better than the so-called therapist I saw last week."

She was keenly aware of how strange it felt to lie beside a man again, even two feet apart. How long had it been since she had done this, just been with someone, just talking?

"To answer your question, I think I'd already started obsessing about this stuff before then." She looked at the dark sky. "It started when my parents were killed in a weird accident."

"Seriously?"

"Uh-huh. About five years before Hugo died."

"God, I'm so sorry. We don't have to . . ."

She shook her head. "No. It's OK. It was a long time ago. On the night of our wedding, actually."

Jago was shocked. "And so that's when it started?"

"Yes, I started obsessing about the accident."

"Can I ask what happened?"

She shrugged. "Bad luck. My parents were in a taxi coming back from the reception. They were traveling up the mountain road to our house in Shropshire and came round a bend and drove straight into the body of this big stag, which had been shot by a poacher. It must have escaped, then collapsed on the road. I remember wondering, what are the chances of a stag dying right on that road? I mean, why not by the side of the road, or not on a bend? Why at night, and not during the day when the driver might have seen it? Why on the night of my wedding? I mean, I found out afterward that fifteen people die each year in Britain in traffic accidents caused by deer. Fifteen out of sixty million. So why my parents? Anyway, they were going fifty miles per hour. Probably too fast. The taxi swung sideways across the road and overturned down a hill into the river. The taxi driver, Stan, from our village, was in his sixties, and I remember a doctor telling me that reaction times slow with age. That you had a fifty percent chance of braking quicker if you were in your fifties like my dad. And I kept wondering if my dad had been driving if they would have survived. I was angry at Stan for a long time. I was at school with his granddaughter, and I couldn't speak to her."

Jago whistled. "Wow. I just, I don't know what to say. I'm so sorry."

Kate pushed her hair behind her ears. She wanted to talk more. It felt good to talk like this with someone. "Don't worry. Really. There's nothing to say."

"God, you've had some bad luck, Kate."

She faced him, resting on her elbow. "Ah, now there's a question. So tell me, do statisticians believe in luck?"

She watched his silhouette in the moonlight. He had a neat-shaped head and sharp cheekbones that suited a crew cut.

"What? In a mathematical sense? No. I mean, you will always have people at either end of statistical calculations. The one who gets struck by lightning seven times. The person who wins the lottery four times. But no. It's totally random. There is no formula for luck."

"Well, I'm not convinced about that." She sighed. "Don't laugh, but sometimes I think I'm cursed. I think I am that person at the end of the statistical calculations. I am the person who gets struck by lightning seven times. I mean, it has to be someone, doesn't it?"

She realized how crazy her words sounded, but somehow she didn't feel embarrassed or self-conscious.

Jago made a piffing noise. He was smiling. He touched her arm and said, "Well, I'll tell you, that's nonsense, Kate. Being cursed is for fairy tales. Not for kind souls, which I know you are."

There was a note of paternal kindness in his voice that reminded her of her father.

"Thank you," she said quietly.

There was a long pause. The branches of the willow danced in the breeze. Jago lay on his back. After a while, he cleared his throat. "Kate. I'm just wondering something."

"Yes?"

"Well, obviously I was joking about this being a guerilla experiment. But I'm curious . . ." He ripped some more grass away. "Would you mind if I spoke to my publisher about what you've told me? See what the psychologist he told me about is doing in the States with this kind of anxiety?"

Kate regarded him appreciatively, realizing that he was offering to help. "I suppose it would be interesting. You wouldn't mind?"

"No, I mean, I'm interested from an academic perspective. That's my thing, doing interdisciplinary work with other departments. But also because I . . ."

There was a rustling past Kate's ear as a rabbit lolloped past the pond and up onto the unlit lawn.

"Fuck," Jago muttered.

A light abruptly illuminated the whole lawn and the pond. Kate and Jago blinked and shielded their eyes.

"Run!" called Jago, jumping up and grabbing her hand.

There was no time to think. Kate let him pull her blindly across the lawn and back toward the hedge. Somewhere behind her she heard a door opening, flooding the hedge with light.

Jago reached the gate and stood back to let Kate go first. He put a strong hand on the small of her back to help her climb up. To her amazement, she heard a chuckle behind her.

"I can't believe you're laughing." She gasped as she hauled herself up over the gates, her legs trembling.

"Go!" he shouted.

"My helmet!" she yelped. "I've left it on the lawn."

"No time—go!"

She jumped on her bike and waited for him to get over the gate and grab his, then followed him up the dark lane. She could hear him up ahead, still laughing, a mischievous laugh, warm and full of fun. Surprisingly, the corners of her own mouth turned up in a nervous smile.

When they hit the towpath, Jago didn't stop, but sped back to Oxford, checking occasionally that she was behind him. She pedaled hard, trying to keep up. Her thighs protested at being asked to work so hard, but the adrenaline pumping through her body kept her going.

It didn't even feel to Kate like she was cycling. Perhaps it was the two glasses of wine, but it felt like she'd lifted off the ground, and was speeding above it.

Like she was flying.

Kate lifted her chin into the wind. An image popped into her head of the man with the jester's hat on Cowley Road yesterday. Was this how he felt? She imagined her features set like his, bemused expression, whistling lips.

And before she could help it, she did something extraordinary.

She lifted her hands off the handlebars for a second, ignoring the water beside her. The bike sailed effortlessly onward.

"Oh!" She gasped as the bike began to wobble.

"Woo-hoo!" came a shout.

Jago looked back, pedaling slowly, waiting for her to catch up. Seconds later she reached him, and he sped up again. She fell in behind him, into his slipstream. Their legs began to move in tandem, in a shared rhythm.

They were flying together through the dark.

She had forgotten what it felt like to be connected and talking with another person. Kate shut her eyes for a second. Another sensation she hadn't felt in so long flooded back to her, of falling, and falling, and falling. Of floating into nothing, her body relaxed completely, not tense and rigid like it always was now. Of tumbling at speed into a beautiful void but not being scared. Free from worry and physical restraint. Of having no choice but to let everything go and . . .

Crack!

Kate's front tire hit a stone.

She yelped and pulled hard on the handlebars to straighten up. The bike wobbled, then steadied. She made herself slow down. They were nearly back at the pub. Houses and lights emerged on their right. She saw Jago duck under the bridge, and followed him. Seconds later, they swerved back up the alleyway. Jago stopped, and Kate pulled up beside him.

He got off his saddle, straddling the bike frame, and grinned. "You OK?"

"Just about. I can't believe you made me do that," she said, panting. "What was that place?"

He touched his nose. "Ahah. The less you know, the less you'll try to predict."

She giggled, unexpectedly, trying to draw breath. "No. It was fun."

She was surprised at her own words. But it was true. Unbelievably, she'd actually had fun.

Jago sat back on his saddle. "Thank God. I was starting to think the extent of my social life in Oxford was going to be talking to Gunther from Austria about algorithms in the lecturers' bar." He swatted an insect away. "Right, do you want me to cycle you home?"

Kate shook her head, touched by the gesture. It was the type of thing Hugo had offered to do when they first met at university in London, even though she'd lived north of the river, and he'd lived south.

"Listen," Jago said, checking his new tire. "Thanks for telling me what was going on. It wouldn't be the first time a woman's run off on me half an hour into the evening."

Kate smiled. Somehow she didn't believe it.

All of a sudden, Jago's shoulders slumped. He opened his bag and searched frantically inside it. "Damn, I forgot to bring you that book."

Kate tried not to look panicked.

"You know what, though?" Jago said. "Perhaps we could call this the next phase of our guerilla experiment. Step two: binning the numbers. See if you can do without it?"

Kate stood there for a moment, thinking of the airline statistics she needed desperately if she was going to book tickets for Mallorca. "What was step one?" she asked.

Jago put his finger on his lip, as if thinking. "Step one: not thinking about it—riding off into the night with a weird Scottish bloke and doing a bit of breaking and entering." He watched her closely. "Could you do it? Cope without the book for a bit longer?"

"Um, OK . . ." She knew her struggle was written all over her face.

Jago shot her a sympathetic look. "OK, well, what if I promise to keep one for you in my bag at all times in case you change your mind?"

She nodded gratefully.

"Brilliant." Jago gave her a grin. "Kate. Listen. This was the most fun I've had in, well, a while. Can we do it again sometime soon?"

"I'd like that."

"Good. I'll give you a ring. Tomorrow?"

Then without warning, Jago leaned forward and kissed her

cheek. "Right . . ." The warmth of his skin on hers stunned her. "Better go. OK."

"OK."

"See you," Jago called. He stood up on his pedals and cycled to the junction, turning left toward central Oxford.

Kate stood paralyzed, waiting for him to disappear. She lifted a finger to touch her hot cheek, where the brush of faint stubble from Jago's chin had grazed her lightly. It had been so long since she'd felt the touch of a man's face against hers. The smell of soap from his skin mixed with the damp saltiness of his T-shirt assaulted her senses.

She shook herself. What was she thinking? It was dark and she needed to get home. She cycled to the junction. Iffley Road lay in front of her. The turn for Hubert Street was two hundred yards away on the right.

The brief sense of elation she had from riding along the riverbank with Jago lingered. Could she do it now, by herself?

On the road, without a helmet?

She looked left, then right. When there was no traffic in either direction, she stood up on her pedals and pushed hard out into the empty road, gripping the handlebars tightly.

As soon as she did it she knew it was a mistake. Out of nowhere a car came speeding around a bend and up behind her.

Kate started to wobble. A bass line thumped through open windows as the car started to pass her.

What was she doing? Idiot! Kate shut her eyes, terrified, bracing for impact. The numbers appeared out of nowhere suddenly, and filled her head. She needed to get off this main road without a helmet and stop being a bloody fool.

Eighty-five percent of bike casualties are not wearing helmets.

The car sped dramatically past her, with angry red rear lights. She pushed her bike over the curb, shaking.

Just don't think about it. Just don't think about it.

Desperately, she tried to push the thoughts away but they wouldn't leave her. No. She wasn't quite ready for this yet.

But tonight something had changed.

She had taken a step forward. Tiny, but still a step.

She'd had fun.

By the time she reached home five minutes later, the lights were out. Saskia and Jack must be in bed. Kate crept in, feeling a little guilty.

She locked the inner doors downstairs, turned on the alarm, and tiptoed upstairs. At the top, she saw the cage door. It stood wide open. With a shiver she walked through it, ignoring the impulse to run to the garden and find the padlock.

She heard Jago's voice in her head.

Just don't think about it.

She passed the spare room where Saskia slept and then Jack's room, on her way to the bathroom.

She was about to turn off the upper hall light when a noise stopped her. It was a heavy scraping noise that seemed to be coming from Jack's room.

That was odd.

His door was half-open. Kate peeked in and tried to focus in the dark. A heavy breathing from the bed told her Jack was asleep.

The noise started again, like something substantial being pushed along the floor.

It was coming from his wardrobe.

Kate's stomach did a somersault. Jack wasn't imagining strange sounds—they were real.

Nervously, she crept toward the door, and carefully picked up Jack's guitar. She grasped its neck with her right hand like a bat, her heart thumping, ready to scream out to wake up Saskia.

"What are you doing?"

Kate jumped.

Jack was sitting up in bed, staring at his guitar in the shaft of light from the hall outside.

"Oh, hi! Nothing," she barked, sharper than she intended. "I was just . . . um . . . putting away your washing. Sorry."

She opened both wardrobe doors wide, hoping Jack wouldn't spot the absence of laundry, and surreptitiously swept the back of the wardrobe to check no one was there.

"Did you hear the funny noise?" Jack asked.

Kate berated herself. This was exactly what Helen was concerned about. Kate was transferring her anxiety to Jack.

"Uh-huh, and it's nothing to worry about," she replied brightly. "It's just someone next door moving something around in their room. The walls in this house are so thin. I hear noises sometimes, too—from the bedroom next to me."

But not nearly as loud as that weird scraping, she thought.

His voice came back uncertain in the dark. "Oh, OK."

"You OK? Sure?" She tried to sound reassuring.

"Yeah." He turned over in his bed. "Night, Mum."

"Night, Jack."

Kate tiptoed to the bathroom, trying to ignore the uneasy feeling that had crept back over her. She brushed her teeth and washed her face, replaying scenes from the cycle ride to distract herself. Soon she was lost in thought. Happy, she walked to her bedroom, turning off the hall light. She shut the door, turned on her bedside lamp, and took off her shirt. It smelled of the grass from the walled garden. She did a double take in the mirror. Her cheeks were flushed, her eyes bright. She sat on the bed and smoothed moisturizing cream onto her skin.

She lay on the bed, running the evening's events back through her head.

That feeling she'd had, as she'd climbed the gate. That tension in her stomach. What was it? It hadn't been fear. She knew that. It was different. It had arrived as she climbed up to the top of the gate, and seen the dark garden beyond. A kind of tension she hadn't felt for a very long time. A kind of . . .

And then she knew.

It was excitement.

Kate climbed in between the sheets and looked at the pile of unread books on her nightstand. Saskia kept giving them to her from her village book club. Poor Sass. She was only trying to help. Her nervous blink had been back tonight. It's not like her little sister-in-law's life had turned out the way she'd planned it, either.

Kate turned out the light. She felt the cool sheets on her body. And as she did, Jago Martin and his blue eyes passed through her mind. The touch of his hand on her arm and . . .

Kate jerked upright. A strip of light appeared under her door and she heard footsteps in the hall. Jack had turned on the light again.

He was still scared.

Kate lay back, cross with herself about the wardrobe incident. If ever she needed evidence of the harm she was doing to Jack, there it was.

"You have to stop this," she thought. Jack had seen her anxious face by the wardrobe, seen her holding the guitar as a weapon. He knew that she, too, feared there were bad men in his wardrobe.

She had to get a grip.

Normal adults didn't check their wardrobes at night.

She thought back to her conversation with Jago in the garden. Just because she'd had some bad luck, it didn't mean she was cursed. Just because her parents and Hugo had been killed, it didn't mean it was more likely to happen to her or Jack. She was not fated to be struck by lightning seven times.

How did that American professor put it? Certain people live with a constant fear of imagined danger, convinced their instincts are trying to warn them but it's all in their heads.

No, she reassured herself, turning off the light again. She and Jack had no more chance of being killed than anyone else. They were normal, too. Not cursed, just unlucky.

She lay back on the pillow, feeling hopeful. Jago was going to help her—he was already helping her to stop worrying about threats that were completely imagined, like the man in Jack's closet who did not exist.

11

Why hadn't Jago called?

Three days after the night in the secret walled garden, Kate looked out of the kitchen window at the magnolia tree, trying not to feel disappointed.

The irony was that, at first, she'd hoped he wouldn't call her.

On Wednesday morning, she'd woken in a panic, wondering what on earth she'd said the night before. About the numbers. About her parents. Jack? She had let her guard down with a man she hardly knew. She'd let his intense blue eyes into places no one was supposed to go. Kate sat up, alarmed, and turned off her phone.

By Wednesday evening, however, when she turned it back on and he hadn't called as promised, she'd been slightly perplexed. By Thursday, she was checking every ten minutes.

Now, on Friday, she was fighting the urge to call him.

She looked back at her brand-new laptop, which had arrived by delivery. She closed down her proposal for David and

Googled Jago for the sixth time today. His own Web site had turned out to be the best: with a small photo of him smiling on a mountain bike, listing his education (Stirling University, MsC; University of Edinburgh, PhD; University of North Carolina, postdoc research), and interests (travel, music, hiking, mountain biking). There was even a sweet little bio with details about his mum (a GP) and dad (a teacher), who lived in Stirling, and his two sisters (teachers). She followed the links, too, to his department at Edinburgh, which had a more official photo, and a few American newspapers that had reviewed his book, and a list of his publications. His specialty, she noted with interest, was applying probability theory to economic models set up by new governments recovering from civil war. That must be why he flew to developing countries so much.

Professor Jago Martin was even more impressive than he had let on.

To her consternation, she realized she really did want to see him again, this man she hadn't even known just one week ago.

Grabbing a pile of fresh laundry, Kate headed up to Jack's room. She looked at the shelf where Jack kept his heartbreaking little collection of his father's possessions—Hugo's childhood toys, soccer medals from school, even shoes—and turned guiltily away, forcing thoughts of Jago from her head. Putting Jack's pajamas in his bag, she realized she would miss him this weekend. They had baked twice more this week. Nothing much had been said at first. Just chatter about ingredients and who was stirring the pot, or rubbing in the butter—but then she saw Jack holding an egg, and the sight sent her hurtling back into a place she hadn't been for years. She remembered sitting at the table in Highgate at Easter, painting boiled eggs with funny faces, then walking to Parliament Hill, where they threw their eggs down the hill alongside other families, chasing after them, falling over, laughing as the shells broke into tiny pieces.

Her and Jack, as they used to be. Mother and son.

And now he was leaving again. He was off to Helen's and . . .

Kate's hand flew to her mouth.

A memory detonated in her mind.

She had completely forgotten, in all the upset about Jack hitting his head on the radiator.

What had he said to her in the hallway, just before it happened?

"Nana lets me walk to the shop alone."

Kate's looked at Jack's calendar. Tomorrow was Saturday.

Oh, God. He'd be walking along the river path with other people's dogs running around off the leash.

She shut her eyes, knowing the numbers were coming.

Hospital admissions for dog attacks have risen 5 percent this year.

In her mind, she saw Jack walking with Helen's dog Rosie along the river path from Helen's house a quarter of a mile to the shop in the village. She saw a horrible dog running around the corner, attacking Rosie, and Jack trying to save her.

She smacked her hand down on his bed angrily.

How *dare* Helen overrule her like this?

Kate tried to remember at what point had she given them this blatant co-ownership of her son. Right after Hugo died it had been necessary, that first year, when she couldn't even lift her head from the pillow. And their moving to Oxford had seemed sensible. Yet now, it had become so invasive: the fortnightly weekend sleepovers at their house, the constant popping in, the upcoming trip with Jack to Dorset at spring break, their copy of the bloody house key, the decisions about Jack's safety with no regard for her feelings . . .

Kate looked over at Jack's wardrobe. The guitar was leaning against the doors again. He was still trying to block in the bad men.

A sense of helplessness came over her. If she tried to cut off contact with them right now, and canceled tomorrow's sleepover, Helen might really blow up and carry out her threat to tell social services about Kate's anxiety, and the detrimental effect it was having on Jack.

No, she couldn't risk it.

There was only one way out of this.

She would just have to learn to control it.

Then, in August, she would take Jack to David's house in Mallorca, away from Helen and Richard's interference, where they could start afresh.

Kate stood up, determined, and headed back down to the laptop, remembering David needed her proposal for the Islington house by six. She could ask him about the Mallorca house in the e-mail.

Then she just needed to work out how to get on a bloody plane. Jago's book with its reassuring pages of airline statistics came into her mind.

Followed by an image of Jago.

Disappointment coursed back through Kate. She had been so convinced this Scottish man with his kind voice and searching blue eyes had the answer, but apparently, she'd scared him off before he could give it to her.

Richard arrived to collect Jack at 5:30 P.M.

"Hello, young man!" he called cheerily as Jack appeared with his bag. Kate stood on the step with the most relaxed smile she could muster and said nothing.

Helen's absence said it all. The threat was clear. The years of pretending to be fond of her for Hugo's, and then Jack's sake, were over. If Helen could take Jack, she would.

Richard kept beaming, as if protesting his innocence in all this, but Kate knew better. His eyes still moved busily, as they had done the first time she met him, and every time since when he was analyzing the situation. Richard looked for ways to maximize everything—be it work, or personal—to his own benefit. Luckily, Hugo had taught her to ignore the ebullience and not trust him an inch.

"We'll have him back by five on Sunday, Mum," said Richard, arm around Jack's shoulder. "Good golly!" he exclaimed when Jack proudly handed him a box of brownies. "Are those for us? Fan-tastic!" Kate winced. "So—Sunday at five, Mum!" he repeated as he left, as if Kate suspected he was in the middle of a child-snatching operation organized by Helen.

"Bye, Mum," Jack said, waving.

As she watched him go, Kate couldn't help it. "Jack?" He turned. She hugged him awkwardly, aware of Richard watching them.

"Please be careful," she whispered in his ear. From this angle she saw the fading scratch on his head. Could she really trust him not to tell Helen about the radiator? she thought shamefully. It was so much to ask of him.

Jack nodded and pulled away. Kate wrapped her arms around herself, and walked back to her front door. As she waved Jack off, a movement in her peripheral vision caught her eye. She looked up and saw the student with the strange-colored eyes watching Richard's car, from a slit in his curtains, as it reversed out of the driveway.

Her phone buzzed in her hand.

are you there? jx

Jago!

Kate shut the front door, and rushed to the kitchen. After various attempts at funny, clever replies, she settled on:

yes . . .

i'm in the juice bar—can you pop down?

She read the message again. Did he mean now?

She looked at the proposal on the screen of her laptop. If she went now, the spreadsheet would be late. David had waited patiently for her laptop to be delivered all week, on the condition that he got the figures by six o'clock tonight to give him time to calculate his bid for the Islington house in the sealed-bid auction tomorrow.

But if she didn't go, Jago might not be there later.

Chewing her pen, Kate stood up. The proposal would be late by only half an hour or so. She'd still get it to David by 6:30 P.M.

This was more important.

Kate picked up her coat, texted Jago to say she was on her way, and flew out the door, hoping David would forgive her.

12

She arrived ten minutes later, trying not to look like she'd been running. Jago was sitting at the same place by the window, reading a *Guardian*. He waved as she passed the window.

Her stomach fluttered.

"Hi, Kate," he said, standing up. Before she knew it he had leaned over and kissed her on the cheek. "How're you doing?"

"Good, thanks." To her dismay, she blushed. She placed her jacket on the back of the high stool next to him, and looked down at the legs as she unnecessarily moved the stool farther away from the counter just to hide her hot cheeks.

"I wasn't sure if you'd be on your own," he said.

"Jack's at his grandparents for the weekend."

"Oh. Does he get on well with them?"

She nodded, allowing herself to look at him straight on now that her cheeks had cooled. "They've got a huge garden and a dog, so he's in heaven." An image of Jack beside the river alone forced itself back into her mind, but she pushed it away.

The waitress with the auburn ponytail came over and did a double take. "Oh, hello again." She grinned at Jago. "You managed to track him down, then?"

"Ah, it was just about buying your book—" Kate said, avoiding Jago's eye. She gave the waitress what she hoped was a dismissive look. "Juice of the day, please."

"Oh. Sure," the girl said, raising her eyebrows.

"So, did I interrupt your work?" Jago said. It was good to see him again. He was wearing a navy T-shirt with the name of a band on it she didn't recognize.

"No. Not at all," she lied.

"Ok. Well. Look," he said, leaning on the counter.

"Yes." She smiled.

"I've been thinking."

"Uh-huh?"

"About the other night."

She took a sip of juice, knowing she had to say it. "Jago. I'm a bit embarrassed about that, actually. I think I probably sounded a bit weird and . . ."

"No." He touched her arm. His voice was reassuring. "You didn't, Kate. At all. And actually, I am hoping I might be able to help you with this obsessional data-anxiety stuff."

Kate glanced around the café. It was fuller this time, the tables occupied by hungover students. Jago dropped his voice. "Sorry."

She shook her head. "No. It's OK. Well. That's nice of you, but what do you . . . ?"

"Well, I rang the psychologist in the States who's writing a book about it."

Kate stared. He had done that for her?

It had been so long since anyone had done anything kind for her. A lump came into her throat.

"I won't bore you with it all," Jago continued, "but I thought you'd find some of what he said interesting. I did."

Kate nodded, curious. "Go on." She tried to stop herself from staring at the arc of his bicep. "Well, part of his theory is that this particular anxiety disorder has developed because of the deprogramming of our flight-or-fight instinct."

He laughed at her puzzled look. "OK. Well, as I'm sure you know, human instinct is wired for survival. To fight the wild bear or run away from it."

She nodded. "Yes. I get that bit."

"But in the developed world we don't generally require that primal instinct anymore.

"Think of it this way." He paused. "If there are no wild bears to escape from, or invading marauders to fight, what do we do? We switch off our flight-or-fight program. We stop relying on our wits to survive."

"Because others do it for us," Kate said.

"That's right. But if we entrust others to protect us all the time, and stop using our own instincts to survive, how do we know we're really safe?"

Kate thought for a moment. "Through information. Statistics?"

Jago banged his hand gently on the counter. "Right. The people who protect us constantly quantify that protection. 'A recent test showed that your family will be blah-blah percentage safer in this car than that car,' and so on."

Kate turned to face him more fully, intrigued.

Jago continued. "But there are hundreds of statistics. Thousands. So what do you do? If you're me, you just get on with life. Accept that nothing is one hundred percent certain apart from that we'll all die. Use a bit of common sense mixed with a few statistics and your own experience. So, for instance, I might fly to an important conference in a country whose airline has a less good safety record, because I know that airlines usually don't crash, so I'll probably be fine. But, I won't go without, say, taking my malaria tablets. Common sense tells me that's a risk not worth taking."

Kate nodded. "Whereas I . . ."

"You don't fly at all. You miss the important conference. You stay at home convinced that by manipulating statistics you are controlling your own fate by keeping yourself safe. You see?"

Kate nodded.

Jago continued. "And that, according to the experts, is why our reliance on statistics is escalating into an obsessional disorder for some people. For someone already suffering from anxiety—and I'm assuming after what's happened to you, Kate, that you might be—it appears to offer choices that relieve that anxiety. Scared of being ill—arm yourself with statistics. Drink two glasses of red wine and you'll be blah-blah percent less likely to develop heart disease, drink three and you'll be blah-blah percent more likely to get cancer. Buy this cycle helmet and you'll be twenty-two percent safer than with that one. But of course, statistics are just an average of something that's already happened. A guesstimate of what might happen next, not of what will happen. You can't predict the future with certainty. You might set off in your shiny new cycle helmet and a truck rolls down a hill because the driver was stuck in traffic for three hours due to a freak accident, and is so tired he forgot to put on the hand brake, and it squashes you flat. You can't avoid danger altogether. But you can spend time convincing yourself that you can, by manipulating the figures—and not living much of a life in the process."

He gave a dramatic gasp as if he'd just finished a sprint.

"I could choke on a peanut in the departure lounge." Kate smiled.

Jago nodded. "Exactly. It's no wonder that when people start trying to work all this out they become . . ."

Kate sat quietly nodding. ". . . neurotic. Like me."

Jago winced. "I didn't say that. . . ."

"No. It's OK," she said quietly. "It's interesting. It's just easier said than done, I guess. It certainly explains some things but I'm not quite sure how it'll help me. I know everything you said is true, I just can't stop the anxiety so easily."

"Ah, well, this is where I bring in what we will very roughly call an experiment. I'm interested to know if it's possible for you to counteract this dependency on statistics." He shrugged. "Who knows. It might lead to an interdisciplinary research paper with the psychology department at Edinburgh some-where down the line. So . . ."

Kate was glowing. He wanted to spend more time with her. She felt a bubble of hope. A glimpse into a future that a week ago did not exist.

"OK. And if I did agree to be your guinea pig—what would that entail?"

"Well. That's the thing, Kate. That's what I wanted to talk to you about. What I'm planning is not orthodox. But sometimes, in the early stages, you have to throw ideas out there and see what works."

Kate sensed a "but" coming.

He grimaced. "OK. Here's the thing. I'm concerned that you might not be up to this."

Disappointment crashed over her. Was Jago trying to tell her he didn't want to see her again, in the gentlest possible way?

Was this a roundabout excuse to extract himself while pointing her in the direction of help?

"What do you mean?" she asked, trying to stop her voice from wavering.

"Well, I'd really need to try to kick-start your instincts so that you react rather than think. I'm concerned that maybe that's just asking too much of you at the moment. You're a little fragile, as you should be, but, you know, I don't want to mess with . . ."

"Jago," she said more firmly than she meant to. "I want to try." Right now, all she knew was that she wanted his help.

"Really?"

Their eyes met.

"OK, well, let's see . . ." He glanced out the window. On the pavement there was a woman in her sixties, tall, with a silver bob, glasses, and a Barbour waistcoat. She tied the dog to a lamppost, then disappeared into a health-food shop next door. The dog gave a halfhearted bark, whined, and then settled down onto the pavement.

Jago turned to Kate. "OK. Say I asked you to untie that dog and lead it away. Could you?"

Kate looked at the dog. "No!"

"You couldn't?"

She watched his expression. Oh, God, he looked serious. "I mean, I suppose I could. You really want me to steal a dog?"

Kate laughed, waiting for Jago to do the same.

He didn't.

"Um, OK, I suppose I could, temporarily."

"Great," Jago said, slapping the counter. "That's what I want you to do. Go untie the dog, walk down to the pedestrian crossing near Tesco, and wait for me."

Kate shifted on her stool.

"You really are serious?"

"I am."

"Jago. This is a bit crazy. That woman will think I've stolen her dog!"

"As I said, Kate, what I'm planning isn't orthodox. But if it makes you feel better, I know the woman, the dog's owner. Well, to say hello to, anyway. Her name is Margaret—I think— and she's the wife of a colleague at Balliol. I promise, if you do it, I'll tell her it was us, and that it was a controlled experiment. I'm sure she'll be fine about it if I apologize. And if she's not, I'll take the flak. So you don't need to worry about it. What I want to find out right now is, can you do something spontaneous?"

Well, if Jago knew the woman, that made it a little different. Kate stood up reluctantly and hesitated, her hand on the stool. When Jago didn't stop her, she slowly moved toward the door. Jago just watched her.

He was really going to let her do this?

Kate opened the door, praying that he would call her back and say she'd passed the test. That she called his bluff.

But he didn't. Instead, he peeked out the window. "By the way, if Margaret does happen to catch you, you're not allowed to mention me."

The thought of Margaret catching her made Kate halt mid-step. "Jago, look, this is—"

He interrupted her. "Come on, Kate. See what happens."

She sighed and forced her body out into the warm early summer day. She decided that no matter what, she would not go back inside the café. If this is what he wanted her to do, she would do it.

Close up, the dog appeared younger than she'd realized. It

looked up at her with hopeful brown eyes. Kate peeked into the health-food shop. Margaret was chatting to a girl behind the counter.

Kate shook her head as she felt the anxiety envelop her.

"For goodness' sake," she said, kneeling down as if tying her shoe. She felt her heart starting to thump. She reached out a finger and touched the dog's leash. What would she say if Margaret caught her? She decided she'd pretend she thought the dog had been abandoned.

Feeling safer now that she had a story to tell if she was caught, Kate undid the leash, checked again that Margaret still had her back turned, and led the dog away.

"Come on," she urged it. Kate began to run toward the traffic lights up ahead, cursing Jago as she went.

"Quick, before she spots us," came a voice behind her. It was Jago, pacing up behind her, looking ridiculously relaxed. He pushed the traffic light button.

"I can't believe I'm doing this!" she hissed. "I can't believe you've made me steal a bloody dog! What are we going to do with it?"

Jago chuckled. "Go," he said calmly as the green man appeared. She crossed the road. The leash had turned damp in her sweaty palm.

Once she reached the other side, she glanced, panicked, toward the health-food shop. Margaret was halfway out the door, her head turned back toward the counter, still talking.

"What now?" Kate asked.

He motioned with his head. "That lamppost. Quick."

Kate threw the leash frantically around the lamppost as if it were burning her fingers. The dog sniffed at her, and sat down again on the pavement.

"Now run!" Jago grabbed Kate's hand and pulled her up to where they'd come from.

There was a tinkle as they passed the health-food shop, and Margaret exited, shouting back a cheerful good-bye. Jago began to unlock his bike.

"Ginny?" Kate heard Margaret call out. "Ginny!"

There came a bark.

"Ginny?" She saw the woman speed walk down the road, astonished. "Gosh. How did you get over here, girl?"

To her shock, Kate felt the corners of her mouth turn up. Jago saw it, and grinned at her. It made it worse. An unexpected bubble of laughter came out of Kate's mouth in a snort. Jago threw back his head and laughed in his laid-back boyish way that she realized she was starting to love hearing.

"Don't. I feel horrible and mean. I better have passed your bloody test."

"You already had," Jago said. "I just fancied a laugh."

"You . . . !" Kate gently punched his arm. To her surprise, he caught her hand and put an arm around her shoulder.

"So, madam. Are you free tomorrow night?" he asked cheerily.

Kate panicked. This was Cowley Road. Someone might see her. Saskia. Jack's friends.

"Uh, yes. Sorry," she said.

"Excellent," Jago beamed. He grabbed his bike from the railing. "So, say, the Hanley Arms, eight o'clock?"

"OK, great."

Jago winked as he pulled into the road. "You did well. We'll have some fun tomorrow. Don't worry about it."

"And you will tell her? The woman, Margaret?" Kate called, nodding in the woman's direction.

Jago nodded. "It'll be fine. I promise."

Kate watched him go, then saw Margaret walking down the Cowley Road with her dog leash firmly wrapped around her hand. There had been no harm done, Kate reassured herself. The dog was safe. And Jago would explain it all in the name of a psychological experiment. Since Margaret knew him, she'd laugh it off.

Then, Kate noticed someone watching her.

It was the waitress in the juice bar.

Their eyes met through the window. The waitress, who Kate suspected fancied Jago, was not smiling anymore. She looked watchful and wary. Had she seen them take the dog?

Smiling innocently, Kate turned on her heel to set off back home.

But she didn't get two steps when there was a rap on the window.

Kate's stomach lurched. Had she been caught?

Without Jago, she didn't feel so brave.

The girl was beckoning her over.

Apprehensively, Kate crossed the road. The girl met her on the sidewalk holding a bag.

"The Scottish guy—he left this," she said.

"Oh, thanks," Kate said, taking it from her.

"You kind of rushed off there," the girl said.

Kate looked at the ground. "Thanks. I'll get this to Jago."

"Interesting guy," the waitress said, her gaze burning into Kate, who shifted uncomfortably.

She nodded. "He is. Anyway, thanks for this."

And before the girl could make her feel any more awkward, Kate set off back to Hubert Street, not quite believing but suspecting that a beautiful twentysomething girl was a little jealous of her.

As she marched away, Margaret and Ginny were climbing into their car. What would Jack say if he knew what his mum had just done? It had been like a student prank—silly but also a little fun. Dangerous, even. How long was it since she had been silly, or thrown caution to the wind?

Kate opened Jago's bag and found the book inside.

Touched, she realized he'd left it there for her on purpose, in case she needed it.

Well, did she?

She took it out and felt the weight of it in her hands.

It was all here. Everything she always thought she needed to survive—if she wanted to carry on being a complete lunatic.

Kate put the book back in Jago's bag. No. This was going straight in the shed. She was locking it away. The obsession with numbers had to end. She would call Jago later to let him know she had done so. She smiled at the thought, knowing he'd be proud.

However crazy his methods were, they might just be the antidote she needed.

13

The small, hard cricket ball still sat in the middle of the trampoline, waiting for the blond boy to come home and hit it with a bat.

Spoiled brat, Magnus thought, looking out the window and onto the gardens at the back of Hubert Street. All these toys, in the garden and in the bedroom. And a scooter, too.

He rubbed his nose, and clicked one more button on the laptop in front of him. A message popped up. "Installation five minutes," it said. Magnus glanced at the clock. She could be back any minute. He needed to get out of there.

He sat back on Kate's swivel chair and stretched his long legs under her desk.

It had been thirty-five minutes since he'd seen her turn right out of the gate, and walk toward Cowley Road, and two minutes less than that since he'd squeezed himself through the ragged brick hole behind her son's wardrobe. He ran through the numbers again. It would take her ten minutes to walk to

Cowley Road, and ten to walk back, plus the time she spent there. Five more minutes at her computer was all he needed.

He looked around Kate's study, inhaling the faint leftover fragrance of her vanilla hand lotion. He liked it. So much, in fact, he'd taken some in a little saucer to keep in his room. He tapped his fingers on the table as the new laptop in front of him said, "4 minutes 39 seconds." He opened the drawer and took out the photo of her and the man. He'd seen that one before.

Four minutes and three seconds. He stood up and wandered out into the hall, noting that the cage at the far end, across the stairs, was open for the first time. That was interesting. He smirked. Silly woman.

He turned right and entered Kate's bedroom.

It wasn't as tidy as usual today. The bed appeared to have been made hastily, a duvet chucked on top, its four corners untucked. Her nightclothes lay strewn across the pillow. And it wasn't the flimsy nightie with the holes he usually found in her drawer, but a new, long gray T-shirt. He inhaled the scent. It didn't have the same soft silkiness of the other nightie against his bristles, but still he liked it.

The fitted wardrobe door was open, with two pairs of jeans hanging over it. Idly, he took a pair down and held them up to himself at the mirror. She was definitely too skinny. He placed one hand inside the top, and pushed his arm all the way down the leg. It nearly fitted his arm.

As he put them back, the photo by the bed caught his eye. It was new. A black-and-white image of a man and a woman in their fifties looked back at him. The man was handsome, not unlike Magnus, with dark-blond hair and glasses, and a small nose. The woman not so much. Her nose was sharp, and she was almost as skinny as Kate. Magnus took out his camera and photographed it. Then he snapped the gray T-shirt on the pillow.

Sighing, he sat on the bed and pulled his long legs up onto the duvet, turning his head to sniff the pillow. He pushed his buttocks and thighs into the duvet and wriggled a little.

Then he looked over at the dressing table. A lipstick he hadn't seen before lay on the glass top. It looked new. Magnus reached out and took it, flipping the deep-pink waxy color up and down from the tube before placing it in his pocket.

Suddenly, there was a click of a key in a lock downstairs.

He sat up abruptly.

Shit. She was back already?

Magnus paused to listen. *Beep beep beep* the alarm went before Kate turned it off.

Had to be quick now.

Walking swiftly and silently, he reentered the study. "39 seconds" the message on the screen said. "No problem," he murmured in English to keep himself calm.

He heard the woman unlocking the door into the kitchen at the back of the house. That meant she'd be walking right under his feet in a second, so he'd have to be careful not to creak the floorboards.

Calmly, he counted down with the computer, "three, two . . ." then ejected the disk he had installed in the side of it. He tiptoed to the door and peered out of the study.

Damn! She was running up the stairs now. He couldn't make it back to the boy's room.

Before she reached the top of the stairs, Magnus slipped into Kate's room. Checking he'd put the photograph back on the table, he lay carefully under her bed.

A pair of ankle boots with worn-down heels got in his way.

He shoved them and tucked his big feet in under his bottom, out of view.

The air was warmer and stale under the bed.

He'd done this before, twice. He'd just stay for a while. He heard her reach the top of the stairs then walk up the corridor. She was humming, then her mobile phone rang.

"Hello . . . Oh, hi, David . . . I'm so sorry. Give me another twenty minutes. I've had a difficult week with Richard and Helen. I'll tell you when I see you."

Magnus listened, interested. He didn't get to hear Kate's voice that often.

"When I see you . . ." Magnus mouthed under the bed, trying to copy her vowel sounds.

Magnus stretched out among dusty boxes, and relaxed, as best he could, holding his nose tight so he didn't sneeze. It was only twenty minutes before he could make his escape.

Of course, ultimately, he could just pop out right now and give her a right old fright.

But it wasn't time for that yet. There was a lot more to do first.

14

Kate sat herself down at the computer, typed in the last few figures, and sent David the document twenty minutes later. Relieved it was done, she wandered back out of the study to go downstairs.

A whiff of something drifted into her nostrils. A male odor. Hormonal. Cloying and unfresh. It wasn't the first time she'd smelled it, but Jack wasn't even home. She poked her head inside the little boy's bedroom. His deodorant was lying on the shelf as normal.

She looked around for discarded gym clothes, but there were none. Compared to most boys his age, Jack was tidy. Bed made, toys in boxes. The only thing that was out of place was his wardrobe door, which must have fallen open again when she'd been out with Jago. The guitar that Jack had rested against it had tipped sideways with the motion of the door swing. Kate walked over and ran her hand over the catch of the door, vaguely wondering why it was no longer working properly. Perhaps it was Jack banging it shut with too much force, or maybe it was the floor. She shut it, and ran her foot over the hundred-year-old Edwardian floorboards, feeling to see if there was a new slope that was making the door bow out of shape. There wasn't.

Another wave of the unpleasant smell hit her. Where the hell was it coming from? Maybe Jack's preteenage hormones were just going into overdrive right now but she couldn't find the source. She sighed. If only Hugo was here to guide him through the secrets of male puberty.

A pang of guilt stopped her. If she started something with Jago, how or when would she even begin to broach the subject with Jack? How would it affect her efforts to bring them closer again?

But without Jago, would it even happen?

She pressed her lips together. It was too early to think about all that. She'd only just met him. She left Jack's bedroom in search of some lip salve.

She paused midstep. That was strange. The smell was in her room, too. Kate wandered to the dressing table and slicked some salve across her lips, looking around for the source again.

As she turned to go out, something caught her eye. The ankle boots she'd meant to have reheeled ages ago were sticking out from under the bottom of the bed.

Kate leaned over and picked them up. For a second, she started to worry about how they'd moved but was able to stop herself.

Pleased, she headed back downstairs to place them by the front door, and realized there was a new bounce in her step. And she knew why. For the first time in a long time, she was looking forward to something. Eight o'clock tomorrow night at the Hanley Arms.

Back in the kitchen, she saw Jago's bag on the floor, and she felt a new resolve take over. She marched out the back door and locked the book in the shed. Back in the kitchen, she grabbed the kettle. As she waited for the water to boil, she looked at the magnolia tree outside, the only plant she had brought from their Highgate home. The tree was so much taller than when Hugo had last seen it. Its boughs and branches were thickened and matured. They had grown up and away, in different directions.

A band of pain tightened around her chest so fiercely, so unexpectedly, that Kate started.

Tears welled.

After five years, was she going finally to leave Hugo behind, and move on?

"I'm sorry," she whispered. "But I think this man will help me. Please, don't be cross. It's for Jack, too."

At that exact moment, a bird flew off a branch, sending two dark-green leaves floating to the soil below.

Kate watched, startled. Was that a sign Hugo was watching her? Was he trying to tell her not to do it?

No. It was time to stop looking for imagined signs. There had been a time when she thought she would never let Hugo go. She thought she would die old and lonely, holding on to the shirt he wore that night, splattered with the blood that spilled onto the floorboards, covered the table, the half-eaten food, the table runner. Now, she could see that she had to let him go, and take Jack with her into the future. Whatever this thing with Jago was, it was time to at least try. . . .

A thud from upstairs practically stopped Kate's heart.

She stood stock-still. The sound had come from Jack's room.

Her mind shot back to the break-in of two weeks ago. The sickening terror of seeing the dining-room window broken, shattered glass on the floor.

Was it another intruder?

She glanced, terrified, at the alarm box in the hall. It had definitely been on when she came home.

Kate felt the color return to her face as she remembered Jack's wardrobe door. It must have fallen open again, and pushed the guitar onto the floor.

Calm down, she thought. Calm down. She shut her eyes and tried to summon the peace she'd felt on the riverbank on Tuesday night.

She took long, slow breaths.

One thousand, two thousand, three thousand, four thousand . . .

Kate opened her eyes once she felt better.

Amazed, she realized she could wrestle back a little control.

As she prepared her tea, she wondered what Jago had planned for tomorrow night. She bit into a brownie, surprised at its sweetness. It felt chewy and spongey between her teeth. The sugar and chocolate exploded into her mouth. She looked at it with surprise. How delicious. She kept chewing.

This thing Jago kept saying. That the statistics were just exacerbating her anxiety. It was interesting. They really were making her feel even more unsafe than she did already.

She took another bite, a touch of optimism flushing through her.

Things were going to get better.

Then she remembered Jack would be going to the shop in Richard and Helen's village tomorrow morning by himself.

She looked up at the kitchen clock.

"Don't panic," she whispered to herself. There were still seventeen more hours to decide what to do.

15

It was Saturday, lunchtime, and the river was crowded with boats.

Rosie pulled hard on the leash, panting, and Jack followed. They made their way back to Richard and Helen's house, the paper bag of warm bread from the village baker and Granddad's newspaper under Jack's arm.

He looked at the river on his left, wondering if any of the boats motoring past were Granddad's. Everyone knew that Saturday morning was Granddad's alone time. He had been out for an hour already, and had said he was looking forward to the chicken and vegetable soup that Jack and Nana had made together this morning.

A small feeling of dread grew in Jack's stomach as he looked around the bend, ahead.

Rosie pulled on the leash, her nose leading her to some interesting smell in the reeds.

"No, girl," Jack said, pulling her back.

He didn't have many memories of Dad, but the few he did have were becoming brighter all the time. The clearest one was Dad telling him about his dog Pip, who'd drowned in a river when Dad was young. Jack remembered because Dad said that he had cried for two days. He remembered feeling stunned that big men like Dad ever cried.

Jack came around the bend and finally saw what he had been dreading.

Up ahead, the narrow path disappeared into a canopy of trees that created a tunnel that lasted for a two or three minutes' walk.

Jack would never tell Granddad, whom he suspected had never cried even about a dog or anything, or Mum, who was already too worried about him walking on his own, but sometimes, when he got to this part, Jack felt scared.

He felt that someone was watching him.

"Come, girl," he said nervously. Often, he managed to cross through behind some dog walkers or a family, but today the path was quiet. The only other pedestrians had passed in the other direction.

Jack quickened his pace. He'd just have to be brave.

The smell changed instantly, as it always did. Now it was musty and earthy, because the ground was slightly damp. The light in here was a sinister gray.

Jack pulled Rosie's leash lightly to tell her they were going faster, and fixed his gaze on the gravel, glancing up occasionally to check how close they were to the other end.

It was no good.

As usual, the sensation of being watched descended upon him. And as it did, the distance to the patch of sunlight at the other end stretched farther ahead.

If anyone had asked him, he would have found it hard to describe. There was nothing real, just a sense of a blurred shadow that melted into the foliage. Jack could sense that if it wanted to, the thing behind the trees watching him could travel more quickly than a car. If it wanted to catch him, it would.

Jack quickened his pace till the muscles inside his legs were stretched as far as they could go.

"Come on, girl," he repeated, jerking Rosie's leash harder than he meant to.

She looked up at him timidly.

Then, behind him, there was a noise.

It was a sound he had never heard inside this tunnel before, but had always feared.

It sounded like heavy feet breaking into a trot, right behind him.

"Quick, Rosie," he said, gasping, too scared to look back.

Something had come out of the bushes, and it was coming to get him, just like he'd always feared it would.

"Don't run," he told himself, remembering what Mum had instructed him to do if he ever came across an aggressive dog. "If you run it really will go for you."

But as Jack quickened his walking pace, the padding behind him became faster, too.

And then . . .

Ruff! Ruff! Ruff! Ruff!

The barking came out of nowhere.

It was only when he felt the vibration in his hand that he realized the barking was coming from his mobile. Why had he put on such a frightening ring tone?

Someone was phoning him.

"Hello?" he shouted, hurrying on along the path, praying the thing behind him would be put off. Only fifty yards to go.

"Jack, it's Mum," came a voice.

"Hi, Mum." The sound of her voice in this dark, scary tunnel helped.

"Jack, I just wondered where your PE kit was?" she said. She was trying to sound casual, he could tell. "I was going to wash it. Did you take it to Nana's or have you left it at school?"

Forty yards, thirty yards. Jack raced on desperately, willing his legs to move more quickly. He knew what Mum was doing. He'd told her he went to the village shop at twelve o'clock, and she was checking on him, but pretending she was calling about something else.

Right now, though, he didn't care.

"I put it in the wash basket," he said, ready to shout in case the thing grabbed him. Only twenty yards to go. "Oh, and Mum," he said, trying to keep her on the phone till the end. "Nana says can you pack my raincoat for going to Dorset at spring break because it might rain."

"Oh. OK. You've got your navy one for school. That'll do, won't it? Jack, why are you breathing so heavily?"

The padding was so loud now that Jack broke into a run. As he reached the opening in the trees, he dived through it, as if he were crossing the finish line on sports day.

"Jack! What's going on?" he heard his mum ask. "Are you all right!"

An elderly couple was reading newspapers on the deck of their boat to his left. The woman looked up and smiled.

Jack stopped and twirled around. "Yes . . ." He panted. "Um, Rosie was running toward the river in Nana's garden, so I chased after her. Anyway, thanks for ringing, Mum."

She paused again. "OK. You're welcome. Look forward to seeing you tomorrow. And hey, Jack? I was thinking. Perhaps you could bring back some blackberries from Nana's garden and we could make jam? Remember—like we used to?"

"OK. Bye," Jack said, turning off his phone.

He stood, catching his breath, humiliated at the shaking he felt in his legs, hoping Granddad wouldn't sail past right now and see him looking like this.

Yet the sound was still coming from behind him.

Swinging around, he looked inside the canopy. It was long, gray, full of shadows—and completely empty.

That's when Jack realized, the sound was his own blood, pounding in his ears.

That Saturday evening, Kate was ready at 7:45 P.M. sharp. She was showered, and wearing her new jeans again, this time with a white T-shirt, a thin, new navy cashmere sweater she had bought in a shop in the High Street this afternoon, and socks and hiking boots, in case they would be climbing over any more gates. She had applied some makeup, and blow-dried her hair.

Today was surprisingly relaxed. She was pleased with herself at the way she'd managed to check on Jack without making him suspicious, or causing conflict with Helen, while putting her own mind at rest. Once she had got to grips with this anxiety, maybe she'd even be able to let Jack walk to the shop herself.

As she left her bedroom, the laptop caught her eye through the open door of the study. A little thrill of anticipation ran through her. Of course! She hadn't done that yet.

She paused for a moment, then, feeling like a teenager, wrote Jago's name with "wife" and "girlfriend" beside it.

A small, grainy photo came up in Google images. It was from someone else's Facebook page. It was a photo of Jago laughing beside a pretty, petite girl with white-blond hair and dark eyebrows. "Jago Martin and his girlfriend, Marla Van Dorsten, at Thomas and Julia's wedding," said the caption. Kate stared. Was that the ex-girlfriend?

She felt a pang of jealousy. Where had that come from?

As she stood up, the numbers came out of nowhere.

Seventy percent of all homicides are committed by someone you already know.

"Kate, shut up!" she said out loud. But hang on, was it really that stupid to be careful? After all, she'd met Jago in the street, no less.

Her mind was trying to tell the difference between irrational fear and reasonable caution instead of jumping to the conclusion that she needed to be afraid.

She was a single mother. She should be cautious of strangers, for Jack's sake, as well as her own. This was actually progress!

She decided to trust her instinct while staying in control. She grabbed a pen and a Post-it note and scribbled on it.

"Dear all, I've gone out with Jago Martin, a visiting professor at Balliol. This is his phone number. . . . I should be back by midnight, Saturday. Kate."

She reread the note.

Was that mad?

No, she thought firmly, grabbing her bag and walking back to the door of the study.

It was sensible. Probably the first sensible decision she'd made in a long time.

Next door, Magnus stood looking in the mirror in his bedroom. Thoughtfully, he picked up the saucer of hand cream he'd taken from Kate's house, and put a little on his hands. Her rubbed the cream up and down each finger and over each nail, till he felt his hands become softer, enjoying the sensation. He'd almost used it all up now; it would be time to fetch some more soon.

Then he picked up Kate's lipstick, and smeared the dark raspberry color over his pale, dry lips. It was difficult to keep it within the contours of his mouth, and it kept running over. He tried to fill out the wonky lines he created above and below his mouth, running the lipstick back and forward firmly, adding waxy layer upon waxy layer of pink, until his lips were nearly twice the size.

Finally, he reached down and picked up a plastic hair band with a small bow on it that he'd taken from Kate's dressing table on another trip through to next door, and placed it carefully into the front of his hair.

He turned to the side to examine the effect, giving himself a long, slow wink.

There was a flicker of movement on his stolen computer. Flustered, he turned quickly.

An image of Kate walking away from him appeared on the screen.

"Yes!" he hissed, clicking on a button to magnify it.

Magnus sat down, watching Kate through the built-in camera of her own laptop, walking down the corridor as she disappeared down her stairs.

And then there was nothing. Just the open door of the study, and the empty hallway beyond.

Magnus grinned through smudged raspberry lips.

16

Kate arrived at the Hanley Arms five minutes early. The pub was busy tonight. Saturday night crowds spilled into the little beer garden at the back. She stood nervously, in a small space between the front door and the garden gate, moving from side to side, letting people come and go through the two entrances.

What on earth did Jago have planned?

A few men glanced at her, a couple behind their girlfriends' backs. She turned nervously, unused to the attention.

By five past eight, Jago was officially late. Kate was checking her phone every few seconds, with a growing sense of unease.

Had she misunderstood?

Suddenly, she became aware of someone waving at her from a car.

It was a woman in an old white sedan, parked up on the pavement, engine running. She was winding the window down manually.

"Kate?" rasped the woman through the gap.

She had short bleached-blond hair and dark roots. Her stomach ballooned beneath her navy T-shirt. She had dark eyes, and heavy bags beneath them.

"Sorry?"

"*Are you Kate?*" The woman's voice was not unfriendly, just firm and good-natured.

Kate nodded, confused.

"Taxi, darling. Out to the Warwick Arms at Chumsley Norton?"

Kate was bewildered.

"No. Sorry, I didn't call for a cab."

The woman held up a piece of paper that had been on her lap. "I think it is you, darling. Your bloke ordered it. Jay-boy or something?"

"Jago?"

"Something like that," the woman said, giving Kate an expectant smile.

Kate was silent, unsure what to do.

"So, do you want it or not, love? Makes no difference to me. He's already paid. You'll have to hurry up, though, I've got another pickup back in Cowley at nine, so . . ."

He was trying to get her to go in a taxi after what she'd told him? About her parents being killed in one?

Obviously he was trying to make her face her fear, but that was too much. She was not getting in that car. There was rust on the back door, and there was a growling noise coming from under the hood. Absolutely no chance.

"No, I think there's been a mistake," she said, shaking her head. "Sorry."

The woman shrugged. "OK, darling. No problem." She put the car into gear and it rattled off down to the entrance of the narrow alleyway. Kate looked around desperately, hoping that Jago would appear and explain. The chances were low, though, since he was probably waiting where the taxi was going to drop her off. Her phone buzzed.

Kate! Get in the taxi.

She spun around. Where was he?

The woman had reached the end of the cul-de-sac where the alleyway started, and was doing a clumsy three-point turn.

Kate watched as she began to point back toward her. The woman was talking to someone on a radio.

The numbers buzzed around Kate's head.

People who drive for business purposes have a forty percent higher chance of road accidents.

She tried to focus.

The car looked even more banged up from the front.

Another buzz.

Kate. You said you could do this!

Where the hell was he? She looked around helplessly. It seemed like he must be in the vicinity, watching her.

What should she do? She visualized the alternative: sloping home and spending the evening alone again.

Jago's words crept into her mind. "You wouldn't go to the important conference. You'd stay at home trying to be safe."

If she didn't let Jago help her, she'd be sitting with Sylvia in her somber sitting room for years talking about her feelings.

She had to take a leap of faith and put her trust in Jago.

The taxi picked up speed as it headed past Kate to the T junction.

Kate hailed it.

*   *   *

She and the woman didn't talk all the way to Chumsley Norton. The driver was too involved in a conversation with her sister on her headset, about their mother's sciatica.

In eighty percent of car crashes, the driver is distracted.

Kate tried to ignore the anxiety, gripping the seat, and pushing her body against it, as if she could control the car's speed with her thighs. She was sweating inside her new sweater, consumed with the effort of "not thinking about" what was happening, as they sped through traffic lights on the ring road, the engine roaring grumpily, and then took a road west, under a bridge.

"Nine miles, eight miles," Kate mouthed as they passed signposts for this mystery village. She tried not to think about the story she'd seen last week on the news about teenagers in another part of England dropping concrete onto a car from an overpass, injuring its driver; a story that had left her hopelessly obsessing about the chances of your car being the one out of thousands that would be hit. She glanced behind them every so often to check if Jago was following.

Soon, they turned off the road, and took a bunch of rural lanes. The names on the signposts became increasingly old English in their eccentricity. Pog Norton. Sprogget Corner. Hedges rose higher, verges widened, and the road narrowed, so that by the time Kate's driver had decided to tempt her mother out of the house with a shopping trip to Bicester Village, the chance of becoming stuck if they came upon another car seemed a certainty.

But they didn't.

"That's you, darling," the woman said, pointing up at a battered sign with pellet shots on it. It read Chumsley Norton.

"Thanks," said Kate. She lunged out of the taxi, dumb-founded at what she'd just achieved. Her first time in a taxi in eleven years.

She looked around. Chumsley Norton had sounded like a pretty, chocolate-box village. Instead, it looked more like an un-remarkable scatter of houses on the way to somewhere more interesting. There were about ten pairs of them, semidetached and redbrick, with the look of 1950s council houses. On the bend before the houses stood an ancient-looking thatched pub.

The village was silent and appeared to be deserted.

"Excuse me. Did he definitely say here?"

"He did."

"OK . . ." Kate said uncertainly, still holding the door. "And he said he'd meet me here?"

"Back in Cowley in twenty minutes, control," the woman barked into her radio. "Don't know, darling."

Reluctantly, Kate shut the door.

This didn't feel right.

Deciding she should ask the driver to wait for Jago to ar-rive, Kate stuck out her hand. To her shock, the taxi accelerated around the bend, past the pub, and down past the houses, pre-sumably taking an alternative route back.

"No! Wait!" Kate shouted futiley. The taxi disappeared into the distance.

As the noise of the engine faded, it was replaced by an ex-pansive quietness. Not the idyllic rural tranquility of a meadow; more the total absence of human life.

Holly hedges down either side of the road obscured the front gardens of the redbrick houses. The air smelled of silage.

Kate hurried into the parking lot to look for Jago.

From a distance, it had looked like an ad for English tourism, but as she neared the pub, its neglect became apparent. White paint flaked off cottage walls; dark ridges of rot streaked the window frames.

If Jago had been watching her back at the Hanley Arms, where was he now? Dusk was approaching. It was 8:40 P.M.

Jago must have somehow got ahead of her, she reassured herself, or taken an alternate route. Kate opened the door to the bar. A large man with rolled-up shirtsleeves stood wiping glasses. His hair was pulled back into a greasy black ponytail. He surveyed her without expression.

"Evening." His voice was gruff.

"Hi," she said shyly.

Three men sat huddled at the bar, backs to her, like wolves around a kill. They turned and stared at her with unfriendly curiosity.

Kate glanced around. Scuffed chairs and tables sat on a flagstone floor.

Her breath stalled in her chest.

Jago was not here.

The barman nodded his chin upward in a "What can I get you?" gesture.

"Um, orange juice, please," Kate said, looking out the window at the darkening road. She took her phone out. No service.

The barman put the orange juice down on the bar aggressively, spilling a bit. Kate was painfully aware of the wolf pack's eyes on her.

"I'm actually looking for someone," she said quietly, aware they were listening. "A Scottish bloke with a crew cut?"

"A Scottish bloke, eh?" the barman repeated loudly.

Kate shrank back, wishing he would lower his voice.

"I could do you a Welsh bloke with a fat arse," one of the wolves, who had a long nose and purplish lips, said, pointing at his mate, a rotund man in a dirty red sweater.

Memories of the Hanley Arms and the soccer fans came back to Kate with unpleasant clarity. She glanced outside again. There was, however, no escape from here. No bike outside. No Hubert Street.

Where the hell was Jago?

Through the window, Kate saw five or six scooters pull into the parking lot. They were all driven by young lads, gesticulating and swearing at one another as they came. Her chest tightened. Were they coming in here, too?

Trying to mask the nervousness in her voice, Kate handed over her money, and said, "Sorry, I can't get a signal. Have you got a pay phone?"

The barman regarded her with hard eyes. "One up the road," he said, turning his attention back to the wolves.

Up the road? What did that mean? She took her drink uncertainly to a table by the window. Peering out, she could see a dim light coming from about fifty yards beyond the houses. Was she going to have to walk up there alone in the dark? The wolf pack talked under their breaths. She could swear she heard the word "tart."

The door banged opened and Kate turned, hoping again for Jago. Instead, a teenager walked in. He had a ratty face, and short hair gelled carefully onto his forehead in fine lines.

"Evening," he said with a sly grin.

The rest of them sat at a table with a broken umbrella in the empty beer garden out back. She felt the fear crushing her chest. She tried to think calmly. Was this a test? To see if she could take a taxi to this village, then walk into a pub full of belligerent drinkers on her own? And then what? Phone a taxi from the pub back to Oxford?

A hard gulp of panic came into her throat when she realized Jago might not know there was no phone signal out here. Kate glanced out at the pay phone again.

What if she used the phone to order a taxi and an old man like Stan, who'd killed her parents, turned up? At least back at the Hanley Arms, she could see the driver. She'd had a choice to get in the car, or not.

There was no choice now; she must get out of here.

She could try calling Saskia, although God knows what questions that would lead to later.

Kate looked apprehensively at the barman, who was pulling pints for the teenager. She walked casually up and put her hands on the bar.

He ignored her, continuing his work.

She waited half a minute, sensing the wolves' attention on her again.

And another.

When she could take no more of the sneering looks and muttered grunts, she spoke. "Uh. Excuse me."

The barman stopped, a tray for the teenagers in midair.

"I'm sorry. I was supposed to meet someone who hasn't turned up. And I can't get a signal. Would you mind if I used your phone?"

Her voice sound tinny and posh among the gruff, spat-out words of the men.

The barman shook his head in astonishment. "Am I talking to myself here? I haven't got a *bloody* pay phone! Up the road!"

The viciousness of his words gave her a shock. "No. Your phone," she tried to say. The wolves howled in delight. The teenager shook his head, sniggering.

"The phone in my house?" the barman said, sounding incredulous.

The barman set the tray down with a bang. He walked to a door behind the bar and opened it. Kate saw rickety stairs leading to somewhere dark. "Go on, then," he said.

Five pairs of mean eyes burned into Kate.

"Um," she said, stepping back. "No, actually, it's fine. I'll find the pay phone."

Face burning, she ran to the door, and rushed outside, letting it slam back into the wave of male laughter. Cheeks smarting, she rushed out into the dark country road.

Why had Jago sent her to this shithole of a village?

This was not funny. This was not silly. This was horrible.

"Idiot," she said to herself, thinking about how she should never have stolen that dog to impress him. Clearly, he now thought she was much tougher than she actually was, which had landed her here, outside a sketchy pub, on a remote road at night, completely out of her depth.

As the lights from the pub faded, the intense blackness of the countryside fell over Kate like a blanket. She tried not to think about what could happen to her out here. The aggressive squawks of the teenagers back in the beer garden floated behind her, and she kept on faster to escape the whole horrible scenario.

And then, as if things couldn't get any worse, Kate reached the second-last house in the row, and realized the teenagers' noise was becoming louder.

Somewhere inside her head, an alarm went off.

Her instinct to flee took charge of her body. Kate dived off the road and into the shadow of the holly hedge. Swiveling around, she saw the teenagers climbing onto their bikes. They'd just ordered pints. Why would they do that?

Holly cut Kate's skin like spikes through the new sweater that she'd so carefully chosen for her date. Right now, however, she didn't care. She watched the gang put on their helmets. They had heard her say she was walking to the pay phone.

They knew she was out here, alone. She would have been safer if she'd stayed in the pub.

Kate watched as they revved up their engines.

She had to think quickly. She had only seconds before they came looking for her.

17

Saskia glanced up from her laptop to the clock on the wall of her mother's vast country kitchen. It was 9:40 P.M.

"Snores!" she shouted.

With a sigh, she lowered the window of the page she'd been reading.

"What you doing?" said Jack, wandering in from the sitting room, already in his dressing gown.

"Nothing," she lied. He walked toward the oak table where she sat. Rosie ran in behind him and dropped her head into Saskia's lap, looking up with her soft brown eyes. "Just catching up on work. Right. Time for bed." She smiled, stroking Rosie's head. "Want some juice or something?"

He nodded. His face had relaxed again, she noticed, like it always did when he stayed with his grandparents.

Saskia stood up. Jack pulled Rosie toward him. She licked his face and lay down on the floor with a sigh.

Saskia looked at him sideways as she sat back down with his glass. "Snores, what's wrong? You've been quiet all day."

He shook his head.

"Is something wrong?"

"No."

"So what really happened to your head?"

He hesitated. "My skateboard, I told you," he mumbled, gulping juice.

"Well," she said, dropping her voice. "I don't think it was your skateboard. I know when you're lying. You're rubbish at it."

She reached out and rubbed his arm. "Come on. This is me."

He shrugged. "She didn't mean it."

Saskia realized he was actually going to tell her something important. "What, someone at school? A girl?"

He shook his head.

Saskia frowned. "So who . . . Wait, you don't mean your mum?"

He glanced behind him.

"Hang on," Saskia said, getting up. She closed the kitchen door and came back. "Tell me what happened."

"Don't tell Nana." She could see the worry in his expression.

"I won't."

Jack put down his half-finished juice cup. "She was trying to stop me going out the front door when the alarm was on, and we were arguing."

"You and Mum?"

"Yes. I was shouting."

Saskia's mouth dropped open. "That's not like you. What about?"

"Lots of things. She locked the gate again."

"But Nana has the key."

"Mum got a new one. With a padlock."

Bloody, bloody Kate, Saskia fumed. Not that she was surprised. She rubbed his arm gently. "Oh, Snores. Is that why you said it was your skateboard?"

He shrugged again.

"And your mum told you to say that?"

He nodded. "It was an accident. She didn't mean to do it."

Saskia blinked. Oh, God. This was all they needed. If Mum found out, all hell would break loose. She tried to sound reassuring. "OK. Listen, mate, you mustn't worry. This is adult stuff. It's between Nana and your mum. And it'll all get sorted, I promise."

"But Nana says I've got to come and live here, and it's making Mum cry."

Saskia wanted to hug him but he looked so angry she suspected he'd shove her away. "Do you want to live with Nana?"

"Sometimes." There was a tiny fissure in his voice. "But I don't want to leave Mum on her own." The fissure widened, and his voice cracked. "And anyway, she says we're moving back to London."

"She said what?"

Jack nodded. "That's why I shouted."

Saskia glanced up at the door again, double-checking her parents couldn't hear.

"Oh, God. OK." Right. That was going to send Helen completely off the scale. Saskia thought for a second, then took Jack's hand. "Listen now, I want you to go to bed and not to worry about this. Me and Mum, and Nana and Granddad, we all love you more than anything. And the rest of it, we adults will all sort out together, OK?"

Jack nodded. "But don't tell Nana."

"I won't. But don't you tell her, either—or about London. Not till I've spoken to your mum about it."

The door opened and they both glanced up nervously. Richard walked in, holding an empty crystal tumbler. Rosie jumped up and ran to him.

"What on earth are you two up to!" He beamed. "Do you want a drink, darling?" he asked Saskia, as he approached an array of spirits on the work top.

"No, thanks, Dad. I'm going to head home. Snores is off, too, aren't you, mate?" She caught her nephew's eye and winked. He nodded.

Jack stood up and gave his granddad an awkward hug, and then Saskia.

"Good night, young man. Sleep well. Don't let the bedbugs bite."

"Not everyone gets bedbug bites, Granddad," Jack replied. "Some people are immune. It was on the news last night when they were talking about all the bedbugs in New York."

"Smartie bum," Saskia said as Richard chortled.

"He seems OK," Richard said, looking at Saskia as Jack left the kitchen to say good night to Helen. "Darling? You think?"

She hesitated, lifting the laptop, hating Kate for putting her in this position.

"Yes, I think so."

"Sure you don't want to stay, darling?" She watched her dad pour himself another gin and tonic, and a brandy for her mother.

Yes, she wanted to say. Anything not to spend another night in an empty bed, staring at the space where Jonathan had slept for four years, but she knew she couldn't. "No, I should get home."

As her finger hovered over the "off" button, she remembered the page she'd been researching earlier, and brought it back up. She looked at the photo Hugo had taken of Jack that hung on the wall. She nearly started to tell Richard about her dreams of leaving the agency and sorting out the mess she had made of her life.

But she didn't.

No, she thought, closing the laptop and standing up. Right now, Jack needed her more.

She'd have to help herself another time.

Right now, she had a battle to fight with Kate.

18

Kate was still crouched down in the small garden of one of the semidetached houses, her heart banging like a pneumatic drill. The garden was unlit, as was the house. She listened to the scooter engines burst into life in the pub parking lot. If she was right about this, there was no way the teenagers could see this far up the dark country road. If they wanted to find her, they'd have to guess where she'd gone, and there were a lot of options in this darkness.

Kate crawled along the holly hedge till she reached the fence that divided this semi from the one next door. A dustbin stood in the corner. Its unpleasant fishy smell mixed with the stink of silage drifting off the fields was enough to make her sick. Kate pushed the bin firmly, slipped into the gap behind it, then let it back in front of her, covering her mouth and nose as she did.

She tried to think calmly. The boys wouldn't have a clue where she was. For all they knew, she'd had her own car outside, or was staying in one of these houses, or had run off into a field.

She sat, hugging her knees, trying to stop them from shaking.

Why was she even so certain they were coming for her?

She thought of Hugo, and those men in the courthouse, and she knew why.

The noise of the scooters grew into a harmonized whine. Kate peeked through the hedge. Her stomach lurched.

Once you have seen evil, you recognize it. It makes a different sound. A splintered, clashing commotion that causes heads to rise in alarm. It has an energy that blurs everything else.

The gang was searching for her, and she knew it.

Bursting out of the pub, they spread out across the road like an air show formation, their headlights on full beam creating a mass spotlight effect, moving forward slowly.

Hunting her.

Kate shivered, and held herself more tightly. They can't find you, she told herself. They can't search every part of twenty dark gardens, every surrounding acre of field, every ditch. It would take hours. One of the residents will hear them and call the police at some point.

"Where'd she go?" someone yelled.

There was a shriek of out-of-control laughter.

Kate sucked in air. She knew she needed to bring more oxygen into her body. She'd learned that from a self-defense program on TV once. It stopped you becoming paralyzed with fear and helped you run. She looked around the garden. But where could she possibly run to?

"Go up to the pay phone, John! See if she's there," a shout came. A second later a scooter roared past. Now they were in front and behind her.

"Oh, my God," she whispered. They were serious. This was not a prank.

She peeked through the hedge again, and saw the headlights go in different directions.

Kate kept trying to breathe steadily.

"We're coming to get you!" one of them guffawed.

"Look in the gardens!"

Kate dug her fingers into the ground. They were doing exactly what she thought they wouldn't, entering each front garden, methodically and one by one, brazenly ignoring the presumably frightened residents hiding behind curtains.

Kate thought of Hugo with a sudden, awful clarity. And in that moment, she knew what he'd felt like that night.

Hunted.

Frantically, she felt the ground around her, looking for something, anything she could use as a weapon. Nettles stung her fingers, and then she felt something wet and spongy that made her recoil. She tried the other side of her and felt something else.

It was a brick. She grabbed it. The hardness gave her strength.

There was a deafening roar to her right. In the tiny gap under the fence she saw a scooter enter the semi next door.

"Not here, mate!" a voice shouted from close by.

Another memory of Hugo detonated in her mind. Of finding him on the floor, a pool of blood soaking into the floorboards he'd so lovingly restored. Of her, screaming and screaming, as she watched all that passion and expertise and love disappear into nothing in front of her, as his brain and his heart shut down. He was gone. Stolen. His life wasted. For nothing.

She looked through the hedge, a seam of anger opening up inside her.

People like these boys had ruined her life. Their willful, thoughtless violence had killed her husband, terrified Jack, and damaged her relationship with her son to the point where his life would be ruined before it had even started.

Kate scraped the tips of her fingers along the top of the brick, feeling its pores.

She was sick of it.

People like this taking the power from others because they could.

Despite the shaking in her legs and arms, Kate decided that if a single one of these boys came near her, if they threatened to do any more harm to her and Jack, she would take this brick and she would fight him. She would hurt him more than he would believe.

"Here, pussy, pussy!" a teenager shouted above the scooter engines. His friend laughed from across the road.

"Try me," Kate mouthed.

The scooter reversed out of the garden next door and finally turned into the one she was hiding in.

"Seriously," the boy shouted, "where the fuck is she?"

"I'll look in here, mate," yelled his friend.

There was an explosion of light. She could see the boy from here. He was small, not even her height. Skinny, too. Slowly, he turned his handlebars, the headlights illuminating the front door, then the bay window. Kate readied herself to take action before he did.

A plan formed. She would strike him as hard as she could, then run out into the dark field where the gang could not find her.

Kate held the brick in her hand ready to strike.

A new noise arrived out of nowhere. It was a car, and it was speeding toward them all.

Kate stopped in midair.

All the boys began reversing now. She saw them gathering around a black hatchback, their engines whining together.

The car door opened. A new voice joined the melee. It was deeper, bassier. She tried to make out if it was a voice she recognized from the pub. Was this her chance to sneak through the hedge next door and make a run for the fields without being seen?

Then, all of a sudden, like a swarm of vicious wasps, the six scooter boys buzzed past her and carried on out of the village.

Stunned, Kate stood uncertainly in the small front garden, holding the brick, listening to the increasingly distant drone.

She heard a man shout her name. He had a Scottish accent.

Her breath came out in painful gasps. She didn't even realize she'd been holding it.

"Kate? Where are you?" Jago's voice drifted over the hedge.

"Here," she shouted, shouldering the dustbin out of the way, still listening out for the boys. But the whine of the scooters was fading. The gang was gone. It was over. Relief shot through her.

A gate scraped open, and Jago's head appeared around it.

She waited for his face to register her state, then waited for an abject apology.

"Hi there," he said breezily, surveying her. "So how did it go?"

Kate wiped mud off her hands, then her face. She glared at him.

"What are you talking about? How did what go, exactly?" she exclaimed. "Why are you looking so calm? Jesus, Jago. I've almost been attacked!"

"The experiment."

Kate peered at Jago. His face looked untroubled. No, more than that—eager.

Jago seriously did not seem to have a clue that she'd almost hit a young boy with a brick in a bid to protect herself from God knows what the gang were planning to do to her.

"Jago!" she said angrily. "Why are you just standing there like that? For God's sake. Do you have any idea what's just happened here?"

"Tell me."

Tell me? What was wrong with him? What did he think had gone on? That she'd called a taxi from the pay phone and was sitting in this scruffy little garden for fun, while a gang of rabid teenagers roamed the road outside?

"Everything went wrong," she said. "The guy—sorry, the fuckwit—in the pub had no pay phone. I had no phone signal, so, I don't think you realize, but I've had to walk down here in the dark, to this pay phone, and those"—she pointed to the road—"little *wankers* heard me talking about it in the pub, and followed me. Chased me!"

She challenged him with her eyes, waiting for him to throw his hand across his mouth, full of remorse at the dangerous position he'd put her in. To beg forgiveness and offer to make it up to her.

But Jago stayed still.

He was observing her.

"Jago!" Kate shouted, feeling the anger seam rip open inside her. "I don't think you quite understand. Those boys were practically hunting me." She flung a hand in the air.

He still didn't react.

"This experiment, the one where you sent me out to this shithole with no way of getting home—it went very horribly wrong. I was nearly really badly hurt." She was yelling now.

Jago just looked at her and smiled.

Kate stared wordlessly, clenching her fists.

"Kate, it didn't go wrong. In fact, it went perfectly. You did brilliantly. Seriously. The boys just told me they had absolutely no idea where you'd gone."

She repeated his words in her head to check she'd heard them right.

"The 'boys'?" she spluttered. "You mean the *gang* who just chased me up a dark country road, shouting, 'Here, pussy, pussy'?"

"Did they?" Jago grimaced. He took a step toward her. "Listen. Kate. That's Liam, he's the porter's son, from Balliol. I told him and his mates to chase you for ten minutes then call me. I was hiding in my car at the pub. I didn't realize they'd be quite so, er, imaginative, and I'm sorry if they frightened you that much."

Kate started back. "Jago. Please tell me you are joking. You could not have set this up."

"You said you wanted to do this, Kate." He reached out and picked a holly leaf off her sweater. "You said you could be spontaneous."

Kate pulled back from him. "I know but . . . This is . . . This is just . . . crazy!" With a surge of anger, she blew past him, desperate to get out of this horrible pit of a garden.

She flung open the gate and let it slam behind her. "Fine," she shouted back, humiliated at the state she was in. "Brilliant. Well done, you. Now could you just please get me out of this fucking place."

But upon reaching the road, Kate felt the brick she still grasped in her sweaty hand, and realized she was not finished. She spun around to see Jago walking unhurried through the gate.

"And actually, it's really not OK," she said. "Because do you know what I nearly did?" She lifted the brick. "I thought that boy was going to hurt me, and I was preparing to hit him. To defend myself. That's serious, Jago. That's a ridiculous position to put someone in, whether you were trying to help me or not."

To her fury, Jago just shrugged.

"I am not a game," Kate yelled, smacking the brick down on the ground with a crack. She walked to his car, feeling her legs start to shake as the adrenaline left them.

Jago continued behind, looking bemused.

"You don't understand. You shouldn't have done this to me. For God's sake, my husband was . . . murdered!"

The word came from nowhere. The word she never said. Kate yelled it out into the country lane and heard it echo around the houses and gardens and fields, taking with it a stream of toxins from inside her.

For the first time since he'd arrived, Jago came to life. He stepped forward and put his hands on her shoulders.

"Kate, I know," he said.

"No!" she said, flinging them off and stepping back. "You don't know. He was murdered by a pack of men who came to our house in London and pushed their way in the front door to get the key to his stupid sports car. And when he fought back"—she said reaching for her stomach—"they stabbed him. Just like that. With Jack upstairs. And now you"—she pointed at him—"strand me out here and set a pack of boys on me?"

For the first time, Jago looked sorry.

Kate realized she was starting to sound completely out of control. This was doing nobody any good. She counted the way she'd been taught so long ago to steady herself.

One thousand.

Two thousand.

Three thousand.

Four thousand . . . Her pulse slowed. She leaned back against Jago's car. She shook her head ruefully and looked at him. What on earth had she gotten herself into? "I'm sorry, I know you're trying to help me, I really do, but you shouldn't have done this. You really don't know enough about me to know what I can and can't handle." She pushed away from the car, and went to open the door. Her voice was calm now. The disappointment of all that Jago had seemed to offer, fallen apart on this empty road, was palpable. "Can you take me back to Oxford, please?" she asked, starting to feel cold.

She felt Jago's hands on her shoulders from behind.

"Kate," Jago said quietly, gently spinning her around to face him. "I do know. About Hugo."

She stopped.

"I know what happened," Jago repeated. "I went on the newspaper Web sites for Shropshire, and worked out from what you'd told me about your parents' accident who they were, and who Hugo was. I know everything."

Hugo's name sounded so wrong on his lips. As if he'd stolen it from her head. Kate was baffled. "You knew? And you still did this to me?"

Jago took her hands in his, and this time, she was too stunned to fight him. Part of her, she realized, wanted this still to be OK. She still wanted to hang on to the hope that he would help her with the numbers. So when he pulled her into his arms, she did not refuse.

"Listen, Kate," he murmured above her head. "I might look like a student but you have to trust me. I know what I'm doing. I read up on what psychologists are doing in the States and spoke to a colleague on the phone, too. You were safe the whole time this evening."

Jago's chin rested on her head. "We had one chance to kick-start your survival instincts. And we did. And you're fine," he said softly. "A bit muddy, and slightly smelling of cat poo, but fine. I mean it, Kate, you were brilliant."

She stayed in the refuge of his arms, away from this stinking hellhole of a village.

"The reason I did it is that you need to have faith in yourself. You lived in London, for God's sake. You have street sense. You know how to look after yourself. You hid. They'd have given up soon and fucked off. You'd have rung me to pick you up, and you'd have been fine. This was *real* danger, in the sense that to you, it was real. And what did you do? You dealt with it. You survived."

Kate listened to him carefully. It was true. After all this time of being scared of shadows and creaks in the dark, it had been a relief to fight back. To know she would have hurt them before they hurt her.

Jago held her tight. She allowed herself to lean against him a little, partly because her legs were shaking so much and she was cold. He gave her a gentle squeeze, then laughed. "I thought you were going to belt me with that bloody brick."

"I might still," she growled. "Bloody hell, Jago. You scared the hell out of me."

He blew something out of her hair. "Well, I'm very impressed. I wouldn't mess with you."

She smiled reluctantly into his T-shirt.

"So how do you feel?" he asked.

She shook her head, self-conscious. "Don't ask."

"I mean it, tell me," he repeated, dropping his head down to meet hers. His lips brushed her cheek as he said it, and she closed her eyes, distracted by the singular sensation on her skin.

"I don't know. Confused."

Jago lifted her chin. "Bollocks. You know exactly how you feel. Now say it."

She looked up at the sky, hating herself. She had thought of Hugo tonight, of that terrible night that had torn them apart. If she said it, it would mean saying good-bye to that. To Hugo. She would be stepping back into the real world.

"Say it," Jago murmured, his mouth getting closer to hers.

But she couldn't say it, so she lifted her chin up, not knowing what would happen, but to her relief, found Jago's lips waiting for hers.

And to her shame, the kiss on that dark road, covered in mud and holly leaves and sweat, was unlike any kiss she and Hugo had had for a very long time.

It was a kiss from before they married.

From before Jack.

From before her parents died.

From a time when there was no anxiety or fear.

"Alive" was the word she wanted to say to Jago, but she couldn't, so she let his kiss remind her of that feeling all over again.

19

After saying good night to Jack, Saskia raced to Kate's house in East Oxford. As she pulled into the driveway, she saw Kate's car was there. Good.

It was 10:15 P.M. Saskia blinked. It was late to burst in, but this couldn't wait. Lights were on in the sitting room and upstairs. If Mum caught a whisper that Kate was planning to move back to London, all hell was going to break loose.

Saskia pulled on her hand brake crossly. How come she had been elected intermediary in all this? She had her own problems. As Saskia turned off the engine, she saw a shadow cross past the curtain in Jack's room.

At least Kate wasn't in bed.

Sass looked around. Hubert Street always felt so quiet at night, despite its close proximity to the bars and restaurants of Cowley Road.

A security light burst into life as Saskia rang the bell. This was the only option, she reassured herself. The last thing any of them, including Jack, needed was social services accusing Kate of emotional neglect or asking for a mental health assessment.

The upstairs hall light shone dimly through the glass of the front door. Saskia waited, tapping her foot, for Kate to appear.

Nothing happened.

Saskia pressed the bell again, then followed up with a rap of knuckles on the glass.

Seconds passed. "Kate?" she called irritated, through the letter box. "It's me—Sass."

Saskia opened the letter box wide, only to find that Kate had fixed a plastic cowl on the other side to stop people from reaching in.

"Kate!" she shouted, aggravated.

Saskia walked backward and took another look up.

The light in Jack's room had gone off.

Scowling, Saskia fumbled in her bag, took out her phone, and rang the house number. A second later, she heard Kate's phone ring out in the hallway. It rang five times before the faint rumble of the answer machine came through the front door.

Either Kate was ignoring her or something was wrong. Had she accidentally locked herself in behind that stupid gate?

"You OK there?" came a man's voice from right behind her.

Saskia jumped. She whipped around, and saw the weirdo from next door standing in Kate's driveway.

"Yes," she exclaimed abruptly, her heart hammering. "I'm fine."

He was so tall close up. Towering above her, with his pale husky eyes, staring from behind greasy glasses.

"I thought you were maybe a burglar," he said, grinning. "I keep an . . ." He pointed his fingers at his eyes, then at Kate's house. "For her. You know?"

"Er. I'm not a burglar, but thanks," she said, turning her back on him and rummaging in her bag for Kate's spare keys.

She turned back. The man watched her with chilly eyes.

"Hey." A joky tone entered his voice. "Hang on. How do I know you're not a burglar, huh?"

"Listen," said Saskia, employing her finest public school accent. "I'm her sister-in-law. But thank you. Good-bye."

To her annoyance, the man didn't move. Mouthing a swearword to herself, she turned and jammed the key into the door, blinking. Thankfully, it slipped in on the first attempt, and Saskia shoved the door open with relief.

Beep beep beep.

Saskia jumped again. The alarm was on!

Yanking the door behind her, and shouting, "Kate! I'm here!" she dashed to the hall cupboard, desperately trying to remember the new code. What was the number? Hugo's birthday. Third of March—0306? Or was it the month and the year—0375? She turned on the cupboard light and pressed at the buttons with fluttering fingers. The alarm stopped. Quickly, she turned around.

The weirdo was standing right behind her in the hall.

She must have not shut the door properly behind her.

"What are you doing?" she gasped. "Can you get out, please?"

"You want me to look around?" he said, pointing upstairs.

"No, I don't," she said firmly, trying to herd him out of the house with a hand held in front of her. "Really. I'm fine. I'd like you to go, please."

"OK. Bye," he called.

"OK, fuck off," she mouthed as she slammed the door behind him.

Her heart was thumping. What a freak.

Now where the hell was Kate? Saskia turned and saw that all the inner doors were closed.

"*Kate?*" she called crossly up the stairs.

Tentatively, Saskia switched on all the lights and climbed the stairs.

The cage door lay wide open at the top.

"Kate?" she called more quietly. "Answer me. You're creeping me out."

She crept into the spare room first, but there was just an empty single bed and chair, lit by a lamp on a timer switch. Next, Jack's room, which was still dark. She switched the main light on and looked around. Nothing. Ten seconds later, it was clear that there was no one in Kate's bedroom or the study, either.

Saskia crept back downstairs.

"Kate?" she said more timidly, scanning the downstairs hall.

Had she fallen? Saskia reached up above the door frame of the dining room, and used the key to unlock each inner door, one by one, checking behind sofas and tables.

Finally, Saskia opened the kitchen door.

Another lamp on a timer switch was on in here, too.

Saskia's eyes roamed the room until they settled on the kitchen table.

There was a note.

The journey back to Oxford was quick. The roads were quiet at this time of night. They drove from Chumsley Norton back to the dual carriageway, and then when they reached the city center, Kate guided Jago over Magdalen Bridge and back through East Oxford. Gratefully, she noted that Jago had switched on a device that heated her seat. She stretched back against it, drained.

The heat felt good on her bones. She watched the students in their evening dress, running through the streets.

Tonight she didn't feel so different from them.

She'd had an adventure.

She rubbed her lips together, fascinated by the musky taste of Jago that lingered there.

"Better?" Jago asked, glancing over.

She nodded, and curled up tighter into the seat. She shook her head. "I still can't believe you did that."

He grimaced. "I just felt we had to take the risk."

She sighed. "And I can't believe you know about Hugo."

"I'm really sorry, Kate. I'm not surprised it's left you with this kind of anxiety. It would any of us."

Kate shook her head sadly. "You know, the irony was that Hugo wasn't bothered about money, not like his dad. Richard's a businessman, totally money and power obsessed. Hugo just wanted to do something he loved. But, probably because he did love it, he was good at it and this one time, he made a lot of money unexpectedly just when the property boom happened. And he'd grown up with Richard having all these nice cars, and I think it was just a whim left over from his childhood."

Kate's hand moved automatically to below her rib cage for the thousandth time.

Jago tapped the wheel. "And they tried to steal it?"

She nodded.

"I'm sorry. That's shit, Kate. For you and your little boy. The newspaper said they got the guys?"

Kate nodded. "Yeah, but the trial was horrible. Their DNA was at the scene so they couldn't deny the car theft—but they wouldn't admit to Hugo's murder, and when they were found guilty, they shouted these awful things at me in court. Honestly, Jago, they were evil. It was terrifying."

Jago turned into Iffley Road, nodding. "Well, I'm not surprised it left you feeling scared. Not many people ever see real evil. You hear about it, but you don't see it."

His kind tone belied his boxer's looks. She liked watching him drive. He was a confident driver.

"How did you know to choose that pub, by the way?"

He raised his eyebrows and shifted gear as they accelerated up the long stretch of road. "Ah, well, that was a bit of luck. One of the visiting American professors made me go there one night with him. He'd seen it on a Web site, and had some romantic idea of English villages. Of course, we turned up and met the tosser who runs it. I remembered I couldn't get a phone signal and there was no pay phone, so it seemed perfect."

Kate pointed ahead to Hubert Street. Jago signaled and pulled in right, parking in an empty space.

"That's weird," he said, looking around. "This looks like my road in Edinburgh. So . . ."

"So . . ." she said. Her limbs felt like they were made of cloth. She waited, wondering what she would do if he asked if he could come in.

"So," Jago said, leaning over toward her and taking her hand. "Seriously, are you OK?"

"I think so. Yes. I am."

He pushed away a damp strand of her hair from her face. "Kate. I really do promise, you were never in any danger."

She sat, intrigued by the touch of his fingers on her skin, the sensation familiar in some ways, brand-new in others. "I know. I do actually believe you."

"Good. Out of interest, what did it feel like when it was hap-pening? What you saw, what you smelled . . ."

Kate looked out at her house. "It's funny you say that. I smelled things so strongly I almost gagged. Like the holly bush and the silage. And sounds, too. Even though I was behind the hedge, I could sort of tell where each of the scooters was by sound."

He nodded. "All your senses were on alert."

She nodded.

"Like an animal under attack."

"I suppose so."

He nodded. "That's interesting."

His hand was resting on the gear stick. Tentatively, she put her own hand on top of it. Their fingers entwined, and he leaned over to kiss her.

This second kiss was longer. Kate didn't know where she wanted it to go, she just knew she didn't want it to stop. Their breathing deepened.

Suddenly, however, Jago broke free from her lips.

"Kate," he said into her ear.

"Hmm?"

"I'm going to go."

She hesitated, not sure if she was relieved or disappointed. "Is it the cat poo?"

"Maybe a little." He smiled. "But seriously, you've had a fright tonight, it wouldn't be fair of me to, well, not to go." He seemed nervous himself. "If you know what I mean? I don't want you to think I'm . . ."

She nodded, gratefully. "No, you're right."

"Sorry. Didn't say that very well." He lifted her hand with his. "This is a bit weird for me, too, you know." On an impulse, she lifted her other hand and hesitantly touched the side of his head, letting the stubble of his crew cut run lightly under her fingertips. He leaned his head into it like a cat. "That's nice."

"Did you go out for a long time?" Kate asked, doing it again, remembering the photo of the girl on the Internet.

"Felt like it, sometimes." Jago sighed. "No. I'm joking. About five years?"

"When did you split up?"

Jago looked sideways. "About three months ago. We were . . ."

He stopped talking and looked past her to the house. He leaned his head to the side, a curious expression on his face.

"Is that someone looking for you?"

Kate turned, and saw Saskia peering out of the curtains in Jack's bedroom.

"Oh, my God." She pushed Jago away abruptly. "You've got to go. Sorry." Kate grabbed the door handle, panicked. "She can't see you." She saw the uncertain look on his face. "It's my sister-in-law. . . . Hugo's sister. It's complicated. But listen, ring me, OK?"

He nodded and placed a hand on her shoulder. "I will. But wait till she goes back inside. She'll see you when you open the car door and the light comes on."

Kate waited till Saskia disappeared behind the curtains.

"I'm going. Thanks for going to all that effort to completely petrify me," she said sarcastically, leaning back to kiss him briefly.

"You're very welcome." He grinned. "I'll ring you tomorrow. You did well. Stick with it, we'll get there. I'm convinced this will help you."

"Thank you," she said, and meant it. With that, Kate jumped out and ran inside to find out what her bloody sister-in-law was doing in her house.

20

"What the hell are you playing at?" Sasksia exclaimed, leaning forward to pick a holly leaf off Kate's sweater.

"What am I playing at?" Kate walked past Saskia, lowering her head in case Saskia could see the glow in her eyes. "What are you doing here?" she barked. "Where's Jack?"

"At Mum's, he's fine. Let's lock the door before that bloody weirdo comes back," Saskia said turning the dead bolt.

Kate dumped her bag in the front hall. "What weirdo?" She checked her reflection in the mirror. Jago was right. Her face was smeared with streaks of mud.

"That guy next door. The student. What's that smell?" Kate saw Saskia look suspiciously at her shoes. Kate ignored her, taking them off. "Which one?"

"The tall one. With glasses."

Kate shook her head. "They've all got glasses. I mean it, Sass," she said spinning around. "What are you doing here? Why are you in my house?" Kate tried to remember when Saskia had turned from her sweet, shy little sister-in-law, into this morally superior woman who seemed to think she had some ownership over her life.

Saskia pursed her lips, and held up a note.

Kate cringed.

"Sass!" she exclaimed, grabbing it. She felt like a teenager, her secret stash of cigarettes discovered by Mum under the bed. "For God's sake. That's private."

"I can't believe you did that!" Sass exclaimed, pointing at the back door.

"What?" Kate asked, bewildered.

"Ran out the back door. If you had a man here, you should have just answered the front door, told me it wasn't convenient and I'd have come back tomorrow. Not sneaked out and hidden in the bushes. Look at you!" She pointed at Kate's muddy face. "Where is he? Still out there?"

"What are you talking about? I've just got home."

Sass exaggerated disbelief. "I saw you, Kate! Or him," she said pointing at the note. "Upstairs in Jack's room."

What was she talking about? "Sass! No—you didn't."

"I did, Kate. Walking behind the curtain. I can't believe you. And the reason, by the way, that I let myself in is that I thought you'd fallen and hurt yourself."

Kate felt a shiver pass through her. "Sass. I'm not lying. I've been out since eight. I've just got back." She looked up the stairs. "Have you been up there?"

Sass nodded. "Yes, I've been right round the bloody house. There's no one here, Kate. And the alarm was on, too."

That unnerving sense of unease crept over Kate again. She felt it eating away at the new sense of empowerment Jago had given her this evening. Throwing up her hands in frustration, she stomped off into the kitchen.

"Sass! One minute you're all telling me off for being overly anxious, the next you're winding me up!"

She turned and saw Saskia's cheeks turn as pink as her mother's.

"Kate. I saw someone at the window. And then the light went out in Jack's room."

Kate tried not to let her nerves seep back in. "Maybe you were looking at the bedroom next door."

Sass hesitated.

"What?" Kate growled. "You look like you're dying to say something."

"Well, I was just thinking . . . that it sounds like we're both imagining things at the moment. Doesn't it, Kate? You know, like Jack falling off his skateboard, for instance."

Kate tried to hold Saskia's gaze angrily, but was overcome by a wave of shame.

"He told Mum he fell off his skateboard. And then he told *me* that you told him to say that."

"Jesus, Sass, are you spying on me? For your parents? Is that what it's come to? You record every mistake I make with Jack, and what? Helen writes it on her report? You and I used to be friends. What's happened to you?"

Saskia tried to hold her ground. "But is it true?" she demanded.

"What do you expect me to say, with your mum ranting about calling social services? It was an accident, Sass, and if Helen wasn't causing all this upset in the first place, it wouldn't have happened."

Kate stomped across the kitchen and switched on the kettle.

"And who is he, this Jago Martin? This visiting professor? Where's he visiting from—London? Is he the reason you're moving back there?"

"Oh, for God's sake!" Kate said. "What do you do to my son! Sit him down in a bright room and interrogate him the minute he gets to Helen's? Honestly, keep this up, Sass, and I'll be the one ringing social services!"

They held each other's furious stare for five seconds.

"What if Hugo could see us now, Kate? He wouldn't believe it." Saskia's voice cracked.

Kate pulled down two cups from a shelf, tasting her betrayal of Hugo on her lips as she did it.

A twinge of sadness passed through her.

Despite all their problems, she and Saskia had trudged together, side by side, for five years, struggling together with their grief over Hugo's death. But this week, Jago had given her a glimpse of the future, and if she knew anything, it was that she needed to keep going now, even if that meant leaving Saskia behind.

Jago had reminded her tonight what it felt like to feel alive. And she wasn't going back.

"Sass," Kate said. "Hugo can't see us. He's gone."

Kate looked distracted, Saskia thought, as she put coasters down on the kitchen table. There was a dangerous light in her eye, and holly leaves stuck to her sweater. What the hell had she been doing? Saskia bit her lip. She needed to calm down. She'd already said more than she meant to. Any more and Kate might tell her to leave.

Already, she wished she had broached the subject differ-

ently. Made peace with Kate, not poured more petrol on the
fire, like she had the other night when Mum threatened to take
Jack away. She hated getting angry. She'd always been so rubbish
at it. Hugo had laughed out loud on the rare occasions she lost
her temper.

Saskia leaned over and plucked off another leaf as Kate put
down two mugs of tea and a plate of brownies. "So is it true?
About London?" she said in what she hoped was a more reasonable voice.

Kate was still avoiding her eye. "No. I don't know. I've been
thinking about it. Oxford's not home for me. It never has been."

Kate coming to Oxford was supposed to keep the family
together after Hugo. How had it ripped them further apart, like
a rotten seam?

"And him?" Saskia said, trying to keep the hurt for Hugo out
of her voice. "Does he live in London?"

She stopped, astonished, looking at Kate's mouth.

Kate was eating a brownie.

It was so long since Saskia had seen her sister-in-law eat
casually, and not push her food to the side of her plate as if it
were contaminated. Tonight she looked like the old Kate, stirring those giant dinner-party pots in Highgate, beating eggs
and flour, adding stock and saffron and spices with deep con-
centration, dancing around the kitchen as she tasted sauces, a
contented look on her face.

And now, just for a second, Kate looked like that person
again. A woman enjoying eating again.

Kate shook her head. "No."

Saskia couldn't help herself. "So, who is he?"

Kate rolled her eyes and Saskia decided she better take a
step back. If Kate had really met someone, the last thing Saskia

needed was to alienate them because of her disapproval, perhaps creating a new ally for Kate; someone who might later encourage her to take Jack away from her and her parents altogether. "No one. Just someone I met."

"Nice name," Saskia tried, fumbling about. "It's a cross between Jack and Hugo. Uncanny, really."

Kate glanced up.

"Like it's meant to be, or something." There was a note of bitterness in her voice.

Kate sighed. "Sass, nothing has happened."

She couldn't help it. She had to know. "But it will?"

Kate pushed her hair behind her ears. "I don't know. I've just met him. It's been five years. I have to start again somewhere."

Tears welled in Saskia's eyes. Before she could help it, one ran down her face. "Sorry." She sniffed. Tonight's unexpected glimpse of the old Kate—Hugo's Kate, not this moody, strange, Oxford Kate—had exposed old wounds.

Old Kate would have reached out and rubbed her arm, with a kind look on her face. This one held her tea tightly in both hands. "Oh, Sass, please don't," she said.

But Saskia couldn't stop the tears. "It just feels scary, Kate," Saskia continued. "If you meet someone, you'll stop being our family. You'll join someone else's. You won't be my sister-in-law anymore, you'll be theirs."

There. She had said it.

There was a silence at the table.

Kate rolled her eyes. "Don't be a pillock, Sass."

There was a moment of tension and then they both burst out laughing. Sass sniffed and sat back, feeling better. "Well, I've got to admit, he's doing something right. You look happier. And you're going out again. I wish I was."

Kate chewed a bite of brownie. "What's happening with Jonathan?"

Saskia took one for herself. They never talked like this anymore. She bit into the brownie, thoughtfully. What would she give to tell Kate everything right now? To tell her the truth about her marriage to Jonathan. The awful truth that she had to keep hidden from everyone; from Helen and Richard, Kate, and most definitely Jack, who desperately needed the remaining functional adults around him to be rock solid, not foolish and unreliable.

"He just sent the divorce papers," she said carefully.

Kate looked genuinely surprised. *"Yes,"* Saskia would love to have said, *"things go on in other people's lives, too, Kate. You're not the only one with problems."*

"Wow. I'm sorry, I didn't realize."

Saskia shrugged.

"Sass. I still don't really understand what happened there. It all seemed so sudden."

Saskia heard the sympathy in Kate's voice that she remembered. She wanted it back for good so desperately. A wave of temptation to tell Kate the truth overwhelmed her. Could she trust her? Or would she just blurt it out in front of Richard and Helen, and even Jack, next time there was a big argument?

Saskia thought about the way Kate had blatantly lied to her about not being home this evening, when she so clearly had been with this new man, and her distrust of the "new Kate" returned.

The old Kate never lied.

She swallowed the brownie. No, maybe she'd tell Kate one day, but today was not that day.

"Um, I don't know." She shrugged. "He just got bored with

me. He hated that I complained about working for Dad all the time, and never did anything about it. He said that when he met me at college, I seemed like someone who was going places and it turned out that I wasn't. I couldn't even stand up to my own father. So now he is going places on his own." She sighed. "He's right, though, Kate, and I know it. I'm a bit of a failure. I make coffee for Dad for a living."

Kate frowned. "That seems unfair, Sass. . . . I mean, it's certainly not grounds for divorce. And what about the Charlbury lot? You don't seem to see them much at the moment."

Saskia sighed. "They've all sided with Jonathan. Actually, Marianne and Christian are throwing a party for his thirtieth tonight with a nineteen-sixties theme. I'm not even invited."

Kate sipped her tea. "Well, Christian is his best friend, and I suppose he and Marianne have to take sides. You know, Sass, I remember at your wedding Jonathan told me that he'd had an Italian girlfriend for three years and never bothered to learn Italian. I always thought you deserved the kind of man who would learn Italian for his partner."

"Why didn't you say anything?"

"It was after Hugo. You needed Jonathan at the time, and, to be honest, I didn't have the strength."

Saskia remembered. Old Kate would have sat her down with a bottle of wine, and told her the truth, because she wanted only the best for her.

Saskia sat forward, wondering. There one thing she could tell Kate. "Well, if I tell you something, will you not tell anyone?"

"What?"

"I'm thinking of finishing my degree."

"Have you spoken to your dad about it?"

Saskia laughed bitterly. "No."

"You should."

"You know, I was just looking at that amazing photo Hugo took of Jack this evening"—she pointed at the photo, blown up and framed on Kate's kitchen wall—"that one, at Mum and Dad's today. Do you know that I took up photography before Hugo?"

Kate shook her head.

"Well, I did. And my art teacher said I had potential so Dad bought me a really nice Nikon. Anyway, Hugo got interested and borrowed it and, well, you know how brilliant his eye was. And then Dad came to that exhibition at school when I won the photography prize, and was saying how great my photos were. . . ." Saskia sighed. "And I said—as I always did, doing my self-deprecating thing—'Thanks, Dad, but you know, Hugo's already way ahead of me.' And Dad said, 'Well, I know, but he's just more imaginative, darling.'"

"Sass . . ." Kate said.

"Well, it's true!" Saskia exclaimed. "You know how much I loved Hugo, Kate, but the way Dad treated him . . . his precious 'golden boy' . . . It wasn't easy, growing up with that. You know, he never once considered I might be as good as Hugo at something—or even better."

Kate pushed back in her chair. "It's just the way your dad was brought up by his dad. Men were expected to have the big careers, women weren't. Hugo didn't like your dad's attitude, either. He felt bad about it for you . . . but really—who cares what Richard thinks? You know you're talented. And so did Hugo. So what does it matter what your dad says? He's just your dad. He's not the bloody king of the world."

"Easy for you to say, Kate. You stand up to him."

Kate shook her head. "No, Sass, that's not true. Standing up to Richard is exhausting. I step around him, just like Hugo taught me. I wish you'd do the same."

Saskia tapped her fingers. "I've missed this. Talking to you."

Kate picked at her coaster. "I'm always here, Sass."

She felt the tears coming again, but rubbed them away, as she always did in front of Kate. It had never felt right to cry in her presence. As Hugo's widow, Kate's grief automatically took priority over hers and everyone else's. "But that's not true. You're not."

Kate sighed. "Don't start, Sass."

Saskia pushed her hair away from her face. It was time to stop, while the going was good. "So, can I meet him? This Jago?" she said.

Kate looked away. "I've only just met him myself." She pushed back her chair. "Anyway, listen, I'm exhausted. I need to go to bed. Are you staying over?"

"No, I'll go."

Saskia picked up her coat. They walked into the hall together.

"Kate, I've got to tell you, Jack was upset tonight. He says you're still locking the gate upstairs. He's terrified that Mum's going to ask him about it."

Kate threw her hands up. "God. Not this as well! Look. I bought a padlock and used it, but then I threw it away, OK? And they're coming to take the whole bloody gate out next week. And that's the last thing I'm saying about it."

"I didn't tell Mum," Saskia said, allowing the hurt to come into her voice. "It's not easy, you know. Being in the middle of you all like this."

Kate softened a little. "I know."

Saskia opened the front door, and motioned toward the cage.

"Although, to be honest, after talking to that weirdo next door, maybe you've got a point. He's odd, Kate. He smells of drink and I saw him staring at this woman in her house in Walter Street the other week."

Kate walked behind her, locking the inner doors in the hall. "Sass. Please." She sighed. "Don't do this to me. You're encouraging my anxieties now. He's just a piss-head student—just like we were once. Really.

"Anyway, as you said yourself, there's no point having the gate if I've got the alarm on the windows and doors. What's he going to do, climb through the attic skylight?"

Saskia picked up her bag. "I know. I just want you to be OK." She looked at Kate tearfully. "I always have."

She saw a glimmer of sadness cross Kate's face, and she hoped it was a longing for their old friendship. "Let's worry about things that are real, shall we?" She gave Saskia a half smile and shut the door behind her.

Sass walked to her car. In the old days, they had never parted without a hug or a kiss.

In her heart, she knew now that was never coming back.

21

It was Tuesday, 6:00 P.M. Cricket practice was over, and Jack arrived back at Hubert Street with a lot on his mind.

Gabe wasn't helping.

"Go on, J," Gabe said, sitting on his bike. "Ask her now! I'll wait."

Jack shook his head as he typed in the number combination to the side gate lock, and opened it into the back garden.

"No. Later." He scowled. Gabe didn't understand. He didn't know what it was like to have a mum like his. Gabe's mum let him do anything he wanted.

"Aw," Gabe said, frustrated. "But before we go to the park to play cricket tonight, yeah?"

Jack nodded, even though he knew that might be a lie.

"Bring the ball, J, yeah?"

"OK. Come and get me after tea."

Jack shut the gate behind him and checked it was locked again, as Mum had taught him, and leaned his bike on the wall. He looked through the kitchen window.

She was walking around licking a spoon.

She turned and saw him.

She waved—and smiled.

Jack stared, bewildered at the sight. His mum was smiling? Not a fake version of Gabe's mum's, but her own. A smile that he recognized from long ago in a way he didn't understand. It lit up her eyes, and made them shiny, and changed her face. It made her look pretty, and younger. A lot younger than Gabe's mum.

Jack waved back hesitantly.

He went to fetch his cricket ball from the trampoline, but it wasn't there.

He looked around the garden. There weren't many places it could be. There wasn't much here. Just a lawn that looked like it had been laid like a carpet, its edges meeting the fence on three sides. Granddad cut it sometimes, and was going to teach Jack to do so soon. There was a patio without any seats, a shed, the magnolia tree, and a giant trampoline.

Jack looked under the trampoline, thinking. Maybe if Mum was in a good mood, now would be the time to ask her.

He tried it out in his head: "Mum? You know Gabe's sleepover for his birthday on Saturday? It's outside in the garden, on the trampoline. Can I go?"

He imagined that cheerful expression he'd just seen disappearing, and the worry wrinkles coming back. Jack sighed. The thing was, he wasn't completely sure he even wanted to go to Gabe's sleepover.

His mind flew to the three year-eight boys who'd befriended him on Facebook. At first it had been exciting. Damon said the boys were "cool." Damon's brother Robbie knew them at secondary school, and one lived on Gabe's road. But then the year-eight boys read about Gabe's sleepover, and said they'd come after Gabe's mum was asleep, and bring cider and cigarettes and it would be "a laugh."

Jack wanted to tell Mum. Get her to talk to Gabe's mum and make sure the sleepover was safe, so he wouldn't have to worry about it. How could he, though?

He stood back up again. The ball wasn't here.

"Hi," he said, wandering in the back door.

She looked up. "Hi! How was cricket practice?"

He shrugged. "Good, thanks."

A smell took him by surprise. Rich and meaty with spices. His taste buds popped. It smelled like the cooking at Nana's house, but spicier.

"What are you making?" he asked, peering at the cooker. A large red pot he recognized from a high-up cupboard was inside the oven.

"I am making lamb tagine," his mum said. "Well, trying to. I used to make it in London. It's an experiment, though. I'm a bit out of practice. It might be rubbish."

Jack gawked. The table was set, too. For the two of them. With knives and forks, and glasses, and she'd lit a candle even though it wasn't dark outside.

He leaned against the work top curiously. The trays they used to eat on in front of the telly remained stacked in their normal place.

He saw his mum pick up her mobile, look at the screen, then put it back down by the cooker.

"Who was that?" he said. Not many people rang his mum.

"No one. I thought I might have a message. Do you want to help?" she said.

Jack's ears pricked up. Not only had she smiled but she was

talking about Dad. Not in the sad way that made him feel she was pulling him under a murky river, but in a new, happy way.

She pulled out a packet, and handed it to him. Jack watched her, fascinated. What was happening?

It was almost as if she was . . . He stopped himself from lingering on the thought, knowing it was too much to hope.

"You need to put that in a bowl, then pour on the boiling water. Then when it's soaked in, pour some olive oil in— then fluff it up." She winked. "I'm sure you'll do it better than your dad. You've got my hands." Kate reached out a hand and touched his fingers, which were slim like hers.

She nodded. "And you could put in those almonds in the packet over there, and chop that mint for it, too."

"OK. I'll do it in a minute," Jack said. "Can I have the key to the shed first, please? I can't find my cricket ball."

"Wasn't it on the trampoline?" Kate asked, reaching up and grabbing the key.

"That's what I thought, too," he said, walking out. He unlocked the shed and went inside. It smelled of cut grass and chemicals. Objects from their old house in London were stacked on the shelves, things that were never used. Gardening equipment. His old inflatable paddling pool that he couldn't remember using but recognized from an old photo. A giant suitcase he'd never seen before. Dad's skis.

Jack pushed a spade away and sat on a box, running one hand over the metal catches of the skis, thinking about what had just happened in the kitchen. Those men in London had been put in prison for stealing Dad's life, and his dad's car, but they'd stolen lots of other things from Mum, and from him, too. Things that were difficult to put in boxes and measure.

Jack measured his feet against the fixings. Granddad had said Dad was planning to take him skiing when he was six, and that he could have Dad's skis when he was older, so it would be like he was skiing with Dad after all. As usual, his foot sat in the middle, with space at both ends. Dad had big feet. He knew that because he tried on his shoes sometimes, wondering if his toes would ever reach the end.

It was while he was sitting there that Jack's eye was drawn to a book underneath the table.

Beat the Odds and Change Your Life.

Jack picked it up. What was this?

The cover opened up. "To Kate. What are the chances? Jago Martin," it said inside.

Who was Jago Martin? How did she know the man who wrote this book?

He started to flick through. This was the mad stuff that Mum always talked about. Numbers, and bad things that might happen to you. He glanced through the airplane figures, then the traffic figures. Did she hide this in the shed and come and read it in private?

He didn't want Mum to talk about these weird numbers anymore. He wanted her to laugh more.

So, he hid the book under his sweater and stood up. Maybe she'd just think it had got lost. Grabbing a tennis ball to play with at the park instead of his cricket ball, he locked the shed behind him, and walked through the kitchen, realizing to his surprise that there was music playing. A CD cover lay beside the dusty old player in the corner, and Mum was swaying a little as she stirred a pot.

Jack did a double take. Mum was *dancing.*

"Five minutes till tea, Jack," she said.

"OK," he replied, astonished, running upstairs to hide the book under his mattress.

He couldn't ask her about Gabe's sleepover. Not today. He didn't want to spoil this good mood she was in, wherever it had come from.

He had seen a peek of his old mum through the glass amber eyes and he didn't want to scare her away.

22

An hour later, Kate cleared plates, and checked the clock.

Seven o'clock, and still no text from Jago.

Where was he?

She had actually enjoyed today, and wanted it to continue, sitting at the table with Jack and eating their dinner together. For the first time since she could remember, they'd both had second helpings. They talked about his cricket practice and Jack mentioned a film he wanted to see, which gave her an idea.

She blew out the candle.

If only Jago would text, this might be the closest she'd had to a normal day in a very long time. Having something to look forward to again was becoming addictive.

She put the dirty dinner plates into the dishwasher. She hadn't been able to stop thinking about Jago all week, and the crazy night in Chumsley Norton. The episode came back to her in waves. Disbelief at what he'd done, how she'd reacted, and then a guilty thrill at what happened afterward. But now it looked like he wasn't going to text her. She had a good mind to go to the shed and read his book after all.

That was funny, she considered, hesitating by the recycling bin. Jago hadn't mentioned his lost bag, and she'd completely forgotten to tell him the waitress had found it.

Lost in thought, Kate then noted with surprise that the recycling box was already full. She lifted it and took it to the front door. They normally only half-filled one box a week.

The thought came out of nowhere.

A third of sexual crimes are committed on children under sixteen.

"Shit," Kate murmured, slamming the front door shut again and dropping the recycling box in the hall. Where the hell had that come from? She stood against the wall, perturbed. There had been so few like that today. Only three instead of the usual ten or twelve.

"Don't think about it," Kate thought. She sat down on the stair. "It's nonsense. An average of what has happened doesn't guarantee it *will* or *won't* happen to you or Jack. And if you don't give him some independence, he'll never grow up."

She forced herself to her feet, opened the door again, took a deep breath, and realized she was fine.

She stood on the doorstep, waiting cautiously.

It was really gone that quickly. This was actually working, she smiled at the thought. Jago and his advice had improved things already.

And she was thinking about him.

Constantly.

Especially about the kiss on the dark country road, and the one in the car.

Kate walked to the mirror. She ran a hand down over the flat front of her new T-shirt, stopping at her hipbones. She had woken at 3:00 A.M., and found herself imagining Jago was lying next to her on the opposite pillow. In the dim light of the moon coming through her curtains, she had thrown back her covers, lain sideways, and slipped a hand under her nightshirt, allowing it to rest on the dip in her waist, as if the hand were his. She had explored her body, to see what he would find. What she discovered was a mountain range of jutting hip and clavicle bones, and sharp ribs that made bridges across her chest above the hollow valley of her stomach. Two quiet little mounds of breast in the middle that no longer filled the old bras she couldn't be bothered to replace. The rough terrain of dry skin on neglected knees and elbows.

What would she see in his eyes if he ever saw all this, she thought again, looking in the mirror?

Hugo had loved her body. All of it. Pregnant, ill, stretched, shrunken. From the start, and to the end.

Kate had turned over onto her stomach and pulled the covers close. She had only kissed Jago. He had made it clear he didn't expect more unless she wanted more. She still had a choice, so there was no point in anticipating her own self-consciousness.

But as she looked at herself now in the hall mirror, she knew that wasn't really true. She was wearing earrings for the first time in years, bought before she knew what she was doing, this afternoon in Oxford. The small silver hoops hung under her hair, in reopened holes stinging slightly, emphasizing the cut of her cheekbones. A lace bra that was the only one that still fit her sat under a pretty charcoal top that set off the blackness of her hair and the amber of her eyes. The choice was slipping away from her. Jago's kisses had jump-started her body out of a five-year slumber, whether she liked it or not.

And now her body was waking her up at 3:00 A.M. to think about him lying opposite, while her mind told her to proceed slowly.

You have a child. If this man can help you, fine, if he can bring you and Jack back together, fantastic, because your priority must always be fixing your relationship with Jack, not what you want. You need to get to know this man before you think of doing anything serious with him because . . .

Drriiiiinggg.

Kate jumped.

Sass. Please, be Sass.

She walked to the front door and looked through the peephole.

It was a tall man with glasses, standing very close to the doorway. She recognized him as the man in the garden next door the other day. She opened the door.

"Hi," Kate said.

"Magnus!" he said, not moving back, but holding out his hand. "Your neighbor."

"Hello," Kate replied, holding out hers automatically. The man took her hand in large, damp fingers. He shook it hard. Too hard. It was all she could do not to say "ow." She stepped back to give herself more space.

This must be the guy Sass had been talking about.

"You know when the bin men come?" he asked, waving an arm toward his house.

"Tomorrow," she said. "Wednesday." How could the students not know that? No wonder there were bloody bin bags all over the front of their garden.

He still stood there, too close to her doorway. She felt herself withdrawing farther. Didn't they have personal space where he came from?

"Tomorrow? Hey, great. Thank you." He paused and looked at her, then walked off.

Kate nodded uneasily. "You're welcome."

Relieved, she shut the door. She walked quickly to the kitchen and washed her hands. Saskia was right. He was a little strange.

Her phone buzzed on the kitchen table. She dried her hands and grabbed it excitedly.

"Yes!" she hissed, when she saw it was from Jago.

Blackwell's at 7:45 p.m.

Kate's face broke back into a happy grin. "Bit close to the bone there, mate," she said.

She walked around tidying the kitchen, imagining telling Jago about the weird student.

"Kate, he's just a student with a nervous handshake who turns into a tosser around women," she imagined him saying. "Trust me, I have six of him in every class. You've got to tell the difference between real danger and imagined danger."

She looked at the clock. Only a short while till she saw him.

"Please, Sass," she said under her breath before running upstairs to clean her teeth, her thoughts about the odd student next door left downstairs.

Saskia arrived at 7:20 P.M., full of apologies. To Kate's relief, Jack arrived back at the same time, with Gabe and Damon in tow to drop him off. Kate congratulated herself for the second time this week. She had managed not to phone Jack to check up on him, and he looked like he'd had fun.

This was all going even better than she'd hoped. And now she was going to try something she hadn't done in years. She challenged herself to cycle to Broad Street on the road.

Determined, Kate pulled on her denim jacket and, at the last minute, remembered to grab the bag with her ankle boots. She buckled up her new bike helmet, checking the straps twice, and went outside. "Jack, show Sass where the dinner is, will you?" she called, taking her bike out of the side gate.

Then she saw Jack and the other two boys muttering to one another.

"Kate?"

The call came from Gabe. She turned as she walked down the drive, where Jack was hitting Gabe's arm crossly.

She stopped reluctantly, anxious for the task at hand. "Hi, Gabe."

"Can Jack come to my sleepover on Saturday? My mum says he's got to ask you, and he keeps not asking you because it's in the garden and he thinks you'll say no. And if you say no, I'm going to ask Sid. So can he?"

The smile slid off Kate's face.

In the garden? What was he talking about?

"Oh, like, camping, in a tent?"

"No—on the trampoline. In sleeping bags."

He was joking? Three ten- and eleven-year-olds, lying out-side at night, alone in a city, with foxes, and burglars and . . .

The numbers began to buzz annoyingly at the back of her mind.

Kate realized that they were all staring at her. She tried to pull it together.

Gabe was waiting.

"It's just my mum thinks you might worry about it. . . ."

"Shut up, Gabe," Jack glowered.

"My mum said yes," Damon piped up.

Kate saw Saskia open her mouth, probably in order to tell some irritating story about how her and Hugo used to camp in their garden. Kate shot her a dirty look.

Don't dare, it said.

Then to her sorrow, Kate saw Jack jut his jaw tensely as he had in the car the day she'd gone to Sylvia's. He was embarrassed. In front of his friends.

The buzz of numbers grew louder in Kate's head. She tried to ignore them, cursing Gill, Gabe's mum, for putting her in this position.

"Um, listen, I'm in a hurry, Gabe," she said, trying to keep her tone bright. "Can you tell your mum I'll ring her tomorrow? And, Sass, don't wait up, I might be a bit later tonight," she said, pushing off on her bike before Saskia could interrogate her.

Kate waved at Jack, and pulled into the road, aware of the astonishment between Jack and Saskia as they realized that she was not riding on the pavement. She cycled to the junction and regarded Iffley Road nervously, and the long stretch of it that ran right into Oxford.

But it was no good.

Gabe's request had rattled her and made her question her good intentions.

She looked up and down Iffley Road. This afternoon, on the way back from Tesco to buy ingredients for the tagine, she'd managed half the ride on the road, the rest on the pavement. But now she felt less brave. Kate gripped the handlebars, waiting for a long break in the traffic, then pedaled hard across the road, trying to concentrate only on her pedaling. She cycled as fast as she could, desperate to get it over with.

But the idea of Jack sleeping outside, with no adult to protect him, was starting to make her feel sick.

A third of children do not report sexual offenses to an adult.

"Don't think about it," she whispered. A truck went past, making her swear out loud.

Two-thirds of road accidents happen on 30 MPH or slower roads.

She tried to ignore it.

More crimes take place at night than at any other time.

It was no good. Panting, Kate pulled by the ivy-strewn school on the corner of Magdalen Bridge.

Bloody Gill and her bloody laid-back, hippie ways.

And this bloody, bloody road.

Kate leaned against a wall, raging at herself. The figures were flying at her so thick and fast now she suspected she might have to push her bike all the way to Blackwell's, which would make her late for Jago.

"Get a grip," she thought. "Jack won't be on his own in the garden; the others will be there. And if you don't allow it, he'll be left out of the group."

One thousand.

Two thousand.

Three thousand.

Four . . .

Within seconds, she began to relax. A minute later, she felt almost back to how she had been before Gabe had spoken. Tentatively, she climbed back onto her bike, and headed shakily across Magdalen Bridge.

Almost immediately, she found herself among a pack of other cyclists. They were mostly students, and a mother, to her alarm, with a toddler in a child's seat. Kate stayed in the middle, hoping the pack would protect her, and gritted her teeth. The toddler was laughing as his mother cheerfully sang "The Wheels on the Bike Go Round and Round." Kate gripped her handlebars as if she were hanging from a trapeze as the road dipped around to Longwall Street, to the quieter Hollywell Street.

Eventually, the welcome width of Broad Street loomed ahead.

"Come on," she said. "Just a bit farther."

But her rhythm started to escape her. Her legs felt as if they were jamming down randomly on the pedals now, at risk of slipping off with each push.

Finally, the Sheldonian Theatre came into view, and then Blackwell's.

She was nearly there.

She had done it!

Kate drew up in the central parking area and dismounted. Her hands were trembling.

She looked behind her, amazed. For the first time in five years, she'd cycled the whole journey on the road. It had been horrible, panic-inducing, but she had done it.

She looked across the road with a shiver of anticipation. Broad Street was packed with pedestrians on this early summer evening. She couldn't see Jago. She pushed her bike through a group of Japanese tourists to the bike rack by Blackwell's, conscious of a tremor in her leg muscles, too. Locking her bike, she looked around. A "ghost walk" tourist group was gathering on the pavement. A boy cycled past her in college robes, a carrier bag of wine balanced on each handle.

Kate stood by a wall, glancing intermittently toward Balliol. She wandered over to Blackwell's arched windows and peered inside. She checked her watch for the fifth time—7:52 P.M. Oh, God, this wasn't part of another experiment, was it?

"Hey. Good timing!"

She turned, and saw Jago walking toward her, holding a rucksack. He was wearing a white T-shirt and dark jeans, and looked really pleased to see her.

"Hi," she said, suddenly wondering how you greeted a man you'd kissed on your last encounter. Jago had no such reservations. He leaned down, smiling, and kissed her confidently on the mouth, the smell and touch of him sending a shiver through her—then stepped back and hit himself on the forehead.

"Shit." He held out his rucksack. "Can you take this, Kate— my bike's just there." He pointed. "I've left my jacket in my room."

Kate nodded.

"You look nice," he said with a wink, walking back to his room. Kate pushed her hair behind her ears awkwardly, try- ing to remember how to behave in this situation. She had met Hugo when she was twenty-one. It hadn't felt awkward then, just normal. The last in a steady succession of teenage and college boyfriends. She took the rucksack over to Jago's bike, noticing a clinking noise coming from inside it.

As she went to put it down, a high-pitched sound like the rape alarm Dad had made her take to university, came from inside Jago's bag.

The tourists from the ghost walk looked over.

Kate ran her hand along the front of the bag. She felt a hard lump in the front pocket.

The noise stopped suddenly.

She hesitated, about to stand up . . .

Then it started again.

"Ooh, shut up," she muttered. Customers inside Blackwell's were looking out the window now. Not knowing what else to do, Kate unzipped the pocket.

Marla ringing, the screen of Jago's phone read.

Kate paused.

Marla?

The noise was increasingly desperate with each ring.

What should she do?

She hovered her finger over the "answer" button.

Then as quickly as it had started, the noise stopped.

You missed a call from Marla, a message popped up.

"Right," Jago said, coming up behind her, his jacket over his arm. "Let's go."

"Oh," Kate exclaimed, jumping up. She glanced at the open pocket of his bag.

"I'm sorry, I was just—" she stuttered.

"Was it going off?" Jago said, bending down. "Sorry. I switched it to the alarm ring tone and turned up the volume so I could hear it from the shower. My publisher in London was supposed to ring. Was that him?" He picked up the phone.

Kate said nothing.

Jago looked at the screen. A dark look passed over his face.

He looked at Kate. "Did you answer?"

"No!" she stuttered. "No. I wouldn't—I just—I—it was just ringing and ringing and—"

"No, don't worry. I better just listen to this voice mail, though." He held the mobile to his ear. When it had finished, he changed the ring tone back to the one she'd heard before, an acoustic guitar strumming.

He made a face. "Well, that's unexpected." He stood up, zipping the bag. "Marla, my ex-girlfriend. I'm supposed to be seeing her in August in the States, but she's at a conference in Paris, apparently, and wants to stop off in London."

Kate tried to stay expressionless.

Jago looked stunned. "Sorry. That's thrown me a bit. We haven't spoken for three months."

Kate hesitated. "Well, do you need to go and ring her? I mean, we can do this another time. . . ." She stopped awkwardly, praying he wouldn't accept her offer. "I mean, I can go."

Jago punched her gently on the arm. "Oh, you're not getting out of this that easily, mate. No. I'll ring her back later." He unlocked his bike. "Come on."

"But if you two have stuff to . . ."

"Kate, let's go," he said, climbing on his bike. "If I'm not mistaken, you and me have business to take care of," he said, looking back with a heavy-lidded, ambiguous look.

"OK," said Kate, blushing and climbing back onto her bike. The plastic bag on her handlebars swung against her. "Just a sec. I need to hand this in to that shoe-repair shop on the corner first." She pointed to the end of Broad Street. "It's open till eight."

Jago pointed where she now saw steel shutters across the door. "It's five past. You've just missed it." He put out a hand. "Give them to me—I'll drop them in for you in the morning."

"But . . ." Before she could say any more, he took the bag from her, hung it on his own handlebar, and headed off Broad Street toward town, waving for her to follow. Kate pulled uneasily back out into the street.

"Hey. Look at you. You're cycling on the road," he called back, before picking up speed.

She smiled, pleased with herself.

Jago went in front, turning right at the top of Broad Street, then on up Woodstock Road. Kate followed, feeling like a new colt, her skinny, unsure legs pushing awkwardly against the pedals as two trucks thundered past her.

Trucks are involved in nearly a third of all road accidents where people are killed or injured.

Thankfully, a minute later, Jago turned left and coasted past rows of mews houses in Jericho. As the traffic died away, he beckoned Kate forward to cycle by his side.

He scrutinized her face.

"So how've you been after Saturday? No aftereffects?"

"No." She shook her head. "How are you? You looked a bit surprised back there."

He shrugged. "Sorry. I didn't expect to hear from Marla again. I'm only going back to North Carolina to pick up my stuff. The last time we spoke she hung up on me shortly after calling me a 'motherfucking piece of shit,' if I remember correctly."

Kate sat back a little more comfortably on her saddle.

"So, why do you think she's coming over to London?"

"I really don't know. Anyway, it's not important. What is important," he said, turning onto a bridge, "is this. Right. So step three was jump-start Kate's survival instincts by completely terrifying her in an Oxfordshire village and nearly get brick on head for trouble," he said. "And tonight . . . step four: Kate fucks with the statistics and shows them who's boss."

"Oh, God," Kate said as Jago sped ahead with a grin. She picked up her speed to stay with him. At the point in the path where she had veered right toward Sylvia's last week, Jago forked left. Quickly, the path emptied of joggers and pedestrians. It was narrower, darker, overshadowed by the hanging branches of willow trees.

They passed a fisherman packing down a small red tent as he finished up for the day. With a sudden rush, she remembered Jack's sleepover. Her chest tightened again, and she tried to breathe through it. She could deal with it tomorrow. Now she needed to concentrate on tonight.

The lights of the last houses started to disappear behind her.

It was amazing how in Oxford, just a few hundred yards from the High Street, you could feel you were in the countryside. As the light dimmed, Kate fixed her eye on the reflective spot on Jago's rear mudguard. They cycled for five more minutes.

Then Jago stopped.

Kate braked behind him. He held up a hand as if listening to something, and put a finger over his lips to quiet her.

"What?" she mouthed.

He jerked his head toward an opening in a hedge. They pushed their bikes into it, laid them down, and emerged on the other side, into a meadow. Kate heard her feet squelch and looked down. This was wetland. Her nostrils filled with the potent smells of wild grass and water mint.

"OK?" Jago whispered.

She glanced around nervously. He took her hand. "Come on." They set off across the soggy grass, Kate feeling her fingers stiffening in his grip. He was so unselfconscious about these things. Why couldn't she be? With Hugo, she supposed, there had been no boundaries between their bodies, but this was new territory. A new hand, a new size, a new grip. Strange and foreign.

Two minutes later they arrived at a gap in the hedge. Jago peered through it.

"Come here."

He put a hand around her waist and guided her forward so she was nestled between his arms, with her back against his chest. She tried to concentrate on what he was showing her.

A small canal boat sat chained to the path. She could just make out its name—*Honeydew*—in faded yellow paint. Piles of logs sat on the deck. Plant pots were scattered across the top, some of them cracked, full of herbs and flowers. A dim light shone inside.

A figure passed across the window. Kate drew back.

"Someone's in there."

"Sh . . ."

He was a man in his sixties wearing a navy cowl-neck pot-ter's top. He had waist-length gray hair matted into dreadlocks, and a crumpled, round, red face.

Kate watched the man as he shut each pair of curtains on the boat. A murmur of a radio started up from within.

"What are we doing?" she whispered.

"You are going to steal his boat," he said with the same voice he'd used when he told her to take the dog.

Kate shook her head.

"Sh." Jago laughed. He pointed. A rowboat with a small outboard engine sat bobbing on the river. One end was tied to the canal boat, the other to a hook on the riverbank.

"No way," she whispered. "The dog was enough, Jago."

He squeezed her tight, his arm around her waist, his breath tickling her cheek. "It's just an exercise."

She turned her mouth to his ear, feeling his bristle brush her cheek. "In robbery?"

"No. Taking control of the numbers. You let these stats bully you. If you steal this boat, you change the crime statistics for Oxford tonight. I want you to fuck with them, like they're fuck-ing with you."

Kate shook her head again. "No. That's really horrible. I know what it feels like to have things stolen from you and I'm not doing that to someone else."

He thought about that. "OK, look. Kate. Have you felt any different since the other night? You're cycling on the road. That has to be good, yes? Trusting your instincts to keep you safe?"

She shrugged. He hugged her closer. It was all she could do not to turn around and kiss him again.

"Yes, but I'm still not doing it. I'm not going to be responsible for making him feel as terrible as I did when we were burgled."

Jago groaned in her ear. "All right, well, what if I told you that I chose this bloke on purpose?"

Kate glanced up at him, curious.

"That when I cycled past here a few days ago in the evening," Jago continued, his face pressed into her hair, "I saw him watching something dodgy on a screen."

She turned and saw his raised eybrow. "What do you mean 'dodgy'?"

"Er, child dodgy."

She gawked. "No!"

Jago shook his head. "Sorry, I didn't really want to tell you. But I was thinking about it this morning when I woke up—it's probably why he's moored out here in a boat on his own. He'll be trying to keep his head down if he's on the police radar, especially if he's been inside for it before. These guys have to live somewhere after they come out of prison."

Kate shook her head. "But if he's still doing it, we should call the police."

"Well, if you want to tomorrow, we can. But first I want you to do this. Because right now, this is about you, not him." He turned her by the shoulders back to look at the boat. "Now, listen, if he sees you, we'll run back to the bikes. But honestly, he looks so stoned, we could probably take his whole canal boat with him in it, and he wouldn't notice."

It was a funny joke but she didn't feel like laughing.

"Kate. Do it. We're on the right track here."

He stroked his hand down the side of her arm, easily, comfortably. She stood, watching the boat through the gap.

To her surprise she found herself, just for a second, intrigued instead of frightened at the unpredictability of the situation. Interested to see what might happen. After all, Jago was right, it wasn't as if she should be feeling sorry for the boat owner.

"Just do it, don't think about it," Jago said.

She felt herself move forward.

The man was whistling. She could hear him walking around inside, clattering some pans. Bastard, Kate thought, thinking of Jack. She used the thought to spur her on.

She crouched down in the hedge. Checking that Jago was watching, she crawled out onto the path as the dim light from the canal boat, diffused through red curtains, guided her.

The rowing boat bobbed on the current. Painstakingly, Kate moved one hand and one knee together at a time in tandem till she reached the metal rope cleat on the bank.

This was crazy.

Her breath coming in heavy waves, she fumbled her fingers, undoing the rope, trying not to think how deep the water was. The first knot came easily and she dropped the rope into the rowing boat. The freed end of the boat gave a buck of excitement, and glided away.

It was too late now. Kate sized up the other knot, at the canal boat end. She crawled forward, wanting to get this over and done with as quickly as possible. But when she reached it she saw it was a different type of knot. Tighter.

"Halfway there," Jago called quietly.

Kate glanced up at the canal boat to check that he didn't see her. It was a such strange concept. That the horrible man inside had no idea she was out here. That she was the bad person in the shadows.

She began to pick the second knot. Luckily, it came away more easily than she expected.

A loud bang exploded above her. A light burst onto the deck.

Kate's heart began to pound so heavily it felt like it had dropped into her stomach.

The man walked onto his deck. He coughed, and the faint smell of incense drifted toward her.

Kate crouched down, holding the loose rope. The urge to run overwhelmed her. But if she stood up, he'd see her. He'd be able to leap off the canal boat and grab her.

She lowered herself as flat as possible into the shadows, glancing with panic to her right.

The man doesn't know you're here, she tried to tell herself to calm her growing panic. Just like the teenagers in the village. You are in control. If you jump up now, he'd be more scared than you.

Kate began to count to calm herself.

One thousand, two thousand, three thousand . . .

She listened to the man picking wood off the woodpile, praying for him to finish and go back inside. A discussion program about the use of music in film on Radio Four blared from somewhere.

Radio Four?

Then there was a movement. Kate peeked up and saw, to her dismay, that the freed end of the rowing boat was moving farther away from the bank.

She shrank back down, clenching her jaw. If the boat owner looked up, and focused his eyes in the dark, he would see it. He would . . .

"Oi!"

The man's yell burst into the night.

"What you doing to my bloody boat? Who's out there?"

"I—I—" she began to stutter.

Before he could say another word, a dark figure came out of the hedge and ran straight up to the man.

"What the . . . Get off . . ." she heard the man growl.

She saw Jago reach the side of the little fiberglass canal boat and shove it hard. It moved only about a foot off the riverbank, but it was enough to catch the man off balance. He staggered one way, then the other, then flew over the side with a splash.

"Get in!" Jago yelled to Kate.

She pointed. "What? No! He's in the water!"

"It's shallow. Get in the boat," Jago said, running toward her.

Shakily, she did what he said, placing one foot inside gingerly, and gasping as the boat rocked underneath her.

"Fuck," Jago hissed, jumping in beside her. He grabbed her waist to steady her, sat her firmly on the bench, then reached for the outboard engine cord, still standing up. "That went a bit tits up."

"Jago. Stop . . ." she hissed as the boat roared into life.

"Get off my fucking boat!" the man shouted from the water.

Jago leaned over expertly and shoved them off the side. Quickly, he maneuvered the boat into the middle of the river, ignoring the impassioned yells.

Kate looked around frantically. "Jago. There's no life jackets."

"You'll just have to swim," he shouted. He sat down and accelerated the boat back up the river toward Oxford. Kate looked back. To her relief, the boat owner was pulling himself up onto the bank, his dreadlocks flattened around his ruddy face.

He looked like a tree monster.

Jago watched him. He looked like a child who'd done something very naughty.

She shook her head, checking back again to ensure the man had made it out of the water safely. He might be evil but she didn't want to be responsible for seriously hurting anyone.

They turned a bend, and the boat carried on, its cheap engine spitting and growling into the night. At a safe distance, Jago pulled into the bank to retrieve their bikes, then carried on, the bikes balanced in the middle of the boat.

After a moment, he cut the engine and pulled out the oars.

"Er, OK. Sorry about that," he deadpanned.

"I can't believe you, Jago," Kate exclaimed, looking around nervously. "We're going to get arrested."

"No we're not," he said, pulling back on the oars. "He won't call the police. Not with all those dodgy DVDs on his boat. He'll probably be scared that we're child-porn vigilantes who know what he's up to. In fact, I bet he'll move on down the river tonight before we go back to harass him any more—or he'll just hope that we're drunk students and go looking for his boat in the morning."

Unconvinced, she rested her head back and watched the thin bloodred stripe across the horizon to the west, as the last of the day's sky collapsed into embers. Jago rowed on.

She'd never met anyone like him. While her conscience was telling her that stealing this boat was wrong, whatever the owner had done, she trusted Jago. He'd run at the monster with the dreadlocks to protect her.

As Jago turned to check that the boat owner wasn't following on the bank, she appraised the neat shape of his close-cropped skull and the sharp cheekbones that always softened when he smiled, surprising her. She didn't know why, but instinctively, she knew that being around someone brave, if a little maverick, who was not scared of boundaries and rules, was exactly what she needed.

The ebb and flow of the oars through the reeds rocked her.

The boat moved on under the moonlight. The hard knot in her chest, as she thought about the man with the dreadlocks, started to soften. There was no point dwelling on it, or she would ruin the point of this evening. The man had climbed out of the river. And tomorrow, she'd call the police anonymously and give them a tip-off about what he was up to.

For now, she had to relax or she'd ruin this experience. She'd hardly been out in the dark for years, to say nothing of floating along on a magical river.

Kate concentrated on the navy sky above and the rich smell of foliage. It was so unusual for her to be out at night, she'd forgotten how water and trees shape-shifted and became charged with new meaning. How at night they displayed an entirely different type of beauty.

She had no idea where they were going, but for the first time since she could remember, it felt OK.

As they passed the spot where she'd seen the fisherman's tent, the thought of Jack and his nighttime sleepover pushed its way uneasily into her mind again.

So she tried something different. She concentrated on seeing Jack's sleepover from the perspective of tonight.

As Jago rowed toward a fork in the river, Kate told herself that if she denied Jack the chance to go to Gabe's and do something exciting and different, he would never have what she had now.

An adventure under the stars.

Jago rowed for another five minutes. The air was lush with the smell of foliage.

"Do you know why night smells different from day?" he murmured.

Kate shook her head.

"It's to do with convection. Heat moves molecules around in fluid. So when the sun's shining it stirs it all up, and the smells are diluted in the air. Then when night comes, the heat goes, and things stop moving. Smells become more intense."

"Really?" She nodded, impressed. "It's a shame."

"What?"

"That when we stop this boat how much useful stuff's going to be lost when we get onto dry land and I kill you for making me do this."

Jago snorted. She threw her head back, pleased she had made him laugh.

She opened her mouth to speak, then stopped.

"What?" Jago asked.

"I was just wondering, how did you get into academia?"

Jago carried on rowing steadily. "Well, my dad says that my brain just seemed to understand numbers from early on. I made him set me sums all the time. And I suppose I get the teaching thing from him—he teaches English, so do my sisters—and the maths stuff is probably from my mum's side. They're all doctors."

She tried not to give away that she already knew this. "And you didn't want to be a doctor?"

He shook his head. "No. I like working in a university. You get the freedom to explore areas you're interested in. Paid to go abroad. Long holidays. I'm sure that sounds very selfish, compared to my mum. She's amazing. She works with geriatric patients."

"But you do work for new governments in postwar countries—that's not selfish." Jago shot her a curious look.

Damn. Kate kicked herself.

"Did I tell you that?"

She pretended to look back at something in the water. "I don't know. Didn't you say you flew to developing countries, or something. I just thought that . . . ?"

"Oh. Yes. No, you're right. Yes I did." He nodded.

Silence descended upon the boat.

"You Googled me, didn't you?" he said after a second.

"No!" she exclaimed, mortified.

"Yeah, you bloody did. Don't worry. I'd probably Google me, too. Scottish skinhead with a penchant for dog-rustling." He wiped a fly from his face. "I'm going to do you later. Find embarrassing photos of you at school."

"Fuck off." Kate giggled. It felt good to swear at someone again without it holding any menace.

There was a small lane of water up to the right.

"That's it, I think," Jago murmured.

Kate saw a white jetty in the moonlight, up ahead of them. It sat at the bottom of the garden of an Oxford college, whose name she couldn't remember.

"Come on." Jago took the boat in, tied it up loosely, and climbed out. "We can hide out here for a while."

She passed out the bikes and the rucksack to him, then he held out a hand. She took it, glad to be back on dry land.

Jago took a blanket out of his rucksack and laid it down, then pulled out a bottle of red wine and two plastic cups. Kate was surprised. It was the kind of good French wine that Hugo used to buy in the old days. She had only vaguely noticed before, but Jago's T-shirt and jeans were always good makes. Expensive brands. Book deals in America and Britain, she suspected, sip-

ping her wine, probably meant he was far from being a poor
lecturer. Relieved, she realized that would make things simpler.

"You really think he might be looking for us?" she asked,
sitting down.

"Nah. He's probably still drying his hair."

"Don't," she said, feeling mean as she smiled.

"So," he said. "You did well. How do you feel?"

How did she feel? "Er . . . I'm not sure."

"Like a terrible person?"

"Would it be bad to say not really?"

"Not at all," Jago said, looking at the bottle with apprecia-
tion. She liked the way he did that, like Hugo would have. She
sipped her own wine, watching him. He was so like Hugo in
some ways. They were both people who created fun out of the
most mundane moments. But Jago had a love of adventure that
Hugo had never had. Then again, Hugo would not have stolen
someone's boat. He would have bought them a boat if they
needed an adventure.

Jago put down the bottle. "No. I think it's interesting," he said.

"Why?"

"Because I think normally you'd feel bad about doing something like that. You'd worry about the old guy, because you're a
kind person, but, in the context of what we're trying to do—"

Kate interrupted him. "It feels . . . I do feel bad about stealing a boat. But I know why we did this. And I suppose just for
once it feels nice. For it not to be me who the bad thing is happening to." She picked up a flat stone and turned it in her hand.
"Can I tell you something?"

"Hmm?" Jago asked. He sat closer to her, then lay back so
they were touching, side by side and looking at the stars.

"All evening, I've been worrying about Jack going on a sleepover in someone's garden. Worrying about the bad things that might happen to him outside at night."

She cringed as she heard her inner fears voiced for someone else to hear.

But Jago looked genuinely interested. "Ahah! And now you *are* that bad thing, outside at night? For someone else?"

She nodded and took another sip. It followed the last one to the back of her throat and gave her a little boost of courage.

"And how does that feel?"

"Empowering, I suppose," she said after a second. "In a very weird way."

"Did you ever feel like this before your parents died, too—anxious about things?" He rubbed his hand over his head, and she remembered the feel of it, the soft stubble under her fingers, and wanted to do it again.

Kate shook her head. "Oh, God, no. No. I didn't worry about anything then. Who does when they're a teenager? Plus we lived in the countryside. I rode horses—jumped five-bar gates, that kind of thing. Spent my teenage years bombing around country roads in Minis at ninety miles per hour with drunk farmer boys, feeling invincible."

"Seriously?" Jago checked her glass. There was a gentlemanly manner about him that reminded her of her dad.

"Yeah. And that's just the start of it," she said. "Me and Hugo were going to go traveling after uni but he stayed in London to set up the business, so I went with some friends. I did all sorts of stuff I can't even imagine now. Hitched through Vietnam. Bungee-jumped in Thailand. I even worked at a parachute center in New Zealand for three months as a receptionist. Learned how to skydive on my days off."

Jago's mouth fell open. "You're fucking joking?"

She giggled. "No, I'm a qualified skydiver—got my international license and everything, believe it or not."

"I've always wanted to do that. Kate, I'm impressed. So you weren't always such a wimp."

"Oi." She sat up and sipped her wine. "It's funny. I've been thinking a lot about that recently. How it felt."

"You haven't done it since?"

She shook her head. "I almost did. For my thirtieth birthday— a sort of symbolic reentry into the world after losing my parents—but it didn't happen."

"Why?" Jago shifted toward her so that his leg brushed against hers.

She tried to make hers relax against it, unfamiliar with the physical contact. "Well, I did a refresher course and went up in the plane. But the wind changed, and we couldn't jump. Hugo was watching me down below. Jack was with him. I think something rattled him. The day he died, he was trying to persuade me not to reschedule the jump." She lay back. "I sometimes think he had a premonition of death when I was up there." She looked at Jago. "Only it wasn't mine. It was his."

A crack came into her voice. She put down the glass, and sat up, biting the soft part of her cheek, cross with herself for tearing up.

That time was over now.

Jago gave her a moment, then touched her gently on the leg, as if he sensed that she was struggling.

"What's it like?"

"What?"

"Jumping out of a plane."

How long was it since she'd spoken about that time in her life?

"Oh, it's unbelievable. Like nothing else. There's all this noise from the plane engine, and you're sitting at the edge feeling more scared than you ever will in your life. Then you step out and throw yourself into this vast open space. You count slowly, and your parachute opens and you've survived. You're flying. And then there's this sense of total euphoria." She shook her head wryly. "Honestly, I can't even get on a bloody airplane to go to Spain now. Feels like another lifetime."

Jago rubbed her arm.

She wrinkled her nose. "One in a million."

"What?" Jago asked.

Kate looked up at the sky. "The chances of both your chutes not opening. It has to be someone, though, doesn't it . . . ?"

"Your luck is the same as anyone else's, Kate, that's what I keep telling you. The same as that old guy on his canal boat right now, thinking, 'Why me? Why my rowing boat and no one else's?' That decision was random. It wasn't about him in particular. Tonight you fucked with the crime statistics. Thefts in Oxford have just gone up, reported or not. It's that simple."

Jago stretched out his arms above his head.

Kate registered what he said.

"Hang on . . . you said it wasn't random. You said you'd chosen him because you knew he'd watched child porn."

A long, lazy smile appeared on Jago's face.

"Jago! Did you make that up?"

"Well—you wouldn't have stolen the boat otherwise." He laughed, grabbing her arm playfully.

"You . . . bastard . . . !" She shoved him away, and pointed up the river. "That poor old man! That's a terrible thing to say about him. And we knocked him in the water! He might have drowned."

"Listen. I wouldn't have left him if I hadn't been sure he was OK. I'm sorry. I just really wanted you to do it and I could see you were going to back out. It was a little white lie."

Kate tried to pull away, but Jago pulled her gently back down. "Listen, what's important is that you did it. You took charge of the thing that's scaring you—these stupid statistics. And you did. He'll be fine. We'll leave his boat here and he'll find it to-morrow. He's probably used to pissed students playing stupid pranks by the river at night."

Kate shook her head, refusing to talk. She pushed his hand away, and he returned it to his side. "So what about the woman with the dog—Margaret? Was that a lie, too?"

Jago shook his head. "No, Margaret is real—and I told her about us taking the dog as part of a probability experiment. Actually that was quite funny. She said she was glad I'd told her, she thought she was going doolalley."

Kate tried to work through the confusion in her head. He'd lied to her and made her steal the old man's boat. She should be furious. She knew she should be. Yet, she wasn't. He'd lied to help her. Deep inside, she knew he was right. Part of her had enjoyed being the monster in the dark and not the victim for once. And Jago had stolen the boat with her. Taken a risk to help her . . .

They lay there for a while, side by side, as they had done in the secret garden a week ago, but this time touching. Gradually, she became aware of a small patch of warmth on her skin. Glancing down, she saw that the little finger of Jago's hand, which was still lying on his side, had come to settle just where her sweater had ridden up, exposing an inch of skin.

On purpose or not, she wasn't sure.

She shut her eyes, listening to the distant sounds of traffic and chatter in the nearby High Street, savoring the sensation.

Willing his hand to move.

She wasn't even sure how it happened, when it did, but there was friction.

A tiny movement of skin on skin.

Kate heard her own breathing expand into the warm night.

And this time, when his hand moved, there was no confusion about his intention. Kate kept her eyes closed as Jago, slowly and quietly, trailed the edge of his nail across her side. She heard his weight shift. She knew he was watching her now.

He traced shapes on the skin under her sweater, his own breathing becoming louder close to her ear. This is strange for him, too, she reminded herself. His first time, possibly, with someone new since Marla.

Either way, he wasn't in a hurry. As if he sensed her self-consciousness at being touched after so long, he trailed his fingernail lightly and slowly across her stomach, giving her a chance to stop him at each border, his breathing gentle beside her ear. Higher and higher his finger moved, circling her belly button, tracing across the mild stretch marks left by Jack, up the sides of her torso, making her shiver, till she felt it trace its way across the bottom of her bra strap and wait there awhile.

He kept her gaze, watching, as he slowly lifted the cup of her bra with his finger, pulled it down. He waited for her to stop him. When she didn't, he moved inside.

Where his fingertip came, gently, to rest.

Kate inhaled deeply and lifted her head, seeking out his lips with hers.

Suddenly, a guitar began to play right beside them. They both opened their eyes and looked at each other, confused.

"Phone." Jago sat up, letting Kate go.

"Quick, in case the man from the boat hears it," Kate whispered, looking behind her into the meadow.

"Shit. Fuck," Jago swore, pressing buttons in the dark.

The screen went bright. "Fuck," he mouthed at Kate, holding up a hand. Jago jumped to his feet.

"Hello?" There was a pause. "Oh, hi. How are you?"

Kate sat up, straightening her bra and sweater. He rolled his eyes at her. "No, I did get it. I'm just . . . busy . . ."

Kate felt her heart sink. It was obviously Marla.

"Well, what do you mean, you're going to . . . ?" Jago's voice took on a stern tone. "That's not what we said . . . I mean. Look. Can I call you back in half an hour? I'm in the . . . library."

Kate froze. He shrugged a "sorry" at Kate.

"OK. Ring me then."

He put the phone down and sighed.

"Sorry!" He groaned. "I didn't mean to answer it. I pressed the wrong button." He looked at Kate apologetically, and rolled his eyes. He leaned down with a small groan and hugged her tightly. He looked around at the bikes. "I'm going to have to go and sort this out. She's a bit . . ."

Kate waved a hand. "Don't worry. It sounds complicated."

Jago sighed. "Trust me, it was. We spent last year flying back and forth across the Atlantic for the weekends to sort it out, then just arguing when we got there. But, listen, I do need to sort this out. Kate." He dropped his hand onto her cheek. "She wants to come to London tomorrow. There's no rush here, is there? We have plenty of time, yes?"

Tomorrow? Kate tried not to show her anxiety at the news.

Instead, she made herself nod and he pulled her up, and hugged her again. "She's not going to let this go, so I need to sort it so you and me can get on with what we're doing, OK?"

She nodded against his chest, realizing she was becoming more familiar with the shape, the wide, neat boxer's shoulders, the flat muscular wall of his rib cage.

It was time to take a risk. Move on. Trust someone.

"Hey, look," Jago murmured.

The rowboat was drifting in the current.

"We can still take it back. Do you want to?"

She thought of the poor man with his wet dreadlocks, and the truth was that she really did want to take it back. But this exercise was about making a leap of faith. The least she could do was try. As Jago said, he'd find it in the morning.

So she shook her head.

"OK, then," Jago said, packing up quickly and climbing on his bike. She followed. He leaned over and looked at her intently.

"You have amazing eyes, you know that?" he said. "I know it sounds cheesy, but I have to say it. I was trying to think what they remind me of. It was this lake I saw in India once at sunset. It looked like the water was made of liquid gold."

Kate tried to smile, her worry about life jackets and being arrested and drowning and trucks and sleepovers all put away for a little while, and replaced by one single thought: Marla.

23

Saskia turned Kate's dishwasher on, turned out the light, and shut the kitchen door into the hallway, eyeing the clock as she went.

Kate was late tonight.

Had she gone out with this Jago character after her therapy session?

Pausing in the hall to check there was no sound coming from Jack's bedroom upstairs, she walked into the sitting room and put her cup down. Turning on a late-night arts panel program, she sat on the sofa and pulled Kate's laptop onto her lap.

Her face was burning with embarrassment.

Images of what happened after work kept firing into her brain.

If she'd walked out of the office just five seconds later it wouldn't have happened.

But she didn't. And there, in front of her, on the High Street, was Marianne, her black bob shining in the sunlight, carrying a dry-cleaning bag. Probably, Saskia thought bitterly, containing her dress from Christian's thirtieth birthday party that Saskia had not been invited to.

"Oh," they both uttered awkwardly, stopping face-to-face. "Hi."

Marianne glanced about nervously, as if seeking an escape route. "How are you, Sass?" There was a chill in her voice. They had been good friends for years, but Christian was Jonathan's best friend. It was clear where Marianne's loyalty lay.

"Good, thanks. How was your, um, birthday?" Saskia said, before she could help it. "Good," Marianne replied quietly. "I'm sorry I didn't . . . it's just, with Jonathan and . . ."

Saskia couldn't help herself. "It's fine. Marianne, how is he?"

Marianne pulled a face. "OK, considering."

Saskia felt a touch of hope. "Considering? You mean, considering the divorce?" she asked. Was it possible Jonathan was having second thoughts?

Marianne shook her head sharply. A shadow of anger cast across her face. "No, Sass—considering what you did to him." They regarded each other nervously. Marianne looked up the road. "Listen, I'm sorry, but I've got to get the six o'clock train back." She lifted an arm awkwardly. "I better go."

"Bye."

Saskia nodded, stunned. Jonathan had told Marianne? He'd sworn he'd never tell anyone! What, now the divorce papers were signed and the money was amicably divided—including the deposit Richard had given them for their house—he was breaking his promise?

Saskia watched Marianne marching down the road, terror creeping over her. Marianne and her husband, Christian, used the same contractors as Dad. If they knew what she'd done, it wouldn't be long before Dad did, too.

*   *   *

Saskia took a sip of tea, and sat back on Kate's sofa. Her eyes felt dry and sore. She imagined Richard's face when he received the news. Jonathan had been a coup for him. Bright, well connected, and successful on his own terms, yet never a threat to Dad. Everything Richard had wanted in a son-in-law. A perfect marriage to boast about at the golf club. Divorce had most certainly not been in Dad's plans.

Saskia stared at the laptop. If ever she needed to get away from Richard, it was now. Pulling up an application page, she read through what would be required of her.

Hugo had escaped. Now it was her turn.

It took Saskia half an hour to complete the first part of the application. As she stood up to fetch more tea, she heard a movement above her.

"Where's my mum?" a voice said.

She looked up. Jack was leaning over the banister in his pajamas.

"Snores—you've got to get to sleep! It's half-ten on a school night. Your mum will be cross with me if she finds you up."

"Why's she so late, though?"

Saskia sighed. Why did Kate always have to lie to him? "She's just out with some friends."

He gave her a look that said they both knew that wasn't true.

"Or one friend. I'm not sure, really. Maybe someone she works with?"

"Mum works at home. By herself."

Saskia exhaled and sat on the bottom step. Bloody Kate. She tried to sound reassuring.

"Listen, Snores. Don't worry too much about it. If you want to know where she is, just ask her. Going out is a normal thing for an adult to do. You're just not used to her doing it, that's all."

He shrugged.

"What's that you're reading?" she said, trying to distract him.

"Found it in the shed. It's about maths and stuff."

"Is it, now? Your dad was good at maths, too. You get it from him. Time for lights out now, so see you later."

He stood there stubbornly.

"Jack, what's the matter? Are you hearing noises again? Want me to check in your wardrobe?"

He shook his head. "But who's she gone out with?"

Saskia stood there, tired of being the go-between. Kate needed to sort this out. "Listen, your mum will be back soon. You can ask her tomorrow, OK? Now, listen, I have work to do. I'll come and check on you in a minute."

She waited till he disappeared, then went to switch on the kettle. She checked the clock yet again, irritated with Kate. It was nearly 10:45.

Where was her sister-in-law?

Magnus sat on the other side of the wall, upstairs, reading through Saskia's application on his link to Kate's laptop.

Interesting.

Hopefully, she'd come back soon. He liked this blond one. Liked watching her close up on the screen. Those big green eyes and that little worried face that you just wanted to squeeze into a smile.

He stopped and picked up Jack's cricket ball from the floor of his bedroom, and threw it up in the air, and caught it.

Next, he flicked onto Jack's Facebook page, and then onto Jack's friends' pages.

His pale eyes widened behind his glasses as he looked at one belonging to "Gabe." What was this? Sleeping on a trampoline on Saturday night. Out in the garden?

Magnus whooped loudly. A door slammed.

He made a face at the wall. These students weren't being very friendly to him. One of them kept asking him suspiciously which course he was doing at Oxford Brookes, because they never saw him there. He'd made up something that sounded real: integrated visual computer studies. "The smell comes right into my room," he heard the boney one whine in the kitchen last night.

Never mind. This would all be over soon.

24

It was Friday afternoon, and the traffic was light.

Kate coasted down Headington Hill so fast that the wind pushed back the hair below her helmet. A supermarket delivery truck overtook her, only feet away, but she hardly noticed.

Her mind was elsewhere.

It was three days since the night she and Jago had stolen the rowboat.

Three days without a word.

Kate checked over her shoulder, then pulled out past a man in a T-shirt and a secondhand suit on an old bike who was putting his brakes on every few seconds.

She moved back in, and carried on sailing down the hill.

No, not a word from Jago since they'd ridden back along the river path to Blackwell's on Tuesday night without even a suggestion of when they'd meet again. They'd kissed again as he tied up his bike, but he sounded distracted when he said, "You did well, safe home."

Kate coasted through the green light at the bottom of Headington Hill, cycled in a steady rhythm toward Magdalen roundabout, sailed around it, and headed over the bridge and up the High Street passing the grand frontages of some of Oxford's most famous colleges without a glance. Three minutes later she stuck out her hand at Carfax crossroads, waited for the traffic to break, turned right, and dismounted.

And finally paused for breath.

She looked around.

Cornmarket was packed today. The tidal pattern of the city was changing again. Tourists were starting to outnumber students, signaling the start of summer. It was unusually warm, and legs were making their first nervous outings of the year in a variety of shorts. Kate took off her helmet and looked around, hoping for a glimpse of that cropped head or a reassuring snatch of Scottish accent. She tied her helmet to her bike, and allowed herself a little internal self-congratulation. Two-and-a-half miles today. The farthest she'd cycled for five years on the road nonstop. And the fourth time she'd managed to cycle in traffic without stopping. All since stealing the rowboat on Tuesday night.

Kate chained up her bike at Carfax. The numbers were quiet, too. Present but less insistent.

And it was all thanks to Jago.

Who'd bloody disappeared, it seemed, presumably with Marla.

Kate yanked the chain harder than she needed to, to check the bike was secured properly, then stood up and walked off down Oxford's main shopping street, trying to put Marla out of her mind, at least for the next ten minutes.

Winding her way through the tour groups and parents with

strollers and boys on skateboards, she reconsidered the revelation she'd had only twenty minutes ago. She'd been standing in a line to buy a chicken from the organic butcher in Headington to roast for Jack tonight. She'd been thinking about telling him about her new idea to have a weekly movie night at home for the two of them, and showing him the film she'd bought, when, out of the blue, she suddenly remembered something.

There was a clue about where Jago might be.

A clue that, for a moment, at least, would give Kate a break from the film that had been running in a loop in her own head for three days. "Based on a true story," it could have been billed. It started with the facts. The scene where Jago disengaged from her on the jetty that Tuesday night, as the significance of Marla's second call finally registered on his face.

His ex-girlfriend desperately wanted to see him after three months.

The next scene had him waving Kate off before heading into Balliol to call Marla to find out what was going on. "I'm pregnant," Marla said, in Kate's best American accent. "From our last night together. I need to see you." In Kate's imaginary narrative, Marla had then jumped on the red-eye from Paris, while Jago had driven straight to Heathrow. He had arrived to see Marla standing wanly at a distance. Not tall, dark and skinny, like Kate, but petite and curvaceous, with white-blond hair, dark eyebrows, and a cute little nose. They had run to each other, tears spilling down their faces, as Marla declared that she wanted to give it another try for the sake of the baby. She missed him. She'd move to Oxford, Edinburgh, anywhere, to be with him. It didn't matter how darn cold and damp it was.

And that was it.

The end.

Kate moved sideways to avoid a man drawing an image from a famous painting on the sidewalk in chalk.

But then, in the butcher's today, as Kate had looked down at the Dr. Martens of the student in front of her, she remembered.

Her ankle boots.

Jago had put her ankle boots in his bag that Tuesday night to take to the shoe-repair shop for her the next day, because it had been closed.

So if she were right, if he had driven off to London on Tuesday night, and been lying blissfully in Marla's arms ever since, Kate's boots would still be in his rucksack, lying abandoned in haste in his room.

Or . . .

Kate prayed.

The little shoe-repair shop loomed ahead of her at the end of Cornmarket, its window half the width of the neighboring French children's boutique and organic café.

Kate turned into a scruffy entrance, shuffling sideways to avoid hitting a rack of umbrellas and shoe polish right inside the door.

The shop was gloomy and cramped. It appeared empty at first. Then a movement behind the counter told her she was wrong. A tiny, ancient man with gray hair slicked into a sculpted wave on his head stood behind the counter. He was looking down at something with great effort, like a tortoise in its shell. He lifted up his head to peer at her through his glasses.

"Oh. Hi," Kate exclaimed. "I was just wondering if my boots were ready. Black ankle boots, should be under the name Kate?"

The old man stopped. He wiped his hands on his apron, and turned slowly, a deep bend in his back, to a shelf. He rummaged through a pile of plastic bags, then brought one out.

Kate's heart leapt.

"Sorry," she said to the elderly man as he handed them to her. "Do you know what day these were brought in? I can't remember myself," she bluffed.

The old man's whole body looked like it was sighing. He peered at the ticket.

"Wednesday," he said.

She smiled. So Jago hadn't gone straight to London the night of the canal boat. She could erase that awful scene from the film.

"How much do I owe you?" she said brightly.

"Ten pounds," the old man said weakly, as if he was too exhausted to add "please." She handed him a note, thanked him, and headed out of the shop, boots in tow.

Jago had still been thinking about her—on Wednesday, at least—regardless of Marla's intentions.

Kate returned up Cornmarket to Carfax, and retrieved her bike. She was about to turn back to Headington to buy her abandoned chicken, when a thought occurred to her.

Perhaps Jago had never gone to London at all.

Perhaps he'd said "no" to Marla on the phone that night, that he didn't want to see her. That he'd moved on. Met someone new? Perhaps he was sitting in his room right now working. Thinking about Kate. Planning their next night out.

She looked over her shoulder.

If she went back down Cornmarket, she could take the route past Balliol back to Headington.

What harm could it do?

Kate turned, a flutter of anticipation in her stomach. Balliol's entrance was just visible from here. She cycled over to the left side of the road, and took her time approaching the porter's gate. The gate was open for visitors, half of its wooden arch pushed back, revealing manicured lawns beyond.

She glanced through cautiously.

The wooden gate was as impenetrable to casual passersby as a castle keep. To gain entry, she'd either have to ask for Jago blatantly at the porter's lodge, or pose as a tourist and pay an entrance fee. Either way, if she did see Jago, they'd both know there was nothing coincidental about it at all.

She couldn't risk it.

She'd just have to hope that he'd spring one of his last-minute calls on her when she was least expecting it. And pray that in the meantime, she didn't spot Jago and Marla rocking around town like the young couple from the other week, all tousle-haired and fresh from bed.

It was just as Kate was starting to accelerate up Broad Street back to Headington that she heard her phone ring.

She stopped abruptly, forcing the cyclist behind to swerve around her with a cross look on his face.

She took the phone from her pocket so fast she nearly dropped it. Fumbling, she managed to push the "answer" button.

"Hello?" she said hopefully.

"Kate? It's Gill."

Shit. Gabe's mum. They'd been swapping phone messages all week, and she'd forgotten to try her again today. "Hi, Gill."

"Hi-ya," Gill answered in her lazy voice, tinged with its student-protest, self-righteous edge that Kate suspected she kept firmly as a rebellion against ever growing up, despite being close to her forties.

"Calling about tomorrow night," Gill's tone was antagonistic. "Kate. Listen. Before you say anything, they'll be fine, love."

Kate took a breath to calm the irritation Gill always provoked in her. "I'm sure they will be, Gill. It's just, Jack said they were sleeping outside? By themselves?"

Gill gave a little tinkle of laughter, her humor at Kate's concerns clearly being relayed with exaggerated facial expressions for whoever was in the room with her. She then turned on the slow, patronizing voice that she presumably used for the elderly people she cared for at the retirement home in Cowley—probably irritating the shit out of them, too. "Listen, love. They'll be right outside in the garden at the back. It's not exactly the middle of a war zone. They're really looking forward to it, Jack especially."

Kate grimaced into the phone. She hated it when Gill did this. Implied that she knew what Jack wanted better than Kate. It was too painful to believe that Jack's guard might come down in Gill's noisy, messy, laid-back house, with its Indian throws and candles and general air of stoned inertia, in a way that it never did with Kate.

When Kate said nothing, Gill carried on. "Honestly, Kate, love, I can hear you worrying. You worry too much."

Kate felt her hackles rise. If she said no, Jack would never forgive her. He might even mention it to Helen, who would in turn accuse Kate of stopping him having fun at what Helen would surely perceive as a "harmless" sleepover. She sighed. "OK, then."

Gill hesitated, clearly shocked. "You're all right, then?"

"I said, it's fine."

"Ooh. Well, that's a first!" Gill exclaimed in what was supposed to be a playful voice. "We'll send him back with Gabe on Sunday, yeah?"

"OK, bye." She took a deep breath. "Thanks."

She ended the call. "It will be fine," she whispered to herself. "You are not cursed. Let Jack have his adventure, like you had

yours by the canal boat. Just because he's outside does not mean
he'll be in danger."

Yet the anxiety was flooding her in a way it hadn't done for
days.

She couldn't slip backward. She couldn't.

She needed to speak to Jago. She rang his number.

To her consternation, it went straight to message. She took
a deep breath.

"Jago. It's Kate. I'm outside, just passing Balliol. Just wondered if you fancied a coffee or a drink or something." She
paused, aware of the panicked tone of her voice. "But maybe
you're not there, so . . . don't worry."

She pressed the red button, and was about to put it back in
her pocket when it rang.

"Kate? It's Jago," said a Scottish voice.

"Oh. Hi," she said, relief flooding through her to hear his
voice. "Sorry, I just . . ."

"No, it's fine. It's great to hear from you. It's just that I'm in
London at the moment. I'm not there."

She paused, shocked. She was right. He'd gone to Marla.

"Oh, well, don't worry, I just . . ."

"No, it's fine. How are you? Not been arrested by the rowboat police yet then?"

She forced a laugh. "No." She tried to think of something
else to say but all she could think of was Marla sitting right
beside him.

"Listen. I'm glad you rang. I was going to find you later anyway. What are you doing tomorrow night?"

She moved to let another cyclist past. "Um, I haven't decided yet. Jack might be going to that sleepover I told you about
but . . ."

"Brilliant," Jago said. "So you're going to let him go? Well done. Fancy coming up to London then?"

She pushed her hair away, recharged with the anticipation of seeing him again. "Uh, I don't know. What did you have in mind?"

"Ah! Step five of the experiment, of course."

The thought of seeing him tomorrow thrilled her so much she didn't allow herself to feel nervous about what step five might consist of. "Yes."

"Excellent. Well, can you meet me at . . . hang on, let me just check this . . ." She heard a rustle of paper. "Highgate tube?"

Kate frowned. Highgate? That's where she used to live.

"Or, if you don't fancy it we can wait till I get back to Oxford next Friday. . . ."

He was in London for another week? Could she do this? Leave Jack outside on a trampoline at Gabe's, and go to Highgate?

"No. I can come," she said.

"Great. I don't know what time yet so I'll ring you tomorrow. And don't worry about getting home. I've got the car, so I'll run you back to Oxford afterward."

Kate nodded. At least she would only be around the corner from Jack on Saturday night. "Oh. OK. Great, see you then," Kate said.

"See you then!"

She put her phone away thoughtfully.

Highgate.

She tried to remember. Had she told Jago that she and Hugo lived there, that night they were in the secret garden?

And why hadn't he mentioned Marla?

She got on her bike and cycled home, arriving back just before Jack and Gabe.

"Did you talk to Gabe's mum?" Jack called out as he came in, taking off his blazer.

"I said yes. But God, Jack, I'm trusting you. If there's any funny business with Gabe or Damon. I mean it. You stay on that trampoline and don't move, unless it's to go inside."

She watched his face, waiting for him to explode with delight. And he did smile, but a flicker of something else passed across his face.

"Jack?" Kate asked uncertainly. "What? You do want to go?"

"Yeah," he said, putting his bag down, and running into the living room to switch on the television.

Confused, she stood in the hall trying to work out what she'd glimpsed in his expression, and couldn't. To her sorrow, Kate realized she'd lost so much precious time with Jack over the years, she couldn't read him. She couldn't read her own son.

Determined more than ever to change now, she absentmindedly dropped her bag and set off up the stairs to check train times for London.

In her haste, she didn't see the cricket ball tucked in on the stairs. She didn't see it till she stepped on it as she ran, and her foot skidded away behind her, forcing her forward with a jerk.

"Argh!" Kate shouted. Her hand shot out, and caught the banister, taking her weight just before her jaw came in contact with the stairs. Her bent leg banged into it instead, sending a sharp pain through her knee.

Magnus saw Kate arrive back home, then the boy, in his school uniform, with his friend. They waved briefly at each other, then he entered the house.

Magnus sat back, fingering the silver necklace he'd taken this afternoon from that brunette woman's house on Walter Street. The window had been open again, so it was easy. Took him two seconds to lean in and whip away her bag. He also had her phone, which had some interesting photos on it. Very interesting photos.

He sat on his unmade bed, flicking through it, eating a chicken dish he'd found in Kate's fridge. It was good. He'd taken five spoonfuls then wiped around the top with his finger before he put it back in the fridge so that the previous tidemark disappeared and didn't give him away.

Suddenly, a movement caught his eye on the computer. He sat up and saw the skinny woman, Kate, had opened her own laptop and was glaring at him crossly. He jumped back, covering his mouth with his hand, for a second thinking she could see him.

"Jack," she was shouting behind her. "You must have left it on the stairs. You have to be more careful. I nearly broke my neck on the bloody thing."

Magnus laughed out loud gleefully, trying to listen to the boy's protests that it wasn't him, as he came up the stairs to see what had happened. It had worked!

"Careful, lady. Don't want to have an accident," he said to the screen.

Then he told himself off. He'd have to be careful, too, with his little games, or the long-term planning would all be for nothing.

25

The next morning, Jack jumped out of bed, almost banging his head on his bookshelf in haste. Ten past nine, his Arsenal clock said. The earliest he'd been up for a long time on a Saturday morning.

He grabbed the curtain and looked outside, squinting.

It was sunny.

He frowned.

Ever since the year-eight boys had been on Gabe's Facebook again this week, saying they were definitely coming on Saturday night, he'd been hoping for two things. One, that Mum wouldn't let him go to Gabe's and he could blame it on her; or two, that it would rain today and they couldn't sleep on the trampoline.

Jack opened his wardrobe to find his jeans.

His sneakers were lined up again on the bottom shelf, not how he'd left them. Had Mum been in here, rooting around in his things to see if he had any secrets?

With a gulp, Jack thought about his Facebook page. The last time he'd used it on her laptop when she'd been out, he'd forgotten to click on the "clear history" button, and it was just luck she didn't find that he'd been on it. Jack bit his thumbnail. If she ever found out . . . He couldn't bear to think about how worried she would be. Now that he'd glimpsed his old mum again in the kitchen, he wanted her back twice as much.

Feeling a little sick, Jack put on his T-shirt.

He padded to the door, and opened it quietly in case Mum was still asleep. Her door, however, was open, her bed already made. The men had come to take away the gate yesterday when he was at school. He perused the holes in the ceiling and floor they had filled in with plaster yesterday. He and Mum hadn't even discussed it at dinner last night. The gate had just gone. There were other things to think about anyway. The year-eight boys, obviously, and the roast chicken and the rhubarb crumble that Mum had made, that was so delicious, he'd had two portions of each. The film that she'd surprised him with was good, too. Not that Mum had properly watched it. It was supposed to be movie night for the two of them, but he saw her drift back and forth to her secret place in her head, and back in, but at least she was trying.

Jack started to pad across the hall to the bathroom when he heard Mum's mobile ring down below in the hall.

"Oh—hi, Jago. . . ." she said in a happy voice.

Jack stopped. The floorboard creaked heavily.

"Oh. Hang on," Mum said, lowering her voice. He heard her move to the sitting room and shut the door.

Quickly, Jack tiptoed back into his room. Very carefully, he crouched down, lifted his rug, and lay down, his ear at the gap in the stripped floorboards.

"Uh, eight? That should be OK," came a muffled voice from the room below. "Should I bring anything?"

There was a pause. Then his mother laughed.

Jack put his hand flat on the floor.

A proper laugh.

But not with him, with this man called Jago.

Jack half-crawled to the bed, retrieved the book from the shed, and checked the name.

It was him.

He flicked to the man's smiling photo.

Was this the "friend" Mum was out with when Aunt Sass was here the other night?

He flicked through the pages, reading some of the numbers.

That was interesting.

Picking up a red felt-tip that was beside his bed, he marked something in the margin.

"Jack!" his mum shouted. "I'm going to head up to London for the evening to see an old friend while you're at Gabe's. What time are you going?"

An old friend? Jago wasn't the name of any of her and Dad's old friends who sent him birthday cards. Why didn't she just say "friend"?

"Six."

"Could we go slightly earlier?"

"Probably," he replied, his stomach starting to hurt.

Before he'd just been scared of the year-eight boys, but now he was worried about this Jago man, too.

He didn't want Mum to go.

Mum came downstairs at five o'clock, wearing black jeans and her old black leather jacket with a hoodie underneath. She had makeup on her eyes again, and her lips were pink and shiny. She smiled that nice bright-eyed smile again.

"Do you need any help?" she asked, pointing at Gabe's books, which he was trying to wrap. "No, thanks," he said even though he'd had to rip off the sticky tape twice because it kept wrinkling up.

"Well, we better get going," she said, putting on her ankle boots. Jack watched her.

He wanted to tell her so badly about the year-eight boys.

Yes, Gabe would be furious at him, but anything right now was better than knowing the year-eight boys were coming in the middle of the night, when all the adults were asleep.

Could he tell her? She had been better recently. Maybe she wouldn't panic. Maybe she'd just be calm and talk to Gabe's mum about it and it would be OK. And she wouldn't go to London.

Jack took a deep breath.

"Mum?" he started.

"What the hell is this?" she exclaimed.

She was staring at her ankle boot, turning it sideways.

"What?" he mumbled.

"The heel's too short. Has he given me the wrong ones back?"

Jack shrugged.

Kate whipped off the boot and looked inside. "That's so weird. They're definitely my boots but that old man's chopped about an inch and a half off the heel. How strange."

"What do you mean?" Jack said, starting to feel cross with her. He was trying to tell her something important and all she was thinking about were boots and dressing up for this Jago Martin.

She shook her head in confusion.

"Can you still wear them?"

"Good question."

His mum stood up, flexing her toes inside the black leather, and moved from foot to foot. "They actually still work because the leather's so soft. It's odd, though. Maybe the old heel was so worn down he had to make them shorter. Never mind."

She picked up her bag, and put her hand on the doorknob.

"Right—sorry, Jack, what were you saying?"

Even though they had been shortened, the heels still made her taller. She looked pretty again, Jack thought. Damon's big brother Robbie had said she was "hot" the other day, and he supposed that's what he meant, too.

How come this man Jago could make her happy, but he couldn't?

He tried to think. If he did tell her about the year-eight boys now, it might ruin everything.

He realized she was regarding him closely. "Jack? Are you OK? If you don't want me to go to London, I won't."

He forced himself to smile. "I'm fine."

"Sure?"

"Uh-huh."

"OK. Got your stuff?"

He nodded.

Then, without warning, she pulled him in for a hug. Not an anxious, sweaty hug, but the type of kind cuddle Grandma gave him—soft and reassuring, where the adult was in charge. As he moved away from her awkwardly, she caught him on the side of the face with an unexpected kiss.

He guessed she was trying to find the right words.

"Jack, please, be sensible tonight. And if you're worried about anything—and I mean anything—call me, OK? I'll come straight back."

He went to pick up his bag. She carried on talking.

"You know what, Jack? After what's happened to you, I think it's amazing how well you do at so many things. And you have good friends, too. Dad would be so proud of you. And when I get back I want to tell you about two more nice things I've got planned. I really enjoyed movie night last night. I think it's time we had a bit more fun. Shall we do that?"

He turned to hide his face, feeling tears spring up.

"*Please don't go,*" he wanted to shout.

26

Kate arrived at Paddington Station at six thirty, having fought the urge twice to text Gill that Jack had the beginning of a cold so could the boys sleep inside tonight.

Don't think about it, she told herself.

As always, after Oxford, London appeared to be midtornado. Heels, suitcases, hands, and words blew in all directions. Laughter, yelling, requests for directions to the start of a new life, maps, interview suits, couriers, squealing brakes, and frustrated horns.

The mass purpose of intent of this massive city lifted her up and shot her along, like flotsam on surf.

Kate stood among the crowds feeling her energy levels instantly rising, her posture straightening out.

One word echoed around her head, as it always did when she arrived here.

Home.

*   *   *

The tube from Paddington to King's Cross was jammed. The Saturday shoppers and tourists were working their way around central London like giant multilegged creatures, carrying coffee, bags, maps, and matinee brochures, swaying from handles and racing for seats.

The last time she'd been here was a few weeks ago for the hospital scan. She had ridden amid the throngs of the tube, thinking London was where she and Jack needed to be again. Away from Helen and Richard's disapproving looks and endless excuses for popping in. Back in a world where life raced on, it didn't float.

But today, as Kate stood on the Northern Line platform at King's Cross, she felt less sure.

The Northern Line had been their tube, their carriage to Highgate.

The journey home.

It had been four years since she had been on the Northern Line. Four years since she had been to Highgate.

The sensation of loss was so sudden, Kate stumbled back when the first train came, and stood, back against the wall.

She let that tube go, and waited three minutes for the next, and then the next.

As a fourth train came, she steeled herself. If she was going to move on in her life, repair her relationship with Jack, start a relationship with Jago, she had to go and say good-bye to Hugo properly now.

So, when the fifth train came, she pushed herself away from the wall. She propelled herself through the doors before the urge to run took over, and sat down in the half-empty car.

*   *   *

The train kept stopping.

Each time, inside the dark tunnel, the window reflected back to Kate the reason why it had been four years.

The empty seat beside her, where Hugo used to sit.

Flashing at her as the train picked up speed again. Empty, empty, empty.

The seat of a ghost.

The hundred steep stairs from the bowels of Highgate tube station up to the pavement teetered above her.

If she shut her eyes, she could feel Hugo's hand on her back, pushing her up the stairs after a night in town, his voice echoing along the tiled walls.

"Come on, you lazy cow. Hurry up. I've recorded Match of the Day."

"Can I just say that I am not lazy—I am drunk."

"Lazy and drunk."

She touched the handrail where she had bent over laughing, as he waited, that sweet smile on his face.

"Come on, I mean it. Hurry up," he had said, with a slap of her butt. "Or I'll leave you here for the muggers."

"No, you won't, because if you do that, then you won't be getting any later."

Hugo had snorted. "Yeah, well, I'm not going to get any later, anyway, am I? Five quid, you're asleep on the bed with your jeans on three minutes after we get in."

And she had sniggered so hard, she'd bent up double, and

he'd given this sort of roar, and wrapped her up under his arm and raced her up the stairs, squealing.

Today, she walked the stairs alone, each one a mile high.

And then up the steep lane alone, toward Highgate Village.

Some of the Edwardian house fronts looked familiar, once owned by people she'd known. Anouk, the Dutch mum, from NCT; Jean from the Highgate History Society, who had told them so much about the history of their house; Hugo's old school friend Frank who had moved in with his wife, Sarah, just before Hugo was murdered, and joined their Tuesday night pub quiz team. Kate peered in and saw a child's bike. Were Frank and Sarah still there? Leading the life she and Hugo would have had?

She made her way to the top of the lane, and the busy main street of Highgate Village. Nothing had changed. Beyond it, at the bottom of the steep drop of Highgate Hill, lay central London miles in the distance, the skyscrapers like icebergs emerging from the Arctic mist of today's overcast sky. A couple in their thirties walked across the junction in front of her, both in well-cut black coats, the girl laughing, a flash of red lipstick and white teeth.

They could have been her and Hugo, on their way back from pushing Jack's stroller around nearby Hampstead Heath, cheeks flushed, eyes bright, venturing to buy cake from the deli before returning home. Or after a shopping trip to the farmers' market, Indian breads and Moroccan harissa in rucksacks on their backs, Hugo's arm around her shoulder, as they strolled along the cobbled, narrow streets of this old London village, with its walled gardens and studded wooden gates, pleased with themselves that after all that had happened to Kate, they had created a good life for their family.

"A fine, fun-loving, and hardworking young couple, ready to walk through life shoulder to shoulder," as her dad had said in his speech the night of their wedding, none of them realizing he would not be there to see it.

Just trying to make a good life for Jack.

The shutters were half-open.

It took her a minute to check, but they were indeed the ones Hugo had tracked down in the salvage yard in Enfield, and painstakingly stripped back to their natural pine in his workshop in the garden, one by one, then lovingly waxed.

The new owners had painted them white.

Kate walked around the square twice, fighting a new wave of nausea at the sight of it, peeking over at the four-story house from different angles. The half-open shutters on the ground floor revealed a glimpse of the jaw-dropping view across London at the back of the house. There was a dining table, just where theirs used to be. The table they had sat at talking about their plans, looking over the Soviet-scale 1970s estate in the distance, with its ever-changing life stories played out on stacks of balconies and in rows of windows, imagining how the magnolia tree would look in spring when its branches reached their own.

Then there was the front gate, where Kate and Jack and his nursery friend Olivia had sat at a table one hot summer day, selling homemade rose-petal and lavender "perfume." She had been a different mother then. One who helped Jack and a friend pick petals in the garden and make potions, then sat, laughing proudly, as he and Olivia sold it to indulgent neighbors and passersby for five pence "a squirt," before jumping in Kate's car and giving the proceeds to the local cat shelter.

Kate took a seat on the bench opposite and scanned the house further, trying to remember what it had looked like when those windows were full of chattering guests drinking champagne at Hugo and David's famous "open house" parties, to celebrate their latest restoration project and show house to prospective clients. It had been a different life. One she could no longer believe she'd been part of. Windows full of their friends and family, real-estate agents, architects, work contractors, old clients, new clients, lawyers, bank manager, Georgian Society friends; all of them drinking Hugo's fine wine, celebrating Hugo, David, and Kate's latest project and toasting the next. She glanced up to the square black roof and small windows of the Georgian attic. Jack's playroom. The place she would sit rocking him, looking down at his tiny face, wondering secretly if it would be possible to love her and Hugo's next child as much as she loved this one.

A child who would never now exist.

She wandered back through Highgate Village, listening to passing chatter about rugby scores and film reviews and property prices. The bulletin board outside the public toilet was crammed with notices. Hundreds of leaflets, in eye-popping colors fluttering off all sides of the board, offering sessions and lessons in tai chi, Japanese meditation, singing, Brazilian dance, osteopathy, theater, book groups, writing groups, mother and baby jogging, craniosacral therapy . . .

The endless promise of the city. A promise of an exciting race through life.

As Kate turned, she spied her old theater-actress neighbor,

Patricia, with her distinct gray beehive, emerging from the deli-catessen, chatting with a bespectacled man holding a Chihua-hua. Desperate not to be seen, Kate dived into the nearest pub and ordered a bourbon from a barmaid she didn't recognize.

Did any of their old friends even live here anymore?

She had stopped answering their Christmas cards years ago, tired of their awkward messages and the addressees on the en-velopes that made Hugo's absence even more obvious than it already was.

Mrs. H. Parker and Family.

Kate And Jack Parker.

The Parker Family.

The Parker Family Minus Hugo Who Was Brutally Murdered.

The old familiar thick belt of grief tightened around her middle and squeezed hard.

Kate jumped up and chucked back her bourbon.

No.

She had to get out of here.

Grabbing her coat, she walked out of the empty pub.

The sun had completely disappeared now behind the murky clouds gathering ominously above her, the early June air thick and warm. She ran across the intersection, picking up speed as she hit the lane back down to the tube again. Her newly heeled boots clicked on the pavement as she set off at a pace down the hill.

"Kate?" she heard Patricia shout, surprised, the well-enaunciated, loud vowels of the actress reaching out down the street to catch her.

She kept running.

She left Patricia behind.

Left Hugo behind.

Left it all behind.

She couldn't let herself feel the grief anymore.

It was time to move on.

This was not home.

London was not home.

This was a place of ghosts, and memories that had rotted like old fruit.

She had to find her way to the future.

She needed to see Jago.

Jago was the only person who could unlock her anxiety.

Jago was the key.

27

Maybe it was the change in the weather, but London looked monochrome compared to the pale gold of summery Oxford. Archway Road roared unpleasantly with thick lines of traffic. Flowers that had burst forth in bright shades in the unusually early summer sat with their heads bowed in the still, fume-filled air.

Kate crossed back over Archway Road and started down the steps in the hill toward the tube entrance.

"Please be here," she whispered.

She reached the bottom step and peered around to the left.

Jago was there, reading the *Guardian* just under the tunnel entrance at the top of the stairs leading down to the platform.

Just seeing him gave her back a surge of the strength she thought she'd lost today.

"Hi!" She had to stop herself from exclaiming too loudly, and walked toward him.

"Hey!" He was wearing the fitted dark jacket again over a T-shirt, and walking boots under dark khaki trousers. "You look nice," he said, giving her a hug. She wrapped her arms around him and stood there, against his chest, feeling the pulse of his body beneath. She waited a beat before pulling back.

"You OK?" He laughed, squeezing her gently.

"Hmm," she said, staying there. "Just glad to see you. Strange day."

"Ah," he said, rocking her gently. "Shit. Of course—Highgate. I didn't think."

She pulled back reluctantly. "I thought that's why you'd chosen it."

Jago shook his head. "No, not at all. It was actually Highgate Woods I wanted to bring you to. Sorry. I didn't even click that they are the same thing. I don't know London. Is it a bit close for comfort?"

She shook her head, relieved. "No. No, it's fine. As long as we don't have to go into the village."

"I think a drink's definitely in order. I saw a pub on the main road?"

She nodded.

And with that, he rolled up the newspaper, and offered her his hand.

She took it and walked up the slope with him, trying not to think of the hundred times she had done it with Hugo.

The pub was not one she and Hugo had visited, for which she was grateful. It was large and anonymous, with rows of tables and a sports screen in the corner. She sat down, and Jago went to the bar.

"What's that?" she asked as Jago rested two drinks on the table. He winked. "Whisky doubles. For courage." He looked around approvingly. "Nice. Good table. Not a toilet or fire extinguisher in sight."

She made a face at him but was secretly pleased. He was right. She hadn't even thought about it. She waited for him to take off his jacket.

"Aren't you warm?" she said, taking a sip. The whisky followed the bourbon down, igniting her insides.

"Yes. But I can't take it off."

"Why?"

He smiled mischievously.

"What? The jacket is part of the plan, too, is it? Oh, God. Is that why you told me to wear a hoodie?"

"All will be revealed," Jago said, sipping his whisky. "So, how've you been? You let Jack go on his sleepover then?"

She made a face. "I'm trying not to call the mum and make sure they're all right."

"Really? Well, don't. He'll love it."

She nodded. "But I am feeling good. Better."

Jago put down his glass. "You look much brighter." He looked at her appraisingly, then grinned and leaned forward and kissed her softly on the lips. "Sorry. Been thinking about doing that all week."

Kate blushed. If he'd been thinking of getting back with Marla he wouldn't have said that, surely? "Don't be sorry. Well, I don't know what you've done, but I'm really not thinking so much about the numbers at all. Just a few times a day and I can stop myself quickly."

Jago grinned. "Seriously? That's amazing, Kate. To be honest, after the canal-boat debacle, I thought you might pull out. . . ."

Kate sipped her whisky. "No, it's been a good week. The best

I can remember for ages—anyway, how are things with you?" She hesitated. "With Marla. What happened?"

Jago sighed heavily. She scrutinized his face, searching for something that might say: "Since I last saw you I have been in London making passionate love to my American ex-girlfriend, who has dropped the amazing news that I am about to be a father, so after tonight, you won't see me anymore—bye."

But there was nothing.

"Or should I not ask," she tried, searching for some sort of idea of whether it was really over or not.

He put his glass down. "I'll tell you later, I promise. Right now, however, we have my dastardly plan to carry out, so no distractions. I'm a bit nervous about this one myself."

"You're nervous? What the hell are we doing then?"

"Well, it's a bit risky, but as you've now foolishly revealed you do have a rather impressive adventurous past, I think we should go for it."

She grimaced. "OK. But can we please not do something illegal this time? I have to think about Jack. And no more boats."

Jago laughed. "Ah. OK. Well, what about bats?"

She thought she'd misheard. "Bats?"

"No bat phobias?"

She scrutinized his face. "Bats? No, but . . ."

"Good, because I'm taking you bat-watching in Highgate Woods. Have you done it before?"

She took another gulp of whisky. "No. I'm surprised you got tickets—don't you have to book months ahead?"

Jago winked. "Ah. Now, I said I was taking you on a bat-watch. I didn't say I was taking you on the official bat-watch. And it may not end up being bats that we actually watch."

"What do you mean?"

He took a final swig, put his glass down, and laughed. "Now, that would be spoiling the fun. Right, come on. Drink up." Jago looked outside. He checked his watch and looked back at her. He folded his arms on the table and leaned forward.

"Did I say, I've got the car? I can take you home afterward."

Kate felt her cheeks flush again, remembering the gentle trail of his finger across her body. He beckoned her, and she leaned forward to meet him for a second, longer kiss.

They entered Highgate Woods ten minutes later, through On-slow Gate, standing back to allow the last of the day's strollers and joggers and dog walkers out. A thick canopy of horn-beams and oak trees announced the start of the dense, ancient, seventy-acre wood. Jago pulled up his hood, obscuring his face, and nodded to her to do the same. "This way," he said, taking her hand.

There was a noise behind her. She turned to see two separate groups enter behind them. They were heading down the main path that she knew led to the ranger's office and café in the middle of the wood. One group consisted of two loud, well-spoken men in their late thirties, accompanied by—and happily ignoring—two boys a little younger than Jack, with fashionable long, shaggy haircuts and expensive fleeces, who fought with sticks and yelled at each other in confident miniversions of their fathers' voices. A few steps behind, on their own, were two women in their early twenties, speaking to each other in broken English, one with a Spanish accent, one possibly Polish. Lonely au pairs who've met through the school playground, Kate guessed. A night away from their host families for a welcome evening in the hope of making new friends in London, no doubt.

"Oi," Jago whispered, touching her arm.

"What?"

Keeping his head down, he motioned sideways. Checking that there was no one else behind them, and that no one from either group was looking back, he led Kate abruptly off the main path to a smaller one that forked to the left. Still holding her tight, he broke into a fast walk.

"Where are we going?" she whispered.

Jago held his finger to his lips. He led Kate down yet another path, then forked left again. Then, without warning, Jago pulled her off it.

A giant fallen oak lay on the ground. Jago crouched down behind it. How did Jago know where they were, she thought, doing the same. She'd come to this wood at least twice a week for years with Jack till he was five, and she still occasionally got lost, due to the lack of landmarks. Had Jago memorized a map?

"OK?" he said, turning around.

"Oh, yes. Having a lovely time, thanks," she deadpanned, swatting an insect away from her face.

He laughed. "It won't be much longer. The rangers are going to lock the park gates in a minute. They'll come through looking for stragglers, so stay down."

"They're going to lock us in?" Kate suddenly felt queasy.

He nodded.

On cue, a distant roar of an engine could be heard.

"Sh," Jago said.

The ranger's truck passed on the other side of the tree trunk.

She looked around at the darkening wood and thought of Jack. Quickly she whipped out her phone.

are you all right?

She waited, but nothing came back. He probably was too embarrassed in front of his friends to reply, she thought, putting her phone away, as Jago swatted at her hand for fear that someone might see the light from the screen.

Jago leaned in to her ear. "The bat-watchers gather by the wild-life hut, for the ranger talk. Then they give them bat detectors and they set off when it's properly dark."

"Right. So what are we doing? Stealing the rangers' sand-wiches?"

"No, but that's not a bad idea. I haven't had any tea."

She snorted suddenly, and put her hand over her mouth as he poked her in the side. "No. We're going to build on our canal-boat escapade. Step five: monster in the dark." He pointed at her. "That's you, by the way. You're the monster."

She regarded him nervously. "What do you mean?"

Jago pushed her hair away from her face, trailing a finger across her cheek as he did it. Any resistance she felt started to drain away.

"I'll tell you in a minute." He looked back up. "Right. They've gone. Scared?" he whispered.

"What do you think?"

She watched him take a black box out of his pocket. He shook it and it made a crackling sound.

"What's that?"

"Bought it off the Internet. Are you ready?"

He grabbed her hand and headed off through the woods.

They crept along the lane toward the rangers' hut, staying among the trees. Gradually, a murmuring of voices could be heard. The wildlife hut loomed ahead. Kate surveyed its familiar shape with a shock.

This place?

She'd completely forgotten about it.

A hundred potent memories flooded her mind. Jack had loved that hut. How many times had she lifted him up to see inside the wildlife exhibits, opening the nesting boxes and crouching down beside the stuffed fox.

As they crept along through the trees, even more intense memories flooded back to her. Jack had been a different child then. A child who whined like normal children. Cried if she didn't let him stop to color in the sheets the rangers left in the hut. Laughed if she chased him around the cricket field. Let her kiss his cheeks and ears again and again, when she caught him, then returned them to her, the kisses of a child; soft, wet toddler lips on her cheeks.

As Jago led her, Kate looked back in the direction of Highgate Village.

And then those men had come to their house one night and . . .

For the first time in years, a feeling of sickening loathing shot through Kate.

Maybe it was being back in Highgate after four years, but with suddenly painful clarity, she hated those men for what they'd done. At the time, they'd just stolen Hugo. Now she saw how much else they'd taken. They'd ripped Jack and her from their home and friends, from Jack's school, and forced them to move far away. They'd forced Kate to rely on Richard and Helen and turn into a nervous wreck. And Jack had become a fragile, frightened boy who could only rely on Richard, Helen, and his friends, even his friend's mother, because Kate was so messed up, so lost.

Kate tried to gather herself.

"OK. We'll wait here till they start moving across the field," Jago said, stopping behind another large tree.

"I still don't get this."

She heard the latent anger in her voice. It wasn't Jago's fault. He took her hands in his.

"Kate," he whispered. "You're convinced you're cursed. That you and Jack are fated to fall into the path of bad people. The burglars in Oxford. The poacher who shot the deer. The robbers who stabbed Hugo . . ." She winced. "But you're not. You've just had some really bad luck. We all do at some point. Now, you took control of the numbers at the canal boat. Now I want you to take control of those monsters that you feel are waiting for you."

Kate shivered, despite the warm air.

"How?"

"I want you to become one. See how that feels."

The sky was darkening now, but in the distance, crossing the wide open acres of the cricket field encased by forest, she could see the flashlight movements and shadowy outlines of a group of twenty bat-watchers. She could hear the boisterous boys with long hair shouting, and two rangers with flashlights talking.

"Them," Jago said, pointing to the young au pairs at the edge of the group.

28

Jack sat on Gabe's bed, looking out the window into the garden, the lacy outline of the tall trees waving against a darkening sky. Gabe's house wasn't as big as theirs but the garden went on forever, disappearing around a bend where Gabe's mum grew her vegetables, and down to the fence, where the trampoline lay, not visible from the house.

Gabe's mum hadn't been completely truthful with his mum about where it was situated. She'd made it sound like it was right outside the house, but you couldn't even see it from there.

The clock said half past nine. They'd had their pizza and watched a film. It was time for the sleepover to really begin.

Gabe's mum looked out his bedroom window.

Jack prayed, his hand on his stomach, trying to calm the fire inside.

"You know, I think it'll be fine, boys, yeah?" she said. "I

thought it was going to rain earlier but it seems to be holding off. You still up for it?"

Jack looked at Gabe, hoping he'd say he was scared of the year-eight boys, too, and call it off.

"Yeah!" Damon said, jumping off the bed.

"Yeah!" Gabe copied him.

Jack tried to smile.

"Right, you lot, grab your sleeping bags and let's go then, yeah?" Gabe's mum said.

"But what about . . . ?" Jack whispered to Gabe. Gabe tried to look unconcerned, probably because Damon was there. "It'll be cool, don't worry."

Jack stood up uncertainly, and they all trooped downstairs. Suddenly he didn't like Gabe's mum as much. His mum did lots of things wrong but at least she tried to keep him safe. Jack gathered up his sleeping bag and felt his mobile in his pocket, remembering Mum's words that he could call her.

It was hot and sticky outside. They tramped down the long lawn in the dark, till they reached the vegetable patch, the light of the house disappearing behind them as they turned around the bend. Damon was making silly faces in the flashlight.

Jack looked around, worried. Gabe's house was semi-detached with an alleyway next to it, so the year-eight boys could get down the side and climb over the fence.

"Right, you lot, have fun!" Gill called. "I'll leave the key under the mat at the back, Gabe, if you need to use the loo—no peeing on my carrots, yeah? See you in the morning!"

She walked off, leaving them to line up their sleeping bags on the surface of the trampoline. They put down their *Deadly 60* cards and flashlights.

"This is fucking wicked." Damon laughed, swearing like they all did whenever adults weren't there.

"Yeah!" Jack said. In the light of the flashlights, Gabe was smiling, but Jack saw him look at the fence a couple of times, too.

Jack checked his watch. Only 9:40 P.M. Nine hours to go. He crawled inside his sleeping bag.

29

The moon emerged from behind charred clouds, making it easier to see them.

The Spanish au pair was slightly heavy, wearing a light-blue coat, and she had a bright smile. The other one had a long dark ponytail and a square face, and was as skinny as Jack, and not much taller, either. Kate watched their awkward stances, knowing they were new to all this. They were still finding out where they fitted in, in this enormous metropolis.

"Why them?" she turned to Jago.

"Why not?"

"Because they look nervous and new to London. And they look like nice girls."

"You've got to get out of this way of thinking. Fate is fate. Behavior doesn't control it. We all have bad luck sometimes."

"But they're young. That guy on the boat at least looked like he'd . . ."

"Kate. You're not going to murder them. We'll be out of here in half an hour and I won't let anything bad happen to you, or them, I promise. I just want you to follow them for a bit in the dark. See what it feels like. It'll be good for you. Now, listen, I'm going over to the field."

"What?" she said, alarmed.

"It's so dark, the rangers won't notice me now. And whilst I'm doing that, I want you to head that way"—he pointed to the right—"and take the path behind the trees. Try to end up near the cricket scoreboard. Wait behind it. Just make this noise"—he made a five-beat clicking noise, with his tongue— "and I'll find you."

"But . . ." she began to protest.

He squeezed her hand. "Try it."

Kate tried out the noise, shaking her head at the ridiculousness of it. To her shock, he then finally unzipped his jacket, revealing underneath it a dark-green fleece. With his khaki trousers, he looked exactly like a Highgate Woods park ranger.

Jago pulled out the bat detector and slipped off into the dark.

She was on her own.

Half an hour, he said. And then it would be over.

Nothing bad would happen, he promised.

She waited until she could make out Jago's shadowy outline emerging from the trees. She could see a few of the bat detectors being pointed at the sky, and hear the young boys yelling as a crackling noise over the airwaves indicated a bat was near. Small groups scattered in the darkness, the two rangers accompanying some of them, as bats were spotted. It was then that she saw Jago do it. He stepped close behind the two au pairs who were at the edge, waiting for the young boys to share their bat detector. Jago smiled and handed the Spanish au pair his black box, checking that the rangers weren't looking over. The second au pair turned to them, and the three of them began chatting.

Uneasily, Kate crept to the rangers' hut, then down behind the cricket field.

She crept along the boundary, deep in the shadows. A gloomy circle of sky was visible above the tall trees around the cricket field. The shouts of the bat-watchers drifted across. The boys with sticks were just running around randomly, yelling and play fighting.

Kate found the scoreboard and settled behind it.

From here, she could see the wildlife hut again. So many happy memories with Jack in this place, destroyed.

She couldn't get Hugo's killers off her mind.

She pictured them leering at her, swearing at her in court.

Those angry fists they had gestured angrily with, the hands that had ended Hugo's life so cruelly. All Hugo had ever done was be true to his heart and loyal to his family. He had tried to lead a good life and they had viciously ripped it to shreds, like animals.

Kate watched the groups of bat-watchers.

It was an intriguing sensation, Jago was right.

None of them knew she was here.

She was the shape in the shadows, the noise in the wardrobe.

She was the one in the dark, waiting.

Just for a moment, she shut her eyes and let herself feel the sense of power.

She heard Jago's voice drifting toward her.

"You're right, well done. I'm Irish."

"Ah. From Dublin maybe?" the Spanish au pair said in heavily accented English.

"Very good!" she heard Jago exclaim. "Not many people would get that the first guess."

He was flattering the girl, Kate realized. Drawing her and her friend toward Kate. She peeked out from the scoreboard and saw Jago had taken them away from the crowd.

"I'm afraid we're not having much luck here," he said, pointing his fake bat detector box at the sky. "Probably the noise of the children. I think we might take a few of you up this path and see if we have more luck."

To Kate's amazement, Jago took his phone from his pocket.

"Janet. Robin here. I'm taking my group down Hazelnut Path. Do you want to bring a few others over here? See if we have better luck? . . . OK. See you in a minute."

He turned to the au pairs. The Polish girl was still holding the bat detector to the sky, giggling. It made a crackling sound.

"Well done!" Jago said. "There must be a bat up there. We're close," Jago continued. "Let's see what we can find."

And with that he led the au pairs off the cricket field and into a narrow path behind a row of hornbeams.

Kate paused, unsure of what she was supposed to do. So she followed them.

Jago kept talking to the girls, leading them onto an even narrower path, then left again. Soon, they were deep inside the woods with only Jago's flashlight for light.

"Up there," Kate heard him exclaim. Then Kate heard him say, into his fake phone, "Janet. Are you on your way? We're on Oak Path now."

The au pairs smiled innocently. "The others are just coming," Jago said. "You keep pointing up there, and I'll just pop back and shine my light to tell them we're here. You girls OK here for a minute?"

They nodded, beaming.

Kate watched. It was a strange kind of power, them not knowing she was here.

Jago walked down the path, and with the girls' backs to him, switched off his flashlight.

He took a quiet step into the trees about ten feet from where she stood.

He glanced around, and she made a gentle clicking noise with her tongue.

Jago came over, grabbed her hand, leaned right in to her ear, and whispered, "They're lost now. The bat-watch finishes in ten minutes. I'm going back to the field to fill out the numbers. That gives you ten minutes to follow them around a bit. Then come back to the field in case the rangers do a head count and we need to make up the numbers again."

"But what do you want me to do?" Kate whispered, glancing around the tree trunk at the girls, who were still looking up at the sky.

Jago breathed heavily into her ear. "Kate. Those men who killed Hugo had no morals. If you really want to know what it feels like, you have to lose yours. Even just for a few seconds."

A timid voice drifted toward them in the dark.

"Where is the man?"

The other one now: "Eh. Hello?"

"Do it, Kate," Jago murmured into Kate's ear, before disappearing off into the woods.

Kate stood uncertainly, trying not to crack the twigs under her feet.

She crept forward to the side of the tree trunk, and saw the girls glancing anxiously up and down the path, whispering to each other. The light from the fake bat detector sat under the

Polish girl's chin. Her eyes were round and scared. The girls turned around once, then again, looking disoriented. Then began to call out.

"Excuse me!"

"Hello? Sir?"

"Are you there?"

Kate stepped back. Her heel pressed into a twig. It broke in two with an explosive crack.

She saw the girls freeze.

"Hello?" they whispered.

Kate watched, knowing they would start to feel like she did in Chumsley Norton. Their senses heightened. They would hear every sound magnified.

One of the girls spoke breathlessly. The other took her hand, and they began tentatively to walk down the path away from the noise Kate had made, presumably trying to find their way back to the cricket field.

But they were going the wrong way.

Farther and farther into the woods.

Kate watched, knowing how they were feeling. Their hearts were thumping, their palms sweating, their hackles up, waiting for evil to jump from the shadows. Just like she did when she got home to Hubert Street every day. Walking around the house, shoulders hunched, anticipating the monster who would leap from behind a door, or inside a wardrobe.

Kate hung her head. She was so sick of being scared and traumatized because of those men who had killed Hugo and left him in a pool of blood for her and Jack to find. The poacher who had carelessly shot an animal and left it to die in pain, in the path of her parents' car. The burglars who had smashed her window and broken into her home. Together they had done this. Created the shadows in her bedroom at night that made her start awake with a gasp. The creaking floorboards. The broken windows and muddy smears, the imagined footsteps on the stairs.

The people who made her and her child sleep inside a cage in their own home.

Kate watched the girls and saw her own fear on their faces, as they tried to escape from the footsteps crackling twigs behind them in the woods.

Her footsteps.

The moon disappeared behind the clouds, shutting off the light.

Jack lay on his side on the trampoline, praying for it to return, listening for the footsteps of the year-eight boys on the lawn.

He glanced at his phone again, hoping Mum had texted him again. He lifted his head for the twentieth time, and scanned the fence at the bottom of the garden, as Gabe and Damon threw down cards and laughed more loudly than normal. He knew Gabe was as nervous as him but was trying not to show it.

"Be quiet," he wanted to say. "If someone comes they'll hear us. They'll know we're here."

"What's up, Jack-off," Damon said, whacking his arm.

"Nothing," he replied crossly, turning and looking at the trees.

"I'm going for a pee," Damon announced, climbing out of his bag and jumping off the trampoline.

"Me too," Gabe said, following him. "Deal the cards, J."

"Wait . . ." Jack said, trying to keep his voice calm. But they had already jumped off, making him bounce upward.

"Your mum said we couldn't pee on the carrots. But she didn't say we couldn't do it on the flowers." Damon was laughing.

Jack sat up nervously and gathered the cards.

Trying to focus on the numbers, he dealt them out, one by one, straining his ears for the other two.

And then he felt it.

The feeling from the river path. The heavy, blurred shadow that emerged from the bushes and settled its weight on him.

He tried to ignore it. But this time there was a different sound. A crack.

Jack spun around.

And there, looking through the fence, were two bright eyes.

Watching him. Not moving. Not blinking. Just staring at him through the crack.

Gabe and Damon were around the corner, giggling.

He grabbed his phone and looked at Mum's text message.

are you all right?

He wanted her here, now.

But she was in London with that man.

So he concentrated on Mum's words, shaking, as if she were here, and keeping him safe.

Kate didn't mean to chase the girls, she just did.

As she came up behind them, cracking more twigs behind the trees, they moved more and more quickly along the path. Their breathing was so loud she could hear it. The Spanish girl was whimpering.

She'd stop in a moment, she told herself. Just a minute longer to know what it was like to be on the other side.

"Who's there?" the Eastern European girl called out hopefully into the trees. When Kate didn't reply, she kept running.

Kate kept a few feet behind them. When they reached the top of the next path, they came to a fork.

The girls backed against a tree at the side of the path, and looked left, then right.

Kate watched as their faces turned toward her and caught a shaft of moonlight along the path.

They looked terrified.

Kate stared.

Is that what Hugo had looked like in his last moments? Eyes bulging, forehead sweating?

Is this what her parents had looked like as their car lay up-turned in the river, the water rising?

Why had the monster of fate done this to everyone she loved?

The truth would not leave her alone. As she watched the girls, she realized she had believed what she had wanted to believe, because it was endurable. She believed that her parents had died instantly before the car sank in the river. That Hugo, big, brave, and ebullient Hugo, had fought those men to the very end, until he had fallen fatally, thinking of her and Jack in his last seconds.

Kate looked at the fearful au pairs, frantic, gasping, desperate for help, their dignity stripped away like animals.

They were both whimpering now. The Spanish girl opened her bag, and took out a mobile.

She was going to call someone.

Alarmed, Kate tiptoed forward till she came silently to a stop behind the tree where the girls now stood, their backs against the trunk, watching the path.

If the girl rang someone, this would be over in minutes.

"Say to him to ring the police," she heard the Polish girl whisper.

Seconds, even. The police would contact the rangers straight-away.

Can you do it, Kate? Jago's words came back to her. Have no morals? Even just for a few moments?

The Spanish girl began to shakily tap numbers into her phone.

Predators have no morals.

Tap, tap, tap . . . One, two, three numbers . . .

Behind the girls, Kate lifted her hands, knowing that all she had to do was grab their shoulders in this dark forest, and they would feel the kind of terror that had haunted her so many times. Yet this time, she would be the cause. She would be taking back the power. . . .

And then her hands froze.

In her imagination, she heard their screams, saw their trau-matized faces.

She looked at the au pairs' shoulders, hunched helplessly against the dark. . . .

No.

She couldn't do this. She just couldn't.

Kate shut her eyes, forced herself to see all the people who had hurt her family.

But it was no use.

Kate gave up. Jago would just have to be disappointed with her.

She thought of the words she should say to reassure them she was a member of the bat-watch group, come to find them, and began to step forward to introduce herself as gently as she could, without startling them.

But as she did, Kate's shin banged hard into a hidden tree stump.

With a shriek, Kate fell forward, her hands flying out to stop herself. In an effort to break her fall, she accidentally grabbed the Spanish girl's hair, yanking it hard sideways.

"Oh!" she gasped.

"Aaaa-ieeeeee!"

The girl's agonized scream shot through the woods like a flash of lightning. Immediately the other au pair joined in.

"No . . ." Kate gasped, untangling her hand as she righted herself, but only tugging the girl's hair more. One strand, she realized too late, was caught in her watch.

The Spanish girl dropped the phone with a yelp, and without looking back, ripped her hair from Kate's watch, and the two girls raced off along the unlit path, grabbing at each other's hands, frantically sobbing.

"Oh, no, please. Wait!" Kate shouted, picking up the Spanish girl's phone, but they were stumbling away fast, already disappearing into shadows, till all she could see was little streaks of light as a trainer or watch caught the moonlight. "You're going the wrong way!" she called.

But they were gone. Their sobs faded into nothing as they ran farther into the woods. Kate stopped, and looked around her desperately. She dropped back into the shadows.

What the hell had she done?

She had to get help.

She hurried off in the opposite direction to the girls, till minutes later, the large patch of moonlit sky opened up ahead of her signaling that she was nearing the cricket field.

As she approached at a half jog, she saw the distant movements of the bat-watchers and dropped again behind a tree. They were gathered in larger groups and heading back toward the hut. Checking that there were no rangers walking around with flashlights to see where the scream had come from, she crept behind the cricket scoreboard and crouched down, waiting for Jago.

Nettles stung her ankle but she didn't care.

She sat in the dark, heart thumping.

Idiot. How could she have done that?

A hand suddenly appeared around the back of the score-board and grabbed her, making her jump.

"Quick," Jago whispered. "They're about to do a head count."

"No!" she replied. "You've got to help me—I scared the girls and they've run off. We need to tell someone. They'll get lost in here."

Jago nodded and walked off. She followed him around the perimeter hedge of the café toward the rangers' hut.

"Did you hear the scream?" she whispered as they crept along.

"It sounded like it came from the road. Kids messing around. Nobody took much notice."

It took her a moment to realize that Jago was heading to the rangers' hut.

"No! This way," she whispered, grabbing his hand and pulling him toward the path, where the girls were.

Jago ignored her.

"Jago!" she hissed. He charged ahead toward the dark mass of the group.

"Put your hood up," he said, "hide your face."

"No. We need to go back!"

Just then a ranger shone his light in their direction. Ducking down, she pulled up her hood and stood still as the ranger counted out loud.

"Twenty?" he said.

"Yup. Twenty," the other ranger agreed.

Kate felt Jago grip her hand as the rangers began to lead the group back to Onslow Gate, one in front and one behind.

She tried again, tugging on his hand. "They're on their own—one of them dropped her phone."

He kept moving, resisting the pressure.

"Listen, Kate," he said under his breath. "I know you're worried, but if we go after them in the dark, it'll just terrify them more. The rangers will get suspicious if we turn around, and someone will call the police when they realize we shouldn't be here, and the girls are missing. Do you want that?"

Kate shook her head angrily. This was not OK.

"They'll be fine," Jago continued. "Look. It's just a city wood—it's not the middle of the bloody Yorkshire Moors on a stormy night. I bet the other girl has a phone anyway."

It was no use. Jago kept guiding her toward Onslow Gate. She glanced behind her every few seconds, desperately searching for the shape of the girls in the dark, in the hope that they weren't still on the other side of the woods, about to be locked in for the night with no flashlight and possibly no phone.

Before she knew it, she was standing on the pavement, cars rushing by, back in the city.

"Look," he said as the bat-watching group dispersed up the road, laughing and waving. "Look at that."

Kate peered at the six-foot-high wooden fence he was pointing at.

"They can easily climb over it," Jago said. He was smiling and his tone was reassuring. "They'll hear the traffic, and find their way to it in five minutes, once they've calmed down."

"I'm not sure. . . ." she said, looking around anxiously. "Jago, I can't believe I did that to them."

He took her shoulders in his hands and kissed her forehead. "Kate. Don't worry. I promise you, they'll be fine."

Before she could reply, he led her across the road to his car. She followed him, her will weakening, a terrible sense of guilt descending upon her.

*   *   *

"What up, J?" Gabe yelled, arriving back.

Jack was standing on the trampoline, desperately grabbing his sleeping bag and bedroll.

"Where are you going?" Gabe said, his nerves finally showing.

"I saw something. Over there. There's someone watching us."

"Where?" Damon shouted, coming up behind him.

Jack pointed behind him, trying not to cry. "Someone over there. Behind the fence."

"Where?" Damon shouted again.

Gabe peered over. "I can't see anything."

Jack stood up. "There is!" he shouted at them. "I'm not lying!"

The boys looked at him, stunned.

Jack stared back. They'd never heard him shout before.

"There," he said, dropping his voice.

He turned and pointed at the fence, his sleeping bag in hand.

But the eyes had gone.

"You're just imagining it, Jack," Gabe said, sounding nervous himself.

"Come on," Damon said, sitting down and picking up his cards. "Ignore him. Want us to call your mummy?" He sniggered. "Oh, no. That's right. You can't. She's in London with her boyfriend."

"Shut up, Damon," Gabe said, looking at Jack. "Come on, J, it's all right. Look, there's nothing there."

Jack shook his head. He put his sleeping bag back down and picked up his cards, knowing they were wrong and he was right.

The eyes were gone. And now nobody would believe him.

30

Magnus arrived back from Gabe's garden at 10:30 P.M., took off his jacket, and sat on the bed, satisfied.

The woman was in London and wouldn't be back till late.

The boy would be outside all night.

Lifting Kate's laptop up from the floor, Magnus climbed into Jack's bed, put the laptop on his knee, turned on the small reading lamp beside Jack's bed that no one could see from outside, and stuffed a cookie in his mouth, which he'd taken from the kitchen.

This was his third. He'd also had a spoonful of half a lasagna he'd found in the fridge.

As he finished the cookie he burped loudly then settled back down.

Right, it was time.

Magnus pulled up a blank document and thought for a long time about what to call it. It had to be something the woman wouldn't notice, that could sit among the documents on her computer, unseen by her.

He thought of the perfect phrase in his own language, then translated it to English as best he could.

Then he carried on typing, carefully looking at each word, checking back on the handwritten note he'd brought from next door to make sure he had the words right.

When he'd finished he sat back with a sigh, contented. He saved it, and hid it among her folder called "accounts." The last time she'd looked in there was when she's done her tax return in January.

Magnus lay back, shut the laptop, and closed his eyes for a moment on Jack's bed.

He preferred Kate's room. It smelled of that nice vanilla hand cream.

But after the blond woman nearly caught him in the house last Saturday night, he was going to stay in the boy's room, with the main lights off this evening, just in case she turned up again, sticking her little pointy nose into his business. It was nice and cozy here. With a tinge of sadness he suddenly realized that tonight would be his last night in the woman's house.

He'd nearly done what he came here to do.

Magnus shut his eyes, just for a moment.

31

Apart from a few cars heading back from a night out in London, the M40 was quiet by the time Kate and Jago reached it. The motorway stretched ahead into the black night, with just the odd glow of rear lights flitting by like fireflies.

Kate and Jago drove in silence for thirty miles. It was when they reached the top of the hill overlooking the Chinnor Valley and descended steeply upon the lights of farms and villages spread for miles across the flat landscape before them that Kate realized she was looking forward to going home.

And by that, for the first time in four years, she realized with surprise that she meant Oxford.

Jago drove slowly, watching the road thoughtfully.

A truck with Spanish license plates overtook them, making good use of the empty night road to deliver its goods north of London.

Madrid, it said on the side.

Kate looked away, replaying the scene in the Highgate Woods in her head.

"What?" Jago said.

"One of them was Spanish, I think."

"Kate, listen. Don't worry."

She watched the truck disappear into the dark, its brake lights flashing back at her like dragon eyes. Kate rubbed at a raindrop on the outside of the window, even though she knew she couldn't wipe it away.

What on earth had she done? She'd never be able to tell anyone.

"Kate! Cheer up! They'll be fine. As far as they're concerned, they just got lost from the ranger. Their English wasn't very good—when they try to explain to people what happened, that's probably what they'll think happened, too—that they just got lost, panicked, and freaked themselves out." He touched her leg. "Listen. This was about you, not them. Don't worry. It's not like you hurt them."

Kate looked up at the black sky. In the daytime, she knew red hawks hovered in it, searching for prey, wings held aloft menacingly.

"But it was interesting, huh?" Jago asked. "Being a predator." He growled when he said the word, and made a claw shape with his fingers, then laughed.

She looked out the window. "I don't know."

The thing was, she had hurt those girls. She hadn't stabbed them or punched them but for the rest of their lives, they would find themselves wondering who had touched them that night. She ran through the implications.

They might never go out at night alone again.

They might even give up their dream of living in London.

She thought back to the intense hatred she'd felt in Highgate

Woods toward those men who killed Hugo. What had she let those feelings do to her? The preyed upon becomes the predator. The bullied becomes the bully. In some ways, she was as bad as those men.

Jago turned the CD player on. American alternative folk music drifted into the car.

"Anyway," Jago said, "I think we're probably pushing our luck now. One more step to finish off next weekend. And I'll make it a fun one, I promise. No more scaring people or breaking the law."

"I can't do something like that again, Jago. Involving other people."

"Kate," he said, overtaking a minibus. "We won't, I promise. And seriously, don't worry about it. They'll be fine and you've proven a point to yourself."

As he pulled back into the slow lane, he reached out and touched her leg. She turned and met the long look he gave her.

She fought the urge to tell him to drive off the road now, and take her somewhere dark, then hating herself for it.

Wondering for the first time if the person she was becoming was any better than the person she was leaving behind.

32

It was the screeching call of an alarm that woke him.

At first Magnus thought he was back in the prison cell at home, lying above Jorgen, a fellow burglar, and that it was the brutal morning wake-up call.

Beep beep beep.

Magnus tossed and turned in Jack's bed. It was warm. He didn't want to get up.

"Do you want a drink?" a woman asked.

Magnus sat upright in the pitch-black.

Where was he? He put out a hand and felt the edges of a small bed.

A light came on downstairs in the hall, illuminating a corner of the Arsenal poster beside his head through a crack in the door.

The boy's room!

He'd fallen asleep.

"Have you got a whisky, by any chance?" he heard a man say in a Scottish accent.

Magnus froze. Kate was downstairs, and she wasn't alone.

It felt so strange to have Jago in her house.

Kate dropped her bag on the kitchen table, horribly self-conscious of everything she saw as she looked around, as if she'd been ripped open and he was looking inside at all her secrets. Jack's soccer shoes by the door, the pile of ironing in the kitchen, the photo Hugo had taken of Jack watching her plane on the wall. She saw Jago look at it.

"Great picture. Great house, Kate." He turned around. "It's beautiful."

She smiled demurely and took off her coat. "Thanks."

What would happen if Jago became part of her life, she thought, grabbing glasses from the kitchen cupboard. Would she have to remove the photos of Hugo? Take away his Georgian furniture? His CDs? How would Jack even start to understand?

As if he sensed she was lost in thought, Jago came up behind her. She felt his hands on her shoulders.

He leaned his face on her shoulder and inhaled deeply.

"I've got something to tell you," he murmured.

She paused. "Hmm?"

"I saw Marla in London on Wednesday night."

Kate tensed.

"She came on the Eurostar from Paris, and I met her in a bar at Waterloo. She was in a state, talking about getting back together again and . . ."

Kate turned to face him and stared at his chest, unable to look at him. "And I told her that I was seeing someone. And that I wouldn't be coming to North Carolina on my way to Utah in August now, and I'd get a mate at the university to pick up my stuff from hers and get it shipped back here."

Kate waited for more.

"Then she got the late train back to Paris.

"Was that OK?" he said, peering down at her. "To say that? That I'm seeing someone?"

Kate couldn't help it. She turned around with relief, and he met her with a kiss. She fell into him against the wall, knowing now that she was ready.

It had gone silent downstairs.

Magnus gave it another second, then turned around in the dark. How had this happened? He scrambled out of the bed, noticing too late that the boy's night-light was on a timer switch that had turned it off while he slept. In the dark, he tried to throw the cover over the bed as he'd found it.

Turning, Magnus peered at the other end of the bedroom. There was only one thin slice of light on the wall, coming through the almost-shut bedroom door. Using that as a compass point, he tiptoed toward where the wardrobe door should be.

His toe touched something springy.

He withdrew his foot quickly, and for a moment, thought he'd got away with it.

Then, in front of his nose, a breeze blew by, and the most almighty crash rang through the house.

Shit.

*   *   *

"Jesus!" Kate yelled, jumping back. The crash upstairs was ten times louder than the thud the other day. She looked up, startled. "Oh, my God. There's someone in the house."

Jago stepped back and looked up.

"Kate, listen. Don't panic. Where was it? Upstairs?"

He appeared unruffled, just as Hugo would have. "At the front. In Jack's room, I think. The big bedroom at the front."

"OK, stay here and I'll go look. . . ." He started to walk out of the kitchen.

"No!" Kate yelled. "No, Jago."

Tears came, and for the first time in a long time, she didn't fight them. She couldn't let Jago go up there. It was all too much after Highgate tonight, and those agonizing memories of Hugo.

"You can't."

"Kate, relax. I'm just going for a look. If there's someone up there, they'll be as frightened as we are, and make a run for it. I can handle it, OK?"

The memory of Hugo lying on the floorboards, blood soaking into them, was right in front of her.

"No, Jago," she begged. "Just stay here and call the police."

He hesitated. "OK, tell you what. Get the phone, ring nine nine—then if there is someone up there, which I'm sure there isn't, I'll shout, then dial the third nine, OK?"

She felt hot tears running down her face.

Jago took her face in his hands. "Kate! Don't worry. I'm here."

He put her hands down by her sides, kissed her, then walked off through the dining room, picking up Jack's tennis racket as he went.

*   *   *

"Just stay there," Magnus heard the Scottish man shout.

Desperately, Magnus put out his hand in the dark, found the old chimney breast beside the wardrobe, and stumbled across the floor. Luckily the wardrobe doors were still open. He lay down on his stomach and aimed his feet at the hole in the wall. Pushing hard with his long arms, he propelled himself backward. He managed to get his calves through into next door, then, with another big push, his upper thighs.

The Scottish man was coming up the stairs quickly, thump, thump, thump. Was the woman coming with him?

Magnus was sweating now, trying to push the rest of his body through the gap.

He went for one last push but something stopped him. Panicking, he moved his stomach off the ground. A jutting piece of shelf bracket had caught on his shirt. Shit, shit, shit, this would ruin everything. He wriggled desperately to free himself.

Magnus's body was three-quarters through, just his head and shoulders still protruded.

As he went to shut the wardrobe doors, the Scottish man turned on the light. He was holding a tennis racket.

Magnus froze, his head sticking out between the bottom doors of Jack's cupboard. The Scottish man scanned the room quickly, taking in the rumpled, unmade bed and a fallen CD rack that Magnus had knocked over.

Then he turned to the wardrobe.

Their eyes met.

Magnus saw the Scottish man take a moment to register what he was seeing.

His expression changed. "Kate!" he called back down the stairs. Magnus's heart thumped. "You're OK. A CD rack just fell over. It was probably just a draft when we slammed the front door."

And with that the Scottish man turned back to Magnus with a furious look on his face. He leaned down, grabbed Magnus's hair with one hand, so tight on his scalp his neck hurt.

Magnus groaned.

The Scottish man put his lips close to Magnus's ear.

"You stupid, stupid fuck," he growled. His other hand came flying up and punched Magnus sharply on the side of the face.

He stood up, and walked to the door.

"Just going to use the loo, Kate," he shouted down the stairs, then he turned, put his fingers furiously to his lips, turned off the light, and shut the bedroom door.

Oh, great, Magnus sighed to himself.

Now he was in trouble.

Kate paced back and forth across the kitchen, waiting for Jago to come down.

How the hell had a draft knocked over Jack's CD rack?

The feeling of unease had soaked back into her bones, as it so often did in this house. Maybe they should move. Buy a new apartment in the center of town without these creaky old doors and drafty windows. Unsettled, her mind flew to Jack, lying outside in the dark.

Kate took out her phone and started to text, not caring what Gill or Jack's friends thought about it. He'd probably be asleep anyway.

how are you? Ok?

His answer flew back.

no. bit scared

She stared. Oh, God. She looked at the clock. It was 11:30 P.M.

why?

don't know

want me to come and get you? Im home.

His response brought a lump to her throat.

yes but don't because they'll laugh at me

Kate heard Jago in the upper hall, and her body, newly awakened, responded with a shiver.

Her body was betraying her, begging her to have Jago stay the night.

He'd have to understand.

jack, im coming now. I'm going to sit outside in the car

i thought you were with your friend?

you are more important than my friends jack—than anybody.

Jago started down the stairs.

Jack's next text brought more tears to Kate's eyes.

im tired of being scared mum

we'll sort it out together I promise. coming now

Jago walked toward her, that easy smile on his face.

"We had a fight, and the CD rack won," he said, lifting his hand. The fingers were grazed.

"How did you do that?" Kate said, grabbing them.

"It's fine. I scraped it on the wall looking for the light."

Kate took him to the sink and ran the cold water. Gently, she placed his hand under the stream. She turned apologetically. "I'm sorry, I just panicked."

"Is this the kind of thing you were telling me about?"

She nodded. "I hear strange noises all the time here."

"Well, it's an old house. The floors are quite uneven in Jack's room, I noticed, and do you want me to fix that catch on the wardrobe?"

Kate sighed and turned off the tap, but held his hand still in hers, hoping he'd understand.

"Jago, you don't know how much I want you to be here tonight, but I'm so sorry." She held out her phone. "I have to go. It's Jack."

If he was disappointed, he didn't show it. "Oh, God, of course." He hugged her. "Don't worry. We're not in a hurry here, are we?"

"Hmm . . ." She groaned playfully, the tone betraying that she wanted nothing more right now than for him to stay.

"I know." He laughed, stroking her back. He kissed her head. They stood there for a second.

"Right," she said, grabbing her stuff. Jago picked up his coat and they headed together down the hall. She locked up behind them.

"Next weekend, I promise," Kate said on the doorstep, turning on the alarm. "Jack will be with his grandparents."

"Worth the wait," Jago said, kissing her ear as he put his arm around her and walked her to the car.

She drove around the corner to Gill's at 11:45 P.M., and parked in a space outside. Too late, she realized she should have brought a sleeping bag.

Crossly, she stared up at the dark house. Gill was probably snoozing away in there, stoned out of her tree, while Jack lay terrified outside.

She texted Jack.

i'm outside in the car

thanks mum. sorry.

don't say sorry. i should have realized you were scared. I'm sorry. try to sleep and i'll stay here till the morning right outside.

night mum

night x

Kate pushed back in her seat, thinking about her crazy night with Jago.

An unpleasant image of the au pairs in the woods came back to her. Where were those girls now? At home, crying, unable to sleep? Talking to their own mums tearfully on the phone?

Jesus—what had she done?

Kate felt the cold creep into her body and allowed it to.

She deserved every freezing minute she was going to experience tonight in this car.

The bullied became the bully—but only if they let themselves.

That's not who she was, and she needed to tell Jago that.

33

The following Tuesday, as arranged, Richard arrived at six to pick up Jack.

Kate opened the door to find Helen there, too.

"Hi. Come in," she said cheerily, for Jack's sake.

Helen gave her a small smile, the coldness of their last encounter three weeks ago still present. In the hall, she looked up.

"It's gone," Kate said.

"Some of Jack's school things that he left," Helen said, holding out a plastic bag, as if she hadn't heard her. "I've washed them."

Richard hung up their coats, still smiling, but analyzing the situation with his busy eyes, as always.

"There he is! Hello, darling!" Helen said, wrapping Jack in her pastel-clad arms. "Looking forward to the seaside?"

He nodded, beaming.

"Come and tell me about your sleepover, darling," Helen said, leading him into the kitchen to fetch his coat. "Sounds like you boys had a real adventure."

Kate glanced at Jack, and gave him a tiny wink.

When he returned it, in that second, she felt a little owner-ship return to her, and smiled with relief.

"OK, darling," Richard boomed. "We're heading down to Dorset tonight. Got the place till Friday, so, what, bring him back Sunday? Give you a chance to do some work?"

The doorbell rang behind him, and Richard turned without compunction and opened it.

It's my house, my door! Kate wanted to say, but didn't.

Saskia stood there, with pink cheeks, like she'd been running.

"Oh, great, I was worried I'd missed you. I came to wave you off," she said, walking in behind Kate and waving at Jack in the kitchen.

The dreaded triumvirate. Jack was disappearing into their fold again.

"Here's his bag," she said, handing it to Richard.

Right then, she made a pledge to herself. Next time, she would announce to Richard and Helen that she was coming to Dorset with them, invite or not. They would start to follow her rules and respect them, whatever they were.

Jack and Helen returned from the kitchen.

"Well, we might as well head off, folks, if you're ready?" Richard said.

Kate nodded. She gave Jack a casual hug, resisting the urge to squeeze him tight and tell him to be safe. "Have a good time. I'll miss you."

Saskia gave him one, too.

"Well, if they're all heading off, fancy a drink, Kate?" Saskia said.

Kate knew everyone was pausing to listen to her reply. They were lifting bags and opening doors, but their ears were point-ing directly at her. Jack glanced up, hopeful.

He wanted her to go, Kate realized, wanted her to make things better with Aunt Sass.

"There's the new place on Magdalen Road," she said, picking up her coat.

"Great," Saskia said, the shock registering on her face, and they all left together.

The pub was packed when they arrived. At Saskia's request, Kate went to find a table. Saskia returned five minutes later with a whole bottle of wine, causing Kate to raise her eyebrows.

"We're getting pissed," Saskia announced, sitting down. "How else are we going to get through this? How long's it been since we went for a drink—three years?"

Kate raised her eyebrows and held out her glass, already dreading Saskia's questions.

"So," Saskia said with a challenging look on her face. "You've done it, haven't you?"

Kate regarded her, confused. "What?"

"You know what. You've got this kind of sexy walk thing going on."

She suddenly realized what Sass meant. It was the kind of sweetly guileless comment Sass would have made in the old days, and it took her by surprise. Kate burst out laughing, nearly spitting out a mouthful of wine in the process.

"Actually, I haven't!"

"Really?"

Saskia was trying. She could see that. Kate smiled. "Not quite yet. It's been five years, Sass. For him as well. I suppose it'll happen when we're both ready."

Saskia took a sip of wine. "This weekend?"

Kate made a face at her. "Stop it."

Sass sighed. "But is it definitely over? Him and his girlfriend."

Kate nodded. Saskia ran her finger down her glass, thought-fully.

Kate took a sip of her drink, and watched her. "What?"

Saskia groaned. "Kate. If I tell you something, will you promise not to tell anyone? I have to tell someone or I'm going to die."

Kate nodded.

"Jonathan. The business I told you about him being bored with me. It wasn't exactly true. I mean, it was. He did get fed up with me moaning about working for Dad and not going back to do my degree, but it wasn't the reason he left me."

Surprised, Kate sat back. "OK . . . ?"

Saskia sighed. "I had an affair."

Kate slammed her drink down on the table. "You are fucking joking? You!"

Saskia nodded ruefully. "You remember when Dad made the whole agency go on that terrible team-building week in Gloucestershire? I met him there, at the hotel, on the first night. He said he liked the ladder I'd made out of a tree trunk."

Kate sniggered into her wine. She'd forgotten how funny and self-effacing Sass could be.

Saskia hit her arm. "Don't, Kate. Honestly. He was called Tony, and he came from Essex, and he'd just got divorced. He was on business, and he was lonely, and he was very sweet to me."

"Oh, your dad would love that." Kate smiled, imagining snobby Richard being faced with the prospect of announcing at the marina that instead of "Jonathan from Surrey" Saskia was now seeing "Tony from Essex."

Saskia rolled her eyes. "Exactly. Anyway, I just needed to get away from everyone—you know what Dad's like when he holds forth to a captive audience at the bar. I said I had a headache, and Tony asked me to come for a drink in the village. I told him about all the arguments me and Jonathan had been having, and I really don't know how it happened. I was feeling low and he just kept telling me he was sure I would make a fantastic architect one day. I drank too much and we ended up back at the hotel. And then it just kept happening every night that week. Honestly, I've never done anything like that before and I still don't really know why I did."

Kate sighed, knowing that Saskia would never be able to bear the guilt of something like that. "Please tell me you didn't tell Jonathan?"

Saskia sighed. "I didn't realize how seriously Tony was taking it. He started texting me when I got home. I tried to stop him, but when I didn't return his calls, he rang me at the house when I was out. Jonathan answered."

"Oh, Sass!"

"He looked so sick. And the worst thing was, Tony wasn't even my type. He had this spiky hair with too much gel in it. And wore a business suit. I honestly don't know why I did it."

Kate felt a tug of old affection for Saskia. She had been cast into the role of big sister when they first met, and loved it. "Maybe it's not too late. If you finish your degree and give Jonathan some time, maybe he'll come round?"

Saskia shrugged. "No. Do you know, I'm starting to wonder if this is the best thing. I'm not sure Jonathan really wanted the best for me. Not the way Hugo did for you. So, now it's my decision and no one else's. And I'm going to tell Dad tomorrow that I'm going to apply to do my Part Two, then do my Part Three the year after next, and qualify as an architect. And that I don't want his money. I'll pay myself."

Kate sat back, imagining Richard's fury. It had taken Hugo a year to tell his father that he'd swapped from a degree in architecture to one in architectural history and design, and would not be following Richard's dream for him to be an architect like himself. It was a sweet irony that Saskia, who Richard had no plans for whatsoever, would be adopting the dream for him. Becoming Richard's equal. Kate sat forward. "I'm pleased for you. Actually, I think Hugo should have stepped in and made you do it years ago."

Saskia gave her a searching look that made her pretend to find something dirty to rub away on the side of her glass. "What's he done to you, Kate?"

"Who?"

"This man? He's changed you. You're glowing."

Was it that obvious? "I'm not sure what he's done. He just seems to get what's going on inside my head. He helps me. With the anxiety."

"Him and the therapist."

Kate looked away. She and Sass had shared enough truths for one night. "Yup."

Saskia took a long sip of wine.

A frown appeared on her face.

Kate watched her. "What?"

Saskia blinked hard.

"Sass, what now?"

Saskia shook her head. "It's nothing. It's just . . . I don't know how to say this, Kate."

"Hmm?"

"It's just . . . well, I know Dad's always been worried."

"About what?"

Saskia sighed. "Do you remember when Hugo was killed,

there was all that publicity in the papers about the case? The tabloids kept saying things like, 'The gang targeted Hugo Parker's million-pound home in Highgate,' and 'Hugo Parker's parents traveled from their one-point-five-million house in Oxford to the hearing today. . . . ' And stuff like, 'It has been a second tragedy for his widow, whose parents were killed in a car crash on her wedding night on the way home to their house in Shropshire.' . . . That kind of thing."

Kate did remember. She remembered the relentless invasion of it into her grief, the pain of seeing photos of the people she loved, laid out on newspaper pages next to car ads. "So?"

"I'm just saying. It wouldn't take anyone long to work out there's a lot of money sloshing around. All the life insurance. The property you inherited. The business. And then, a load more coming to you and Jack one day from Mum and Dad."

Oh, my God. Kate put down her glass. Saskia was talking about money. She was accusing Jago of being a gold digger.

Kate bristled. "Well, that kind of doesn't surprise me at all, Sass—as Richard's whole life revolves around money, he can't imagine anyone having any other motive in their life. For your information, Jago's a visiting professor at Oxford, with a best-selling book in the States. He drives around in a hatchback and listens to indie bands, and goes mountain biking. I'm sorry, I really don't think he needs anyone else's cash, and even if he did, he's not the type who would go looking for rich women."

Kate knew as she said it, that a boundary had been crossed. Her feelings about Richard had always been implied to Saskia, never spoken.

Saskia sat back, looking shocked. Her voice went cold.

"Kate. Richard is my father," she said quietly. "I know he has faults, lots of faults, but he's still my father, and I won't sit here

and let you talk about him like that, any more than you would
have let someone talk about yours like that. . . ."

She broke off. They sat there, an almost-full bottle of wine
between them, knowing that it was never going to be drunk.

Kate pushed back her seat. It was time to go. This had been
a mistake. She and Saskia were never going to be friends again.

"Hugo would find this so sad," Saskia murmured.

"He would find it unbelievable," Kate replied. She touched
Saskia's shoulder, feeling sorrow for Jack and his hopes for her
and his aunt, and walked out of the pub.

She marched up to Hubert Street, Saskia's accusation about
Jago ringing in her ears. She gave it a moment of thought then
dismissed it completely.

Jack sat in the back of Richard's car on the M25, looking through
Jago Martin's book, even though it was making him carsick.

He looked down at a page on road accidents, then up at the
motorway.

Something wasn't right.

34

It was Friday afternoon, and the roads were unusually quiet, perhaps now that the colleges were starting to close down for summer. Kate cycled into town, not believing what she had just done.

The sun was out again. The trees were a rich, dark green. The air was filled with the fresh smell of summer.

The numbers were there today, but like text on a computer that was unhighlighted. Present, but flat. Unsummonable.

She cycled easily up the High Street, going over what she'd just done in her head.

She dismounted in Carfax and walked toward the end of Cornmarket Street, enjoying the newfound spring in her step. It had happened gradually, but she no longer had to force a leg in front of the other to get through each day.

Vaguely, she noticed a couple of people glancing at her as they walked past. It had happened a few times this week, mostly men. It was strange to realize she was visible again in the real world.

There was a buzz on her phone. She checked it and her stomach lurched.

It was too late now.

An e-mail sat in her in-box confirming the two flights she had just booked to Mallorca for August.

She and Jack were going on a trip on a plane.

She felt a frisson of excitement at the thought of the warm sun on her skin, and swimming in the sea, forcing herself to sidestep the stats about skin cancer and drowning, and concentrate on what it would be like to have so much time alone with Jack.

Richard and Helen would be nowhere to be seen.

They could discuss their memories of Hugo. Take some photos. Talk about their future. She could even bring up the idea of Jago.

The thought of Jago sent a thrill through her.

She crossed the street, swinging her bag of ankle boots, recalling each word of their phone call last night from London.

"Kate, I had to tell you," Jago had enthused down the phone. "That psychologist guy in the States rang to see how you were. I told him what we'd been up to and he was fascinated. He mentioned us doing an interdisciplinary paper together on this new anxiety disorder—I'm going to stop off and see him in New York when I go to Utah in the summer."

"That's brilliant," she'd said, pleased.

"But he thinks we should stop after this weekend, so we don't go too far. And he said that you're welcome to ring him to discuss the kind of CBT he would recommend if you want to try a different kind of counseling in Oxford."

"Thanks, Jago," she'd said, touched by his effort. "Thanks for doing this for me."

"You're very welcome." He laughed. "Although, of course, I have dodgy ulterior motives, which would be seriously unethical if I were actually a psychologist. But we statisticians are allowed to be dodgy as fuck as long as we can count . . . so I was thinking, that if you fancied it, maybe we could sneak you into my room at Balliol on Saturday after we get back to Oxford?"

She had hesitated, feeling a spark between them along the telephone line that made her smile awkwardly.

"I mean, if you can steal a boat and terrorize innocent people in a wood, that'll be old hat for you by then, missus."

She had smiled. "No, I'd like that."

"Good," he'd said.

They had arranged to meet at eight o'clock tomorrow morning at an M25 service station.

And it was after that phone call that she had felt so positive about the future that she had, terrified, decided to book the tickets to Mallorca.

Kate arrived at the shoe-repair shop a minute later. The old man was working behind the bar again, as irritable looking as last time.

"Hi," Kate said, taking out the boots.

He lifted his head slowly again, and peered at her.

"Sorry, but I picked these up from you last week and when I got home, I realized the heel had been shortened by about this much." She held up her fingers. "I can wear them but I really preferred them the height they were. Could I ask you to redo them, please?"

The old man took the boots from Kate, and peered through his glasses. He put them down on the counter and looked at her.

"He asked me to do it. The bloke."

"Who?" Kate said. What was he talking about?

"The bloke that brought them in."

"Who?" she said, confused. "A Scottish bloke?"

The old man shrugged. "Can't remember."

She frowned. "I'm sorry, but no, I mean, why would he?"

"Seen it before," the old man said, tucking in his tortoise neck.

"Sorry?"

"Some blokes don't like it. When their wife is tall. They ask me to shorten their heels."

Kate shook her head not believing what she was hearing. "I'm sorry," she laughed. "First of all, I'm not his wife. And secondly he's about six foot, and I'm five foot seven. Even with heels on I'm shorter than him."

He turned away from her, putting his hand up between her face and his. "I'll redo them if you want. But he did ask me."

"OK. If you say so," she said, craning her neck to see in the back of the shop, where maybe a more rational employee was hiding. The old guy was even madder than she'd first thought. She gave him her name again, put the boots on the counter, and walked out.

Kate arrived home later with a bag of new holiday clothes for Jack and her. There was a commotion on the pavement.

She looked up to see the tall student with the glasses and spiky hair leaving the house next door, with two large duffel bags. A woman in her twenties was standing in the doorway talking to him with a harassed expression in her face.

"But we need it before you go, Magnus," she was calling out. "None of us can cover your share, and there's the electricity bill, too, that's due soon."

"I send it to you!" he yelled, placing the keys in her hand and waving in the air.

"But we don't have an address for you and . . ."

"I send it!" he boomed again.

He stopped when he saw Kate. She noticed he had a bruise on his face that ran from under his eye down the side of his face.

Something began to register in her mind, then slipped away, like a foot off a pedal.

"Hey. I'm leaving!" he shouted.

Kate looked sympathetically at the female student, to show her support if she needed it, but the girl just turned away.

"Too many crazy fucking people round here," the spiky-haired student called out.

He walked off down the street, leaving Kate standing on the doorstep.

Oh, well, perhaps Saskia had been right. If he was no longer living next door, that was one less thing to worry about.

Inside the house, Kate walked up to Jack's bedroom and put away the new clothes.

Then she sat on her son's bed and looked around. Jack's world, where he had lived on his own for so long while she had been lost in her head, worrying about how to keep them both safe. With one hand, she reached up and took down the little snow globe. Jack had loved this when he was a baby. Asked for it again and again. She shook it and a glittering snowstorm rained over the little plastic mountain inside swirling glittering rain, feeling like her life for the past five years.

She lay back and thought of Jago.

With him, there could be a real possibility of something. She sensed he felt it, too.

Just one more step in his experiment.

The glitter settled.

And then life would really restart.

But first, she knew she had to be honest with Jago about who she was.

35

It was eight o'clock on Saturday morning. Kate pulled into the service station on the M25, twitching with anticipation about the last step of Jago's experiment. In fact, she had been so preoccupied, she'd hardly noticed the trucks behind her on the M40. Instead, she'd found an old Johnny Cash CD in the front compartment and played it, his comforting, mellow voice drifting out of a window she had opened to let in the already-warm June air. To her surprise, she felt a small sense of joy descending upon her.

She spotted Jago immediately as she circled, looking for a parking space.

He was standing at the main door of the café area, a coffee in hand, sipping it carefully as steam drifted up into a blue sky that, if all the bike carriers and boat trailers were anything to go by, was already summoning a weekend crowd to the outdoors.

Kate found a cramped space beside a four-by-four topped with mountain bikes, and turned off the engine. She sat back and observed Jago surreptitiously in her side mirror.

He looked even more tanned than usual, as if he'd been out cycling in the sun. He wore a slim-fit gray T-shirt that showed off the taut muscles of his arms and torso, and a black top tied around his waist. He was wearing tracksuit trousers and sneakers, as was she. He had been specific about that on the phone. "Something comfortable," he'd said. "Something you'd go running in on a cold day."

So. This was it. After today, when they saw each other again, it would be a normal date. How would that feel? Would she be able to do things with him that were planned ahead, without trying to take control?

At least, now, Kate knew she had a chance.

She felt a tremor in her stomach, remembering something else.

Tonight, she would sleep with him. She looked at him again, something niggling her mind.

But first it was only fair that before she took that step, she told him what she had done.

She climbed out of her car, and crossed toward him. He spotted her and picked up a coffee he'd clearly bought for her as she crossed the line of arriving cars to reach him.

"Hello!" He put out his arms. There was no awkwardness on his part or hers now. She fell into him, his body still familiar from last week in her kitchen.

"You smell nice," he murmured. "How are you?"

"Hmm . . ." She growled, prodding his chest gently. "You better have a good reason for getting me up at six thirty A.M., mate."

"Ahah!" He leaned down and kissed her. "Let's go and find out, shall we?" He pointed at her car. "Can you drive?"

"Uh, yes, but how did you get here?" she asked as they crossed back over the road.

Jago opened the passenger door. "Someone gave me a lift on their way to London this morning."

"But I thought you just came from London?" Kate said, climbing in her side and starting the engine.

Jago grinned.

"What?" she said, putting on her seat belt and reversing out. She followed the exit sign back onto the M25, waiting for his reply.

"Kate. I haven't been in London."

She did a double take. "I thought's that's where you've been—working?"

Jago sipped his coffee. "No. My classes finished at Balliol in the week we went to Highgate Woods—the Oxford summer school doesn't start till next Monday."

Kate accelerated onto the motorway, feeling confused. "So where have you been?"

"Now, that's what we're about to find out." She threw him a worried look.

"Come on. One more step, then you can relax. We can relax. Actually, I was just looking at those mountain bikes back there, wondering if you fancied coming cycling with me in the Cotswolds next week—someone at Balliol told me about a good trail."

She tensed, waiting for the numbers to fly at her about mountain-bike accidents, but nothing came. "Um, yeah." She shrugged, amazed at how easy it was to say yes. "I suppose so. That sounds nice."

And it did sound nice. Cycling outdoors in the sunshine in a beautiful part of the country.

"Great. And we'll find a proper country pub this time."

That sounded nice, too. As Jago looked for a radio station, a thought occurred to her. How much else had she missed these past five years, tiptoeing around, frightened of shadows?

They turned off the motorway at the next signpost, and Jago directed her onto a two-lane country road surrounded by high hedges. He found an alternative-music station and sat back, tapping his fingers on his leg. They carried on for ten miles, chatting about Kate's new plans for the foundation, then turned into a much narrower road that soon disappeared.

"Why is this making me uneasy?" said Kate, slowing down.

"Oi. Stop trying to predict."

"Sorry."

As she took her time, it dawned on her that Jack would be home next weekend. How would she explain the Cotswold trip? She glanced at Jago, wondering. Would it be too weird?

She chewed her lip. "Jago. Could I ask you something? What would you think about meeting Jack?"

He dropped his head to the side, as if listening to a strange noise.

"I'd introduce you as a friend," she added.

"Yeah, absolutely. When?"

"Really?" She glanced appreciatively. He hadn't even hesitated. "Maybe next week?"

"Absolutely," Jago repeated, tapping his fingers to the music. "Take him to the Cotswolds, if you like. Does he like cycling? I take my niece, Clara, sometimes in Scotland. She's about the same age."

"Do you?" Kate glanced at him. She liked the way he talked about his family. He reminded her of Hugo. "He'd love that, actually. We never go cycling."

"Great. Me and him can talk science."

Her heart expanded a little. "Thanks. That would be amazing. I'm sorry, it's just—"

He interrupted her. "My sister—Clara's mum—is divorced and the dad is never around. I know a bit about what it's like." He started singing along to the radio. Kate watched him. He was so relaxed. So relaxing to be around and . . .

She looked at him.

But something was different. She had noticed it at the motorway station but now it was becoming more obvious. Jago's foot was tapping incessantly. His legs and buttocks were tensing, too, in turns, moving a centimeter up and down, like a boxer on his toes before a fight.

"So. Come on," she said. "What are we doing?"

Jago froze.

Then, without warning, he threw himself forward and put his head in his hands. "Ah!" he groaned.

"What?" Kate said, alarmed.

Jago threw back his head. "You're going to kill me."

"What?" she exclaimed, swerving at the last moment to avoid a pheasant.

"OK. Right. Can I just say, when you start shouting at me, because you will, that it's your own fault?"

What was he talking about?

Jago turned sideways to face her. "Well, when you mentioned it, last week, I realized it was something that I'd always wanted to do. I had last week off so I thought why not? I've just got a royalty check from my American publisher, so I went for it."

Kate slowed down as they approached a bend, desperately searching her memory. What had she said?

"Jago?" she said nervously. "Talking about what?"

"There." Jago grinned, pointing. Kate looked ahead and saw a field with a hangar appearing on their right.

The yellow wing of a small aircraft came into view.

It took her brain a second to register what was written in large letters on the sign in front of them.

WELCOME TO BINDWOOD PARACHUTE SCHOOL

36

Jack woke up at ten o'clock that Saturday morning, not knowing where he was.

At first he thought he was in the white bedroom with the sloping roof in the thatched holiday house in Dorset, but then he saw Dad's old Arsenal posters on the wall and remembered he was back at Nana and Granddad's. They'd arrived at ten last night after getting stuck in traffic on the motorway for hours.

Then he remembered something else.

The computer!

Jack sat up with a gasp and looked at the clock. He hadn't meant to sleep in so late, but Aunt Sass had been here to meet them with some dinner she'd cooked last night, so he'd been up quite late. Since then, he'd lain restlessly, counting down the hours till he could run to the kitchen, and check if he was right. And now he'd slept in.

Jack jumped out of bed and ran to his bag on the floor, yanking out clothes and brushing aside the shells he'd collected with Nana. He found Jago Martin's book hidden at the bottom.

He ripped it open triumphantly.

At first, back at home last week, he'd noticed something odd about the book, and marked it with a red pen. And then in the car.

In Dorset, he'd decided to go back through it.

Now the margins were covered in red marks.

Jack was triumphant. He hoped Dad was watching him.

Saskia sat at the computer in her parents' kitchen, a cup of coffee and a plate of toast by her hand, reading the e-mail message she had just received, unable to believe it.

She had an interview next Tuesday to do her Part Two workplacement at a small architect firm in Banbury.

She sat back, excitement and worry weaving together inside her. How the hell would she tell Richard? "Dad, I'm leaving your agency. Oh, and by the way, I'm stealing your big dream for your beloved son, Hugo, to be an architect like you . . ."

The kitchen door opened, and she jerked back, thinking it was Dad.

Jack stood there in his pajamas, his hair sticking up, holding a book determinedly in his hand. He looked so cross, she laughed.

"Morning, Snores, what's up with you?"

"Can I get on the computer?"

Saskia looked at her e-mail. "Can you give me a moment? This is important."

She started to type her reply, assuming Jack would fetch his breakfast, but when she looked up, he was still there. His normally tranquil green eyes raged like a rough sea.

"What's the matter?" she asked. "It's not your Facebook, is it, because I'm a bit worried about what I've been reading on . . ."

"It's not that," Jack said loudly.

Saskia stopped midchew. She'd never seen him so worked up.

"Mum's got a boyfriend."

Saskia hesitated. She tried to sound casual as she picked at her toast.

"Oh. OK. Did she tell you that?"

"No," he said, staring hungrily at the computer like he wanted to rip it from Saskia's hands. "I worked it out."

"Is it true?" he asked more gravely.

Saskia sighed. Great. Another Kate mess to sort out. "Snores—I can't . . . your mum has to . . ."

"So it is true?" he asked.

She sighed. "It's your mum's business, Jack. If she hasn't told you, it's because she's not ready to do that yet."

"Well, it's not! Because there's something wrong with him."

"Who? How do you know?"

Jack held out the book and lowered his voice. "Look."

Saskia read the front cover. "Jago Martin . . . oh, that's him. This is the book he wrote?" she said, remembering her conversation with Kate.

Jack nodded. He flipped forward a couple of pages and pointed at the red pen in the margin.

Saskia peered at the statistics on the pages. "So?"

"They're all the same."

"What do you mean?" she replied, patting Rosie as she laid her head in Saskia's lap, hoping for some toast.

"They're all in a different order, but he keeps using the numbers from the pages at the front of the book on all the pages at the back. It's like they're fake numbers to fill the space. Like he's copied and pasted them over and over."

Saskia put down her toast, and took the book from Jack. He'd always been good at math, just like Hugo. Following his pen marks, she flicked through. That was odd. She sat back uneasily.

"Is this a proper book?" She looked at the cover again. "Perhaps it's just an early proof."

Jack shrugged. "It's a book."

Saskia ran a finger down the front inside cover. "Underline Publishing? OK. Haven't heard of that before." She pointed at the laptop. "Put 'Underline Publishing' in Google, Snores. See what it says."

She leaned over and watched the page as it loaded.

When it did, there was silence as they both read it.

"Always wanted to get that novel published? Turn that special holiday or event into a beautiful photo book? Underline Publishing is a self-publishing Web site with an array of predesigned formats to choose from . . ."

Saskia wrinkled her nose, confused. "This is not a real book, then. It looks like one but he's just self-published it." She turned it over.

"Give it here," Jack said, pushing in front of her at the screen. She moved to let him take half of her seat, amazed how easily the little boy worked his way around the Internet. He brought up Amazon, and typed in Jago Martin's book title. Popular books about statistics with similar titles popped up, but not Jago Martin's. Jack pointed at two, excited.

"Look—he's copied the cover of that book, and the title of that one." He then clicked on a third book that offered the option of looking inside. Saskia read the first ten pages in silence on-screen, as Jack clicked through them for her.

"Wow, that is weird," Saskia said. "He's used some of these pages, too."

"But he's changed the headline and some of the numbers," Jack said.

Saskia sat back, trying to work it out. "It's like he's scanned different bits of all these books, then put them together in a self-published book, added a few things, and put his name on it. Why would he do that?"

"I want to tell Mum," Jack said triumphantly.

Saskia blinked, starting to feel uneasy.

"Look, hang on. Let's Google him."

They did and Jago Martin's own Web site came on top of a list of five Web sites that mentioned his name.

"Click that one first," Saskia said, pointing to it. They both stared as it came up, with a small photo of a man wearing black sunglasses and a helmet on a bike. "Bio, journals, press . . ." Saskia said. She pressed on a few links to other sites. They all looked impressive.

"Try the next one," she said. It took them to Jago Martin's entry on the University of Edinburgh's Web site.

Saskia stared at it. Something wasn't right here. A word in the title was spelled wrongly. "One of the worlds top universities . . ."

"Hang on . . ." She leaned over Jack and put "Edinburgh University" in Google.

She pressed "enter" and waited, feeling Jack's nervous breathing on her neck.

An almost identical page came up, but with "world's" spelled correctly.

Saskia typed "Jago Martin" into the search engine built into that site.

"0 results."

"Oh, my God," she said.

"What?"

Saskia searched two more newspaper and education links in Jago Martin's own Web site. They all went to the other four

listed Web pages in the Google search, all of which she started
to realize mimicked real ones.

"I can't believe it, he's . . ." She turned and saw Jack's wrinkled brow, and hesitated. She patted his shoulder. "Listen, there's
probably an explanation."

She tried to sound calm. "Really, don't worry. When I take
you home tomorrow, I'll tell Mum and she can ask him. Have
you met him, Jack? Has he been to the house?"

Jack shrugged. "I think so, because sometimes I can smell
this horrible aftershave smell in my room."

"In your room?" She paused. "But you haven't met him?"

"I've seen a photo."

"That one?" Saskia pointed to the Web site.

Jack shook his head. He flicked to the back page of the book.

"Is that him?" Saskia gawked, grabbing the book from him.

She peered at Jago Martin. Then she looked again, and felt
the blood drain from her face.

"What?" Jack said, sounding scared.

"Jack? Is this a joke?" She sat back unsteadily.

He looked bewildered.

Saskia tried to stand up, and stumbled in shock. "Right. Jack,"
she said, trying to keep her voice normal. "Leave this with me.
You've done really well. Why don't you go and have a shower, and
get dressed? Then later you could take Rosie out for a walk and get
some bread for lunch at the shop? Nana's making soup, I think."

"But . . ."

She put her hand on his shoulder, knowing there were only
so many seconds she could keep her face composed.

"Jack. Please."

37

"No, Jago," Kate said, braking on the single-lane country road right outside the airfield. She knew her action would block traffic. She didn't care. "Not a chance in hell am I going skydiving right now."

She put her hands on the top of the steering wheel and tensed her lower jaw.

Jago snorted with laughter.

"What?" she snapped.

"I was just thinking I'm glad you didn't have a brick in your hand."

She realized he was trying to stop smiling. She shook her head, determined not to be coerced into joining him.

"Listen. Hear me out," he said.

She sat stiffly, feeling the tears coming. "I can't believe this. Why on earth would you think I would want to do this?"

His tone softened. "Kate, listen. I've always wanted to do it. After the canal boat, I looked it up on a whim, and found this course. I had nothing else to do last Sunday so . . . and I think it's exactly the last step you need."

She looked out the window at a small plane taking off, praying for him to say this was a joke. That they were now driving on to some nearby Buckinghamshire village pub for lunch.

". . . so I came here and did a one-day static-line course. Did my first jump on Monday."

She looked at him, disbelieving. She realized he was beaming.

An enormous pressure came upon her, like she was going down a water slide at a swimming pool. What had she done? She should never have told him.

"Please tell me this is a joke," she whispered. But then she saw his tapping feet, the wired tension of his body, and realized he wasn't joking.

"Four times!" Jago exclaimed, making her jump. He laughed at her reaction. "Sorry, I'm completely wired. The adrenaline just . . ." He blew out his cheeks. "Whoo! Sorry, I've hardly slept. I'm completely high on it. Addicted. Do you know what I mean?"

Kate knew exactly what he meant. It's how it had been for her the first week she'd jumped, too.

There was a loud beep behind them. She looked in her mirror and saw a truck approaching from behind.

"You better, um . . ." Jago said, jerking his head toward the opening to the airfield.

A minibus appeared from behind it, and followed her in the gate, forcing her to continue toward the airfield.

Jago perched on his seat, like a schoolboy who'd done something naughty and got away with it.

"OK, listen. I know you're mad but it's going to be amazing."

Was he insane? "I'm not jumping, Jago," Kate said resolutely as they drove into a half-full parking lot. She swung around in front of some hangars and pulled on the hand brake hard, without turning off the engine.

Jago just kept tapping his foot.

She looked around. Ten small two-seater aircraft, their wings like flattened rabbit ears across their little mousey noses, sat in the grass airfield beyond the fence, signposted to keep spectators out. A group of grinning charity jumpers stood lined up on the other side in matching T-shirts, having a photo taken.

Hang on. Kate swiveled around. She knew this place. This was where she had done her refresher course five years ago, with Hugo and Jack in tow.

A ball of fear settled inside her stomach.

"Kate. Come here," Jago said gently after she turned the car off. She was so shaken, she let him, but kept her body rigid in protest as he wrapped his arms around her. He sighed in her ear. "Right, listen. First of all, I'm doing it with you. And second, it's incredibly safe. We did all that stuff on Sunday about how to deal with line twists and cell-end problems, and you know yourself that even if the main parachute did malfunction, you have a reserve. You know all this. I mean how many times have you jumped—twenty?"

Kate shook her head gently. "Twenty-six."

"Shit. Have you really? Well, there you go."

Panic pulsed through her. "No," she said. She wriggled out of Jago's arms, pushing him aside. "I'm not doing it. There's no way."

But he wouldn't let it go. "Listen. You're not doing a free fall from twelve thousand feet. This is just a little static-line jump from thirty-five hundred feet. A piece of piss for someone who's done free fall. All you have to do is jump, let the static-line pull out your chute for you, then enjoy."

She looked past Jago's shoulder, where she saw a man and woman doing the "pre-jump dance" she recognized from New

Zealand, sucking too fast on their cigarettes, turning randomly one way, then the other, as they waited for their jump, grinning at each other manically.

She felt Jago appraising her. "Come on, Kate. Last step. Face the final fear."

"Jago, it's just not that simple," she said, shaking her head, desperately looking for a way out. "I can't just jump. I don't have my license."

He sat back. "OK, well, don't be mad but I gave them your details and they found it on the international register." She stared at him, unable to form words. He was serious about this. "As long as you match the online photo, and you show them a bank card or something. And they want you to do a half-day refresher course, too."

A droning noise approached. Kate looked up and saw a nine-seat Islander far above them. A little figure appeared midair. There was a burst of yellow in the bright blue sky as the static-line from the plane pulled out a parachute. She watched the tiny figure wriggling for a moment then relax back into the jump.

Right at that moment, Kate had a flashback to New Zealand. It was so powerful she almost gasped.

She was up there, thousands of feet up in the sky.

Hearing the loud drone of the propellers dropping away into silence.

Feeling the wind whistling on her face.

Her limbs losing all resistance.

Relaxing like never before.

Falling into the void.

Utter euphoria descending.

Flying like a bird.

Unbelievably, Kate realized she wanted that feeling again.

She had loved it.

"Oh, my God," she whispered.

Jago murmured in her ear. "Listen, you were going to do it after your parents died. This time it's even more important. You need to restart your life, Kate. You said it yourself, Jack needs you."

She watched the jumper gracefully turn in a semicircle back toward the white arrow on the landing field.

Could she do that again?

Jago carried on, hypnotizing her. "And for us, too. Let's make it the start of how we plan to go on. Having fun, throwing caution to the wind."

She let him move in closer. He kissed her cheek, once, twice, three times, playfully. For a second, she thought of Jack and the way they used to show their love to each other so unabashedly, when he was a toddler, and how she wanted that again. She imagined telling Jack she had jumped out of a plane today. Seeing the pride in his eyes as he told his friends. His mum was not weird and anxious. She was fun and brave.

"So we jump once and it's over?"

His eyes shone with delight as he realized she was considering it. "Once and it's over. Then we head straight back to Balliol and lock ourselves in my room for the rest of the weekend."

His words reached inside her and opened a door. She felt the anxiety rush out of her in a long breath, and turned and met his lips full on. The waves that had started in her kitchen last Saturday when he kissed her pounded back through her body.

As Jago kissed her, she thought of what he'd done for her. He'd faced his own fears up in that plane, to help her. He was giving her a chance to jump back into the real world, faster than she'd ever imagined, and he was going to do it with her.

"OK," she whispered.

38

Jack ran around Nana's garden kicking his ball. He knew that he was going to do something bad. He didn't normally do bad things, but today he didn't care.

Aunt Saskia said they would tell Mum about Jago Martin tomorrow. But he wanted to tell her now.

"Nana?" he shouted, running into the house. "It's nearly twelve o'clock. Can I go and get the bread for lunch?"

"Yes, darling, please do," Nana said from the stove, where she was making soup. She turned to find him some money. Aunt Sass was still at the computer, looking a bit lost in her head, like Mum did sometimes. "And can you get Granddad his newspaper, and another pint of milk?"

"Sure," Jack said, grabbing the money and Rosie's leash. Rosie leapt up at him and pawed at his leg.

To his relief, Aunt Sass didn't even look up. Jack shouted, "Bye," and ran out, through the garden gate and onto the river path. He set off past the boats, with Rosie pulling ahead.

"I'm going to look after her, Dad," he said, looking up at the sky.

He waited till he was out of sight of Granddad's house, then grabbed his mobile from his pocket and pressed Kate's number, nervously wondering what she would say. Would she be pleased with him, or cross?

It went straight to voice mail.

He took a long breath.

"Mum. It's Jack. Don't be angry with me but there's something wrong with that man Jago Martin. I've got his book and all the numbers are fake in it. He's stolen bits from other books on Amazon and made them into a book with his name on it and he's pretending it's his. Don't be angry at me, but he's weird. Come home, Mum . . ."

Back at the house, Saskia got up, a nauseous feeling in her stomach.

She picked up Jago Martin's book, then walked into the sitting room and shut the door. She picked up the phone and rang Kate's number.

"Kate, it's me. You have to ring me back straightaway. I don't know where you are or how to tell you this but that guy Jago Martin . . ."

She spoke for another whole minute before putting the phone down.

She sat staring at Jago Martin's photo, hoping to God she was right, because if not, this would really be the end of her and Kate's relationship for good.

She tried to imagine him for the twentieth time in a suit, with black gelled hair, and hoped that this wasn't a horrible mistake. That last time she had seen this man, he really had been called Tony, and really had come from Essex.

39

Kate couldn't believe how quickly everything came back to her.

"I'll wait for you in the canteen," Jago had said when they arrived, after introducing her to her instructor, Calum, and giving her a reassuring kiss.

"Right, this should be a doddle for you, Kate," Calum said. "Let's go."

At his request, she demonstrated flaring the parachute before hitting the ground, then pointed to the altimeter, her reserve chute handle, and the slider, telling Calum what each was for. She pushed her riser straps apart and kicked to demonstrate how to remove a line twist, and mocked up reinflating the cell ends with the steering lines. He made her jump from the dummy plane five times to check she knew the positions and how to breathe. He also made her jump five times in a harness from a twenty-foot-high scaffolding rig to show she could land with her feet together and roll.

All through the morning, as Kate heard the planes droning

above, and saw the jumpers pulling on their suits, she waited for the figures to come.

One in eighty thousand jumps will end in a "serious incident."

But she knew that that would most likely be because she'd done something stupid, like not buckling up her chest strap.

The chances of both chutes malfunctioning are one in a million.

And probably better than that here with qualified packers who checked and rechecked.

The figures did come . . . but they went, halfhearted, on their way again.

They had absolutely no control over her.

They would not stop her from doing this.

And even better, to her astonishment, she was looking forward to it.

"Right, you obviously know what you're doing, Kate," Calum declared at the end of the morning. "We'll have to get you to come back and jump with the club jumpers one day."

It was funny, she thought, this stranger's perception of her as being a brave person.

"That's great that you can access my international license online, is that new?" she said as they crossed the concrete area back to the canteen.

Calum frowned. "Can you? Never heard of that before. I thought you had to bring your license and show it—but then, I don't work in the office . . ."

They shrugged at each other as he dropped her off with Jago, who was sitting outside reading a newspaper at a table.

"Right, you guys. It's twelve fifteen now. We'll jump at one. We'll take the little Islander up. I'll call you," Calum said, walking off to the canteen with a wave.

Jago gave him a thumbs up and beamed at her as she sat down.

She saw him check his watch, and then his phone screen, before he looked back up at her.

He smiled. "How was it?"

"Good, actually," she said, smiling back.

She noticed him checking his watch and phone again. Saw him drumming his fingers on the table.

She nodded. "Jago—are you OK? You look a little bit . . . eh, distracted . . ."

"Shitting myself," Jago blurted out. The irony hit them both and they laughed.

Kate took a sip of his coffee. "I can't believe I'm doing this."

"It's amazing, honestly. I'm proud of you," Jago replied. But his words sounded distant.

She reached out and took his hand, no longer self-conscious. To her surprise, he didn't grasp hers warmly, as he normally did. His hand was rigid. His fingers pushed against hers, were patting them reassuringly, but then he pulled them away. A rush of gratitude went through her. Here she was, worrying about herself, when Jago was having to face jumping out of a plane, too—and he was doing it for her.

"You know, I'd probably never have done this again, if you hadn't made me," she said softly. "I just remembered today how much I loved it."

She waited for him to give her a reassuring hug or a kiss, but he didn't. Kate sat back.

She saw him check his watch again. And then his phone. His shoulders tensed, and he took a deep breath. What was up with him?

"Well, I can't tell you how pleased I am to hear you say that," he finally replied. There was something odd about his voice. It was almost brittle. He must be really nervous, Kate realized. Much more than he was trying to let on. "Right. What do you want?" he almost barked, standing up. "Coffee?"

"Er, thanks." She nodded. She'd just have to let him work through it himself. Clearly, he was feeling as anxious as she was, and with good reason—he was still a novice jumper.

Jago walked off to the canteen line with a brief smile, checking his phone again.

As she waited, Kate looked around the garden. Most tables were busy. The air was full of tension and excitement. She'd missed this. This world of people with adventurous purpose. The horse riding. Traveling with her friends. Skiing. Working at the parachute school in New Zealand. And then when Hugo died, she thought nothing would ever be fun again.

She'd forgotten, this was part of who she was.

Kate stretched, feeling the sun on her face, watching an experienced-looking group of free-fallers walk toward a fourteen-seater Caravan plane. They strode with the heroic gait of firemen or helicopter doctors. They must be the club members that Calum had mentioned. She saw the beginners at the tables around her watch the group with admiring glances.

That had been her once.

She thought about Calum's offer.

Was Jago right? Could it be again?

There was a soft buzz in Kate's bag. She pulled our her mobile, and saw two voice messages that must have arrived earlier when she'd been training with Calum. One was from Jack, one from Saskia.

She raised her eyebrows at what they would both think if they knew where she was.

She lifted the phone to her ear, looking through the window at Jago. He was standing with his back to her in the canteen line, now holding his own phone to his ear.

She wondered who he was talking to.

"Mum, it's me. You're not picking up. I've got something bad to tell you about that Jago Martin man. Me and Aunt Sass looked at his book and . . ."

As Jack's message continued, a cloud passed over the sun. The temperature dropped. Her bones felt suddenly chilled, her face thrown into shadow.

When Jack's message finished, she listened to Saskia's.

And when that message stopped, Kate looked up and realized there was no cloud. The sun was shining as brightly as it had been before.

Jack walked slowly back from the village shop at 12:15 P.M., clutching the bread, newspaper, and milk in one hand, and Rosie's leash in the other. He didn't normally defy Aunt Sass and now he was worried. Would she be cross with him that he'd told Mum about that dodgy book before she did?

He strolled under the canopy section of trees with Rosie, so lost in thought he didn't get the strange feeling he normally had under here of being watched.

So when a very big man stepped out of the bushes, he nearly jumped in the air.

The man was wearing a black beanie even though it was a nice day. He had a mobile phone to his ear and was talking into it.

With a gasp, Jack stumbled. He tried to right his footing and race ahead, but Rosie saw the man, and strained her leash in his direction.

"No, girl," Jack said, his chest pounding. He pulled her hard, too scared to look behind him.

"Jack!"

He stopped, and turned around.

The big man was putting away his phone.

"Hi! It's me. Your neighbor, Magnus! What on earth are you doing out here?"

With relief, Jack recognized the man from Hubert Street. He looked around but the path was still empty. What should he do? He didn't want to be rude. "My grandparents live here." He pointed vaguely behind him down the country lane.

"Oh. That's funny. Hey, nice dog!" the man said cheerfully, coming over. "Jack, listen this is good I bumped into you—can you maybe help me, please?" He pointed out at the road behind the trees. "I've broken down in my car back in the lane. I was just walking to the village to find a bus back to Oxford. The phone in my house is not working and I need to phone my housemates to come and pick me up. Could we ring your mum, and ask her to go next door and knock on my friends' door? Tell them where I am? Then I won't have to get the bus home and leave my car here."

Jack hesitated. Rosie whined, pulling him.

"Can't you ring the AAA?" he mumbled.

The man laughed. "Good idea, but it costs money. I'm a poor student, you know?"

"Um. OK," Jack said awkwardly.

The man leaned down and patted Rosie. Rosie ignored him. "Your mum was telling me in the garden that you're an Arsenal fan, huh?" the man said.

Jack's shoulders dropped. He nodded shyly.

"Me too! You think we're going to get the championship next year, huh?"

Jack shrugged. The man stood up.

"OK. Listen. Do you know your mum's number?"

Jack nodded.

"Well, could you tell it to me and I'll ring her? Maybe you could speak to her for me? My phone is back at the car, actually—could you come with me?"

Jack shrugged again, not sure if he should, but went with him anyway.

He was their neighbor, after all.

Kate sat frozen in the canteen garden.

Her mind raced, trying to think what possible motives Saskia could have for making this up.

"Kate?"

She turned and saw Calum walking out of the canteen with Jago.

"Ten minutes in the packing shed," Calum called, with upturned thumbs.

Jago sat down. "That's interesting."

"What?" she whispered.

"He was saying that they're filming a stunt for a Hollywood film here next week."

Kate tried to calm the rush in her head.

It had to be a mistake.

Why would Saskia say this? Because she was bitter? Could she have really made this up? And involved Jack?

Why on earth would she say Jago was Tony from Essex?

She felt a hand on her arm. Jago was watching her. "Oi, mate. You're not flaking out on me, are you?"

She shook her head.

"No," she said, trying to sound normal, starting to stand up. She'd call Saskia right now, that's what she'd do. "I'm, uh, just going to ring my sister-in-law and check Jack's all right. I want to speak to him, tell him I'm jumping. If anything happened and . . ."

Jago's hand came out of nowhere and settled on her arm. Firmly.

"Kate. Please. That's not a good idea. Nothing's going to happen to you, and you'll just worry him."

"No, but I . . ."

Jago shook his head and grabbed the phone out of her hand. He held on to it. "I think it's a really bad idea. You don't want to make him more anxious, do you? Tell him when you get back down—then he'll be really proud without the worrying bit."

"OK. Well . . ." She looked around. "Actually, I'm just going to get some sugar for my coffee. . . ."

Jago jumped up before she could move. "Stay here—I'll get you some. . . . Least I can do after making you jump out of a plane!" He grinned. His former jolliness had suddenly returned.

As he walked off—still with her phone in his hand—she sat rigid.

Anger surged through her. Why would Saskia lie? Tell Jack the book was fake? Jago's small leather rucksack lay in front of her. She glanced into the café and saw him rummaging at the counter among the salt and pepper. She had to do it. Quickly, she grabbed it.

As she began rummaging, looking for his mobile, something red caught her eye. Her shoulders stiffened.

How the hell did Jago have this?

She heard the tinkle of the café door and he emerged.

Their eyes met.

He looked at her hands. Quickly he came and sat beside her.

"I don't understand," she stuttered. "Did you take this from my home?" She placed her international skydiving license on the table.

Jago said nothing. He reached over for his coffee, and put her phone on the table.

"Jago," Kate whispered. "Please tell me. What is this all about?"

"Hmm?" He sipped his coffee.

She looked about her, seeing the couples around, feeling the dream of her future with Jago cracking. She wanted to be wrong but knew she wasn't.

"I want you to jump out of an airplane, get back to life, et cetera?"

There was a new tone in his voice she hadn't heard before. Hardened, cynical.

"No," she said quietly. "What is taking things from my house about? And pretending to be a professor of mathematics from Edinburgh?"

Her eyes met his. She desperately hoped he would say something to reassure her, to tell her she'd made a mistake, and so had Saskia and Jack. At first she saw the familiar warmth and humor in his blue eyes, but then he registered what she knew, and a cloud of icy mist passed across them. They froze in front of her like an Arctic ice field. She tried to look away but couldn't. His pupils so cruel and lifeless that it made her shudder.

Jago leaned forward, so close to her face that she could smell coffee on his breath. She tried to move but he was gripping her upper arm painfully tight.

"Jago. Let go of my arm," she said, scared.

She looked around the garden for help, but the jumpers were talking in tight-knit groups, lost in their own world of facing their own fears.

"I mean it, get off me," she repeated. But Jago's grip only tightened. Tears formed as it began to hurt. "I said, let me go," she tried to say firmly, but it came out so weakly, it was hardly there at all. She summoned everything she had. "Look. If you don't let go of my fucking arm, I'm going to scream."

Jago held her so tight she thought the bone would break.

"Uh-uh, and if you do, I'll tell my friend the Viking—who you might know better as the bloke next door—to throw your son in the fucking river."

His accent had changed. He was speaking in a different accent. English. West Country. Why was he doing that?

Kate tried to breathe, but her throat felt constricted with fear.

"No . . . how could you . . . ?" she tried, her words fading away to nothing.

"Nana lets me go to the village shop by myself to buy bread at twelve o'clock for lunch every Saturday," Jago whispered in a falsetto voice.

Kate's eyes opened wide as she recognized her son's words, spoken inside her house just the other week. How had he heard them?

Jack walked with Magnus back to his car on the lane.

He opened the door, and Jack glanced around nervously.

"Hey, please, don't worry, Jack. Your mum told you not to get in cars with strangers. That's good."

He shrugged, waiting nervously as the man got his phone.

"What your mum's number?"

Jack told him and watched the man put it in with his big fingers. That was strange. He could tell the man wasn't typing in the numbers Jack was telling him.

Magnus saw him looking, and turned the phone away. "This is great, Jack. Really helpful."

From the front, Kate knew that Jago's hold on her must look like an embrace. A boyfriend, hugging his nervous girlfriend, before her jump.

"Why would you want to hurt Jack?" she said. "Get off me!"

Jago's phone rang. He checked his watch. "And on cue . . ." he said.

He took it out with his free hand and answered it away from her. He murmured something into it, then he turned to her. "Someone who wants to talk to you."

He was holding her so tight, she could hardly move her arms. She moved one painfully within his embrace and took it, with shaky fingers.

"Kate!" a man's voice said in a foreign accent.

"Who is this?"

"Magnus from next door. I have your son, Jack, here by the river. He's just giving me a hand."

"What are you talking . . . ?"

"Mum?"

"Jack! Where are you?"

His voice was timid. "By the river near Granddad's house. I got bread for Nana at the shop. Magnus said can you go next door and tell his friends to come and pick him up. His car's broken."

Kate opened her mouth to shout, "Jack—run!"

But Jago pushed his lips into her face so tight it held her jaw rigid, and whispered. "I would advise you strongly to say yes."

Kate shook her head, and tried to pull away from him, but he stayed there pressed up to her face. Frantically, she pushed her arms sideways to loosen his grip, but he held her so tight she was suffocating. "Jack!" she called.

"If you don't want him to end up going for a little swim right now in Granddad's river, say yes," Jago growled into the side of her cheek, squeezing her upper body so hard it felt like her ribs might break.

Kate tried again to move her body sideways to release herself but he wouldn't let go.

"Kate," he said in the strange new accent. "Stop now, or we're going to kill him. Right now." With each word he pulled his embrace tighter till she thought she might faint.

Kate twisted her head and saw in his eyes a cruelty she could not believe.

He was serious.

Panicked, she looked around her again, frantically, but nobody was looking at her, lost as they were in their own anxiety and excitement about jumping from a plane. If they'd looked over they'd just have seen a boyfriend embracing his girlfriend, and talking intimately into her ear.

She tried to think. They had Jack. By a river. Jago and that man who lived next door.

He knew Jago?

The implications of how long this had been planned hit her. This was serious. These men were violent.

And one of them had Jack.

She had to make sure Jack was safe, for a few moments at least, so she could think.

Jago twisted her around till his face was close to hers. He mouthed, "One, two, three . . ."

"Yes, Jack. That's fine. I'll do it," she gasped into the phone. As Jago began to pull the phone away from her face, she called, "Jack, Jack . . ."

But he was gone.

She sat on the bench as Jago put the phone back in his pocket, fighting the urge to scream for help and knowing she couldn't risk it in case the Scandinavian man really did have Jack. "Jesus, is this about the money? Have it!" she exclaimed, desperately trying to think clearly. "I never wanted it in the first place. Just let Jack go!"

"Oh, it's always the same with you lot," Jago said, sounding disappointed. "You don't care about money because you've always had it." He turned his voice into a high-pitched whine. "When I was a teenager I used to jump five-bar gates on my pony."

She shuddered.

"But the thing is, Kate, if it wasn't for me, you wouldn't have had half of it."

"What?" she said, distracted, hating Richard and Helen with every part of her being for letting Jack go to the shop alone. How long before they realized he was missing?

Jago shrugged. "Where do you think the two hundred fifty thousand came from that Richard gave Hugo to start your business?"

Kate froze.

She thought at first she'd misheard him. What on earth was he talking about? "How could you know that?" she whispered.

"How do I know?" Jago continued. She looked at his mouth, unable to believe these vicious, strange words were coming from lips she had found so gentle just an hour before. "Because I know everything. I know Richard and his partner Charley Heavin, the builder, took every penny my dad had one night in the pub and sold him a piece-of-shit house up on a hill in Cornwall with rotten foundations that fell down. I know my dad bought it with the money my grandfather left my mother, and that he did it without telling her because he wanted it to be a surprise, because he loved her and wanted to make her happy with the view. But it didn't. It made her mad, because cracks started appearing in the walls almost straightaway. And I watched the poor sod spend hours in that basement trying to push the cracks back together with a piece of metal and carjack so she didn't find them. Charley wouldn't return his calls, till one day the whole wall came off the side of it. Literally, off the side. My mother was so mad, she screamed at him it was over, and the poor sod was so stressed, he just lost it, and hit her. With one of the bricks on the ground. He didn't mean to do it, but it killed her. Right there. In front of me, when I was nine." He pulled back as if to enjoy Kate's horrified expression. "And then he killed himself in jail because of what he'd done. And then Richard Parker took the profit and started his business. Fucked off out of Cornwall as soon as he could. That's how I know, Kate. Richard Parker ruined my fucking life."

Horror crept over her. "This is about *Richard?*"

He loosened his grip, but just a little. "Well, to be honest, Kate, it probably should have been Charley. But the fat fuck died of a heart attack on the beach in Portugal, so I'm afraid the finger of fate's next option was Richard."

Kate stared, fighting back frightened tears. "This is crazy. What are you talking about? That's nothing to do with me. Or Jack."

Jago sighed. "I know that, Kate. But, the thing is, I don't care."

She saw him look over her shoulder and wave. Calum was summoning them to start preparing for their jump.

"Shall we go?" Jago asked, standing up and holding out his hand.

"No," Kate protested, trying to push his hands away. But he pulled her up, keeping his arm around her as they walked to the giant open-fronted packing shed. Calum pointed to the jumpsuits and their parachutes and Jago pushed her toward them.

He thrust an overall into her hands and motioned for her to put it on. Kate glanced around, terrified. How could she get away? As she pulled on her overall and chute, with shaking fingers, Jago right beside her, she tried to think. This was about revenge?

There was no doubt that Scandinavian man was with Jack. But would he really kill him?

He wouldn't. Not just for money, or certainly not just to scare Richard. Surely? Not a little boy.

Kate looked around.

She had to shout for help. Call Jago's bluff.

But before she could open her mouth, Jago grasped her chest strap, and did it up, pulling it tighter when she instinctively tried to jerk away, revolted as he touched her breast. He shuddered suddenly, as if he was experiencing a little thrill. "You know, this is a big day for me. I've been planning this for five years."

"What do you mean?" she spat at him.

"Well, it's not easy. The important thing is that Richard doesn't find out it's about him. Because that way I can keep going right to the end. So, I mean, the next step. First the dog . . ." he murmured. He put his hands up like two little paws desperately scrabbling in the air, and began to whine.

It took Kate a long, cold moment to register. "Hugo's dog?" She remembered Hugo talking about the dog. How losing it had been so traumatic, he'd never been able to own another one, even as an adult. "You drowned his dog?"

Jago put on his own helmet. "That's what gave me the idea. Honestly, seeing Hugo's face. And how Richard's face looked, not being able to fix it for him. It just helped, you know?"

Kate felt as if she were being submerged in cold water. "Jago, this is crazy. You're telling me you drowned Hugo's dog because of Richard. But that was twenty-five years ago!"

Jago held out a helmet for her. He was so calm.

"I know it's hard to understand, but this is my life. What I do for my parents. Putting cracks in Richard Parker's world, and then watching it crumble, brick by brick. Just like he did to ours. It's nothing to do with you."

Kate could only stare at him. Then, suddenly understanding, she reeled backward.

"Oh my God. What else have you done?"

Magnus waved good-bye to Jack and he set off for home, relieved.

"Snores!" he heard Sass shout as he came up to the house. "Why did you take so long? Granddad's gone that way down the lane looking for you."

"I was helping that man."

Saskia stared. "What man?"

They peered back out the gate.

"Oh," Jack said. That was weird. "He's gone. His car must have started working again."

Saskia looked back down the empty lane. "Well, never mind. Listen, I think I'm going to take you back to your mum's this afternoon. I need to speak away from Nana and Granddad."

"What about?"

"Don't you worry."

He hoped when she found out what he'd done she wouldn't be cross.

"What else have you done?" Kate repeated weakly.

"Guys, over by the manifest, please," she heard Calum shout. He held out a deep, black cloth bag with a string pull. "I'll need to take your mobile, keys, anything loose that could fall out—in here, please."

Jago put his hand on her back, and firmly guided her forward. Her brain felt like it was under fire. Information that made no sense flew at her from all directions. As they approached Calum, and the open valuables bag, she looked over and saw their plane, waiting on the field. Jago was taking her in a plane. Telling her things that made no sense. That he'd killed Hugo's dog? Drowned it? Telling her that if she didn't go up in the plane, he'd drown Jack, too. Her hand flew to her mouth. This didn't make any sense.

Think, Kate thought.

Pull yourself together.

Jack's in trouble.

Think.

She did her best to force a long, deep breath through her body to calm herself. Then took another. And then, from somewhere through the fog of shock, in the tiny space she created for herself, Jago's voice miraculously drifted into her head. Not the Jago standing in front of her, the frightening stranger with the odd West Country accent who was hurting her son, but kind, sweet Jago from last week. From the night in Chumsley Norton, from the canal boat, from Highgate Woods. "Trust your instincts, Kate," said the kindly Scottish accent in her head. "Trust your instincts."

Kate shook herself. She had to stop trying to work out why Jago was doing this. He was clearly insane. There was no time. Instead, she had to work out how to survive it, for Jack's sake. And to do that, she had to at least pretend she was going to get on the plane to give herself time to think.

Jago stepped in front of her and put his phone and keys into the deep bag Calum held out. Kate took her keys from her hoodie pocket. She scrabbled around, trying to think of some way to gain back some control from him. She had to find a way to let someone else know what was happening without harming Jack.

Jago stepped back and turned to her. Calum, too, watched Kate expectantly.

She held up her keys, then stepped in front of Jago, so he was behind her. Not knowing what she was doing, she stuck her closed right hand into the bag, dropped the keys, and heard them fall on top of something hard with a little thump.

A phone. Think.

Stay calm.

And then, suddenly, out of nowhere, Kate knew what to do.

Quickly, she reached out a finger and searched around. Her fingertip touched the phone below the keys.

Jago's phone.

"So you're sure the weather's OK for jumping then?" she said to Calum, trying to buy herself time.

As she said it, she quickly opened the rest of her fingers, ignoring Jago's eyes burning into her back, and formed a sweaty cage around the phone. She clasped them together, so that it was pulled inside her palm.

"Yes, all good, I'm afraid," Calum laughed.

"She's just a bit nervous, aren't you, darling?" Jago said, pushing his finger so hard into her back she nearly cried out.

Kate nodded, making a comedy scared face at Calum, at the same time, pushing the phone hard with her bent middle finger. It shifted up her palm a few inches toward her wrist, and the opening of her hoodie sleeve.

Keep your nerve.

She could do this.

"OK, Kate?" Calum said, looking at the bag.

"Yes, thanks," she said, starting to withdraw her hand. As she did it, she shoved the phone one last time with her finger, so hard that it hurt—and to her relief, felt the phone settle into her sleeve just as her hand came out the bag.

Jago's face appeared suddenly at the side of hers. She felt his hot, angry breath on her cheek. He was looking down at her hand. She gently straightened her other four fingers so it looked as natural as possible, and held her breath, her middle finger still pushing the bottom of his phone, keeping it from falling.

"OK. Time to go, Kate," he said in her ear.

She let out the breath. Jago hadn't noticed.

She had done it.

Calum pointed to their left. "Now could you follow the others over to the manifest board?"

Jago's finger prodded hard between her vertebrae again to move her forward, then he placed his hand around her shoulder, pulling her close. It was all she could do not to hit it away, revulsed. They walked over to the manifest area, where the other two passengers were writing their names on the board. They looked up at Kate and Jago. She knew what they saw: the kind boyfriend, soothing his girlfriend's pre-jump nerves.

"Anyway," Jago said, pulling her off to the side of the board, "now back to my story—do you remember you used to meet Hugo at a pub in Archway when you were at college? Your local?"

Kate froze again.

What was he saying now?

She shook herself. She had to stop listening to Jago, and keep thinking. She had to use that phone to get help.

"Well, I used to watch you there."

She couldn't listen. This couldn't be true.

Think, she yelled in her head. Breathe. Don't listen to him.

"Well, one day, you left, and Hugo watched you," Jago said into her ear, "and I could tell he was thinking about you. Dreaming about the future. And then I thought, What could I do to take the smile off his big, fat face?"

A small gasp released from her mouth. "No," Kate said, shaking her head. "No."

Jago pulled her in more tightly and she pushed her bent finger harder into the phone till the tendons in her wrist felt they would snap.

"What could I do that would make Richard's son's marriage shit from day one? What could I do to put a great big fuck-off crack through it? That no one would trace back to me?"

Kate felt her legs start to shake. Her breathing became so shallow she thought she might faint.

"You can't have," she whispered. "Their car hit a stag. The police told me."

Jago sighed, and released his grip a little, only to tighten it even harder as she instinctively tried to move away from him.

"Honestly Kate, if you're as pissed off as me, anything's possible, believe me. Remember, I lost my parents, too. And no, it wasn't easy, but you can do anything if you take your time and do your research. I thought about making it look like a fallen tree or a rock fall, for a while, but that was too suspicious. Then I heard about a car crash in Scotland where it hit a deer. It was brilliant. Nobody would suspect it. So I just shot that old stag with one of my dad's old poaching rifles—took a few attempts, mind you—and got it up onto the truck with a winch I fixed onto the pickup bed, like hunters do in the States. Took five minutes—then I waited till dark."

His words flew at her, battering at her. She tried to ignore them, gripping the phone with her finger, but she couldn't. "You killed my parents?" she said.

One of the other jumpers, a middle-aged woman, came over with the pen. Jago pulled back and smiled.

"Nervous?" she asked.

Kate managed to nod, knowing her face must be drained white.

"Me too," the woman said sympathetically. "We'll be fine."

"Well said," Jago said, taking the pen from her with a wink.

As she walked off with the other woman onto the field toward the plane, he took the pen and wrote both his and Kate's names on the manifest board, still grasping her with the other arm. The shaking in her legs worsened. She felt so cold.

But Jago was not finished. She tried to shut his voice out, think about the phone in her sleeve, but already she knew there was worse to come.

"And then . . ."

She groaned and tried to pull away again.

"No."

"No, Kate, it's important. I spent a lot of time and effort doing this. So you need to listen. So, every week, I sat on the bench outside your house in Highgate, the one you bought with my family's blood money. Saw him bring that car home. Saw him looking to see what the neighbors thought."

He pressed his nose hard into her ear. "You see, the Viking gathers information from people like you, when I need it, but he also gives it to people. And one night, he opened his big mouth beside these guys in the pub who had a bit of a reputation for stealing cars. Told them about this fifty-thousand-pound sports car his neighbor had bought. All I had to do was slip in after they'd left with his car keys.

The door was open. Hugo was just about to phone the police. And you know what the best bit was?" Jago growled, putting down the pen, and guiding her onto the field behind the others. "I told him all of this. Told him it would be you next. But I'd give it another five years. Because first I wanted to enjoy watching Richard try to keep the cracks together with his big, dopey, desperate face. Waiting until you'd had enough of the cold nights. Were ready to be warmed up again." He forced Kate to look at him. "Hugo particularly liked that detail. Actually, it was a long wait, so I practiced on your sister-in-law and caused Richard and Helen a little embarrassment in the process. . . ."

Kate took his hand, feeling the phone start to slip down into her palm, but not caring for a second. Because she knew now what was coming. "Please, Jago. Not Jack."

He shook his head as if soothing a child. "Kate, honestly, I'm not going to touch him. I've worked it out. I reckon his foundations will be so rotten after I've finished with you lot, I can sit back and watch him fuck up his own life."

She swung around out of his grip. "What do you mean finished with?"

"Well, his grandparents, his father, and now . . ." He pushed her along as Calum marched to the plane fifty yards ahead, her feet almost off the ground.

She looked at it up ahead. "No," she said. "There are people all around us. You can't."

"I know, which is why when you jump out, you're going to . . ." Hugo whispered something in her ear. It was something Calum had reminded her never to do this morning in his safety refresher.

She pulled back, horrified. "But my chute will get entangled."

Jago shrugged. "Kate, don't worry. There's a note on your computer called 'Sorry,' explaining why you did it. That you were a shit mother and you knew it."

She shook her head, trying to keep breathing, but he kept pulling her toward the plane. Forty yards, thirty . . .

He was telling her to sabotage her own chute.

Think! Stop listening to him. Think what you're going to do. There was never going to be a chance to use the phone at this rate.

Jack needs you.

Jago's arm pulled her faster toward the plane. Twenty yards, ten . . . "The thing is, if you don't do it, Kate, if the Viking doesn't hear you did it, in twenty minutes, Jack's going to dive into the river to save Rosie. I'll be out of here before you can check. And thanks to the money the Viking took out of your Internet account yesterday, I'll be gone for a long time.

"But when they stop looking for me—and they will—I'll come back for you anyway. This way, you save your son at least. If you don't, he goes in the river anyway and I come back for you. It might be a year, or five. In a wardrobe, behind a door, in a window, who knows?" He kissed her ear and said in a playful scary voice: "The monster in the dark."

"Get off of me," she gasped as they finally reached the back of the plane.

He hugged her, pulling her into his body, making her want to retch, hiding her from Calum, who strode ahead to talk to the pilot. "It's a shame you had to run off last Saturday, and that we couldn't finish what we started in the kitchen. But it doesn't matter. Because one day, when Richard is an old man, lying in the ruins of his family, just like my mother was, I'll tell him about today, and your sad, scared face."

"All right, Kate?" Calum said, coming over to check her equipment. She saw him note her expression. "You sure?"

Could she tell him, shout for help? Tell him she'd lost her nerve, didn't want to jump?

But what if Jago was telling the truth? What if they hurt Jack?

It had been Jago, the whole time, for the past eleven years. He had killed Hugo and her parents, and had been frightening her ever since.

None of it had been imagined.

She had been right. Her instinct had been right.

And now he wanted to kill her.

The engine of the plane started up. Her eyes danced about. She was nearly out of time.

She looked at Jago and she thought about everything that had happened. Meeting him in the café, the book, the waitress, the dog, the canal boat, the woods . . .

Another idea came spinning furiously into her head.

Jago's book. The one she'd locked in the shed.

She looked him in the eye. Slowly. She saw him register that something had changed. "I've got your book!" she said as Calum looked over her straps. She saw Jago glance at him, checking if he'd heard.

"No, you don't," Jago said casually.

"Yes, I do. You left it in the juice bar. The waitress gave it to me."

Jago dropped her gaze. He turned around as Calum checked his straps.

"No. I went back. Twice. She said I didn't leave it there."

Kate remembered the waitress's earnest expression. "Interesting guy." Had she known something was wrong about Jago? "Well, she lied," Kate said.

Jago shook his head again. He waited till Calum walked away to check the others. "The Viking checked your house, top to bottom."

He had faltered. A moment of weakness. Finally she felt some power return to her. He was the panicked one now.

"It was locked in the shed."

Jago turned his face farther from her. Trying to hide his disquiet, Kate realized.

"Yeah, nice try, Kate."

"Jack has it," she said triumphantly as Calum called out to them that they would board in three minutes. "And this morning, he gave it to Saskia and she recognized you. Tony from Essex, she said. She's showing it to the police right now. She thought you were after my money." The words tumbled out. Desperately she hoped her face wouldn't give away her bluff. She saw the middle-aged female jumper, her shoulders shaking hysterically, laughing nervously with her friend.

She pointed to the gate where he'd been looking. "So, I expect they'll be here by the time you hit the ground," she said.

"Yeah, yeah." He shrugged, but she knew he was rattled. It gave her strength.

"You're not as clever as you think you are, Jago." She forced herself to continue on the attack, desperate to give herself more time to think. "You lost the book. And the man in the shoe-repair shop was right. He knew you'd done it on purpose to keep me in my place. You couldn't show me how much you hated me when you were putting on the act of being my new boyfriend, so you took me down a peg in a way that made you feel better and you thought I wouldn't notice."

Jago forced another laugh and shook his head dismissively, but there was a new look in his eyes. A vulnerability. She was getting to him.

"And another thing, Jago," she went on, trying to keep her nerve, "even if I do what you ask of me, Jack will be fine. Because he has a good heart, just like his dad. He's had so much love from all of us. And I'm sorry, what happened to you was awful, Jago. But what you've done is so much worse. What you have done is evil."

Finally he turned back to her, a sneer on his face. "You too, Kate. I watched you. Hurt people just like you'd been hurt, and enjoy it. I know what you did to those girls—you're just getting started."

She nodded. "I did, but I felt horrible. And that was what I was going to tell you tonight before we went back to your pretend room at Balliol. I bought the old man a rowboat this week and had it delivered when he was out. And yesterday, I sent a note via the Highgate rangers to tell the girls that they were safe. That it was a student prank gone wrong, and we apologize. I sent the same note to the health shop and asked them to tell the woman with the dog next time she came in."

She touched the phone inside her sleeve with one finger, more confident now. She had him off balance. Now was her chance, her only chance. But even if she could use the phone, who would she call?

Richard and Helen? Saskia? The police? But the weirdo might throw Jack in the river before they could get there. Same reason she couldn't call for help from Calum.

As she thought, instinct told her to keep distracting Jago. "The thing is, I am not like you. And my son would never be like you, and if your mother could see you now, she would thank God she didn't live. You have a choice how you let life affect you and we don't all make the same choice as you. Monsters are made, not born."

Jago grabbed her arm again, and pulled her close against the back of the plane. With a growl, the engine burst into life in front of them on the wing.

Jago shouted above the noise. "Let's see, shall we? See what happens if you don't do what I say?"

Calum waved the first two jumpers onto the plane, then turned to Kate.

"OK?" he yelled over the engine.

There were only seconds now.

Suddenly, Kate knew who to call. She pushed Jago's arm off and climbed into the door of the plane, knowing she had only seconds.

As Jago started to follow behind her, she spun around.

"Calum, could you just recheck Jago's altimeter? I don't think he's reset it right," she shouted, pointing at Jago's arm.

Jago looked up angrily. He tried to follow her onto the plane, but Calum blocked him.

"Let me have a quick look, mate."

Kate moved forward into the tiny long tube, with her back to Jago, knowing Calum would not let Jago on till he was happy. Ignoring the smiles of the other passengers, she frantically pulled the phone from her sleeve.

She had to call Jack.

Without any of them seeing, she texted Jack with shaking fingers.

it's mum—where r u?

She turned and saw Calum was carefully checking the little machine on Jago's left arm. Jago was glaring at him, his anger no longer disguised. His hands gripped firmly on the side of the plane door waiting to climb on.

A message pinged back.

at nana's—u get my message?

Kate gasped.

He was safe. Jago was lying.

She held the phone tight inside her hand as Jago climbed on behind her, followed by Calum. She felt him come up behind her but kept her back to him.

Calum checked their hooks were done up to their static lines, then gave the pilot the signal. With a burst of engine power, the little plane roared up the runway like an angry fly.

"Nice day for a swim," Jago shouted, smiling.

Calum talked into his radio with ground control.

As the plane buzzed into the air, bumping on the currents, Kate allowed herself to breathe again.

Jack was safe.

Now what?

Jago shuffled up behind her, his legs touching hers.

The plane flew upward, till it was at thirty-five hundred feet. Calum opened the hatch.

She looked out.

She was going to jump out of a plane, away from Jago, and she couldn't bloody wait.

"Right, guys. You're up!" Calum shouted over the rasping engine noise, signaling from the open hatch.

Kate began to shuffle forward. She felt Jago coming behind her.

"Number one!" Calum shouted signaling to Kate.

Kate turned behind her to Jago, and calmly smiled. She took the phone from her sleeve with Jack's text message and lifted it to Jago's face.

Then she saw it. The ice cracked. Fear flooded into Jago's eyes.

She saw a man alone, stranded alone in a terrible life, and she was no longer scared. She could have said something. You sorry piece of shit, she could have screamed in his face, but she realized she didn't have to.

Hugo's love and her parents' love and Jack's love were wrapped tightly around her.

"Sorry, Calum, I forgot to put this in the bag," she shouted, handing the phone to Calum. He frowned and waved her forward, taking it from her hand.

Jago lunged forward, but Calum was in the way now, helping Kate to the door.

She shuffled along to the edge, refusing to look back. As Calum did her pre-jump check, she pushed her legs into the powerful wall of air that rushed past the open door of the plane, feeling calm descend on her, remembering that this is who she was. She knew how to do this. She placed her left hand on the door, her right on the floor ready to push off.

She looked down and saw fields thirty-five hundred feet below her.

She saw death and knew she could face it, just as she'd faced it twenty-six times before.

"Go!" Calum shouted.

And with that she lifted her arms and jumped.

"One thousand!" she yelled to make herself breathe. "Two thousand! Three thousand! Four thousand!"

She whooped as her parachute exploded into life above her, and she felt the welcome tug.

"Check canopy!" she called, looking up. A beautiful billowing parachute greeted her. Her lines were clean, her slider down, her cell ends inflated.

She pulled her brake toggles down a couple of times to be sure, then leaned into her flight.

It all came back so suddenly, like it had been yesterday.

Hearing the loud drone of the propellers dropping away into silence.

Feeling the wind whistling on her face.

Her limbs losing all resistance.

Relaxing like never before.

Falling into the void.

Utter euphoria descending.

Flying like a bird.

She flew for a couple of minutes, gently pulling her steering line to take her toward the arrow.

She could see for miles in every direction.

Patchwork fields and road and trains, and places to go.

The world laid out before her, waiting for her to grab it again.

Relief surged through her.

It had all been Jago, the whole time.

Her instincts had been right.

She had protected herself and Jack, even though everyone said she was mad, a terrible mother.

She was going to be all right, and so was her son. She knew it.

She had kept them safe. Her and no one else.

"I did it, Hugo," she whispered.

Then there was a movement below her.

People were gathering. Pointing. Running backward as if trying to see better.

Looking up at the sky.

Jago was plummeting headfirst, upside down, toward the ground, his main chute wrapped around his legs. As he hit fifteen hundred feet, his reserve opened automatically, and she thought for a moment that it might save him, but it, too, became tangled in his legs and the main chute, and flapped uselessly.

She looked down again.

Someone had a camera. Someone was filming Jago's fall.

And even though she hated the monster, she couldn't watch his end.

So she looked up at the sky.

It was over.

40

Kate stopped in front of the juice bar midafternoon. It was a Tuesday and the auburn-haired waitress was behind the counter. She locked her bike and went in.

The girl looked up, and came over, her eyes widening.

"Oh, it's you. Oh, my God, was that the Scottish guy, on the news?"

Kate nodded.

The girl flung a hand over her mouth. "That's so awful. I wasn't sure. It looked like him in the photo but I thought he was called Jago, but on the news they said 'Peter something.'"

"It's a long story. But yes, it was him. I just wanted to ask you, how did you know there was something weird about him?"

The waitress grimaced awkwardly. "I'm so sorry. The first time you came in here, he followed you in and gave me fifty pounds to pretend that I fancied him, to say that he had a sexy accent, et cetera. I thought I was helping him out because he was shy. Then when I saw him do that thing with the dog, I felt bad.

You looked so fragile and vulnerable, and he just seemed weird. I thought if I gave you his bag you might find something in it that told you what he was up to. He came back twice looking for it, and to be honest, he scared me. He was so angry."

Kate touched the girl's hand. "Well, thanks. You were right."

"They said it might have been suicide? On the news?"

Kate shook her head. "They don't know yet. He jumped in a dangerous way that you never do on that type of jump. He knew what might happen if he did, so either he did it on purpose, or he genuinely made a very bad mistake and froze and couldn't release his main chute when it didn't open. The odds are tiny of it happening—one in eighty thousand—so maybe he was just unlucky."

"Got to be someone, I suppose, eh?" the girl said.

Kate nodded. "Got to be someone."

She arrived home fifteen minutes later, and Saskia answered the door.

"He's in his room," she said.

Kate smiled. "Thanks."

She put down her bag. "How are your parents?"

Saskia burst into tears. She shook her head. "Dad won't speak to anyone. He just looks so gaunt, Kate. He can't even look at us. He keeps going out on the boat. It's horrible. I think Mum's too scared to come over to see you. She keeps saying that Jago Martin—or Peter Johnston or whoever he was—his dad was an alcoholic, and it was his fault because he took his wife's money without asking and bought that house for cash without a survey or insurance. It wasn't Dad's fault, it was Charley's. That regulations were different back then."

Kate avoided Saskia's eyes. Richard's demons were his own to deal with now.

"How did you get on at the police station?" Saskia sniffed.

"They're telling Stan the taxi driver's family in Shropshire today. And the lawyers for the guys that took Hugo's car have filed for an immediate dismissal of the murder charges."

"What about the weirdo next door?"

Kate shrugged, shivering at the thought of that horrible man so close to her and Jack. How Saskia had tried to warn her, and how she'd ignored her. "He absconded from prison years ago, abroad, apparently," she said, rubbing her eyes, exhausted. "The police think he came to London, and met Jago through some dodgy bloke they both knew.

"Jago helped him get a new identity, then the weirdo said Jago kept blackmailing him into doing dodgy stuff for him." She rubbed her upper arm. "He was so clever—the weirdo thought he was Scottish, too, never even knew his name."

Saskia turned one way, then another in the hall, shaking her head. "Oh, God, all those people. Your parents. Hugo. It's such a mess," she cried. "I'm so sorry, Kate."

"It's OK, Sass, it's not your fault," Kate said, pulling her into a hug, knowing it's what Hugo would want her to do. They held each other tight.

When Saskia left, Kate went upstairs and found Jack sitting on his bed, playing on the laptop.

She sat down, smiling, and smoothed his hair.

"I have something to tell you."

He waited.

"Well, I think it's time for you and me to think about the

future. So I've arranged for all Dad's furniture to be picked up tomorrow to be put in storage for you for when you're older, and then you can decide what to do with it. And then we're going to turn the dining room into a pool-table room so you can have your friends over."

Jack grinned. "Really?"

"Uh-huh."

He frowned. "But wouldn't Dad be sad?"

She shook her head. "No. Absolutely not. And if you wanted to sell that furniture when you're an adult to pay for something you'd love to do, I promise you, he'd be delighted. Your dad loved life, and he'd want us to get on with ours, too, and enjoy. Starting now."

Jack watched her with his big, pale-green eyes.

"So, the other thing is, at the end of term, you and me are going to Spain for a month to stay in David's house. On our own. And guess what, there's a sailing school there. I thought we could try and learn together."

"Woo-hoo!" Jack shouted.

She laughed and leaned forward to kiss him. She stayed there for a second, resting her lips against his cheek, like when he was a toddler, and to her joy, he let her. Just for a second.

"Mum?" he said, pulling back.

"Hmm?"

"Are you going to go parachuting again?" he said.

"I'm going to think about it."

"What was it like?"

She laughed. "Jack. You've asked me that a hundred times now."

"But that man died doing it."

"We don't know why he died. It's possible he died on purpose, or it's possible he was just very, very unlucky, Jack. And

I think you and I have had our fair share of bad luck for now, don't you? But you know what, it might be over now."

Jack smiled and turned over to go to sleep.

She went over to the wardrobe and peered inside.

"Checking for monsters?" Jack asked.

She turned and smiled.

"There's no such thing, Jack."